THE HEART OF THE LABYRINTH
AND OTHER STORIES

"Overall, this is an exceptional collection of speculative fiction stories suitable for both young adult and adult readers. Read it, and then move onto Mok's novels, which are just as exceptional. Mok writes with heart, humour and humanity, bringing light and hope into even the darkest of worlds. Highly recommended."

- Stephanie Gunn, Aurealis Award-winning author of *Icefall*

"Sometimes whimsical, always substantive; Mok's short stories brim with optimism, heart, and wry humour."

- Rivqa Rafael, co-editor of *Mother of Invention*

"Kaleidoscopic casts. Sly humour. Heart-rending allegory. Acute scientific observation. The stories of *Heart of the Labyrinth* have everything I want in short speculative fiction. Somewhere between astronomy and astrology, bouncing joyfully from unexplained whimsical magics to the specific spectra of moonbeams, DK Mok leads us to find the best in ourselves."

- Thoraiya Dyer, author of the *Titan's Forest Trilogy*

THE HEART OF THE LABYRINTH

AND OTHER STORIES

DK MOK

For my family

TABLE OF CONTENTS

THE HEART OF
THE LABYRINTH

The Labyrinth of Varissen was legend. Every child knew the story of King Varissen: first valiant and wise, then eccentric, then obsessive.

Every child knew of the sprawling labyrinth he had constructed, woven deep with enchantments to protect the secret treasures hidden within.

Every child knew of the silver storm that had swept in from the north, harbinger of the sorcerer Sarak—*may she live forever and not smite this house please*—who slew King Varissen for his precious hoard, and yet, despite the passing centuries, had uncovered not a gem of it.

And finally, every child knew of the beast that lurked within the twisting, turning passages of the labyrinth. Indeed, for many children, this was their favourite part of the story, the part involving the slashing of swords and the crunching of bones and, depending on the parent, either a bloodcurdling description of aerodynamic entrails, or a vague tutting about the dangers of running off on adventures instead of staying at home to mind the alpacas.

Yes, every child knew what lurked in that dark, enchanted place, with ancient gold gleaming in its infernal eyes. Monstrous, merciless, ravenous.

Every child knew of the Devourer.

* * *

The Devourer strongly disapproved of these stories, and he disapproved even more of the parents who fed such bloodthirsty tales to their children. While he didn't believe in burning books, he wasn't averse to the idea of hitting some parents repeatedly and quite hard with those books.

However, today, he wasn't thinking of books, and he was trying very hard not to think about parents and children and other things that looked like talkative meatballs. His stomach had been growling for weeks, and had now started to make a kind of sucking noise that threatened to develop an event horizon.

The Devourer resembled an ungainly hybrid of beasts: scales and hide, talons and tentacles. Although, on days like today, he felt that he was barely more than jaws and a stomach. He plodded through the vast and intricate labyrinth, his claws dragging beside him down the sandstone paths. He tried to distract himself by scraping the vines from the stone walls, revealing snatches of pastoral reliefs, and by weeding the terraced flower beds, before realising that there *were* only weeds. That is, if you counted poison ivy as a "weed", rather than a herbaceous thug.

A part of him wished he had someone to tell him amusing stories or to sing him stirring songs, but his only neighbours were the ravens who picked through the bleached bones and scraps of gnawed armour that dotted the central courtyard.

He could remember a time when he'd enjoyed company, although the details eluded him now. It had been a different place, and a different time. More music, fewer bones. Here, the arrival of company inevitably meant being stabbed, burned and blasted, and almost inevitably, a guilty meal of the people too recalcitrant to flee.

From marauding mercenaries to pompous knights, all demanded the same thing of him:

Where is it? Where is the hoard of Varissen?

The Devourer always told them the same thing: there was no

treasure here. It was an ancient myth spread by the greedy and the gullible. He told them they'd be better off investing in a respectable occupation, like pottery or cheese-making. On rare occasions, someone listened, and left the labyrinth with a new appreciation of ceramics. Most of the time, the Devourer made good on his name.

Every year, Overlord Sarak herself came to pry at the stones and dredge the fountains, scrutinising the mosaics inlaid seamlessly into the rock. She dared not shatter the labyrinth, for fear that the stones were imbued with some kind of sorcery that would render the legendary treasure forever lost.

Don't you wish to be free of this place? she asked him every year. *Just tell me where it is.*

And every year, he replied that she and all the others were foolish and mad, and could she perhaps bring him some fruit, because all the meat was playing havoc with his colon.

And Sarak would wheedle and bellow and snarl, and when none of that worked, she would rake the air with cold rage.

Tell me, or I'll chain you to a rock like the Iron Minotaur.

Show me, or I'll bury you in the catacombs like the Socially Awkward Serpent.

Confess, or I'll tear away your mind like the Broken Angel.

Eventually, the Devourer would snap his jaws and wave his tentacles, rising onto his powerful hind legs, his knobbly scales glinting in the sun.

You should have thought of that before you slew Varissen! he'd roar.

She would withdraw then, leaving the Devourer with a strange ache in his chest and vague visions in his mind. He wondered, sometimes, if the other creatures she mentioned paced their prisons endlessly and longed for civil conversation, and if they too were plagued by murky nightmares of blood and ink.

It had been some time since Sarak's last visit. Actually, it had been some time since anyone had visited. The Devourer lay on his side, his stomach painfully sunken. He glanced surreptitiously at the towering acacia that grew in the central courtyard, eyeing the ravens that roosted in the branches. They stared flintily back at him, the only witnesses to his countless transgressions.

When he'd first been imprisoned here by Sarak, he'd nearly starved to death. No fish swam the putrid ponds, and the bitter plants only made him ill, so he'd snatched ravens to feed his hunger. But he'd seen them mourning their fellows, singing dirges with such accusation that he'd sworn off corvids completely.

Death would free him from this place, but Sarak would simply find another prisoner, another sentry—perhaps one who wouldn't give the labyrinth's visitors a chance to depart.

Thump thump. Thump thump.

The Devourer's eyes opened a crack. Perhaps it was the beat of his heart—or one of his hearts, at least. He was quite sure he had two or three, not to mention several proto-brains to control all the tentacles and claws and various other appendages. He was fairly certain he had a fin somewhere.

Thump thump. Thump thump.

The ravens stirred, hopping excitedly about on the branches.

There would be fresh meat soon.

The Devourer's stomach churned, and he shuffled anxiously to his feet. For the briefest moment, he hoped the visitors would be pugilistic and annoying, but then he felt a stab of shame. Sarak had cursed him with an insatiable appetite and chronic indigestion, but his soul was still his own. For whatever that was worth.

He faced the courtyard archway, hoping that the intruders would somehow be an army of soft cheeses and summer fruits. Suddenly, he realised that the labyrinth's visitor wasn't using the passageways. A dark figure raced along the top of the walls, its boots dancing a path over the tangled vines, moving nimbly despite the heavy pack on its back. As it neared, he could see it was dressed in a brown tunic with light leather armour, and it carried a short, hooked sword in each hand.

With an acrobatic leap, the figure landed solidly on the courtyard wall, gazing down at the Devourer. From this distance, he could see her short brown hair twisted atop her head like a nest, and her brown eyes blazed with determination. Even though she remained a cautious twenty feet away, the Devourer's whip-like tentacles could have sliced off her head from where he stood.

One quick bite and no one would know, except for him and the ravens. But she hadn't attacked him yet, nor yelled "Pestilent wretch, surrender thy riches or taste my steel!" which usually led to the Devourer delivering a stern lecture about civility, semantics, and double-entendres. He was near delirious from hunger, and still she stood there, watching him, with an expression that he hadn't seen in centuries. It took him a moment to dredge the word from his memory.

Pity.

He pushed away hungry thoughts.

"Rargh …" He waved his claws listlessly. "There is no treasure here. Really—no gold, no gems, no enchanted artefacts."

The young woman's gaze skimmed the courtyard before returning to the Devourer.

"Devourer of the Labyrinth of Varissen, my name is Kaya Katavan, and I am here to free you."

The Devourer narrowed most of his eyes.

"Do you mean 'free me from my mortal bonds'?"

Over the years, he'd had some very confusing metaphysical conversations with people who seemed to think that "liberate" and "eviscerate" meant the same thing. Most of those people got eaten.

"I mean," said Kaya, "the curse binding you here is broken. You may leave the labyrinth."

"Sarak will find me."

"Sarak is dead."

The Devourer's hearts pounded in the silence. From the woman's stony expression, it was a sensitive subject, so he didn't press for more details. He'd had enough of death, and he could already guess that Sarak hadn't died from sudden-onset old age. He looked at his ragged claws. Was there even a place in the world for something like him? He remembered almost nothing of his life before this place—just sprawling sunsets and jovial laughter and terrible screams—

"Why?" asked the Devourer. "Why did you free me?"

Kaya held his gaze. "I slew Sarak because my kingdom deserves better. I came to free you, or—ahem—evict you, because foolish souls will continue to come here. I'll judge you not on what you did as Sarak's prisoner, but on what you do as a free being. I seek your word that you will slay no more."

The Devourer looked from her glinting blades to his heavy paws.

"I give you my word, on one condition: I wasn't the only creature imprisoned by Sarak, and the kingdom is large and difficult to navigate for one who looks as I do. Come with me, help me to free the others, and I will be in your debt."

Kaya considered this for a moment, and then leapt down onto the courtyard, sheathing her blades. The ravens muttered in quiet disappointment.

"If I help you, I'll demand a reward when this is done."

"If it's mine to give, then you shall have it," said the Devourer, hoping she wouldn't realise that he had nothing of value, unless you counted a respectable vocabulary.

Kaya nodded, and tossed her pack to the Devourer.

"A Happy-Leaving-The-Labyrinth-Day present," she said.

The Devourer unbuckled the satchel to find it brimming with apples, dates, sweet potatoes, and a large round of cheese.

* * *

They left the labyrinth behind them, and the Devourer cast one final look from the crest of a barren hill. He tried not to take it personally as flocks of scarlet macaws and herds of deer promptly flooded into the abandoned labyrinth, disappearing into the verdant sprawl. He felt the faintest twinge of uncertainty—yes, it had been his prison, but from this distance, from outside its high walls, he could see the overgrown boulevards and the secluded ponds, the elaborate carvings and the towering fountains, the single path winding and flowing from the rusted gates to the central courtyard.

He found himself hoping that the deer wouldn't leave too much of a mess on the mosaics.

"Having doubts?" said Kaya.

"No …"

"It isn't as though there's anything keeping you there."

The Devourer glanced sharply at her, but Kaya was busy refilling her pack with pears from a nearby tree. She'd agreed quite readily to this quest, and perhaps she was motivated by more than just a soft spot for oppressed monsters. She hefted the pack onto her shoulders.

"So," she said, "shall we rescue these friends of yours?"

"They're not my friends."

The Devourer gazed out towards the horizon. The world seemed duller, dustier than he remembered. A fog of memory stirred in his mind.

Warm sunshine, the clatter of plates, an infectious, snorting laugh.

"Are you ready?" said Kaya.

He took a deep breath, tasting the distant smoke and the approaching rain.

"They're waiting," he said.

* * *

Onward, they roamed, and the horizons unfolded as they searched the lands. They travelled the kingdom from peak to trough, from volcanic seas to glacial peaks. They snapped the chains from the Haranguing Hydra, and shattered the coral cage of the Kleptomaniac Kraken. They unbound the anchors from the Judgemental Jellyfish, and freed the Socially Awkward Serpent from the catacombs. Or, at least, they rolled aside the boulder sealing the doorway, and spent several hours coaxing the enormous reptile towards the entrance.

"Sarak is gone," said Kaya. "You're free to go."

The Serpent mumbled and hissed incoherently, writhing into panicked knots behind the sarcophagi. Kaya studied the scene with a frown. It had taken them hours, and rather a lot of complicated physics, to shunt aside the boulder.

"I suppose we should leave him be," she said. "After all, sealing a socially phobic snake inside an abandoned necropolis—as far as torments go, it wasn't Sarak's best work."

"Giving someone what they crave isn't always a mercy," said the Devourer.

He sat on the weathered rock outside, and waited for the sound of hyperventilation to subside.

"Do you remember the delicious heat of the sun?" he said gently. "The slither of sand beneath your belly, the tickle of grass against your scales?" He sighed slowly. "I was Sarak's prisoner too. When Kaya freed me, I was terrified of leaving the labyrinth, of seeing the world, or perhaps of the *world* seeing *me*—for a prison can be less frightening than the unknown. But the worst prison is the kind that sits within you, the cage that tells you what you are, what you will always be. It's a prison that few of us escape, but sometimes, we can bend the bars a little, open the door a crack, and perhaps add a nice conservatory with an adjoining larder." He tilted his head towards the sky. "And perhaps, it would be nice to feel the sun again."

A forked tongue darted hesitantly through the doorway. After a pause, the head of a giant snake peered out, slitted eyes shining nervously. There was another tense pause, and then the rest of the

Serpent slithered out, coils of delicately patterned green and gold. Almost half of his scales were missing, revealing patches of pale skin.

"I'm how are thanks fine?" ventured the Serpent.

"I'm thanks fine too," said the Devourer.

"Thirty miles west," said Kaya, "there's a woodland plagued by rabid boar and brooding minstrels. Perhaps you'll find good hunting and sparse conversation there." She paused. "I recommend you only hunt the boar."

The Serpent abruptly dashed back into the catacombs.

"Wait!" said Kaya. "I'm sure you could nibble a few minstrels, perhaps the ones who sing about all their wenches—"

The Serpent reappeared with something gripped in his jaws—it looked uncannily like a giant deflated white snake. He dropped it at Kaya's feet.

"Sarak my scales she harvested most … for shields and armour, but last my shed skin she didn't take. Stronger, lighter … than leather."

He bumped Kaya shyly with his nose, and then slithered away towards the wooded hills. The Devourer watched as Kaya began to slice the skin into a new set of greaves.

"Impressive work with the boulder," he said. "Where did you learn to use levers like that?"

"I was raised by librarians." Her tone suggested that anyone unable to divert a massive stone using the contents of their pencil-box wouldn't have lasted long in that particular library. "Speaking of minstrels, have you heard the recent Ballad of the Woeful Wombat?"

And as they journeyed, she told him tales of banished marsupials, and sang him fragments of songs from distant lands.

* * *

Summer turned to autumn, and their list of targets dwindled until all that remained were the Iron Minotaur and the Broken Angel.

Both names were steeped in rumours of mayhem and monstrosity, but the Devourer was determined to see his mission to the end.

The Giant Dung Beetle of Despair was the only one who'd declined their assistance, stating that he actually found his activities therapeutic, and he'd like to be known forthwith as The Giant Scarab of Soil Maintenance. The Devourer and Kaya nonetheless constructed a sturdy ramp so that the Beetle could leave the canyon whenever he wished.

Despite their steady success, the Devourer found himself increasingly troubled by what he saw of the kingdom. Parched fields and fetid rivers, starving cattle and structurally unsound shanties.

"I haven't seen the kingdom in such a state since the reign of Warlord Sgar, before Varissen arrived."

Kaya shot him a curious glance, but the Devourer was already pointing to a village crusted onto the next hillside.

"They need a windbreak of trees there, and ground cover to hold the soil together. And the town we just passed is being starved by the very dam they've built to water their fields. They've dried up the wetlands, flooded the valley, and now the landscape's crumbling from the inside out. What they need are aqueducts."

"You seem to know a lot about town planning."

He hesitated, his mind stumbling through visions of gurneys and sluices and gleaming hooks.

"The labyrinth has excellent architecture. It would have been a marvel, in its day. What happened to all the architects and engineers?"

Kaya's expression turned grim.

"Sarak spent her reign locking up the learned and killing the clever. My parents were librarians." She faltered a moment, but when she resumed, there was quiet ferocity in her voice. "Without books, without stories, you keep your people mired in their little patch of here, and their tiny slice of now. People are less likely to rise up against you if they don't remember what they've lost, and they can't imagine what they might achieve."

"I'm sorry … I'm sure your parents would have been proud of the person you've become."

Kaya turned her face away, pretending to study the village ahead.

"Perhaps once we've rescued these last two," she said, "you can do something about all this shoddy town planning."

* * *

The Devourer wasn't sure he would ever get used to all the screaming.

"Begone, foul chimera!" cried one villager.

"Return from whence thou came!" boomed another.

The Devourer dodged a flying pitchfork, and Kaya pushed forward angrily.

"That last sentence involved the incorrect usage of almost every word in it, and that is *not* how you use a pitchfork!"

"Save us from the soulless siren!" wailed another man.

"How can you possibly mistake him for a siren?" snapped Kaya.

The Devourer whispered urgently. "I think he's referring to you. See, he's winking—"

The man yelped as a flying pitchfork sank into the door beside him.

"That's not helpful," said the Devourer. "And I thought you said that's not how you use a pitch—"

"I'm sorry," said Kaya. "I just wish they'd stop throwing things at you."

"I told you I should have stayed in the woods."

"You have nothing to be ashamed of. Look, someone here has to know how far we are from the Bog of Tofu."

Kaya grabbed one of the Devourer's claws and dragged him into a nearby hut.

"Excuse me," she called politely, "we mean you no harm. We

seek the Iron Minotaur—"

The Devourer froze at the sound of frightened sobbing, a strange sensation seizing his hearts. At the rear of the hut, a scrawny couple cowered with their arms around a small, grimy girl.

"Please," said the woman, her whole body shaking. "Eat me and Egbert, but spare our daughter. Have mercy …"

The Devourer felt his stomach twist, but not with hunger, not this time.

Another time, another life. Bloodless faces, contorted with fear. Sobs and whimpers, steel and spatters, and screams that meant his work was done—

"Peony, no!" cried the woman.

The girl broke free from her mother's grasp and rushed at the Devourer with a blunt butter knife. Kaya dashed forward, grasping the girl around the waist and wresting the knife from her, while the girl screamed with fear and hatred—

The Devourer ran from the house, ignoring Kaya's calls. Faces, figures, huts rushed past, and he plunged into the dark and cradling woods. Haunting visions chased him, but these were not the faces of rogue mercenaries and gloating knights. These were common folk, men and women, and he couldn't remember why their blood stained his hands—

"Dev."

He snarled, swiping the air with his claws. "Don't call me that."

Kaya took a step back. "Devourer, are you all right?"

"Did you find out where the Bog of Tofu is?"

"Eight miles southwest."

Kaya waited wordlessly while the Devourer regained his composure, his head still swimming with gurgling screams. He sagged against a tree, his tentacles curling into the knotholes.

"Why did you free me?" he said. "Why were you unafraid of me?"

"I never said I was unafraid of you. Although, I'm not afraid anymore."

"I've eaten a good many people."

"Many, yes. Good, that's debatable. In some instances, you may have performed a public service. Especially in the case of Lord Blattersby."

The Devourer shuddered at the memory of the belligerent man and his human-shield of desperate slaves.

"A killer of monsters is still a monster," he said.

Kaya's mouth pressed into a thin line, and the Devourer realised her lips were trembling.

"Am I a monster, then?" she said.

"No, that's not— I mean, Sarak was a tyrant—"

"Is it acceptable to kill tyrants, then?"

"Uh, I think so, maybe ..."

"Because Sarak considered Varissen a tyrant. And Varissen called the half-demon Sgar a tyrant before him. And perhaps, one day, someone will call me 'tyrant' and seek me out."

"Kaya ..." The Devourer touched a tentacle to her arm, expecting her to recoil.

She didn't.

Instead, she drew a shaky breath. "My parents belonged to a cabal of secret libraries. Sarak slew them, trying to uncover the forbidden books they guarded. I was raised by their comrades, surrounded by tales and legends from our kingdom's past. We stayed hidden, spreading knowledge where we could, but the day came when we were betrayed by Sarak's spies.

"We knew there'd be a reckoning, and when Sarak arrived, afire with retribution, we were ready for her. The battle raged for weeks, and we were aided by the witches and alchemists, the poets and etymologists, and in the end, it all came down to a single moment, a sliver of a second."

She was silent a while, as though hanging in that moment of

decision.

"I killed her," she said quietly. "The librarians told me it was self-defence, but to me, it still felt like murder. Some called me a hero, but I suspect they don't fully understand the word. For a time, I felt on the brink of losing myself. And then, one night, I had a dream of fearless captains, yearning automatons, majestic forest gods, and a bearded man in a big black hat. I don't know why, but the dream gave me courage. And when I awoke, I remembered a story I'd once read—a story about a labyrinth, and a creature both terrible and wise. A beast that devoured mighty warriors, but dispensed words of gentle wisdom to those willing to listen."

"You thought I could give you answers?"

Kaya smiled faintly.

"You already have."

* * *

The Bog of Tofu was as intolerable as it sounded. The Devourer grimaced as he sank up to his haunches in the viscous white muck. He didn't have a problem with tofu in general, especially when it was deliciously fried, but this stuff was not deliciously fried. Or even lightly steamed.

"Are you sure we need to free the Iron Minotaur?" asked Kaya. "It doesn't sound very friendly. And I still have reservations about having released the Kleptomaniac Kraken."

"Everyone deserves a chance to be heard. Sarak imprisoned many of us out of malice, and some of us were human, once. Some, she held for our skills or our knowledge."

"Like you and the hoard."

"There *is* no hoard."

"Then where did Varissen's wealth go? The stories describe treasure rooms brimming with gold and gems, and enchanted relics of extraordinary power."

Glittering coffers, cabochon fire opals, haunting moonstones incandescent with energy …

The Devourer shook his head roughly. "Stories aren't always true. If Varissen wanted to hide something, he would have built a maze, with branching paths and dead ends and vicious traps. But a labyrinth, by nature, is a single path, it's a …" The words wisped away from him, and he waved his tentacles vaguely. "It's a … thing. Your books surely tell you that Varissen was a good king. Not the hoarding type."

"Then why— Oh …" Kaya stopped, staring ahead.

Visible over the curdled trees, the bones of a massive ribcage lay half submerged in the bog.

"Are we too late?" said Kaya.

The Devourer's gaze travelled along the line of ribs, up the cervical vertebrae, to the enormous avian skull at the end.

"Chained to a *roc* …" he muttered.

There was a rattle of chain, and a hulking figure sprang from behind a thicket of trees, tearing Kaya's pack from her shoulders. The Devourer leapt to intercept—or rather, he waded awkwardly in the direction of their attacker, who appeared to be a wiry, middle-aged woman with a large bovine head. A length of chain connected her iron collar to one of the roc's enormous ribs, which didn't impede her dexterity as she tipped a pack of rations into her gaping mouth.

"Hey!" said Kaya. "There's beef jerky in that."

The Minotaur didn't seem to mind, polishing off the meat rations before downing a packet of dried currants. The Devourer waded forward crossly.

"If you'd asked, we would have shared our supplies."

The Minotaur gulped guiltily. Suddenly, her eyes widened.

"Saul?" Her surprise turned to delight, and she swaggered over, slapping him hard across the face. "You've changed!" She laughed, a great snorting sound. "I guess we both have. We really got up Sarak's nose, didn't we, Saul?"

The Devourer stared at her, stunned by both her words and the concussive greeting.

"You know me?"

The Minotaur squinted at him, turning her head from side to side, unable to get him into binocular view.

"It *is* you, isn't it? I'm afraid Sarak sliced up my memory, trying to get at my secrets—for all the good it did her. I guess she did the same to you. But we used to work together, didn't we? At the palace of Varissen?"

The Devourer pressed a tentacle to his throbbing forehead.

Marble floors, the aroma of spiced wine, a jovial woman explaining to him in explicit detail the difference between the Butter Mushroom and the visually-identical Exploding Buttocks Mushroom.

"I don't …" Suddenly, the memory of raucous, snorting laughter bubbled from forgotten depths. He blinked. "Rawlins?"

The Minotaur's mouth fell open, then widened into an uncomfortably large grin.

"Damn you, Saul. I haven't heard that name in centuries."

Kaya cleared her throat. "Perhaps we can reminisce after we free you. I believe we're running low on rations."

Rawlins had the good grace to look ashamed. "I've been trying to escape for aeons. I've a stomach like an iron pot, but all this raw tofu just saps my will to live."

The Devourer and Kaya inspected the rib to which the Minotaur was chained. The bone had already been gnawed to half its original width, but it remained wider than a human torso.

"The bone's too robust here," said Kaya. "But towards the sternum, it should be thinner."

Hooking her blades together to form a makeshift saw, Kaya took one handle, and the Devourer took the other. Even with his brute strength and her meticulously sharp blades, it took them a day to cut through the roc's giant rib. Shaking off the lumps of tofu, they handed the chain to Rawlins.

"I suppose you'll have to carry it until you find a blacksmith," said Kaya.

"Where are you headed?" asked Rawlins. "Do you need a Minotaur?"

"No!" said Kaya quickly. "I mean, thank you, but we're travelling a long way."

"To one final commitment," said the Devourer. "We're going to free the Broken Angel."

Rawlins' ears perked forward, the hair on her neck bristling alarmingly.

"Really? He sounds like a sinister bugger."

"That's what Kaya said about you."

Kaya shrugged apologetically, although she collected the contents of her pack rather pointedly.

"Do you know the Broken Angel personally?" asked the Devourer.

Rawlins furrowed her brow—or tried to, but her features remained placidly bovine. "I don't think so … But I think he knows you." She shook her head. "Well, if you're sure you don't need me, I might go have a hot bath, and then desecrate Sarak's grave."

Kaya raised an eyebrow, and the Devourer wondered if perhaps they should have had a screening process after all. Rawlins sliced away through the cold bog, calling over her shoulder.

"If you want my advice, leave the Broken Angel where he is. Some creatures are in cages for a reason."

* * *

Beyond the farms and forests, beyond the catacombs and bogs, there lay the blasted wastelands: a silent desert at the edge of the sea.

"I've never been this far from the heart of the kingdom before," said Kaya, her breath misting in the winter air.

"This used to be the heart of the kingdom, long ago," said the Devourer.

They crested a ridge and beheld the glittering expanse of the Amethyst Sea. And on the dark rocks overlooking the waves, there rose a ruined castle: a magnificent tangle of turrets and spires, pinning the moon to the starry sky.

"You know this place?" said Kaya.

"Yes," was all he said.

He walked across the wasteland, his clawed feet crunching across the blackened earth. Kaya stepped out in front of him.

"Saul, if you go in there, I'll walk beside you every step of the way. But if you turn back now, I'm perfectly happy for our story to go, 'They finally reached the mysterious castle, decided not to go inside, and instead turned around and went back home. The end.'"

"Ours is not such a story," he said gently.

"Saul—"

"That name belongs to someone I don't know. I deserve a chance to know my story, and the Broken Angel deserves a chance to tell his."

Kaya's gaze was fierce with misgivings, but finally, she nodded. And so they crossed the threshold, passing through the tall doors into the desolate castle. Cobwebs draped the chandeliers, and dust blanketed the beds and dressers. Corridor after corridor, floor after floor, they found only echoes until they reached the throne room.

Shadows laced the marble floors, and moonlight pierced through narrow windows. To one side, a stone table stood scattered with the relics of a once sumptuous banquet: tarnished silver platters, goblets of carmine, spoons of pearl. And upon a dais stood a throne of dark red jasper.

A deep, lilting voice came from the shadowed figure on the throne.

"Gifts. What gifts have you brought me?"

The Devourer exchanged a nervous glance with Kaya. This was a world away from the Judgemental Jellyfish.

"Freedom," said the Devourer. "Sarak is dead. You are free to go."

"Sarak?" said the figure. "That flicker of ash? It was not Sarak who imprisoned me, but Varissen."

The figure stood, and starlight caught his features. He had the visage of a handsome youth, but sickly pale, with long dark hair. The tattered remnants of red velvet robes hung from his waist, and from his bare shoulders sprouted broad crimson wings, their tips ragged and frayed.

Words choked their way up the Devourer's throat.

"Sgar."

Kaya's blades flashed from their scabbards, her voice barely more than a breath.

"Warlord Sgar? The half-demon Warlord Sgar?"

The winged man stalked down the stairs, his gait slightly off kilter, as though the world were discourteously tilted. His eyes locked onto the Devourer, recognition lighting in their depths.

"Saul … I knew you'd return to me. My clever, brilliant, *treacherous* Saul."

With inhuman speed, Sgar swept forward and grasped the Devourer by the throat, slamming him into the wall. Kaya rushed forward, blades swinging, and although she dodged Sgar's first strike, a blinding kick sent her flying.

Sgar's eyes never left the Devourer. "I knew you'd come skulking back. Did Varissen fail to grant you the treasures he promised? Did he tire of you and turn you into some monstrous plaything?"

Without waiting for an answer, Sgar hurled him into a stone pillar, and the Devourer gritted his teeth at the faint *pop* that was possibly his swim-bladder.

"How could you betray me?" continued Sgar, his head lolling as he drew nearer. "Under my rule, your talents were allowed to run wild. You built me such marvellous prisons, and oubliettes of such ingenious cruelty."

"I built them only at your command," gasped the Devourer, struggling to his feet, dizzied by the rush of visions and voices and—

"Always such an excellent liar. I saw the joy in your eyes as you devised each new instrument of misery. I saw the pleasure you took in inspecting every rivet, every hinge, every nail. Oh Saul, you could deliver to me screams in every pitch, and sobs of every rhythm—"

The Devourer roared as the memories flooded back, and he pressed his claws helplessly against his skull.

Pages of detailed diagrams and meticulously inked schematics—

Such brilliance, they said. Innovative, exquisite, excruciating—

The needles would become too hot and lose their sharpness, but if he created a cooling system using pistons and the blood of a glacier cod—

The sluice has clotted again. Come fix it—

Whimpers and screams, bloodless faces pleading—

Sgar lashed towards him again. The Devourer whipped his tentacles defensively, but with breathtaking ease, Sgar grabbed a squirming handful and swung the Devourer into the stone table, sending the silverware clattering across the floor.

Wincing with pain, the Devourer glimpsed Kaya crouched beneath the table, her hands pressed against her side. The snakeskin armour had protected her from lacerations, but something had fractured. She glanced at him with fear in her eyes, and for the first time, he thought perhaps she saw him for what he truly was.

"That would be a 'no' to freeing him, agreed?" said Kaya.

The Devourer nodded weakly.

In a shaft of broken moonlight, Sgar stood silently, as though momentarily forgetting about his guests. He strode slowly towards the table, and Kaya held her breath as bare feet paused beside her. Sgar bent down and plucked a dusty goblet from the floor. He wandered to a window and gazed out at the whispering sea.

"I am Sgar," he rasped softly. "Son of the Phoenix God. Behold my castle, behold my empire …"

He stood with his back to them, transfixed by visions only he could see. With a burst of strength, Kaya darted forward, blades drawn—

The Devourer lunged and grasped her arm with a tentacle, shaking his head. Kaya looked from Sgar to the Devourer, her body trembling with tension.

"He'll kill you," she said.

"Only if we stay."

"What if he follows us? What if he decides to reclaim his kingdom?"

The Devourer looked at the murmuring man, whose eyes had ceased to perceive reality long ago.

"I don't think he will. I doubt anyone can free him from the prison he inhabits now."

Together, they edged back towards the exit. At the faint footfalls, Sgar spun around, his eyes widening in surprise.

"Saul, I knew you'd come back to me. Clever, brilliant, *treacherous* Saul!"

His wings beat the stale air as he swooped across the hall. The Devourer and Kaya raced from the room, skidding down corridors and stumbling down staircases, chased by the thunder of wings. They finally burst through the castle doors and continued running, risking only the briefest of backwards glances. A shadow thrashed its wings in the doorway, shying from the moonlit wasteland.

"My castle, my empire …" Sgar's voice echoed from the dark halls, becoming broken mumblings. "I am Sgar, son of the Phoenix God …"

The Devourer and Kaya kept running until the desolate ruins lay far behind them.

* * *

In the stunted woods just beyond the wasteland, the Devourer found a prickly hollow and curled up tightly inside, wrapping his tentacles around himself. Kaya sat patiently beside him, making a fire and tending to her wounds until the sun set and then rose again. Finally, she prodded him gently.

"Saul."

He didn't answer.

"Saul, you look like a squid dumpling that's fallen out of a bento box."

"What's a bento box?" he asked before he could stop himself.

"There's a small island in the sea of Sarshi— Actually, never mind. But we need to move. You'll grow hungry soon."

"Maybe I'll eat *you*," he snarled.

Kaya gave a short sigh.

"What Sgar said—"

"Don't tell me that isn't who I am," he snapped, looming out of the hollow. "Because I *remember* it. I remember every cell, every chamber, every implement. I delighted in my own cleverness, with little thought for the consequences. I was a monster long before Sarak transformed me. She merely changed my outer form to match the man within. I have my answers now, as you have yours. I'm sorry there's nothing more I can offer you, but our journey together ends here."

Kaya studied him quietly, much as she had on that first day from the top of the labyrinth wall. This time, it wasn't pity in her eyes, but the Devourer couldn't describe what it was he saw there now.

"I'd like to tell you one more story," she said. "But first, walk the labyrinth with me one final time. Will you do that, Saul?"

The Devourer shook his head at the thought of returning to that place, and yet a part of him longed to see it. Just one last time.

"It's a long way," he said finally. "Perhaps you'll have time to tell me about the sea of Sarshi and these boxes of bento."

* * *

Spring had woken the trees and warmed the grass by the time they finally returned to the Labyrinth of Varissen. With trepidation, the Devourer approached the wrought iron gates, noting that they'd been polished and every trace of rust removed. He glanced at Kaya, who looked equally intrigued.

"Ready?" she said, holding out her hand.

After a moment's hesitation, the Devourer placed a claw in her hand, and together, they entered the labyrinth. As they walked along the gently curving path, they saw that the ground had been swept clean, and the walls cleared of vines. The fountains bubbled with fresh water, and the newly pruned trees hung heavy with fragrant white peaches and crisp apples.

With every step, his thoughts seemed clearer and calmer. With every length and turn, his heart felt more grounded, more joyous. As the sun began to set, they reached the central courtyard, and the Devourer slumped to his knees, his chest heaving with emotion.

Finally, he *remembered*.

* * *

Five hundred years ago

Saul stood on the scaffolding in the central courtyard, overlooking the completed labyrinth. The final stone had been set, the last fountain activated, the last sapling planted. It had cost them a fortune in artisans and sorcerers, but they'd fused enchanted artefacts into the fountains and trees to keep them ever-fresh, ever-lush, so long as they were tended. Beside him, King Varissen surveyed their opus.

"Are you certain you want that acacia there?" he said.

"It looks silly now," said Saul, "but in two hundred years, it'll be magnificent. And when people arrive at the centre, trust me, they'll want some shade and a drink."

"I trust you."

Saul glanced away, and Varissen placed a hand on his shoulder.

"You're a good man, Saul. Wiser than you were. Braver than you were. You risked your life to bring down Sgar, and now, you've created a thing of incomparable beauty—a true treasure."

However, it wasn't pride Saul felt now. His arrogance had withered the day a visiting ranger, Varissen, had told him wondrous stories of what a kingdom *should* look like, and filled Saul's heart with shame. Now, his labours—his penance—brought him not pride, but peace.

"You've spent all your wealth on this place ..."

"A kingdom does not need wealth. It needs prosperity, happiness, and resilience. Farmers will grow, merchants will trade, poets will dream, days will pass, and so will you and I. But this will forever be a place of wonder and rest, of meditation and insight. Generations to come will walk these paths and find serenity and wisdom, mercy and kindness, here in this place. This is your legacy, Saul."

Saul lifted his face to the breeze, glancing at the silver threads sparking on the horizon.

"Looks like there's a storm coming."

* * *

The Devourer wiped his eyes, his chest aching.

"A labyrinth is a single path," he said. "A walking meditation, a spiritual journey. A labyrinth is where you find yourself."

"And this is the story I wanted to tell you," said Kaya. "When I read of the labyrinth and the beast within, there was another story I came upon. A story about the man who built the labyrinth. A brilliant, troubled man. A man seeking redemption. It was not the advice of the Devourer I sought. It was yours, Saul."

The Devourer bowed his head, and Kaya touched his face gently. Shadows shifted in the shade of the acacia tree, and several figures stepped—and slithered—into the sunshine: Rawlins, the Serpent, and a woman with brown skin and braided hair. Kaya's eyes lit up when she saw the last figure, and she threw her arms around the woman.

"Amala! What are you doing here?"

"We respected your wish for 'space', but when you didn't return, the other librarians and I went searching for you. Everywhere we went, we heard tales of a young woman travelling with a fearsome beast, and we thought 'That sounds like Kaya'. Although we did wonder who the young woman was."

Kaya pretended to scowl, but her eyes shone with delight. Amala bowed to the Devourer.

"Lord Saul, it's a pleasure to meet you. As I was explaining to Lady Rawlins, with Sarak gone, the enchantment extending your lives has been broken. You'll live out your remaining years as you would have."

"I think she just walks around giving people unhappy facts," said Rawlins. "By the way, sorry, I ate all those bones you had lying around."

The Serpent hissed miserably. "I told her you were saving them for last, like the … crispy bits … of fried potatoes."

Rawlins pointed to the Serpent. "In case you find anything broken, he was already here when I arrived, along with some giant dung beetle who was rolling up all the detritus from the paths. You're a lousy housekeeper, Saul. Oh, and the Kleptomaniac Kraken cleaned all the fountains, and she's taken up residence in the eastern pond. She promises to reform her grabby ways, and the Judgemental Jellyfish said he'd keep an eye on her."

"Do jellyfish have eyes?" said the Devourer.

"I didn't say he'd be effective."

The Devourer cast his gaze around the courtyard, barely able to comprehend the transformation it, and he, had undergone. He turned to Kaya.

"Thank you. For finding me."

With the sunset sky ablaze, Kaya looked at him with fiery optimism in her eyes.

"And now," she said, "I request that your debt be repaid. Build me a kingdom, Saul. Where the roads run smooth and the rivers flow clear. Where the soils are rich and the villages less likely to blow away in the rain. You were ever the heart of the labyrinth, growing wiser and kinder with every step. So, with us by your side, build us a kingdom."

And so, the story began.

Note from the Author

I'm one of the lucky ones. I discovered Terry Pratchett's books when I was in high school, and for nearly twenty years I had a new Pratchett book to look forward to every year. Two books, if I was lucky. And I was lucky for a long time. I had the opportunity to laugh, cry, grow older, and hopefully wiser, alongside characters who became my friends and mentors: Sam Vimes, Susan Sto Helit, Dangerous Beans, Tiffany Aching, and Death himself.

There will be no more books from Sir Terry, but the sparks of wonder, rage, conviction, and hope that he cast into the world will continue to burn bright and spread their light. While 'The Heart of the Labyrinth' was inspired in part by the labyrinth of Centennial Park, Sydney, this story was written for Sir Terry Pratchett, who taught us to be kinder, wiser, and braver than we were.

About *The Heart of the Labyrinth*

The Heart of the Labyrinth was Aurealis Award-shortlisted for Best Young Adult Short Story.

The Heart of the Labyrinth and the accompanying Author's Note were first published in *In Memory: A Tribute to Sir Terry Pratchett* (2015), edited by Sorin Suciu and Laura May.

THE MOON COLLECTOR

Starlight rippled across the frost-flecked breeze on the night our moon was stolen.

I was deep into my first solitary hunt. Snow caked the intricate mandala trees, and my heart pounded with such force I almost feared the frantic drumbeat would chase away my prey. Returning with the head of a mud wraith, and its precious swathe of ember-twine hair, would mark my ascension into womanhood. But I had different plans.

I would bring one back *alive*.

"Why slay the mud wraiths?" I'd asked Elder Tirago. "Why not tame them like sheep and harvest their hair?"

"Their hair sheds only in death," he replied. "And they do not die unless their head is taken."

"But Librarian Mahira says there are stories—"

"And while you chase stories, will our leather stitch itself? Will our axes haft themselves?"

Perhaps, I'd thought resentfully. *If you hadn't sealed away the grimoires after that isolated theft many years ago.*

Instead, I said, "But what happens when all the mud wraiths are slain? My mother says there are fewer now than in her youth—"

"There will always be more," said Tirago. "They spawn, like fish and flies."

"Then why has no one ever seen baby mud wraiths?"

Elder Tirago had turned a fearsome hue, and my father ushered me away before Tirago could call for the Gavel of Denunciation.

No doubt, there were Elders who hoped I'd perish on this hunt, and I dearly wished to disappoint them.

"Be careful, Ora," my mother had said as I departed that evening. "The mud wraiths may stand barely taller than a man, but their fists strike with the force of a landslide."

However, it was not only my bones at stake, but the honour of my family, and I'd planned this hunt carefully. Tonight, a full moon shone overhead, inking the world in its bright, clear cast. The mud wraiths were at their most sluggish when the moon was full, basking in the otherworldly light as though they were turned from mud to stone.

I'd tracked my target for weeks—a mud wraith no larger than myself. Still young, perhaps. Still pliable. Unlike most wraiths, it had kept to the wooded hills and gullies near our village, instead of retreating to the densely forested mountains—a sign of its inexperience, I presumed. The mudling—the *wraith*, I corrected myself—could surely be subdued, as long as I kept clear of its fists.

Its tracks glittered in the fresh powder, and finally, through the ornate fretwork of boughs ahead, I glimpsed a satin shimmer of red. They called it ember-twine, but it was nothing so coarse as twine. Supple as gossamer, strong as iron, you could put a thread in the forge for a year and a day and it would emerge unscathed. The wraith stood motionless in a patch of moonlight, its lumpy arms and legs like poorly shaped clay, its formless head little more than a sodden ball. But fine, coppery hair flowed from its scalp down to where its waist should be, a mesmerising cascade that stirred gently in the breeze.

Silently, I drew the stone seal from my belt, curling my hand around the weathered grip. A dozen seals had been crafted by the founders of our village centuries ago, when the arcane powers of the librarians were still anchored in raw sorcery. One blow to the neck would paralyse a mud wraith. A second strike would sever its head.

For twenty generations, the daughters of our village had wielded these seals and brought pride to their families, while I—

Perhaps it sensed my shifting weight, or my shiver of doubt, but the mud wraith turned towards me, raising its leaden arms—

I sprinted across the clearing, my heart in my throat, motes of ice speckling my vision. I leapt at the wraith and dodged a rocky fist as I wrapped one arm around its neck and swung behind it, twisting my legs across and letting the momentum carry me around, wrenching the wraith off its feet. Gravity slammed it hard onto the ground, and I straddled it, plunging the seal towards its neck.

"Wait!" cried a voice.

I halted, my own inexperience now betraying my limbs. I stared at the creature beneath me.

The mud wraith had a face.

Or, rather, it had two uneven sockets the size of clumsy thumbs, and as I watched, the wraith hurriedly pressed a furrow into its visage and beamed a lopsided smile.

"Hullo?" it said. "Please don't hurt me."

The creature's voice undulated wildly in pitch and volume, as though it had learned to speak by reading books and listening to donkeys.

I managed to recover my own voice. "You can … talk?"

"Yes! You see, I found this magic book—"

My mind raced. "The stolen grimoire? You're the one who took it?"

"Yes! I mean, no. I mean, what's the penalty for not returning a library book? Is it a fine?"

"It's stoning."

"That seems excessive." The wraith nervously reshaped his furrow into a frown.

I privately agreed, but appropriate library penalties were not foremost in my thoughts. I tried to focus on my training, on all my imagined scenarios, of which this had not been one.

"Mud wraith, I have defeated you. You will return with me—"

And *that* was when the world went dark.

There was no clap of thunder, no flash of infernal light. Just a sudden, silent darkness, as though a candle had been snuffed.

"What did you do?" I hissed, my fingers tightening around the seal.

The wraith looked past me, and his empty sockets seemed to pool with fear. "It's gone."

I risked a glance over my shoulder and felt a tremor of confusion. It had been a cloudless night, and yet the moon had disappeared behind a—

No, it had just *disappeared.*

I could see faint stars glimmering where the moon should have been, and over the hills and valleys, an eerie, unseen pall was falling.

The mud wraith shuddered. "What have you done?"

"Me? Infernal sorcery appears to be your domain—"

"I was minding my own business when you jumped out of nowhere and pushed me over. If anyone's engaged in suspicious behaviour, it's you." His indignation barely masked the genuine fear in his voice. "My people will die without the moon."

That shook me from my panic. "What do you mean?"

"We feed on starlight, but we need moonlight to make more of us." The mud wraith stared at the unnatural sky, his downward furrow now achingly forlorn. "Without the moon, my people will fade away."

My heart roiled with fears for my own people. What possessed such power as to vanish the moon? My own ambitions now seemed appallingly childish. I'd wasted my time reading wild tales, remaining ignorant to the true dangers that haunted this world. It had been the height of hubris to think that I knew better than my elders, and yet—

My hands shook, the earthy scent of the mud wraith tingling in my nostrils. Two quick strikes and the deed would be done. I'd return home to praise and a handsome feast, the glint of grudging respect in the eyes of all who'd doubted me.

I stared into the creature's misshapen face, the furrow a wobbly line of woe.

I pushed myself to my feet, tucking the seal back into my belt. "Go."

The mud wraith rose unsteadily and took a few steps towards the tree-line, then turned back to me, his expression perhaps a fraction less woeful.

"Do I still have to pay the library fine?"

"Go!" I roared, and the wraith scrambled away into the moonless night.

* * *

It was a small mercy that the shame of my failed hunt was overshadowed by the catastrophe of our missing moon.

"An omen most terrible," said Seer Virek to the assembly. "Did I not warn you that we hadn't sacrificed enough cats this year?"

My mother's tone was clipped. "Not everything is solved by sacrificing cats."

"Agreed," said Elder Tirago. "Our enemies have grown in might with their armies and weapons of war, while we've become meek and drowsy with our sheep and our fields. And now, without the moon, the wolves close in on our shepherds, assassins roam with a bolder stride. We must rise to meet our foes, or all will be lost."

My father crossed his arms. "Librarian Mahira says the tides might change and some moths might get confused, but the absence of the moon is unlikely to deal our world a fatal blow. And there's been no clear indication that any territory is massing armies."

Tirago's eyes caught slivers of lamplight. "Such complacency is why you do not lead our people. You would have our village ravaged by barbaric hordes—"

"Elders." A crisp voice lanced through the frightened murmurs of the crowd, and Librarian Mahira stepped into the circle of lanterns. Her brown curls were held neatly in place by a small legion of bronze pins, and her woollen robe cloaked her muscular frame. A heavy tome lay open on one arm, abstruse images swirling on the vellum. "Before we march to war, we may yet remedy the situation. Our moon has not been extinguished, but stolen from our skies. And every thief leaves a trail."

Mahira swept her free arm towards the constellations, and golden sparks danced across the heavens in a pattern resembling the powdery plumes cast up by an owl plucking its prey from a snowdrift. "Comets have been swept from our skies, the very stars disturbed by the passage of an ancient force. Legends speak of the Galliyar, spirits awoken before the first dawn, possessing unfathomable power and inscrutable intentions. I believe one of these has taken our moon. They dwell in realms that rarely touch our own, but there is a way to reach them. Examining the grimoires, I've uncovered references to leviathan nomads—the Raivi—who traverse the galaxies, following the call of distant suns. They covet enchanted trinkets, and while our offerings would be meagre, I believe we can summon one and plead for a trade. Our charmed artifacts, in exchange for safe passage for a party of brave souls to retrieve our moon from the lair of the Galliyar."

There fell a silence so thick I felt I could hardly breathe. Ancient spirits, leviathan nomads. To hear these words, not in the secretive shelter of the story nook, but on the public stage of the village council, prised at something within me that I hadn't realised lay sealed.

Elder Tirago spoke first, contempt cloying his voice. "You speak of unseen spirits and fanciful beasts. I speak of real armies advancing in the darkness, real tyrants seeking to use this omen as a pretext to seize our lands and slaughter our people. Childish stories have no place in stratagems of war—"

"They're not just stories—" I faltered as dozens of firelit eyes fixed upon me. "You declared the mud wraiths incapable of thought, but tonight, a mud wraith *spoke* to me. In our own tongue, just as the legends said was common long ago." I saw the worry—the doubt—in my mother's eyes, and my moment of courage wilted.

A smear of anger coloured Tirago's cheeks. "Your lies will not deflect the disgrace you've brought upon your family. Your failure to complete the hunt surprises no one. Your cowardice is clear."

Quiet fury burned in my veins, but the indignity paled in comparison to the clear-eyed fear growing within me. Fear for my family under the reckless, unjust reign of Tirago. Fear that the moonless sky would indeed spur other reckless, unjust tyrants to turn their hungry eyes towards my village. And, in an odd flutter of sorrow, I thought of the mudling staring forlornly at the impoverished sky.

I slowly uncurled my fists and strode from the crowd. I would not waste my strength on men like Tirago. I would need my strength for what lay ahead.

* * *

It was almost dawn when I slipped into the library, the scent of old leather and fresh ink evoking memories of bitter winters made warm by fantastic tales. Thimble lanterns illuminated the central desk, where a glut of scrolls and manuscripts formed crests and valleys.

Mahira sat on a drum stool, her fingers tracing the air above the texts, as though the words radiated a layer of meaning that could only be felt. Her hand stopped at my presence, and the words I came to say clung to my throat.

If this were a normal night, moonlight would have streamed in through the circular windows. Instead, only the feeble glow of the lanterns battled the oppressive dark.

"I'll go." I held out my hand, the stone seal resting on my palm. "It may not be enough to summon a Raivi, but we have to try."

My family's seal was carved from humble soapstone, not like the marble and garnet seal wielded by our village champion, Peregrine: a hunter so ferocious we'd restrung the entire northern fence from the heads she'd brought back last year—

Mahira's gaze was full of tender sorrow. "You have nothing to prove, Ora, daughter of Ena."

"I'm not going for pride. You know that." Sensing her hesitation, I tried to smother my own misgivings. "I know I'm neither the strongest nor the wisest of warriors, but I'm willing. Elder Tirago's hold over our village will not ease soon, and if we idle, he may decide that the grimoires should not only be locked away, but destroyed. And then, our moon will truly be lost."

I couldn't tell if it was hope or defeat that clouded her expression; perhaps a little of both. "I cannot protect you on this journey, and I have no guidance to give on how to recover our moon from the Galliyar."

"You've counselled me well over the years. That is all the shield and sword I need."

A melancholy smile flickered across her lips. "Before you set your heart on this course, you must know one more thing. Time turns on a different spindle when you travel the celestial realms. It is almost certain you will not return within my lifetime."

A triptych of visions knifed through me: Mahira's grave, tangled with weeds; my parents, growing old and frail; a pair of cairns, untended and forgotten.

"How long will pass here?"

"It depends on where you go, and how you return."

I tried to shake the visions from my mind, but a sensation remained, like a fishhook caught in my ribs. To leave would be to abandon my family, but to stay would damn us all to a moonless fate. And the promise I'd made the day my mother passed her seal to me was not only to those who lived now, but to all who would come after. I might not be here for my village, but I could give them hope. Hope that, one day, their children's children might sleep beneath their moon once more.

I replied before my voice or courage could fail. "Then I had better leave now."

Feeling slightly numb, slightly electric, I collected provisions from my family's larder, loading dried fish, pickles and cheese into my pack. I unhooked a coil of rope from the shed, trying to suppress the unease gnawing at my conscience. For over five hundred years, my family's seal had been passed from mother to daughter. It was more than just a tool—it was a symbol of trust. It was a promise that you would protect your family, just as those who'd come before had done.

My hand paused over a reel of ember-twine. I couldn't predict what might befall our village in a moonless world, but I was certain it would not be solved by slaying mud wraiths. I left the twine, hefting a bedroll from the shelf before stepping out into the silvery pre-dawn.

"Hullo!" gurgled a voice.

In the shadow of the mandala trees, the mud wraith stood in wait. "Are you going to fetch the moon?"

"I am."

"I'll come with you. No disrespect intended, but it could be a long voyage, and your people have a habit of decaying. I mean, really quickly. A mere six-hundred full moons pass, and your people go—" He mimed something that could only be described as explosive decomposition.

"We don't—" I mirrored his gesture. "And six-hundred moons is a very long time."

The mud wraith shook his head. "Not to the mountain. Not to the sea. And not to me."

His reasoning was irritatingly solid.

"Do you have a name?" I said gruffly.

"You can call me Book."

"Only criminals and ten-year-olds use made-up names."

"In the time it would take for me to say my genesis name, you would have turned to mulch. Your people sometimes name themselves after things they like: Lily, Basil, Pie."

"No one's called Pie."

The wraith shrugged. "I like books."

"Too much, apparently. Will you be returning the one you took?"

"I gave it to my brothers, so they can learn human-speak. But I think they're mostly learning the cuss words."

I suspected that Mahira wouldn't entirely disapprove of this use of her enchanted texts. Somewhat hesitantly, I extended both my fists towards the wraith. "My name is Ora, daughter of Ena."

Book's expression brightened, and he raised his fists to meet mine, gently bumping our knuckles in greeting. His hands felt surprisingly dry and slightly yielding: not unlike a pouch of honey.

My neck prickled at the sensation of being watched, and I turned to see a figure standing in the nearby doorway. My mother's eyes slid from me to the mud wraith to the pack on my shoulders. Guilt sliced my heart, like ember wires drawing tight. My mother backed away into the house.

"Ma!" I raced after her and nearly crashed into her as she rushed back out.

She pressed a woollen coat into my hands, her lips trembling. And wordlessly, she embraced me. I held her tightly in return, trying to commit to memory the warmth of her slight figure, the scent of pomegranates in her hair.

"Don't worry about me," I whispered. "Don't wait for me. I love you, always."

My last memory of my mother was a stoic figure on the crown of a snowy hill, silhouetted against the coming dawn.

* * *

Twenty days' march took me and my sedimentary companion far beyond the borders of my village, beyond the safely bounded world I knew. Tidy fields gave way to unkempt woodlands, which yielded to rocky canyons. We endured twenty moonless nights that simmered with confused cries and ominous silences before we reached the base of Defiance Rock. The summit of the sandstone spire pierced the veil of clouds, and at its peak, a sweeping plateau jutted like an eyrie altar.

If there is a place on this earth the Raivi will hear your plea, it will be at Defiance Rock, Mahira had said.

We climbed for days, taking rest in the wind-carved hollows. Here, the heart of the rock was revealed in rainbow bands of pink and grey and umber. Book stroked his fingers gently down a curving wall.

"These are the libraries of my people. Here, a flood. Here, a fire. Here, an ocean. I've read these tales a thousand times."

"Is that why you broke into our library? You were searching for new tales?"

"'Broke in' sounds very judgemental—"

"You left a six-foot hole in the wall."

"To be fair, I made that on the way out, when I was—"

"Fleeing?"

"—departing promptly." He fell silent, and I wondered if he were pretending to be asleep. Finally, he said softly, "I was looking for answers." And he said no more for the rest of the day.

* * *

The evening stars were just peppering the sky when we reached the plateau. Scraps of cloud swept past our feet, and it felt as though we could see all the world from our altitudinous perch: jagged mountain ranges, vast barren deserts, endlessly shifting seas. And our ever-spreading villages and cities, a multitude of hearths and furnaces burning like a challenge to the heavens.

With Mahira's diagram to guide me, I etched the sigils of the Raivi across the stony stage. Thick, crumbly lines of charcoal; spirals and domes of pale sand. The sallow air chilled the sweat on my face and neck as I struggled to finish the convoluted inscriptions. Arcane circles within arcane circles, and finally, only one element remained incomplete.

I withdrew the stone seal from my pouch, and it lay heavy in my hand like betrayal given form. Without the seal, my family's honour would be gravely diminished among my people. How would they stitch their leather and mend their fences? My fingers closed around the rough stone. I had to trust in their resourcefulness, their resilience, and hope that the kindness they had sowed among their neighbours would yield harvest in their time of need.

With painfully stiff fingers, I placed the seal in the centre of the innermost circle. Out of the corner of my eye, I saw Book shudder faintly as the seal touched the rock, and a strange sense of relief washed through me, as though the guilt I felt now for my family had lifted a deeper sin.

I stepped back from the summoning circle, taking a breath that felt somehow cleaner, somehow lighter, than I'd ever known.

"Don't worry about your parents," said Book kindly. "You'll probably disintegrate before we return, so I asked my brothers to take care of them."

"You did what?"

"You know, just asked them to check in on your family now and then, to see if they need human things done."

"Human things," I said flatly.

"Like digging holes. Or crushing cows."

"Who the hell crushes cows?"

"Well, your parents can, now."

Without warning, the world swayed, the ground seeming to surge towards us before plunging away again. The charcoal lines beneath us darkened, deepened, until they cut into the rock itself, and shadows rippled outward, smothering the fading cusp of the sun.

The Raivi rose from below the plateau like a dark-mirror moon, a circle of midnight, before she rippled and we beheld her true form. She had the semblance of a stingray the size of a village, and her back and fins were a lustrous black, flecked with luminous constellations. Her pale grey belly was the colour of winter skies, and her mouth curved into a delighted "ah" as she slowly circled our position.

Breathlessly, I struggled to recall the rituals from my childhood tales. "Honoured Raivi, we seek the Galliyar who stole our moon. We beg safe passage to the realm of the ancients, in exchange for this ensorcelled artefact."

The Raivi swooped slightly as she passed again, her fin ruffling over the seal, investigating its curves and nicks before she rippled it up onto her back, where it presumably joined her other treasures. She turned ponderously, her fin running curiously over Book before he too was rolled up and out of sight.

"You know I'm not a trinket, right?" he called urgently. "I'm a passenger. A passenger!"

If the Raivi understood, she gave no indication, wheeling as though to leave.

"Ahoy!" I cried. "I'm a passenger too!"

The Raivi didn't slow as she steered away, and I raced across the plateau, chasing Book's startled cries before I took a desperate leap across the widening gulf. I landed on the Raivi's back and tried to find something to cling to as she abruptly plummeted, as though in freefall.

"Shouldn't we be going upwards?" I said.

"I'm sure she doesn't need a back-fin driver," replied Book.

I gasped as the ground loomed closer, and pressed my eyes shut as I braced for impact.

There was a soft hush, a sensation of floating, of passing through sunlight and shade. When I opened my eyes, Book and I were still clinging to the back of the celestial ray, but all around us, above and below, was an unbroken night brimming with stars. The Raivi's fins undulated slowly as she continued on her course through the unseen realms, apparently unconcerned by her new passengers. Or acquisitions.

Across the gentle slopes of her back, mounds of trinkets and treasures formed esoteric hills. Geodes of blood-plum quartz, gold amulets inlaid with pearl, brass orreries arrayed with unfamiliar worlds, and, for some reason, the occasional giant pumpkin.

I found a patch of clear hide on which to pitch my tent, anchoring the ropes with wads of resin. I was pleasantly surprised to find that the skin of the Raivi was neither cold nor damp, but warm and slightly napped, like the worn velvet on a favourite chair. The tent I'd brought was the only one not stitched with ember-twine—a draughty child's cubby, patched with canvas and string. But for now, it would be home.

I glanced at Book, who stood nearby, head tilted, as though listening to a faraway song.

"Why don't your people build things?" I asked.

Book seemed genuinely puzzled. "Why would we need to? Everything builds itself: trees, corals, stalagmites, people. Your people build lots and lots of yourselves. I mean, *lots*."

I quickly steered the conversation to more constructive territory. "Do you think the Raivi understands us?"

"Too well, perhaps."

We stood, for a while, side by side, with the countless stars illuminating the way ahead, and, if time proved kind, lighting the way back home.

* * *

We sailed through glistening strands of nebulae, past the silent maw of collapsed novae. We watched the bright white fire of newborn stars and the dim red forge of dying suns. At times, towering plumes of cosmic dust rose around us like the phantom ruins of a behemoth's city. We braved storms of icy comets—the occasional stray rock scattering a pile of trinkets into the void.

I'd relocated my tent to a more sheltered valley, and Book and I huddled inside during a particularly fierce barrage. I tensed at the clamour of whistling rock and shattering ice, wincing at every *crash*.

"I'm not used to hiding from the weather," said Book.

"I don't think comets count as 'weather'."

"You know, once, back home, it rained continuously for twelve million moons."

I cocked an eyebrow. "Are you sure about that?"

"I was there," he said solemnly.

Over the passing months, his voice had settled into a more appropriate rhythm and volume and developed a musical cadence that, now, carried a wistful air. "When I was just a clod, monsoon phoenixes used to sweep across the skies every summer, their amethyst plumes trailing fresh mists carried in from the snowstorms of the southern pole. Your people hunted them for their feathers until there were none left.

"There used to be giant wombats the size of full-grown baobabs, carving tunnels through the impassable mountains. And there were singing serpents with scales like spattered gold and lapis, and little jewel frogs that caught the morning light like rainbow glass. They're all gone now. The world used to be a carnival of colour, song and scent. It's much quieter now. The colours more muted. And the air smells of dust and memories." He bowed his head in quiet mourning. "You wanted to know what I sought in your library. Long ago, my brothers from the river glades conversed with your people on many occasions."

"Why did they stop?" The question was a penance, for I already knew the answer.

"Your people slew them all."

I had no words to heal a wound that deep. No measure of remorse could bring absolution for what my people had done. Yet what Book sought was not apology, but answers.

"Our people never hurt you," he said. "Why do you kill us?"

I knew that a soul as steadfast as his could not understand the urgent, frenzied and solipsistic existence we lived, but he desired an explanation, and I offered what I could. "We think we're protecting our families, our communities. We feel that's more important than anything else."

"But you know that once everything is dead, there'll be nothing left to eat?"

"We assume things will grow back. That there'll always be more, because there always has been."

"You can't see that it's not coming back? You can't see the deserts spreading further, the forests growing frailer? Is it because your brains are so small and so squishy that they can't think big, long thoughts?"

"Partly, yes." I lowered my gaze to the living velvet beneath us, the muscles of the Raivi rhythmically bunching and releasing as she navigated the storm. "I know it makes little difference now, but I am truly sorry."

We sat in aching silence for what felt like an age, the bubbling sorrow within me slowly crystallising into bright needles, the pain no longer amorphous, but clear and precise, like spears of quartz.

Finally, Book lifted his gaze, listening intently. "I think the storm has passed."

Outside, the field of comets had given way to an expanse of stifling darkness littered with tiny pinpricks of red. A massive world, dwarfing anything I could have imagined, hung motionless in the night, an orb of fetid browns and greys.

But even more arresting was the colossus who loomed beside it, rendering the alien world a miniature in her presence. Tendrils of ebony hair drifted like tentacles from her head. Her skin was black, with rivulets of mercury tracing the muscles of her back and belly. Where her legs might have been, she possessed a massive fish-like tail, the ragged iron scales shifting with a susurrus of haunting *clanks*.

I felt like a mote of dust demanding the attention of a volcano.

"Honoured Ancient, I am Ora, daughter of Ena. I seek the Galliyar who stole our moon."

I wondered if a being so powerful would even register the existence of a human speck like me. Our answer came almost immediately.

The Galliyar leaned down towards the trembling Raivi, and her silver eyes were each the size of a moon.

"I am not the one you seek. I am the Galliyar of Forgotten Seas." She drew away and dropped the end of a gigantic chain into the silent brown waters. She twisted the chain and heaved it back up, a huge sunken galleon now tangled in the links, cascades of water pouring from the sightless portholes. "I salvage wrecks from the seas of long-dead worlds. To find your lost moon, let a piece of her guide you."

"What do you mean?" I called.

But the Galliyar was already moving on, swimming through the primordial dark, trailing a chain of ships behind her like a string of broken toys.

"That wasn't particularly helpful," I muttered.

"Actually, I think I know what she means," said Book. "The moon left fragments of herself with us when she kissed our world, long before the seas were formed. Our mountains and deserts carry pieces of her within them."

"Please don't tell me we have to double back."

Book placed his hands across his chest. "I have pieces of the moon within me. You might have tiny bits of the moon within you, but it probably comes and goes. Your people are very unstable. I mean physically—and mentally—but mostly physically. You're made of mush, and you always have mush going in and mush going out. Whereas my rock has been essentially the same since the mountains went up."

I eyed Book dubiously. "Then why do you look less muddy than when we left?"

"It's the different humidity," he said primly. "Oh, I have a surprise for you!" He rifled through a nearby mound. "I made these from the comet that broke your fort of telescopes last month." He pulled out two prehnite cabochons and pressed them into his eye sockets. "Now I have googly eyes, like you."

"I don't have—" I stopped, and allowed myself a smile. "They suit you. But you look fine without them. And you were right: the Raivi knows where she's going. Or, at least, she's not too proud to ask for directions."

Book seated himself on the ground and placed one palm on the Raivi's back, and one palm on his own chest. I didn't know if I had any moon within me, but I sat beside Book and adopted the same pose.

"Please," I said. "Take us to our moon."

* * *

I had no measure of time, or at least none that made sense to me. My hair grew longer, but my fingernails did not. My hands became rough and lined, but Book assured me that my face remained the same. Although, I suspected that all humans, regardless of age, looked the same to him. I sipped icy water captured from passing comets and was thankful for the Raivi's penchant for giant pumpkins, telling myself she wouldn't miss a few from her ever-growing stockpile. As recompense, I helped her sort her collection into more orderly themes: gemstones, talismans, textiles, perishables.

"I think she has a hoarding problem," I once told Book.

"It's only a problem if it makes you or others unhappy. Or if it becomes a fire hazard."

"It gives the asteroid mites more places to hide. I had to dislodge three of them from her fins last week. One almost broke my crosier."

Book himself did not remain unchanged. His hair had grown to astonishing lengths, like that of the abyssal maidens of myth, riding their chariots of jellyfish. His muddy complexion had progressively hardened and dried until he moved with the stiff, pained gait of a frail elder. Soon, his hair began to fall out, strand by strand, and I spooled them onto wands and staves, in case he had need of it later. At my persistent, worried queries, he'd finally mumbled "diagenesis" before curling up into the boulder-position, and he remained that way for several weeks. Or perhaps it was years.

I covered him with my woollen coat to keep the dust at bay and fended off marauding mites tempted to take a bite of this peculiar rock. Over time, I regaled his motionless form with stories from my childhood. I told him all my favourite legends, followed by the ones I considered acceptable. I left out the ones I'd always thought unhelpful or steeped in questionable values. After I'd expended all my tales of myth and adventure, I recounted the history of my people, my family, myself. That story hadn't found its ending yet, but the middle was … less lonely than I'd expected.

When Book finally re-awoke, the brittle clay flaked off his skin to reveal smooth sandy boulder matrix, shot with lightning veins of vivid opal. I marvelled at the rich tiger's eye hue of his new incarnation, and the blue-green fire snaking over his chest and limbs.

"Why don't more of your kinfolk look like that?" I asked.

"Among my people, diagenesis is the transformation of one kind of rock to another. We only metamorphose to maturity after twelve million moons. Your people haven't been around for one generation yet."

The scale of time pulled my mind into tortured strands, and I was momentarily dizzied by the sense of history, the sense of loss. I swayed on my heels, then realised that Book was also catching his balance.

The Raivi had stopped.

Although I could feel the stillness of the Raivi beneath my feet, the stars around us seemed to shift and waver, and in a giddy visual trick, the space before us drew aside like a curtain.

In the space between realms, in the place after time, there hung a gargantuan castle rimed in stardust. Turrets of smoky green glass rose in twisting spires, and encircling the base of the castle were concentric rings of sapphire shards, spinning in slow, eternal devotion. We glided through glassy gates that yielded like panes of water, and as we drew near the fortress portico, Book refracted a paler shade.

He nodded to a hanging mobile I'd taken for a string of wind-chimes. "Are those moons?"

As we passed beneath the dangling orbs, I could see the craters pocking each sphere. Voices of reason within me urged me to flee, but those old, familiar voices had grown fainter over the years, and other voices had taken their place. Voices I was only beginning to understand.

With wordless awe and dread, we entered the cavernous halls of the Galliyar's lair. Feeble diminutive suns hovered in brass-lattice lamps that occupied alcoves along the walls, illuminating the cabinets that lined every room.

And every cabinet was filled with moons.

Ice-encrusted baubles, glittering with diamond frost; spheres of roiling scarlet gas and caramel clouds, the colour of hibiscus tea at the moment milk is poured; striated balls of coppery light, pluming with ethereal geysers. A myriad of sizes, shades and compositions floated in their glass prisons, but I could not see the moon I sought.

"So," said Book nervously. "What do we do? I'm not good with fast-moving things or complicated, twisty minds."

I dragged my gaze slowly over the arsenal of talismans and enchanted weaponry that lay neatly arranged across the Raivi's back, and I took a deep breath.

"Honourable Galliyar, I am Ora, daughter of Ena, and I have come for our moon."

"Have you, now?" The voice rumbled like the tide of time manifested. She appeared before us as though the entire universe had moved to take its place around her. A halo of malachite beads framed an opaque white face, and her eyes were tourmaline skies from edge to edge, drifting with wisps of white clouds. Jade spines extruded from her back like skeletal wings, and her skin from the shoulders down was a shifting sea of blue, the shadow of giant placoderms skating beneath the waves.

Book pressed in close beside me, the force of so many moons twisting within him. I squeezed his hand and raised my face to the Galliyar.

"Are you the Galliyar who stole our moon?"

"Stole?" The physical force of her word rattled the halls of glass. "You have no greater claim to it than I. I am the Galliyar of Abandoned Moons. What are *you*?"

"I am of the world that captured that moon. We still need it, and we have no others." I risked a pointed glance at the overfilled cabinets.

"Your world captured it from passing debris, and I captured it from you. As for *need*, your people no longer need it."

She raised a watery hand and a vision floated at her fingertips. My heart fluttered at the sight of familiar constellations, a familiar world—

But no, instead of a blue-green globe streaked with white, there was too much grey, too much orange, and black—why were so many of the rivers black?

The Galliyar slowly spun the ghostly globe. "Your people are long gone. Two thousand years after I collected your moon, they finally consumed their world to the marrow. And before you accuse me of triggering their fall, your people were already drawing their final breaths, the decisions that would doom them already made. What's two thousand years, in the grander scale of things?"

Shock and rage scoured away my grief. "The moon was not yet

abandoned when you took it. You don't *know* that my people would have continued on their fatal course—"

"And yet, I do. I have seen a billion worlds just like yours, lapping up their own poison, prying at their world until it breaks. Not unlike a mindless infestation that eventually kills its host. And it's true; your people *could* have averted it. Almost every world like yours *could* have averted it. But none of them *did*. All of them knew what lay ahead, but none of them stopped. None of them changed. Not in time."

"You could have waited. You could have asked." The futility of the exchange, of our entire venture, burned away what was left of me. My family, my village, my world, all lost. Hope fleeted away, and I wondered if it had ever been more than mere illusion.

The Galliyar's eyes deepened to twilight, lashed with spokes of lightning. "Do you wait for the tree to fall in its own time before you carve it into timber? Do you parley with the beasts you slaughter?"

I felt Book's hand hold mine a little tighter. "Yes," he said quietly. "She did. I asked for mercy, and she showed it. And we ask for your mercy now."

We stood together in silence, facing down the Galliyar.

Her twilight eyes threw a lidded gaze towards us. "An offer, then. If you have such faith in your people. I cannot reverse time, but I can open a window, a sliver of a gap for you to pass through." She flicked a finger towards the ghostly vision, and an emerald thread snaked towards the globe. Where it touched the mottled grey surface, the world suffused with colour, once more a blue-green sphere. "I can send you back to the day your moon was taken. You can do what you wish, try to convince your people to defy their nature and avert their fate. But in exchange, your moon stays with me. Your people won't need it."

There was a time I would have wept with relief, with frustration, with all the emotions a human frame could cage. But that girl was gone, the voices of doubt and ambition within her transformed into voices of stillness, patience, and—perhaps—the occasional big, long thought. Time turned on a different spindle here, and I, too, had undergone a diagenesis.

I'd made a promise, lifetimes ago, to protect my family. And now, I understood that one's family was more than mere blood. More, even, than one's own people. It was your world and all who shared it, from the slumbering dust to the blazing stars, and all the glorious, heartbreaking mess in between.

"My people are gone," I said. "But there's a chance that some life persists. And they need their moon."

"Would you call it 'life'?" said the Galliyar.

"They do," I replied. "Our moon, please."

* * *

In the end, the Galliyar had tipped our sad little moon from a silken pouch containing other moons, as though it were a set of marbles. With a rope woven from the scarlet strands shed by Book during his metamorphosis, we tethered the moon to the Raivi's tail and towed it behind us like a kite.

"I thought you might try to fight the Galliyar," said Book. "Or steal the moon back. Or trick her with riddles."

We sat beside a mound of knitted octopuses, which I suspected were charming rather than charmed, but the Raivi wanted what she wanted. "Why didn't you fight me, the night I hunted you?"

"A rock is a library of all the things that came before. We remember every drop of rain, every fall of ash, every friend made, every life taken. Some stories are drenched in blood and victory. I am not that kind of book."

"Is that a pun?"

"What's a pun?"

"Never mind." I watched as the glow of a passing pulsar swept over Book, his skin like polished copper, but his arms and legs as lumpy and mismatched as they were that first night among the mandala trees. "The Galliyar believed my people to be thieves and butchers, undeserving of mercy. Hubris fuelled our downfall. Perhaps humility would be our redemption."

"I'm sorry about your people," said Book.

"So am I."

* * *

Defiance Rock had been shattered millennia ago, felled in the war that created the Infinity Wasteland. So, instead, the Raivi deposited us on the sloping sands of the desert, which didn't seem as desolate as it had from a distance. Rotund kangaroo rats hopped across the dunes like ginger pom-poms, and bleary frogs peered out from the sands, disappearing again when the false cloud of the Raivi's shadow departed.

"I'm sure she won't keep things sorted by category," I said as we waved farewell.

"She might," said Book. "You gave her a very educational lecture about the dangers of mange."

We had released the moon in what Book assured me was the appropriate position, and if it were slightly misaligned, there was no helping it now. We made our way across the hazy desert, the air cooling as the night breathed closer. We had no clear destination, but one didn't feel necessary.

The surface of a nearby dune rippled and shifted, and a lumpy figure rose from the sands, his skin the colour and texture of sandstone. Two thumb-sized sockets were pressed into his face, and these, he turned towards Book.

"Hullo, brother. We missed you." He then turned to me. "Hullo, sister. Welcome home."

Twilight painted the sky in pastel shades of lavender and periwinkle, and the moon shone like the smile of a long-lost friend, casting a silvery wash over the dunes and beyond. My people's story has ended, pressed between pages of earth and rock, but the story of the mud wraiths continued. And, in time, my own volume would join the library of this world, a tale of mud and stone and starlight.

I smiled at the sand-encrusted figure. "Hullo."

About *The Moon Collector*

The Moon Collector was Aurealis Award-shortlisted for Best Young Adult Short Story.

The Moon Collector was first published in *Under the Full Moon's Light* (Owl Hollow Press, 2018), edited by Emma Nelson and Hannah Smith.

TO RUN BETWEEN
THE FALLING STARS

Magnus raced over the amber glass cobbles, gripping the hand—the claw—of the reptilian woman beside her. There was no cover out here on the bare, blighted hills, and the broken chains around the woman's ankles *clinked* a frantic rhythm as she ran.

The path ahead forked and splayed in glassy veins, and Magnus squinted in fierce concentration—she'd run a mock-up of this course a hundred times in the sunny sports oval: map in one hand, stopwatch in the other. Second path to the right, third left, left again. She resisted the urge to break into a sprint—it was still too early. Still six hundred metres to the exit point. Five hundred. She flicked a worried glance at the reptilian woman, who kept stubborn pace with her despite the dull skin sagging off her bones, and the weeping patches of flesh where her scales had been wrenched off.

Behind them, an alarm wailed with bone-splintering intensity, and Magnus swore under her breath. She risked a glance over her shoulder—dots of light streaked from the towering eyrie gulag, and a searchlight swept across her back. Across the dark sky, countless broad white wings beat towards them, silver helms glinted, hooked beaks screamed.

Four hundred metres.

Three hundred.

The spidery jade bridge was still too far away. Magnus tore into a sprint, regrets strangling her breath. She'd promised herself she'd graduate from Crossing High this year. But at least she'd left a letter on the dresser for her parents, as always, just in case. But Ioren had been right, damn him. Magnus had gotten too ambitious. Too careless.

"Get on my back," hissed the reptilian woman.

Barely waiting for Magnus, the woman dove onto all fours and into a blistering scramble. They skimmed the cobbles, the hills rushing past, the bridge looming closer until the stony lacework finally swept overhead.

Magnus slid onto the mottled green walkway, her heart knocking against her ribs as she ran the last few metres towards a mandala of runes scorched into the ground. A fraction wider than a manhole, the overlapping circles and interconnected lines resembled a stylised star chart. Overhead, outraged shrieks shattered the air and a patchwork of huge white wings smothered the sky.

Magnus drew the limping reptilian woman into the circle, wrapping one arm tightly around her. "Stay very still."

As the feathered sentinels plunged towards them, Magnus slammed her free hand against the cold brass dial harnessed over her breastbone. A glimmering green light raced through the runes at her feet, and Magnus squeezed her eyes shut, concentrating on the journey home. Branches of silver fire burned across her brain, and she gritted her teeth, trying to ignore the furious screeches diving closer, the gale of wingbeats tearing across her face, the grey talons slashing towards them—

A sensation like hot needles rushed over her, and in a blinding whip of green light, everything vanished.

* * *

In the moment before she opened her eyes, Magnus could already feel the plush carpet of her bedroom beneath her sneakers. She could smell the faded rosemary wreath she kept on her bedside table, next to the photo of her grandfather. She drew back gently and saw the reptilian woman's golden eyes blinking in the dim light, her slitted pupils dilating and contracting.

"Akatha," said Magnus. "Are you all right?"

The woman's gaze ticced across the messily made bed, the rolls of chicken wire and scraps of vintage fabric, the half-dried tins of varnish, and the walls adorned with posters of forgotten things, like Pluto and numbats.

"I'm alive," rasped Akatha. "Thank you."

Magnus swallowed the lump in her throat. These missions never felt like a victory, only a small consolation. She busied herself unlocking the top drawer of her desk.

"Your starter kit." Magnus handed Akatha a bulky envelope. "Identity papers, useful contacts, currency, and general guidelines. For example, the animals you see running around on leashes—don't eat them. And this will help."

Magnus held out a slim rubber bracelet closely resembling the fitness trackers many people wore here in Flotsam Crossing. Akatha allowed Magnus to slide the band onto her wrist, and pearly runes blinked across the surface. Akatha suddenly shimmered, her form wavering into the semblance of a woman with closely cropped sandy hair, dressed in a cap-sleeved shirt and cargo pants.

"I'll take you to the safe-house," said Magnus, "and in a few days, you'll get a visit from Ioren—the man who first approached you. He'll help you find a place to settle."

Akatha looked at her light brown hands, and then across at the pane of peaceful midnight through the bedroom window. Her expression betrayed only a tinge of all she'd lost, all she'd left behind, and the world she would never see again.

"You're not alone," said Magnus, touching Akatha's shoulder gently. "Come on, I think my mum has a set of bolt cutters in the kitchen."

***

Six weeks passed, winter folded into spring, and on the first day of term, the school corridors smelled of disinfectant and stale deodorant. Last year's faded playbills and vandalised election posters had been replaced by a fresh slew of sign-up sheets and densely typed school notices.

Magnus grinned as an athletic boy with tousled curls and dark brown skin swaggered down the hall towards her, dressed in a deconstructed couture dress embroidered with interplanetary rovers. He raised a hand as he neared, and Magnus gave him a languid high-five.

"Hey, Nick. Nice threads."

One of the things Magnus liked about Flotsam Crossing was that no one ever questioned why Nick wore what he wore. Just like nobody ever questioned why Magnus had a name more commonly associated with Scandinavian kings and supervillains.

She nodded towards the noticeboards. "Give me the subliminal version."

"Perfumes and aftershaves are banned," drawled Nick. "Visorfields are jammed. The coffee dealers have relocated to behind the portables. And, my friend, the countdown to freedom is *on*."

The soporific chime of the school bell gave way to the squeak of unstable classroom chairs, and Magnus tried to focus on the assessment schedules and course modules streaming onto her tablet. But her thoughts sidled and skulked, dipping into her other timetable, her other commitments. It had been six weeks since she'd returned with Akatha. And it was always six weeks between missions. And visits from Ioren.

"Blood," intoned Mr Sethia, the tips of his fingers resting on the knotholed wood of his desk. "Sweat. Tears. Laughter. Heartbreak."

He leaned forward, letting his words sink into the dusty silence. "Triumph. This is *your* year. Your final year."

Mr Sethia was a neat, middle-aged man with a sharp smile and an orator's soul. He was Magnus's art teacher—her favourite teacher—but today, his words skittered away from her.

"Know this," he said, sweeping his gaze across the restless students, "wherever you go, whatever you do, you will always remember this year. So, my question to you is, what do you want to remember?"

Magnus looked down at the blank page of her process diary, her thoughts twisting and splitting into dendritic tangles. She wanted a transcript studded with distinctions, a victorious hockey season, endless afternoons with Nick and Wolverhampton, drinking homemade toffee coffee until their teeth hurt. But she also wanted …

The thing about life was, you didn't always remember the good things, or the important things. Sometimes, the things that stuck in your mind, that gnawed at you, that refused to let you move on, were the things you didn't even fully understand.

And for over a year, what Magnus couldn't forget was a word, a look, a tone. A broken flicker in a stranger's eyes.

And tonight, she had something to say to Ioren.

* * *

Magnus sat cross-legged on her onigiri floor cushion, her dark hair tied back from her face. Towering escarpments of art history textbooks surrounded her, featuring everything from satirically painted amphorae to boldly stencilled Tokyo street art. Afternoon sunlight peered through the curtains, and haunting electronica by Wall of Extinction floated through her bedroom. Nick leaned back in Magnus's swivel chair.

"Mathematics Communication at Aesara University," he said. "You?"

"Maybe Political Fine Arts," said Magnus. "You?"

She turned to Wolverhampton, who was sitting on her bed with an expression of slightly pensive meditation. He was in the same year as her and Nick and looked like a willowy boy of Chinese heritage, although his family background was far more complicated.

"I think I'd like to be a teacher," he said. "I asked Ms Rathbone what I needed to become a teacher, and she said patience. Lots of patience. And self-restraint. Or maybe she said self-defence. My hearing's been a bit wobbly lately. Mind if I get out of this gear?"

Magnus waved a hand permissively, and Wolverhampton shrugged off his overstuffed blue anorak before tapping the black rubber bracelet on his wrist. He shivered, his clothes and flesh liquefying into translucent blue jelly until all that remained on the bed was a large puddle of amorphous goo. With a pair of eyes.

Wolverhampton and his family had been among the first people Magnus had brought over from their dangerous or dying worlds. It had taken four trips, and he'd insisted on being the last to cross over, after his parents and younger sister. They'd adopted the appearance of East Asians after learning that a sizeable proportion of Earth's population were of this background.

Being originally genderless, Wolverhampton had adopted a male identity after learning that men led statistically more privileged lives. His sibling had promptly called him a wimp, and become a girl instead. His parents, being pragmatic types, both took on male identities.

And then, they'd chosen names.

The green light had faded, but the boy was still shivering. In Magnus's arms, he felt like a fragile plastic bag of water.

"What should I call you?" asked Magnus, and the boy turned his cranial blob towards her.

"I ... can have a name?" he said.

"Any name you want," she replied.

"On my world," he said quietly, "low-viscosity people are all called

'Sesh', because that's the sound we make when they beat us."

Magnus lowered her book.

"I think you'd make a great teacher." She stretched her shoulders and gave a deep sigh. "Do you think—the week before Vesuvius erupted—there were people just like us, wondering whether they should become sculptors or mathematicians?"

Nick cocked an eyebrow. "Do you know something we don't?"

There was a brisk knock at the door, and Magnus quickly threw a blanket over the bed.

"Come in," she called, and a tall, energetic woman leaned in, her dark braid falling past her sleeveless black top.

Magnus's mother, Kami, was a founding member of "Shut Up and Listen", a community activist group that thrived on petitions and witty projectiles. Magnus sometimes marvelled at the unlikely confluence of events that had brought her parents together in Kenya, where Japanese-Australian Kami had been sabotaging poachers, and Dutch-Irish painter, Lars, had been couch-surfing his way across the world.

"Have you seen my bolt cutters?" said Kami. "Hi, Nick."

"Protesting at the meat-mesh factory again?" said Magnus.

"Another three workers were crushed by a poorly secured vat," huffed Kami. "You see the irony?"

"Yes, Mum. It's in the laundry, next to the shovel."

"Thanks. Where's Wolverhampton?"

"He had to use the bathroom," said Magnus.

Kami paused. "I didn't see anyone in there."

"He doesn't like using other people's toilets," said Nick.

Kami shrugged. "Let him know I can get hygienic wipes. Don't wait up for me."

The door clicked shut, and two wobbly blue appendages pushed away the blanket.

"Now your mother thinks I'm weird," said Wolverhampton.

"As long as your dads keep loading her up with organic palmiers, you're secure in her good graces," said Magnus.

"You have awesome parents, Magnus, you know that?" said Nick.

His own mother was an epidemiologist from Uganda, and his father a British-Nepalese diplomat. Their dinner table conversations bounced between Sumerian poetry and sustainable sanitation projects, so he was an authority on cool parents.

Magnus glanced at the window, the sun sinking slowly behind a ridge of distant mountains, the clouds billowing pink and gold.

"It's getting late," she said, and Nick and Wolverhampton exchanged a glance.

"Take it easy, all right?" said Nick as he left.

* * *

Magnus sat in her fort of books, the lamplight brushing the ceiling with shadows. Her shoulder harness lay draped over one knee, the circular case empty. The mechanism—the gyroflare, as Ioren called it—sat cool and heavy in her hand: a fretwork of brass with panes of glass. Like a pocket-watch. Like a compass. Gently, she depressed the crown, and the glass cover snapped open, revealing a miniature brass carousel inset with translucent stones that wavered in her vision, like the barely visible edges of a blowtorch flame. She found it soothing to look at, to hold, this mysterious piece of her past and her future.

"It belonged to your great-grandmother," said Ioren. "And then to your grandfather. And now, it belongs to you."

Magnus knew little of her great-grandmother, Hoshiko, but her grandfather had been a gentle, lively man, softly spoken, full of tales of strife and hardship, and of exquisite joy and kindness. He'd had a smile that lit up her world, and then—

Magnus had only just turned ten when that part of her world had caved in. She remembered peering down from the top of the stairs to see her mother in the hallway below, her hand over her mouth as the police officer spoke in hushed, sombre tones. Magnus's dad stood with his arms wrapped around her, as though he could somehow shield her from the news. They'd said it was probably a heart attack, but his sedan had rolled more than fourteen times on its way down the gully. It had been a closed-casket funeral.

Magnus was sixteen when Ioren first appeared to her. From what little she'd coaxed from him, he was a former incubus who'd been fired for talking too much. But more importantly, he'd been a friend of her grandfather's.

The curtains stirred, and Magnus snapped the device shut.

"How's Akatha?" she said.

"Actually, she goes by 'Sandi', now."

Ioren stood by the bookshelf, impeccably attired in a crisp linen shirt and tailored black trousers, his silk vest patterned as though he'd rolled across vintage wallpaper. His chestnut hair was neatly slicked, and he adjusted his pince-nez with black-gloved hands. He reminded Magnus of a pedigree whippet: all fine bones and melancholy eyes.

"Sandi?" she said. "Seriously?"

"I'm sure you would have suggested something like 'Helionephthys', but she said 'Sandi' was easier to remember. Orientation's going well, although she makes the most disconcerting clicking noise when she's angry."

"Then don't make her angry."

"Everything makes her angry. She attacked the Happy Clucker Chicken Dinners mascot at the supermarket last week."

"He *is* pretty obnoxious. Why is a chicken trying to sell me fried chicken, anyway?"

"You sound like your mother."

Magnus paused at the sudden knot of guilt in her gut. She'd kept these extracurricular activities from her parents because, even if they understood—and surely her mother, of all people, would understand—they'd only worry.

Her early missions had been simple enough, safe enough, although Ioren had warned her that there were always risks, to both her and her passengers. But Magnus had pressed him for more difficult assignments, more desperate circumstances. Because there were some places that should not exist, some torments that no one should endure. And there was something that she could no longer ignore. She glanced at Ioren, subtly bracing herself.

"I've decided on our next target," she said. "When we first met, you mentioned something called a crucifer prison."

Ioren's eyes flashed cold, his amiable air gone.

"No."

That seemed to be the end of the conversation, and Magnus's resolve faltered, her arguments squirming like retreating earthworms.

"You said there were terrible places." She tried to keep her voice steady. "Full of hopeless suffering. You said I could help. This is me, helping."

"There are people you can help, and there are those you can't. I never should have mentioned it, but it was late, and you were bombarding me with so many questions." He shifted, anxious and flustered. "I should scrub it from your memory."

He swept a hand towards Magnus and she grabbed his wrist, holding it firm.

"I want to remember. I want to fix it, or at least try. I've been working towards this. I know I can do it. But I need you to make the approach."

He held her gaze, but his wrist trembled ever so slightly. Magnus remembered only snatches of their first meeting, the details lost in a blur of disbelief and excitement. But she remembered the look in his eyes, the catch in his voice, when he'd mentioned that prison. He'd shown her numerous worlds since then, each more devastating than the last, but none had shaken him, haunted him, the way this one clearly did.

"At least show me," said Magnus. "Let me make up my own mind. Please."

She released his wrist and held out the gyroflare. For a long moment, she thought he would refuse.

"I work for you," he said finally. "I honour the same contract I made with your great-grandmother."

Reluctantly, he tapped the dial with his finger. A green light swirled across the glass, spreading to the brass casing, filling the etched runes with an incandescent ink wash.

"It's a fourteen-dimension plunge," said Ioren grimly. "For one fae boy."

Magnus swiped her fingers across the glass, and the light swept outwards into sheets of schematics and scrolling lists. Her stomach twisted.

"There are hundreds of fae in this prison …"

"Only this boy can cross over."

Magnus scrolled down the manifest. "His father's with him. You said cross-over compatibility runs along bloodlines. That's why I can use the gyroflare. His father should be able to cross over too."

"One soul per plunge, and it takes you weeks to recover. They'll be waiting for you if you return."

"We went back three times for Wolverhampton's family—"

"This is a high-security prison, not a lawless ghetto." Ioren's voice sliced like a razor. "Every world is different."

Magnus stared at the glowing pages, her thoughts drawn to memories of wide, warm smiles and twisted wreckage. Her grandfather's passing had been the first time she'd truly understood just how vast a void could be left behind by a single person.

Magnus curled her fingers around the cold device and let out a slow, troubled breath.

"So, when's our window for the plunge?" she said.

* * *

Her breath scorched in her throat, her vision gurgling in the liquid heat. Eight weeks of training had seemed like overkill, but here, now, Magnus feared it hadn't been nearly enough. She wound her way through countless huge white chambers that were shaped like globular ceramic pots, narrowing into constricted chimneys far above. All around her, gaunt figures staggered—gasping, screaming, their protective enchantments evaporating from them as fast as they could cast them, all struggling to stop themselves from turning into ash.

Some cowered, exhausted and defeated. Every few paces, Magnus glimpsed a pile of soot in the silhouette of a figure curled in on itself, one arm reaching out to barely touch another pile of cinders.

The mission data had been clinical, making brief reference to godlike beings who could bottle fear and desire, and used prisons like these to power their empires. But here, there was nothing clinical, nothing objective, about the screams and the stench. All her training buckled in the face of her rage, her horror, that something like this could *exist*.

Through her goggles, she couldn't wipe her eyes, couldn't stop to clear the terrible lump in her throat. The honeycomb maze flowed like a Möbius strip, with no signposts, no landmarks, no way in or out. Save one.

"Stay close," Magnus croaked to the two figures stumbling behind her.

The fae boy—Ryuen—tried to quicken his pace. He was slightly older than Magnus, his feet blackened and blistered, his dragonfly wings singed to stumps. He half-supported, half-carried his father, Gelharon, who looked like an older, horribly skeletal version of the boy.

"I'll say my farewells when I see the gate," said Ryuen. "Not before."

Magnus concentrated on the schematics etched into her memory. Fifty-eight steps forward. Turn thirty degrees clockwise. Twenty-three steps forward and then turn another ninety degrees.

Her heart thudded painfully and her muscles burned with exertion. She could feel the gyroflare whirring furiously against her chest as it strained to prevent her from turning into charcoal. Her right leg suddenly gave way and she staggered several steps. She drew a gasp of searing air, trying to steady herself.

She'd left a letter for her parents, just in case.

Magnus glanced at the two huddled figures, and then back to the hazy path ahead. Adjusting for three wonky steps, she needed twelve more to the right, then—

"This way," she said.

She raced towards the circle of runes branded onto the floor, brushing away a layer of ash with her aramid gloves. Ryuen and Gelharon staggered into her, and Magnus grasped the older man to prevent him from falling. She tried not to look at the tide of blackened flesh creeping up his shins.

Ryuen took several steps backwards.

"You have to stay close," snapped Magnus.

The young man looked at her, his copper eyes steady through the haze.

"I'm not coming."

Magnus's stomach lurched.

"You can only take one soul," said Ryuen. "It has to be my father." Gelharon began to protest, but Ryuen continued. "I can survive this. People have lasted months, even years, in here. I'll find another way out."

"There *is* no other way," said Gelharon.

"Then I'll survive. Those who last the longest are sometimes offered a deal to work for the Duaken. I promise you, Father, I'll die of old age. In here, or out there. If you stay, you have only hours left, we both know that. I can't watch that. I …"

Ryuen's mouth twisted, his tears dissolving into silver vapour that coiled upwards into the hungry chimneys. It was then that Magnus noticed the dark grey veins flowing across the smooth walls and slithering towards them. The purging streams had locked onto her.

"I'll come back for you," said Magnus. "It might take time, but I promise I'll come back."

"Then I'll wait."

Gelharon reached out. "Ryuen—"

Ryuen's fingers brushed his father's. "I love you—"

The lancing veins rushed towards them in a scorching wave, and Magnus slammed her palm against the smoking gyroflare, her fingers blistering beneath her gloves. Green light flooded the chamber, and—

Magnus tightened her arms around the shaking man, silver needles flooding her brain, pathways burning like falling stars. She concentrated on home, a single point of light in an endless constellation. Gelharon's flesh was already cooling—he'd probably lose his legs, but there was a maker in town who printed excellent prosthetics.

Home, she willed. They just had to—

The constellations twisted, the stars scattering into darkness. A sudden pressure crushed cracks across her mind. Magnus tried to scream, but her lungs felt as though they were filled with shrapnel. Something had gone wrong—

She speared her thoughts towards home, maintaining her grip on Gelharon. She saw his eyes widen in fear, his skin rippling, and then he—

Silence.

Magnus stood in the dim lamplight of her bedroom. She couldn't feel the carpet beneath her melted boots. She couldn't smell the rosemary wreath through the stench of smoke and cinders. Her fingers dripped, glistening red. Blood spattered the walls. Sticky chunks plastered the ceiling.

And her arms were empty.

* * *

Magnus spent her spring break locked in her bedroom, cleaning pieces of fae from her walls. Five bottles of ammonia. Eight garbage bags. Her bed sheets, her curtains, and all her posters went into burning bins down at the vacant lot. Her process diary, too. Partially filled with useless doodles and meaningless waffle. And blood.

She'd always facetiously assumed that fae blood consisted of silver dust and sparkles—after all, they were allergic to iron. But on her hands, it looked like blood. It smelled like blood. And it felt like blood.

Ioren would know the outcome by now, but he didn't appear, and Magnus didn't summon him. She locked away the gyroflare, along with the envelope meant for Ryuen. She couldn't go back for him until she knew what had gone wrong. She hadn't done anything differently, but no one had ever—

She would return, once she'd figured it out. She just—

In the following weeks, she didn't read her streaming messages. She didn't answer her phone. She emerged from her room only after everyone else had gone to sleep. With her bedroom door practically fossilised shut, her parents eventually stopped knocking.

"Final year blues, maybe," said her dad.

"Maybe," replied her mother.

Magnus's dad had spent his final year hanging guerrilla hammocks around the city. Her mother had spent hers campaigning to make their senior prom cetacean-accessible for the dolphin students.

Magnus had wanted to spend this year—*her* year—making her grandad proud. Good grades. Lives saved. Graduation, hooray.

Instead, time passed in an arrhythmic pulse of Virginia Woolf and polynomials, her new sketchbook filling with smoky figures wavering into embers. But the smooth white paper made her nauseous now, and the classroom heaters smelled like burning flesh.

Five weeks went by, and every flutter of seagulls, every yell from the sports oval, sent a disorienting jolt through her. Magnus leaned over the steel washbasin trough in the seniors' toilet block, cupping the rust-tainted water to her face. When she straightened, she saw a reflection behind her in the scratched tin mirror.

"I get that you need space," said Nick. "I get that you don't want to talk about it. I just need to know you're okay. Because from here, it looks like you're having a meltdown."

Magnus flinched at the last word. Shakily, her lips parted, but no sound emerged, the words still bottled in her throat. She knew she should talk about it, have a good cry, process her emotions and parcel them away. But her thoughts ricocheted around her skull, dodging out of reach one moment and then suffocating her the next. She wanted to be fine, but right now, she didn't know how.

She didn't know how to explain the way, so often, this world didn't feel real. Her parents chatting at the dinner table. Students bustling through the school halls. Supermarkets gleaming beneath LED lights. So bright and hollow, like a cellophane diorama. But Magnus could see the real world on the other side—

As the silence pooled around them, Nick shook his head.

"You've got to stop doing this to yourself," he said. "Ever since that guy showed up, you've been running yourself ragged. I'm proud of what you're trying to do, I am. Wolverhampton's always blubbering about how you saved his family, and you never asked for payment, or qi, or a piece of his soul. But you've got to slow down. Take a step back. Take care of yourself."

Words finally crawled from her throat.

"But I'm the only one—"

"You're not indispensable, Magnus. The universe won't break if you stop doing what you're doing. But *you* will, if you're not careful."

Magnus felt the knots in her chest constricting, coiling so tightly she could hardly breathe. He hadn't seen dimensions billowing like an endless swathe of tapestries, seething with the lost, the trapped, the hopeless. She wanted him to understand, but that wouldn't be fair.

When she didn't say anything further, Nick headed for the door.

"I'm always here if you need me," he said. "But you shouldn't feel guilty about wanting a life for yourself."

* * *

Magnus ran across the starlit sand, the powdery beach curving away into a crescent, enfolding the town of Flotsam Crossing. She ran because it cleared the noise from her head and swept the ash from her eyes. And because it had been six weeks since the crucifer prison, and she would never run far enough.

She finally slowed, gasping lungfuls of the salt-licked air. A sudden swell brought a slap of seawater over her feet, leaving a tide-line across her sneakers. Magnus wiped the sweat from her eyes, not turning to look at the shadow on the shore.

"When were you going to tell me?" said Ioren.

"You already knew."

It was an excuse for toddlers, cheats, and cowards, and Magnus knew which one she was. For a long while, the only sound was the endless lapping of the waves and the breath catching in Magnus's throat.

"You were right," she choked. "I screwed up."

"No," said Ioren quietly. "You were right. You could have done it."

"But he … he didn't …"

"There will always be losses. Your grandfather's rate was one in five—one in five he couldn't hold on to as he tore through the aether.

You, Magnus, you surfaced ten times without a single casualty. I'm sorry I didn't prepare you better for your first loss."

Magnus turned her face away, the light-flecked waves blurring in her vision. So there would be more, countless more.

"I always tell them the risks," continued Ioren. "They make a choice."

"That's not a *choice*: quick death, slow death, torment with a chance of splatter."

"What do you want, Magnus?" said Ioren gently.

A part of her wished he'd never appeared that night. That all she had to worry about were university fees and broken hearts, shrinking job markets and rising apartment prices. A part of her wished her grandfather's secret friend had been a genie instead of … She didn't even know what he really was.

"I …" In the hushed twilight of the beach, her tangled thoughts washed slowly away, leaving only an old ache in her chest. "I … need some time."

Magnus couldn't decipher the expression in Ioren's eyes as he nodded, brushing imaginary lint from his sleeve.

"I understand."

"Ioren. What do you do … when you're not doing this?"

He remained silent for a long while, as though discarding a succession of answers. Or finding none.

"You know how to reach me," he said.

And with the sigh of the receding wave, he was gone.

* * *

In the following weeks, it seemed to Magnus that texture, colour, and substance gradually seeped back into the world. The days felt less paper-thin. The episodes of unreality, of feeling as though she were crushed beneath waves, slowly eased. She shuttered away her thoughts of Ioren and the gyroflare and the countless worlds glimmering in the darkness.

Summer cruised past in a glorious succession of lingering days. Blazing afternoons of thundering hockey war-cries blurred into spirit-crushing all-nighters in front of constipated essays. Frantic scavenger-hunts through the town's art supply stores ended in muggy evenings on the boardwalk, her toes dipped in the clear green water, a cup of lychee sorbet in her hand. University applications were sent with a swipe and a skipped heartbeat.

Magnus sold caramel-banana muffins at the charity fundraising fair, and went literally stag to the mythical-creatures-themed dance, where Lance Thickett tried to throw Wolverhampton into the cetacean pool. Magnus ended up in the principal's office for accidentally dislocating Thickett's shoulder. Nick ended up there for relocating it.

"Since when is first aid an offence?" muttered Nick, his flashing neon gryphon wings creating a mini-disco in the receptionist's office.

"I think it's more the wedgie you followed it up with," said Magnus, her *Mononoke Hime* antlers tucked under one arm.

"I'm glad I don't have bones," said Wolverhampton in his kraken-print tux. "Or a butt crack."

They were let off with warnings, and the year rolled inexorably towards final exams. Magnus pushed everything else from her mind—this was *her* year. But even so, the whisper of distant worlds kept plucking at her heart, and she tried to drown it out with the jarring beats of Sky Burial Rights.

Therefore, she didn't hear the knocking at her door, and only half-turned when her mother leaned in.

"There's someone here to see you," said Kami. "Do you have a friend called Sandi?"

Magnus leapt down the staircase in a single hip-dislocating bound, skidded down the hall and out onto the porch, where she shuffled the tall, tawny-eyed woman behind a hedge of camellias.

"Akatha," said Magnus. "How are you? Is everything okay?"

"Yes. Your sun is a little small, but I'm fine."

"What are you doing here?"

"I came to say goodbye."

Something odd tugged at Magnus's heart. Most of the arrivals soon moved on to bigger cities, smaller villages, places that reminded them of home, or washed away the memories. Only Wolverhampton's family had stayed, and they said it was because they wanted to be near a good school.

"I've studied your global map," said Akatha, "and decided the Sahel is a suitable habitat. Ioren tells me it's very hot and very sunny, and there are mammals trying to live there with insufficient water-delivery infrastructure."

"Um, that sounds about right."

"Before I go, I had one last question—one that Ioren couldn't answer." Akatha fixed Magnus with a bright, piercing gaze. "Why do you do it? Risk your life for ours?"

"I …" Magnus swallowed. "I actually don't do that anymore."

Akatha studied Magnus for a moment—no disappointment or judgement in her eyes. Finally, she nodded.

"Everyone deserves to be happy," she said, and as she roared away on her beat-up motorbike, she raised a hand in farewell.

* * *

That night, a jangling chorus hummed and murmured in Magnus's heart, her thoughts dancing to swooping wings and growling bikes, sobbing children and kraken-print tuxedos, kilns of flame and captured souls.

Everyone deserves to be happy.

Magnus quietly closed her sketchbook and unlocked her desk

drawer. The gyroflare lay silent and dark, and she pressed it to her aching chest.

I wish I could be as strong as you were, Ojiisan.

It didn't take strength to plunge into dangerous worlds, or to fight your way home. It took strength to admit that some days you'd succeed, and some days you wouldn't. It took courage to triumph and fail and do it all over again. Saving a tiny speck in an endless tide. One soul in a million. One soul in a billion. But one soul was still one soul. It was a woman on a bike in the Sahel. Or a family singing burbling songs together in their pastry shop.

Magnus felt a tingling against her skin and saw a faint shimmer of green swirling at the edges of the gyroflare. She tentatively tapped the glass, and a frosty globe bloomed from its surface, rotating slowly above scrolling statistics, pages of maps, and the image of a child with blue compound eyes. It was one of the missions Ioren had lined up for later this year—data she thought only he could access.

She swiped aside the globe and it was replaced with the image of a cratered planet that floated above a new set of warnings, tactical recommendations, and a photo of something that resembled a frightened fruit bun. She flipped to the next file, and the next—dozens of people who were cross-over compatible, who'd been approached.

People who were waiting.

* * *

The icy world broke apart, slowly sundered by the gravity of unforgiving suns and vengeful moons. Against a terrible symphony of cracking ice and shattering glaciers, glittering palaces crumbled to shards, and Magnus skated across a disintegrating sea. Foggy shadows passed beneath her feet: the frozen bodies of those who'd fled and found nowhere to go. Hugging the shivering girl in her arms, Magnus raced towards the ornate circle of runes scored into the ice. With the world collapsing behind her, she slid towards the circle, pressing the gyroflare just as the ground splintered into frozen plumes.

Week by week, month by month, she raced across plains of rippling fur and crawled through caverns of gnashing stalactites. She sailed beneath skies darkened by schools of armoured manta rays and, one by one, she found them. One by one, she brought them home.

She led each of them to the safe-house, and none of them ended up on the local news, so she presumed Ioren stepped in to guide them. He always had a talent for finding people, even if he didn't have the ability to bring them across.

Magnus undertook one last mission before her final exams began, before quarantining this time for her studies, for herself. She'd selected a world smothered by sorcery and spite. The oligarchy of troglobites had blotted out the sun, watching as the dryads withered and starved.

Magnus dodged through the skeletal woods, bleached branches clawing at the eternal night. She gripped the fibrous hand of the dryad beside her, a woman with moss-green eyes and hazel skin. They leapt into the scorched circle of grass, and their hulking, translucent pursuers recoiled from the sudden blaze of emerald light.

Silver veins spasmed through Magnus's mind, the world tearing away. The dryad shuddered, her flesh wizening and hardening as the dimensions streaked past, until finally, the two of them burst through the threshold of stars—

And Magnus stood in her bedroom, in a cubicle of plastic sheeting, a pile of kindling cradled in her arms.

The next morning, she went for an early jog, ate a breakfast of grilled mushrooms and tomatoes, and ensured that her jacket covered up her most recent cuts and bruises.

"Why is there a dead stick planted in the yard?" said Lars, bringing in the morning paper.

Magnus kissed her father on the cheek.

"So she can see the sun."

As she turned to leave, Lars wrapped her in a quick bear hug.

"You know what you are?" he said.

"Dad …"

"Come on …"

"I'm your magnum opus."

Lars released her with a Cheshire cat smile. "Don't you ever forget it."

From the kitchen window, Kami watched her daughter striding down the sunlit lane, her schoolbag over one shoulder, and just the slightest hint of a limp in her gait.

* * *

Kami's meeting with the Axolotl Preservation Society had run late, amidst brutal schisms surrounding the definition of "preservation". Insults had been hurled, along with several jars of formaldehyde.

The house was dark by the time she hiked up the porch and dropped her keys onto the side table. Lars was out with friends tonight, at Endless Static's post-modern, pre-singularity gig. Magnus was out jogging—probably another of her marathon laps of Flotsam Beach.

God, that girl loved to run.

Kami slid a bucket of fried chicken onto the kitchen bench and deposited her groceries onto a nearby chair. At least, she presumed there was a chair somewhere beneath the pile of tracksuit pants. She borrowed a slender paintbrush from a jar on the sideboard and reached into a grocery bag, withdrawing a packet of dried pig's blood. Warm water and a vigorous whisking resulted in a bucket of pungent, dark red ooze.

It took her nearly two hours to paint the tiled floor with an intricate mandala of sigils, painstakingly tracing the pattern three times over to ensure that none of the lines were broken. Without stepping into the circle of glistening runes, Kami placed the bucket of chicken within the innermost circle. She cracked open a frail leather notebook, gently leafing to a page of faded calligraphy. This would be the third time in her life she'd recited this incantation, but her throat warmed as the sibilant sounds took form.

After a pause, the kitchen light sputtered and extinguished. The lace curtains stirred with the barest breath, and a silhouette stood within the circle.

"You realise that's not actually a sacrifice?" said Ioren.

"Tell that to the chicken."

Ioren frowned, but it wasn't convincing. Kami glanced briefly at Ioren's feet, his toes just touching the inside edge of the outermost circle.

"What's going on with Magnus?" she said.

"You could ask your daughter."

Kami drummed her fingers against the bolt cutters on the kitchen bench, and Ioren raised his manicured hands placatingly, but didn't speak.

"She's taken it on, hasn't she?" said Kami.

"Almost two years ago."

"Is there any chance …?"

"The contract has been sealed."

Kami cursed silently. A part of her had known, of course. She'd recognised the same dramatic mood swings, the same poorly explained injuries that she'd seen in her own father. She found her voice faltering.

"But she's …"

"… just a child?"

"She's *my* child."

"That's why she's strong enough." His tone was gentle, but there was something in his eyes—there'd always been something in his eyes.

"You know the terms," he continued. "I only ask. She has to

choose."

Kami's heart wrenched quietly. All parents lost their children eventually, one way or another. To careers, to distant countries, to families of their own. You couldn't hold onto them forever. All you could do was love them, prepare them, and let them go.

"You'll look after her," said Kami, a hint of a growl in her voice.

"I always try."

A shadow of sorrow clouded his eyes for a moment, and Kami turned away, feeling the pang of shared loss.

"I never said … thank you … for bringing his body back," she said.

In the silent kitchen, the scent of autumn leaves and rain filtered in from outside. Ioren's gaze slid towards her, his face half in shadow.

"It was your father's wish that I spare you this life," he said, "but I've always wondered, if I'd asked, would you have said 'yes'?"

Kami looked steadily at Ioren.

"You know the answer to that."

The faintest rueful smile touched his lips.

"You are your daughter's mother."

* * *

The last pencil clattered onto the desk, the last examination booklet rustled shut, the last school bell chimed its faux-soothing *bloops*, and the school hall erupted with a slurry of joyous, dazed and tearful students.

"Magnus," called Mr Sethia, edging his way through the human tide. "I just wanted to let you know that the fire department decided not to fine the school."

"Oh," said Magnus guiltily. "Glad to hear it."

For her major artwork, she'd constructed a wire sculpture of a phoenix, papered with letters written by fellow students, describing their most vivid memories—both exhilarating and traumatic.

During her final presentation, Magnus had set fire to the sculpture and quickly learned that school smoke detectors were surprisingly sensitive. And connected to the sprinkler system.

"Next time, don't use pyrotechnics without a licence," said Mr Sethia. "Although, it was certainly memorable."

"That's what I was aiming for."

Magnus took the scenic path past the hockey field and out through a narrow side gate, leaving behind the roar of school anthems and the cheers of the newly liberated.

A set of footsteps crunched after her on the gravel path.

"Magnus," panted Wolverhampton. "How'd you go?"

"I was thrown by the essay on imaginary politics. But other than that, I think I did all right."

"Good. I mean, not about the politics, but that you did okay." He wobbled slightly, which he often did when he was anxious. "There's something I've been wanting … There's something I'd like you to have."

He took her hand and placed a soft globule of water on her palm. It was about the size of a mochi, luminous and glassy, and it rolled gently within its pocket of surface tension.

She was about to make a nervous joke about exchanging bodily fluids, but from Wolverhampton's expression, she was witnessing something rare and sacred.

"What is it?" she asked.

"You've never asked my family for anything. And I … The Uruanai are liquid entities, but we have a denser core—our ekaori— which gives us our physical integrity, our strength. If our ekaori becomes damaged or contaminated, we lose our cohesion and die. But we can gift small pieces of it to others. Parents often give their children a piece of their own ekaori, to make them strong. And I … I'd like to gift this to you."

Magnus cupped the shimmering globe in her hands.

"It's a piece of your heart?"

Wolverhampton hesitated, as though urgently trying to remember what a heart was. Then, he smiled warmly.

"To make yours stronger."

* * *

Magnus sat on the carpet, making one final modification to her shoulder harness. She snicked the thread with her teeth for that extra wabi-sabi touch, and smoothed the newly attached pouch. She'd sewn it from faded blue hemp reclaimed from one of her grandfather's old jinbei. Running her fingers across the soft fabric, she could still remember him shuffling down the hallway in his slippers, always with that smile—the one that meant he had something wonderful to show her. A cloud of passing cockatiels, a gilded book of poetry, a freshly baked blueberry pie.

And yet, behind that mask of serenity, he'd seen unforgettable horrors. He'd been so moved, so tormented, that he'd continued his plunges long after he should have stopped. She knew now that his passing hadn't been the result of a cardiac arrest or a slippery road, but a heart that couldn't let go. He hadn't been able to reconcile his domestic life of suburban privilege with the unspeakable things he'd seen. It had called to him, as it did her.

Magnus gently tipped the globule of ekaori into the pouch, and then threaded her arms through the harness, securing the buckle at the front. The pouch rested beside the gyroflare, pressing lightly against her breastbone. A wintry chill breathed through the curtains, and Magnus closed her window, feeling the presence tingling behind her.

"I must say, I'm impressed," said Ioren. "Escorting so many new arrivals to the safe-house without the aid of glamour bands."

"You can thank the popularity of the wearable blanket."

"Your latest friend—the speckled yeast entity—said you wanted to see me. You are aware that you can summon me at any time."

"Creatures are summoned. People are invited."

Ioren graced her with a curt bow, his eyes unreadable. "To what do I owe this pleasure?"

"Tell me about my great-grandmother."

"As I've said before, Hoshiko was a clever and curious—"

"Don't give me the fairytale version. She didn't summon you out of curiosity. She didn't bind you out of whimsy. Why are you really here, Ioren?"

A complicated expression rippled through his eyes, the edges smouldering with silver fire.

"Hoshiko *was* clever. And curious." His eyes darkened a shade. "And desperate. She was studying to become a chemist when war broke out, and all the local schools were closed. In the late autumn, an unfamiliar militia marched into her village, and at her mother's insistence, Hoshiko hid in one of the secluded wells. When she finally emerged, five days later, starving and chilled to the bone, she found the village deserted. Making her way from hostile, frightened town to town, she eventually learned that all the people from her village had been captured and imprisoned in a labour camp.

"She wrote to the provincial officials, brought petitions to their offices, but no soldier, no commander, no government, would divert resources to a rescue. So, Hoshiko turned her attentions to the infernal arts." Ioren's mouth bent into a bitter smile. "She learned of creatures who could travel between dimensions, compromise any barrier, evade any security, and she eventually summoned me, captured me, and bound me to her will. With my assistance, she rescued the villagers and smuggled her family to safer shores, where she eventually met your great-grandfather. A fairytale ending, whether or not you approve."

"Except that wasn't the end, was it?"

Magnus remembered the night Ioren had first appeared to her, the night of her sixteenth birthday, when she'd peppered him with questions.

"What are your powers? How far can you travel? How old are you? Did you know Cleopatra?"

"Limited. Restricted to reconnaissance. I don't remember. You know, not every supernatural entity has met Cleopatra. She was a very busy woman."

Magnus had been so bewildered, and then so compelled, that she'd never revisited the most important question.

"Why didn't Hoshiko end the contract?" she asked. "Why didn't she free you?"

She saw the cold light shiver in his eyes, saw the tension running through his slender frame. When he spoke, every word was placed with the delicacy of a chess piece in an endgame.

"At the time that your great-grandmother summoned me, I was … employed in a situation from which I wished to extract myself. When Hoshiko learned of this, she spent years researching powers diabolical and profane, and finally, she discovered a way to free me from my existing contract—and bind me to her bloodline instead. As part of that compact, in every generation, I ask one question, and … well, you know the rest."

The strange man proffered his hand, a glassy curio hovering at his fingertips.

"Happy birthday, Magnus," he said. "I was a friend of your grandfather's, and I have a present for you."

Magnus closed her eyes for a moment, imagining her great-grandmother as a young woman, full of fire and resolve and compassion. She finally understood how it had begun, with a woman's desire to save one person, and then one more, and then one more …

"She didn't die of old age either, did she?"

Ioren was silent. After a pause, Magnus shrugged on her jacket, tightening her shoulder harness.

"Why can't you leave the crucifer prison alone?" said Ioren softly.

"Because I'm the only one who can help them. That's why my great-grandmother started crossing dimensions instead of helping others on Earth, isn't it? Because she found out what had happened to you, because she learned of the unbearable things that exist out there. People who are beyond the reach of anyone except us—except *me*."

"You don't have to take on everything yourself. You have only one life—brief and precious. There's no need to sacrifice all that you are, only a portion. Each person need only leave behind one stone, well-placed, in order to build a road for all who follow. No solitary person bears the burden of building the road alone. One stone, Magnus. That's enough."

Magnus pulled on her gloves and then turned to him, her gaze steadfast.

"How long were you in one of those prisons?"

Ioren flinched, his gloved hands clenching quietly at his sides. Magnus didn't need to push for an answer to know that her guess had been correct. He'd survived long enough to cut a deal with the Duaken, to sign some kind of demonic contract. Hoshiko had freed him from his servitude. Or, at least, from one kind.

"How I die isn't as important as how I live," said Magnus. "And if every person leaves behind just one stone, then this is mine."

She pulled on her goggles and tapped the gyroflare.

* * *

They swam through the heat, her skin burning, his feet leaving charcoal smears across the white clay floor. The heat scorched fiercer than she remembered, as though the flames recognised her, hungered for her, sending tendrils of blistering heat through her flesh.

Magnus could already see the inky veins rushing along the walls, chasing them as they ran towards the sigils ahead. Ryuen staggered, his bones stark beneath his skin, his hair little more than charred stubble. Magnus gripped his hand, her own legs shaking, but Ryuen grew heavier with every step.

"It's all right," he gasped. "We tried …"

Magnus didn't respond, saving her breath for every painful step, half-dragging Ryuen as the heat swirled around them.

"You can still make it," he said. "And I can join my father … in starlight …"

Magnus faltered, her vision swimming, her careful count momentarily broken.

"You knew?"

"Ioren told me … He said you would try to come back, but I …" Ryuen's voice cracked.

The crust of charcoal swelled further up his shins, and Ryuen slid his hand from her grasp.

Sometimes you triumphed. Sometimes you didn't. Sometimes you tried your best to free someone, only to find that you'd merely changed their prison. And sometimes, your desire to help others became your own cell: invisible bars closing tighter and tighter until you struggled for breath, still clutching the key, unseen, in your hand.

Because the key, the real key, was knowing when to let go.

And when to hold on.

"Hell. No. You. Don't." Magnus growled through gritted teeth.

With the gyroflare rattling fit to break, she lifted Ryuen into her arms and resumed her count, charging desperately towards the circle of runes. A burning gale roared against her, and the purging streams surged across the floor, lashing at her feet. Grey tendrils whipped at her arms and legs, slicing open her jacket as they tried to find purchase on her bones. Against her chest, Magnus felt the cool pouch of ekaori throbbing gently, and a soothing chill rushed over her.

Twenty steps. Ten steps. The heat screamed and clawed, and in reply, a fierce wave of cold radiated from the globe of ekaori, a protective layer of frost crackling over Magnus's skin. As she leapt onto the dark circle, a starburst of green fire flooded the room, and her final, frozen footstep left a crack in the clay.

* * *

A crescent moon hung over the deserted beach, and Magnus sat on the sand, soaking in the stillness. She'd failed to secure a place in Political Fine Arts, but she was warming to the idea of a gap year. According to her mother, the social justice group "Can't Take the Sky" was recruiting designers for their subversive media campaigns. It'd be a good opportunity to build a portfolio, and it'd give her time to think.

Magnus rested her chin on her knees, and after a pause, gestured to the spot beside her.

"You shouldn't lurk," she said.

"Old habits," said Ioren. "In my former occupation, sometimes I'd get shot at, and sometimes I'd wind up bogged in a debate about economic theory. One always proceeded with caution."

He settled demurely onto the sand, his pince-nez tucked into his shirt pocket.

"How's Ryuen?" said Magnus.

"Recovering. Grieving. Grateful." He paused. "What you did—"

"What *we* did."

Ioren hesitated, his gaze shifting to the restless waves. "Thank you."

Magnus leaned back, her fingers sinking into the sand. She'd expected this year to define her, to give her clarity, but her future seemed as impenetrable as an overgrown garden, wild and brimming with menace and wonder.

"What am I supposed to do now?" sighed Magnus.

"Are you really asking for career advice from an unemployed

incubus?"

"A self-employed former incubus."

A wintry breeze stirred, and Magnus stared out towards the edge of the sea.

"You've seen the rise and fall of empires," she said. "And yet suffering continues in this world, in every world. The road we build is never-ending. Ultimately, does it even matter what I do?"

"It matters to you, and to those you help. I *have* seen the rise and fall of empires. But I've also seen meaningful change. I've seen joyful girls filling once-forbidden schoolrooms. I've seen institutions of slavery torn down and drenched in shame. I've seen women fight for, and win, their rightful places in the highest halls of power. Life is unpredictable, and you never know how your actions might ripple through history. Don't waste your energy on doubt, Magnus. Follow your heart, do what you can, and know that you are making the universe a kinder place."

A kinder place.

Magnus's thoughts turned to plates of warm blueberry pie, softly read stories by firelight, and a large, wrinkled hand enfolding hers. There was a kind of power, a kind of magic, in the ordinary moments that stitched together a life. And there was more than one way to save someone.

"We're having a farewell for Nick," said Magnus, "before he heads off to Aesara. You should come."

"I don't think—"

"Wolverhampton's dads are catering. When was the last time you had a pastry with intoxicating levels of butter?"

"I ..."

Ioren's reply seemed to stick in his throat, and he suddenly found an intense need to clean his pince-nez, scrubbing at the glass with a corner of his silk handkerchief.

Magnus watched him quietly for a moment. Hoshiko had

released him from the Duaken's hold, but he'd spent the last few decades in another kind of bondage. Roaming the endless stars in search of suffering, finding the few who could be saved, devising ways to rescue them. And Magnus finally understood the broken flicker deep within his eyes.

"You're not really bound to our bloodline, are you?" she said. "But you need us to bring them across. My great-grandmother might have summoned you, but you'd been searching for someone like her. Someone clever enough, curious enough, compassionate enough to help you save them. She never bound you to a contract, did she?"

Again, he didn't answer, and Magnus didn't press him. She knew there were times when words were too much, or not enough, and his painful, knotted story needed little confirmation. She couldn't imagine how long he'd been without family, without friends, pouring his pain into the crafting of the gyroflare, and then into his search for someone to wield it.

Magnus exhaled slowly, the plume of her breath hanging in the chill air.

"One stone," she said. "That applies to you too. You shouldn't feel guilty for wanting a life of your own. I think it's possible to be part of an interdimensional rescue team and still set aside a part of your life to enjoy pastries and worry about relationships and the rising cost of cheese. I think we can make that work, don't you?"

Ioren appeared entirely focused on the scrap of silk in his hands, his shallow, tremulous breaths a soft staccato. But he made no move to leave, and Magnus sat wordlessly beside him. She didn't know if it was possible to excavate him from the matrix of scars he'd accumulated over the years, but in a way, he was no different to all the others, struggling to overcome the weight of their grief and take a step into the unknown.

He held out his hand, the lamplight creasing shadows across his palm. "Will you help them?" he said.

"Yes," said Magnus, closing her hand firmly over his. "Yes, I will."

Lights bobbed gently on the water over by the distant marina, and Magnus felt the years unrolling ahead of her, a fog of terrifying and fantastic possibilities. The future was an uncertain thing, and it often seemed that she could only ever see a few paces ahead, the ground turning from grass to coal to clouds, ever-changing beneath her feet.

But of this, she was certain: there would always be needs more dire and causes more worthy. There would always be sculptors and volcanoes. And there would always be people doing the best they could, wondering if it was enough.

But Ioren was right—no one could bear the burdens of the world alone. Sometimes, you needed respite, a sanctuary from the endless battle. Sometimes, it was those small, cherished moments of ordinariness that gave you the strength to face the impossible.

For strength came not only from within—from your own wisdom and experience and humility—but also from the connections you forged with those around you. The road might never end, but good company made the journey bearable, and every stone placed eased the way for all who followed.

About *To Run Between the Falling Stars*

To Run Between the Falling Stars is original to *The Heart of the Labyrinth and Other Stories*.

AUTUMN MOON

It could have been a bridge between worlds, on a night like this. The moon was a lamp overhead as I stood on the pedestrian walkway spanning Sydney Harbour. A few kilometres south, Chinatown was bustling with festive lanterns and families celebrating over auspicious dishes.

The fifteenth day of the eighth lunar month—the Mid-Autumn Moon Festival—when Chang'e, the lady of the moon, was at her loveliest. But in Sydney, in the Southern Hemisphere, it was early spring, mid-September. And I was alone.

I'd moved to Sydney with ambitions of becoming a photo-journalist, covering issues like the political battle over poker-machine reform, or the impact of malaria on subsistence communities. But it hadn't quite turned out that way.

On nights like this, I missed the stories my dad used to tell as we lit our dollar-store lanterns, the pink and orange cellophane so prone to self-immolating. He'd recount tales from Chinese folklore, and in my head, they all blended into one great tapestry of immortal archers and heroic monks, dragon princes and rebellions facilitated by lotus-seed cakes.

But the story that had stayed with me, that lingered long after I'd grown up, was one about a poet. Exiled from his homeland, despairing of the corruption engulfing his kingdom, he composed one last, epic poem before throwing himself into the Miluo River.

Mourning villagers tossed bundles of glutinous rice—zongzi—into the waters, in the hopes that the fish would leave the poet's corpse untouched.

My mother always said it was a waste of a life and a waste of good food. It was hard to tell which bothered her more. But the story always made me cry. For the hopeless poet, for the grieving villagers, for kingdoms lost.

These days, the full moon in early spring always reminded me of home, of those childhood festivals, and the melancholy story that still haunted me.

Which left me standing on the Harbour Bridge as bats wheeled overhead, snatching moths as they fluttered in the lights. During the day, it was fifty thousand tonnes of steel, connecting the sticky heart of Sydney to its manicured northern shores. But at night, beneath this cat's cradle of lights and soaring silhouettes, you could forget that you were a failed photographer far from home.

I drew a zongzi from my bag, the dumpling still warm through the tightly wrapped bamboo leaves. To unfinished business and futile gestures. Cheers.

Glancing quickly below to ensure there were no boats, I tossed the zongzi through a gap in the security fence and imagined it sinking past lost poets and sunken dreams.

"It's illegal to throw things off the bridge," came a voice.

A man stood a few metres down the walkway. No uniform, no badge, no weapon. I'd once been mugged in Hyde Park by a man with a bendy straw, but this guy looked harmless. He was in his early thirties, scruffy hair streaked with highlights, white T-shirt, faded blue jeans, and lime-green flip-flops.

"It's a ball of sticky rice," I said. "It's like brushing crumbs onto the pavement."

"You threw a fork," he said.

"I dropped the fork," I replied, wondering how the hell he'd seen the flimsy utensil tangled in the zongzi string.

He leaned back against the railing and considered me for a moment.

"You've got the festivals wrong," he said. "Zongzi are for the Dragon Boat Festival."

"I like the story of the poet better."

The man smiled casually.

"He was a lousy poet, and he never jumped."

"Qu Yuan was one of China's greatest scholars," I said a little hotly. "And 'The Lament' is widely considered to be a masterful work of literary—"

"I'm not talking about Qu Yuan," he said. "I'm talking about the original poet, the calamity he brought, the legacy behind the legend you know."

"Where'd you get your version?"

"I was there," said the man.

I mirrored his pose, leaning against the railing.

"Go on," I said. "Spin me a yarn."

"There's a price."

I flipped him a two-dollar coin. I preferred giving pies rather than cash, but I bought the occasional *Big Issue* from the homeless vendors at Town Hall Station. Plus, my only edible offering had probably just concussed a kingfish.

The man inspected the gold coin before tucking it into his pocket.

"It's a long story," he said.

I rubbed my arms. Standing on a bridge at night quickly lost its appeal once the mosquitoes got busy.

"How about I buy you dinner?" I said.

* * *

We threaded our way back to Chinatown, the hazy neon glow giving way to searing LED signs. Personally, I felt neon had a smoky appeal, a kind of cyberpunk Monet. LEDs had all the charm of a swarm of laser pointers.

We miraculously found a tiny table overflowing onto the sidewalk from a pocket of a noodle shop. I managed to manoeuvre an uncooperative folding chair far enough from the table for me to squeeze in. The man didn't seem interested in introducing himself, so I mentally labelled him 'Joe'.

"Immortal or time-traveller?" I said. I loved a good story, and tonight it made me feel a little closer to home.

"Let's just say when people make offerings, I might show up," said Joe.

"You're like the god of glutinous rice?"

"I wouldn't call myself a god," said Joe with affected modesty. "Not the usual kind, anyway." He ordered a salad and chips, which certainly didn't seem like the traditional fare of deities.

"If you're from Chinese mythology, why do you look like a surfer?"

"I take on a local form when I appear," shrugged Joe. He glanced at his fluorescent green flip-flops. "Can people actually run in these?"

I unwrapped the gently steaming leaves from my tetrahedron zongzi, and settled into my wobbly chair.

"So, this original poet, some kind of calamity," I said.

"Keep in mind, this was long before Qu Yuan," said Joe. "When the three kingdoms were a hundred, and borders clawed and gouged at one another. In a small kingdom, sheltered between a sweep of mountains and a curving river, there lived a young farmer known as Humble Turnip. His plot was meagre and parched, yet it was not for rains and ripe harvests that his heart yearned."

"This is going to be a tragic love story, isn't it?"

"Patience," said Joe, spearing a cherry tomato. "It was a scorching summer's day when Humble plucked the solitary peach from his barren orchard and took it to a sagging bridge above the river gorge.

There, raising his prayers to the heavens, he threw the peach into the sluggish waters. The peach was sour and bruised—the other gods didn't even stir at the ripples. But I was always a sucker for a hard-luck story."

Joe took a draught of his pineapple juice.

"Humble told me of a woman in the provincial militia. She wore red lacquered beads in her braided hair, and she was ferocious with a pole-arm. They called her Winter Gale, because she could knock a man clean out of his shoes. Humble could have asked me for princely wealth or warrior prowess, but what he asked of me was poetry. He wanted to win her with words, and eventually become a respectable scholar in the imperial bureaucracy of the empress. This gift of words, I granted him.

"He continued to make his offerings to me—roast chestnuts, preserved duck eggs. Humble developed fine calligraphy and gained recognition among the local officials for his flowing verse. Yet Winter Gale still failed to perceive his existence."

"Did he actually talk to her?"

"That's what I said to him," said Joe. "When a woman comes home after a gruelling day battling bandits, she doesn't want a sonnet; she wants a plate of freshly steamed buns. We started doing things my way. If Winter Gale caught a cold after rescuing a calf from the dam, Humble would show up with a hot bowl of ginger and shallots. If she tore her coat in a skirmish, he'd be waiting with a needle and thread. I taught him to cook dishes fit for a king, and to listen with love to the troubles of her heart. That's how you win someone over."

There was a tinge of bitterness as he said this.

"You were spying on her?" I said.

"Watching over her," said Joe. "Laws were different back then. But it worked. Her affection for Humble grew, as did his eminence as a gifted poet. The day of the imperial examinations drew nearer—"

"Tess?" A deep voice slid through the crowd. "Fancy running

into you here."

A slick man in a dark suit strode over with a pert brunette on his arm—she seemed to be playing an engrossing game on her phone.

"Remy," I said, getting to my feet in a reluctant show of social grace.

Remy was the kind of man who wore designer cufflinks and owned an espresso machine with more functions than a shuttle cockpit. We'd shared a few visual communications subjects at college, but his idea of visual communications involved 'cheeky' billboards rather than investigative pieces on women's health in Yemen.

"Still working at the copy shop?" said Remy with a grin you could slice lemons with.

"Still working on my portfolio."

"Still living at the dorm with fifteen exchange students?"

"Still living in Ultimo," I said, smiling through gritted teeth.

It was actually a lunchbox-sized apartment, and there were only three students, a high-maintenance physics teacher, and a middle-aged puppeteer who just couldn't get it together.

"And what do *you* do?" Remy addressed Joe, undoubtedly noting his lack of wallet, phone and keys.

"You'll see," said my companion, smiling pleasantly.

"Well, Tess, always a pleasure," said Remy, sailing triumphantly towards the invitation-only seafood restaurant across the road.

My appetite gone, we started walking back up Sussex Street, towards the patter of fountains along Darling Harbour.

"Why aren't you with your family tonight?" said Joe.

I could have gotten on a plane the size of a minibus and rattled my way home to Nimbor, a crusty outback town where the grass was always yellow stubble, and red dust caked everything. My parents always kept a room for me behind the hardware store, just in case.

"I'll go back when I have something to show for it," I said. "So where are you staying?"

"Oh, I never stay," said Joe. "But thanks for dinner."

"Are you going to finish the sto—"

The neon sign above us flickered, and he was gone.

* * *

Later that week, on his way to a strategic meeting on consumer data collection, Remy would find his Jeep engine inexplicably full of steamed mung beans. But that's a different story.

* * *

The following year, I'd moved out of the lunchbox and into a cosy old terrace in Surry Hills with two guys called Steve. In my head, I nicknamed them Boring Steve and Chaotic Steve.

On the fifteenth of the eighth, I went to the Harbour Bridge again, and under a perfect moon tossed a zongzi into the waters. I waited until after midnight, but Joe didn't show. Then again, gods were probably busy, and the zongzi hadn't been particularly good that year.

The year after that, I went home for the Mid-Autumn Moon Festival. I'd finished up a contract temping at Gruthers Art Supplies and was about to start a new marketing and design position for a bargain cosmetics company. I'd begun to realise that the problem with my portfolio was the fact that all the good intentions in the world were no substitute for genuine talent.

It was a crisp night, and my parents made oolong tea in the kitchen while I hung lanterns in the backyard. The lopsided Hills Hoist languished dramatically, cheery lanterns hanging from each spoke.

"Nothing for me this year?"

I turned to see Joe sitting on the dried grass, leaning back to gaze at the constellations. His jeans were darker than last time, and more fashionably snug at the hips. His flip-flops had been replaced by a pair of black and orange sneakers with vaguely hydraulic soles.

"You didn't show last year," I said.

"I had a thing in Bangkalan. Is that the same outfit you were wearing two years ago?"

"It's my celebration shirt."

I hung a yellow, fish-shaped lantern on the back porch, then joined Joe on the grass.

"I think we reached the part about the imperial exam," I said.

"We don't have to keep going with that story," said Joe. "I know a good one about the household god of small fortunes, and a hilarious misunderstanding."

His tone was light, but something in his eyes seemed old and tired.

I'd waited two years to hear the end of his story, but seeing him now, I understood that it wasn't just a story for him. I touched his shoulder gently. "We don't have to continue with that story."

Joe was silent for a while, and then I noticed my dad standing on the back porch with a plate of lotus-seed paste mooncakes.

"Dad," I said, startled. "Uh, this is Joe. A friend from Sydney."

If my dad was puzzled by the abrupt materialisation of this friend, he didn't show it.

"I'll make some more tea," said my dad. He returned shortly with the good china, then withdrew tactfully to the kitchen.

Joe breathed gently on the fragrant tea, cupping the warm porcelain in his hands. We sat in silence, drinking in the swathe of stars overhead.

"Humble asked Winter Gale to marry him," said Joe softly. "And he asked me for one last gift. A wedding ring. A ring of protection, to shield Winter Gale from the bandits' blades and from the ravages of pestilence. I told him such a thing was beyond me—I dwelt in the rivers and the lowlands, accepting offerings of pigeons and pears.

"But he begged me, day and night, bringing me sweet potatoes and rice, fresh melons and dried mushrooms. Finally, he told me to do it not for him, but for Winter Gale. Create this ring for her."

"What was she like?"

Joe closed his eyes, holding the teacup close to his lips.

"I forged a ring of blood-red gold. Seamless so as not to scratch her, warm so as not to chill her. Inscribed with words of power, words of love, it would protect her from the elements, from winging arrows and the breath of plague. From the shadow of the mountains and the tears of the river, I forged this ring for Winter Gale.

"The day of the imperial exam arrived, the first hurdle for any potential courtier, and Humble rode to the capital in his finest robes."

"I'm guessing he passed."

"He never took the exam," said Joe darkly. "With his winning words, he became a senior courtier to the empress. With his attentive ways and skilful banquets, he ingratiated himself into her affections. And with his blood-gold ring, crafted from the shadow of the mountains and the tears of the river, he wed the empress."

The teacup was cold in my hands. With a lump in my throat, I imagined Winter Gale back at the village, waiting patiently for Humble and his promise, her red bridal dress gathering dust.

"Gods and fools," said Joe. "He found himself a gullible god and played me magnificently."

"Only because you have a good heart."

"Do I?" said Joe bitterly. "You haven't heard the rest of the story."

A chill crept up my back, and the glow of the kitchen window seemed distant and surreal.

When Joe continued, his voice was icy. "When I learned of Humble's treachery—his betrayal of my trust, and Winter Gale's love—I brought down the mountains and parted the rivers. I silenced the dust storms of the steppes and let the borders fall. Oh, how they shook when they saw the approaching hordes, the scimitars and spears pouring across the plains. He and the empress, in their palace of marble and zhennan wood—what good were their silk robes and jade lions in the face of a god betrayed?"

Joe's voice was low now, barely a whisper. "Humble ordered every village, every house, to raise offerings to appease me. They filled the rivers with roast pork and shrimp dumplings, white peaches and rice wine. They poured everything they had into the rivers and prayed for me to save them, but it only fuelled my wrath."

His next line was little more than the shape of words on his lips. "I demanded a life."

A red lantern caught alight, collapsing slowly onto the lawn in a sheet of flame. I grabbed a bucket from beneath the stunted kumquat tree and stomped the last resisting embers.

And of course, he was gone.

* * *

I visited the Harbour Bridge the following year, but I'd outgrown my penchant for dramatic gestures. I'd quit my marketing and design job, having decided that a vaguely artistic job in a company selling crap was somehow worse than doing time in a copy shop. Chaotic Steve had eloped and been replaced by Jackal, a former guerrilla tattooist who now worked at a domestic violence shelter, and was actually pretty cool once you got past her avant-garde piercings.

The year after that, I spent the week with my parents again. I felt oddly happy, despite my career fishtailing between cubicle jobs and street corners. I'd just moved into an apartment of my own—it was small, but comfortable, and for some reason it had a decorative fireplace in the living room, which I found inexplicably charming.

I hadn't forgotten about the man in the faded jeans. I'd spent countless hours retracing his story in my mind, and had grown to realise that gifts, used unwisely, were objects of destruction. But a good heart would find its way to a satisfying ending, somehow.

And I dusted off my portfolio.

* * *

It had been three years since that night beneath the lanterns at my parents' house, and I didn't even realise it was the fifteenth of the eighth until I noticed all the elaborately embossed tins of mooncakes in the shopfronts.

I picked up a red-bean zongzi for dinner and promised myself I'd have something healthy for breakfast. I went to bed early, looking forward to work the next day, which meant that life was finally headed in the right direction. A few months earlier, I'd started working at the Sydney Storybook Foundry, where a combination of staff and volunteers helped disadvantaged children write and illustrate their own books. For the more matter-of-fact children who preferred penning non-fiction, I helped them take photos for their publications. I was also the official headshot photographer for the author profiles. The kids came up with some pretty outlandish poses, but they had a heck of a lot of fun.

I woke sometime after midnight and saw Joe sitting at the end of my bed, half-illuminated in the moonlight. He wore a white formal shirt, loose at the wrists, and a pair of black jeans with frayed cuffs. His feet were bare. The bedroom curtain was partially drawn, and Joe gazed out across the terracotta roofs and banana trees.

"You've been busy," he said.

"I'm finding my way. And you?"

"Redecorating." Joe paused. "Since I've seen your home, would you like to visit mine?"

"You have a house?" I said. "Is there a whole district in heaven populated by the gods of yum cha dishes?"

"Shall I withdraw my invitation?"

I laughed, held out my hand, and he took it.

* * *

It was like waking into a dream. Never had I been more lucid, more aware of how transient and fragile the world was. I drifted in a sepia dawn, like a sea of someone else's memories. Seamless parchment flowed on all sides, enfolding me in an origami maze. Across the softly lit surfaces, watercolours streamed, formed and faded.

Above me, brush paintings of mossy mountains rose and weathered. Beneath my feet, gigantic scarabs battled serpentine dragons. And far to my right, a small, forgotten kingdom held its breath.

Joe stood beside me, still holding my hand. In the living inkwash to my right, over and over the rivers filled with sacks of rice. Over and over, the shadows swelled towards the capital in an endless loop.

"I think it's stuck," I said.

Joe tensed as I reached towards the inky image, but he didn't stop me. The vision flinched and twisted, and finally wrenched into the image of a woman riding hard across the steppes. Her leather boots were scuffed thin, her cotton robe was a diligently stitched patchwork, and in her braided hair were wolfberry-red beads. The image spasmed—now a proud courtier, now a crashing gate, now a trail of dust.

"I demanded the life of the poet," said Joe softly. "And as the invaders spilled through the kingdom, Winter Gale rode to the capital and asked Humble for the ring I had forged for him. She had long ago discovered his duplicity, perceived it perhaps before I had. Now, Winter Gale brought the ring to the sagging bridge above the river gorge, and for the first time, she summoned me.

"She entreated me to relent, to spare her people. The gifts I had bestowed upon Humble, he had bestowed in part on her, so she would bear Humble's sins in his stead, and the ring she returned to me, tossing it into the roiling waters.

"She stood at the cusp of the bridge, the clashing metal singing nearer, and she asked if still I demanded a life."

In the flowing image, the woman stood alone on the wooden archway, her feet firmly planted, as though guarding the gates to the kingdom. To defend her home, she would face down a god, and yet there was pity in her eyes. Below her, the dark waters of the river churned, and overhead, the moon hung bright and cold. Joe's grip tightened.

The woman jumped.

I turned away, and it seemed a long time passed before Joe's fingers slowly loosened.

"I sealed the mountain passes," said Joe. "I restored the rivers. And I left Humble to the villagers."

The inky image melted, then resolved once more into a bedraggled Winter Gale limping from the river, cradling her arm and looking slightly puzzled.

"I have a soft spot for women on bridges," said Joe.

"Did you and she ever …"

"I never returned."

The living painting finally faded, and the page was blank. In the real world, this story had long been replaced by tales of other poets, other calamities, other legends that bled into one another to form the heart of the Dragon Boat Festival. But here, this first, lonely iteration was only now just fading.

"I'd been meaning to replace that for years," murmured Joe. He exhaled slowly, as though he'd been waiting a long time to draw the next breath.

"You're welcome," I said.

* * *

We reappeared on the roof of my apartment, the suburb below painted in starlight and shadows.

"Thank you," I said. "For sharing your story."

"Thank you, for sharing yours."

It was true, stories never really began or ended. They interconnected, diverged, changed one another, and given time, turned into different stories.

"Oh, wait a minute," I said, clambering down onto the balcony and grabbing my digital SLR from the study. "Say 'zongzi'."

Joe pulled me around beside him, and the camera flashed.

"That's not going on social media is it?" said Joe, craning to look at the preview.

"Captioned 'Me and the Glutinous Rice God'?"

A breeze swept across the rooftops, carrying the scent of camellias.

"So, was it worth your two dollars?" said Joe.

I shrugged. "I could have gotten more value."

Joe smiled to himself, hands in his pockets. "Well, maybe I've got a few more stories."

"You know where to find me."

An owl hooted indignantly in the predawn, and he was gone.

* * *

Some stories, like Humble's, become scars in need of forgiveness and release. Others, like Qu Yuan's, become legends to be remembered. But the best stories are the ones that become lessons—about hope, persistence, and unlikely friendships. These stories aren't always extraordinary, but they make the best memories, and they are the ones that shape a life worth living.

There's a handmade book on my desk, with thin cardboard covers and a spine bound with string. On the last page, a man with scruffy hair smiles out from a black and white photo, his arm around my shoulders. It's a story about a Winter Gale, an Autumn moon, and a god of endings lost and found.

About *Autumn Moon*

Autumn Moon was first published in *Holiday Magick* (Spencer Hill Press, 2013), edited by Rich Storrs and Jessica Porteous.

ALMOST DAYS

What is time?

It's a question I never asked myself while I was still alive, and now, I suppose time is something that happens to other people. Gainful employment, on the other hand, only happened to me after I'd died.

My colleagues call this place the Wings—we're the before and the after, enfolding the stage of the world. Here, in my lonely turret on the hill, the sun is always noon overhead. Go seaward, towards the misty waters of Unan, and the sun hovers in eternal dawn. Go worldward, towards the Golden Vale, the realm of Transformation, and the sun dips into the cusp of night. Travelling across the Wings can give the illusion of time passing. Long ago, I found it comforting. Now, it makes me vertiginous.

My hill is small, with bald patches where I forget to remember the grass. On its crown sits the cottage I inherited from my predecessor, and despite my best efforts, the building remains shaped like a large barnacle with an oversized turret on its head, so my dwelling resembles a squat fort sitting on a long-suffering crustacean.

All I know of my predecessor is that she retired, and that her retirement had possibly come as a surprise to her. The only legacy of her presence is a single word scratched under a loose paving on the floor.

Enough.

I try not to think about it: the only reminder that I wasn't always here.

In my cavernous turret, a column of glassy green threads—the Flow—streams in my seaward window, and out the worldward arch. Far seaward, where the dreaming of souls fills the sea of Unan, glimmering spray rises from the warm waters, coalescing into liquid threads. My task is to comb and groom each strand until it shines, sleek and supple. Every life runs through my fingers until it tapers to its end, and scatters into the Nimbus above, one day to rain back into the misty sea.

When times are prosperous and uncomplicated, I can comb through weeks in one sitting. But when the world endures upheaval, when doubt and indecision fill its souls, I can spend an unrelenting age combing through the tangles of a single, crucial moment. Today, I've resolved a number of tricky knots. Then again, it's always today.

A thread frays near my hand, someone's potential path splitting off, the loose tendril already ghosting. I smoothly snip its base, leaving the main thread smooth and unharmed. I hold the snippet over the brazier of entropy beside me, but the ghosting thread twists vibrantly between my fingers. In its smoky light, I see a girl searching for firewood across an arid savannah, dreaming of centrifuges and stars. In this path, she abandons her search for twigs, and races to school. This path that never happens.

I take a frosted violet phial from my pocket and place the ghost thread inside, twisting the stopper gently. The sound of clinking bottles drifts from outside, and I hurriedly tuck the phial into my robes.

At the base of my hill stands a low wooden gate strung with mismatched glass bottles. No fence, just a solitary gate to mark the bounds of my domain. A pale blue contrail streams through my window, solidifying into a smartly dressed man in his late twenties, with light brown hair and spotless teeth.

"Tangles," nods the man, brushing imaginary dust from his tailored suit.

Tangles isn't actually my title. My predecessor was known as Reed, but after the Stewards implemented their last round of changes, I became the Flow Optimisation Officer. Naturally, I acquired the nickname Tangles instead.

My guest's title is Timing, but he calls himself Serendipity. He tunes the tension of the Flow, tightening a thread here, loosening one there, so all things move in harmony. At least, that's his task.

It's rumoured that he's fond of reuniting high school sweethearts, taking a morbid delight in how they squirm to discover that the other has filled out, thinned on top, and led a far less exciting life than the future had promised.

"I like what you've done with your hill," says Serendipity.

"I haven't done anything to it."

Serendipity fixes me with birdlike eyes, then smiles brightly.

"My mistake," he says.

Still smiling, his hand darts towards the Flow and tweaks a thread slightly.

"It was aligned!" I slap his hand away. "Now Winston Kerr's going to miss his bus."

I knead gently at the fresh kink, and in the shifting depths of the thread, the single dad stops chasing the huffing red bus, an oversized Hug-A-Planet in his arms. He looks just as Atlas might if he caught public transport.

Serendipity continues to look quietly satisfied.

"On the next bus, he'll sit next to Doctor Madeline Teng," he says. "In three days' time, she'll resuscitate his daughter Liesel at the pool party she's about to be invited to."

"We're supposed to align, not interfere. Smooth their course, not change it."

Even so, I can't suppress the subtle thrill that bleeds through me as Winston's thread transforms along its new course, and the truncated thread of his daughter suddenly sprouts like a fresh shoot.

"Pity," says Serendipity, sauntering towards the worldward arch. "What would I be without it?"

He pauses, looking at me with an expression I don't understand, and then his contrail disappears over the wispy horizon.

* * *

My heart no longer beats, my ribs no longer rise and fall, but the little violet phial hums against my chest like an appropriated soul. I've made no changes to the cottage itself, just a small alteration to the hill. Only a minor adjustment, virtually plumbing upgrades, not worth mentioning to the Stewards.

I descend the turret stairs, and sweep aside the empty bottles and half-blown glass in my cellar. I kneel on the cool, dark earth and trace a circle on the floor. A ring of flat stones rises from my etching, and the centre falls away into a well. Gathering my robes around me, I leap into the void.

We each have our eccentricities, here in the Wings. Distractions to pass the timeless days. Motion creates mesmerising wreaths of light which drift lazily from her rocky spires. Transformation constructs elaborate headdresses, gruffly complaining that she rarely has a chance to use the owl-headed one these days, ever since polytheism fell out of fashion. I have my bottles. And this place.

My feet touch down softly on the floor, and the ceiling curves into vaulted sandstone far above, rising like the petrified ribs of a long-defeated colossus. Thousands of loculi pock the sandy walls, and cradled within each is a softly glowing bottle. Ghost threads float and coil in every glassy vessel, phantom memories of opportunities past.

I climb the lattice of bittersweet vines, past rustic clusters of red and orange berries. I nest the violet phial in a waiting hollow, and brush my fingertips over its neighbours—tiny orbs of golden glass, long necked decanters of scarlet crystal, undulating blue barber bottles. I let myself drift in their fading dreams: a library rich with golden afternoons; an impassioned speech in a jury room; a crowded seminar hall and a lone, searing question.

These fragments of 'almost time' are the relics of choices, like mayflies frozen in amber. They are the split second that stretches forever, the moment that hangs for eternity, intense with all the uncertainty and hope of a decision that cannot be unmade.

All these bottles are filled with choices I never had, brimming with longing and aspiration. My own life had been a shadowplay, brief and stark. But here, amongst these private kingdoms and sugar-glass dreams, I can almost pretend I'm alive again. It's too late for me to change what I had, but it isn't too late for Winston, for Liesel, for those whose threads still flow. And I find my thoughts turning towards reconstituted mayflies.

I linger over a conical green inkpot: a young woman with a runner's build sits beside a dark-eyed man. At their feet is a pond rippling with overfed, geriatric ducks. She reaches over and plucks a leaf from his hair, the moment of warmth flowing into a timeline that never was. The essence of the moment is all but gone, only the almost-time remains.

Three seconds.

* * *

In the brilliant daylight of my turret, I grip the dark green inkpot, strange creatures stirring in the silt of my thoughts. I gently draw a single strand from the Flow, and pour the ghost thread into the glittering skein.

* * *

Name: Evea Dorin
Age: 29
Occupation: Kendo instructor

Evea Dorin was making a cup of ginger tea when the phone rang, and a voice she hadn't heard in two years spoke seven words, then hung up.

In the busy heave and sigh of Evea's life, she would normally have dismissed the message as one of Jackson's odd turns, and made a mental note to visit him the following day, despite their estrangement. However, an odd twinge shivered through her—a half-remembered day in the park.

It took three seconds for the unease in her gut to congeal, and by the time her housemate came to check on the kettle, Evea was already four blocks away.

I'm sorry. I love you. Take care.

Jackson's words looped in Evea's mind, ending in a dial tone.

Let me be wrong, she thought. *Please let me be wrong.*

The words pounded with every step. Her days on the high school track team were imprinted into her muscles, and she sprinted past the peak hour traffic.

Jackson's fibro house peered silently from the corner, and the knot in Evea's stomach tightened as she reached for one last burst of speed. She shoulder charged the glass patio door and swung into the darkened sunroom, crash tackling Jackson just as the pistol fired.

The skylight shattered, and the pair lay breathless on the parquetry, dried leaves drifting down like orange stars.

* * *

There's a peculiar clarity to the silence, as though a background hum I've never noticed has disappeared. Bottles clink outside, and

I hurriedly throw the empty inkpot into the brazier, where it ceases to exist.

A wintery blue contrail materialises into a pale woman—no, a girl—with limp auburn hair. I don't recognise her, and apprehension grips me.

"Hello," says the girl. "I'm Timing."

"There's already a Timing," I say.

"He retired today," says the girl. "Transformation instructed me to watch the nexus of the Flow. She said I'd understand what I needed to do."

I glance nervously at the brazier, and the girl follows my gaze. I quickly turn back towards the threads streaming between us. The girl, Timing, is perhaps sixteen, and has the look of someone newly passed through the Shallows—a little unsure of where she is, who she is, certain only of her title and her task.

She stares into the glowing heart of the Flow, and I busy myself combing away the tangles that have formed. Her expression doesn't change, but tears trail slowly down her face.

"It becomes easier," I say, patting her on the shoulder, as I've seen people do in the Flow.

The Shallows wash away our regrets and affections, the details of the life we left behind. We can't remember how we died, or who we left behind. But still, this is not an Afterlife, only an After.

Timing touches her cheeks, and seems vaguely surprised to find them wet.

"I'm not upset," she says. "I just feel a little odd."

I offer her a handkerchief, but I only know what handkerchiefs look like, and from Timing's expression as she wipes her eyes, I suspect mine is somehow deficient. She returns the stiff square to me, and peers at my face. I pull my hood further down.

"Were you always so amorphous?" says Timing politely. "Or have you forgotten what you look like?"

I've forgotten much of my mortal life, but there's little enough to remember. Always hunger, always darkness, always running. My tribe was savaged when I was too young to comprehend what that meant, and every village I came upon chased me away with stones and fire. When Transformation finally appeared to me, though that was not her name then, she made me an offer. A place with no pain and no hunger. A place where there would never be darkness.

Timing reaches into my hood, and before I can pull away, a tingle burns across my skin and deep into my bones. I stumble against a wall, and raise a hand to my mouth. There are lips now, a straight nose, a deep brow.

Timing parts her hands, and a mirror appears between them. A young man stares back at me: ragged brown hair and startled hazel eyes.

"How did you do that?" I croak.

"I'm Timing," is all she says.

She looks into the Flow again, with brighter, clearer eyes.

"Where are our threads?" she asks.

"We don't have them."

She contemplates this, then vanishes in a blue mist.

* * *

Pity.

It's been a hundred lifetimes since I last ventured from my hill, but Serendipity's last words crawl up my spine and fester in my brain. I gather my gnarled staff, a circular travelling cloak, and a rose-coloured flask inlaid with a silver window.

"Going somewhere?" a voice drawls behind me.

A thunder-grey vapour claps into the form of a tall, bronzed woman, and the bottles at my gate clink in belated apology. Transformation seldom visits, and her presence is still enough to make me feel acutely mortal again. She's wearing a deerskin tunic today, and a crown of quetzal feathers to hide her unruly brown hair.

"I'm going to visit Luan," I say. It's close enough to the truth to keep my voice from shaking.

Transformation's gaze slinks to the pulsing Flow, and her finger traces along a glittering line.

"I thought Jackson's thread finished today," she says.

"Friendships are an unpredictable force."

Her eyes narrow. A willow rod materialises in her hand, the tip touches my cheek, then flicks back my cowl.

"What happened to your face?"

Her hawk eyes probe my entrails, and I try to wish away the sweat on my back.

"I think this is how it's supposed to look."

Her gaze is disapproving, as though faces are a nuisance, and I wonder if she bothers to have one when she's wearing her full-faced helms.

"You can't get to Luan's," says Transformation.

"I can walk," I say stiffly.

Transformation looks faintly disgusted. Her hand clamps onto my arm, and we twist into the aether.

* * *

I'm kneeling on wet sand the colour of sunrise. My vision slurs, and I rise unsteadily. Before me is a shallow bay that touches the sky, beyond which lies the Sea of Unan. The sun is barely a glow on the horizon, and I can't help but think how the beginning and the end look so much alike.

Overhead, a watery aurora streams worldward, forming the threads that will eventually join the Flow. At my feet, foamy waves lap at the sand, and I'm careful not to let the water touch me.

"What's so urgent you had to leave your little hill?" says Transformation. She's standing casually on the beach, watching me with the gaze of an apex predator.

"Brazier maintenance," I say.

Transformation inspects my words, and doesn't seem entirely satisfied.

"I'll make my own way back," I continue, and begin walking towards Luan's shack. I slow after a few steps, and turn back to Transformation. "Did you see Serendipity, before he ... retired?"

She's still for a moment.

"I see everyone."

Transformation turns her face towards the sea, and with a snap, she vanishes in a comet tail across the sky.

* * *

They say Luan is as old as the Wings, far older than the Stewards, who dare not change his name. He disposes of forgotten things. Trinkets, memories, empires. They're all dropped with kindness into the wicker basket at his elbow, from which even the Nimbus can't recall them.

His shack is a giant crab shell, half sunken on the beach, bleached white in the eternal sunrise. Colourful paper flowers hang in the windows, stirring in the breath of the sea.

"The last time you were here, you were wading from the Shallows," says Luan.

He takes the form of a man in his sixties, wearing a long tunic of unbleached cotton, and sandals woven from reeds. No one knows when he died—or if he died—and no one dares to ask. He's the kind of man who likes to answer a question with a question, and his questions have claws.

"Please tell me about my predecessor," I say.

At the sink, Luan holds a tall earthenware teapot beneath a palm-sized cloud, and gently prods it to fill the pot.

"Why did you come here, to the Wings?" says Luan.

I stare at my feet, pale and bare. The blood and the darkness seem so far away, but never quite gone.

"I wasn't ready."

Luan moves towards a large cockle shell on the benchtop, filled with soil that smells like rain. From its depths, a tiny fern is unfolding, and he tenderly pours from the teapot. Luan's shack is filled with conches and clams, all cradling liverworts, delicate grasses, and pine seedlings.

"Are you ready now?" says Luan.

I tense, the rose flask pressing cold against my hip. I shake my head, not trusting my voice.

"Your predecessor presided over the last dark age," says Luan, "when ignorance and confusion reigned over compassion and reason. Threads broke where they should have frayed. Your predecessor lost her focus."

I think of the word carved into my cottage floor, and I wonder whether losing focus had been her transgression. Or whether the transgression had come after.

"Go home," says Luan, watering a rotund cactus.

I bow, and pause at the door. I can remember the sound of my heart, and for the briefest moment, the silence aches.

"Did she put up a fight?" I say.

The teapot is still.

"Why would she fight?"

Luan's question gives me my answer. Triumph and loss belong in the world—there's no place in the Wings for desire or conflict or pity. Perhaps, in the end, my predecessor realised that. And yet, my own answer burned in my throat.

Why would she fight? Because even here, there are things worth fighting for.

My pace is steady as I leave the shack, breaking into a run only when I reach the cover of the weathered basalt on the shoreline. I lower the rose flask by a cord into the pristine waters, and quickly wrap the stoppered bottle in layers of my travelling cloak.

I've never been able to contrail, but I make a concerted effort now. I blurt into smoke every few hundred metres, then back into corporeal form. I pass the windswept gorges where Motion makes her home, and continue past the ice-capped peaks of Insight. I scud by the jungle citadels of Fortune, and the golden towers of Misfortune.

I finally reach the sanctuary of my noonday hill, and drop my damp cloak into the hungry brazier. I hold the rose flask up to the light—there isn't much, but it'll have to be enough. It'll all come down to the—

"Hello again."

Bottles clink, and Timing is sitting on the stone sill beside me. I freeze, the cold flask resting in my palm.

"I brought you a present," says Timing.

She continues to sit on the sunny windowsill, looking at me with pleasant expectation.

"Uh, thank you …"

I see no evidence of a gift, but feel it'd be impolite to question it. She smiles, and I wonder, not uncharitably, where Transformation found this one.

"I thought you should have it," says Timing. "Just in case."

A chill prickles up my spine, and Timing vanishes in a hush of blue, glancing ever so briefly at the bottle in my hand.

* * *

A pale amber wine bottle, a hexagonal pickle jar, a peacock-blue perfume bottle inlaid with pearl. I load up my arms and fill the turret with my subterranean treasures. Glowing bottles cover the floor from wall to wall, coloured glass in every shape and size, beneath the twisting Flow.

I select a slender phial of champagne-coloured glass, and gently pour an hour into a glittering thread.

* * *

Name: Benson Senkai

Age: 34

Occupation: Biochemist

They were alive.

Benson peered through the wire lid of a cage labelled *Team LV223* and savoured the moment. His instincts had been right; the vaccine had only needed minor adjustments. They were one step closer to clinical trials, and it was a huge step.

"They're shutting us down, Senkai."

Benson turned to see his colleague, Quesar, standing in the doorway. Her dark braid looked frizzier than usual, and she wore her lab coat like a gangster Mac.

"Look! Team LV223—" began Benson.

"It's not a profitable field."

Benson refused to let the news sink in. Schendruk Pharmaceuticals had only taken over their facility last week, but already, a third of the staff were gone.

"Antibiotic-resistant tuberculosis is one of the leading causes of death—"

"In low-income countries," said Quesar. "Like I said."

Benson gripped the sides of the plastic cage, as though he could draw strength from the snoozing white rodents inside.

"The vaccine didn't just work," said Benson, "Team LV223 were *already* infect—"

"Stop calling them that," snapped Quesar. "You know why the other researchers don't take you seriously?"

She held up a squeaky toy.

"Pet toys, micro-green salads, rat runs—" Quesar gestured at the colourful lab.

"Sedentary, overfed rats can skew the results—" said Benson.

"All the little rat funerals?"

"I just think their sacrifice deserves a little more respect. Quesar, if we can modify the vaccine to be effective in humans—"

"Senkai, it's over." Quesar rubbed her temples, shoulders sagging. "Security's clearing us out in half an hour. Maybe you should think about another career track. Look at that kendo instructor turned mental-health advocate whose online talks you keep forcing us to watch."

Benson was silent.

"I'll see if I can get you a spot at Vati-Tech," said Quesar. She sighed heavily. "They're trying to develop a vaccine for homosexuality."

Benson closed his eyes, and heard the lab door swing shut. He resisted the urge to grab a flask of radioactive goo from his secret inventory, which he kept in the event that he someday found a way to give himself superpowers.

Instead, he stared dully at the computer screen. Part of him realised that Quesar was right, Schendruk wouldn't waste money on human trials. It was over. But an old memory stirred, of how he'd once dreamed of studying law. Scenes from *12 Angry Men* and *8* had filled him with the conviction that a single voice could change the course of nations.

Benson glanced at the clock. Twenty-five minutes. Not nearly enough, but he'd take what he could get. He moved methodically between the computers, the crowded benches, and the vaccine refrigeration unit. Time seemed to stretch oddly into the longest twenty-five minutes of his life, but by the time the boots reached his door, Benson had only one thing left to do.

The doors swung open, and Benson raised the aerosol chamber to his face, hoping he'd calculated the dosage correctly.

"Kanpai," said Benson, and inhaled.

* * *

Two minutes. Three hours. A day. Bottle after bottle tips gently into its respective thread. The Flow shivers and I swiftly smooth its course. The light at the window flickers, and I risk a glance outside. The sun blinks.

They're coming.

I place the rose flask on the windowsill, and for the first time since my shadow touched the Wings, I draw a breath. Vapour rises slowly from the bottle, trailing outside to form a cloudy perimeter, then a thin shell of fog around my hill. It won't hold, but every moment counts.

Beyond the fragile fog, contrails are circling now. Dark shadows wheel furiously outside the dome, but don't pass through. I continue to empty the phials and flasks, glittering almost-moments streaming into the Flow, becoming moments once more, infused with the spirit of barely remembered days.

At the threshold of my gate, a dark grey contrail crackles into Transformation, with Timing beside her. Timing reaches towards the wispy vapour, and Transformation catches her wrist.

"You can only pass through the Shallows once," says Transformation.

Timing looks up at the window, and smiles to see me. For a moment, I almost regret the path I've chosen. All around the patchy grass, I can see my colleagues standing darkly: Motion, her windswept hair forming a midnight halo around her; Misfortune with his iridescent scales and serpentine shadow.

Bottles clink wistfully, and a white cloud by the gate transmutes into Luan. He lays a hand on Transformation's shoulder, and then steps through the fog. His skin shivers and crackles, his whole body threatening to scatter into mist. For a moment, it seems that something else stands in his place—something of water and light, something that never remembers being human.

Luan labours to take another step, then another, solidifying back into his usual form as he inexorably approaches my cottage.

I know this is how it must end. Had known, perhaps, since Serendipity's words had sliced deep into the hollow place I longed to fill.

One more, just one more.

I grasp a blood-red libation bottle full of golden afternoons, and one minute is all I have left to give.

* * *

Name: Rutger Stone

Age: 43

Occupation: CEO of Jupiter Exploration

Rutger Stone sat gargoyle-like in the auditorium, bored to petrification. The speeches at these events were interminable, but it was less than a minute until they broke for beluga and Romanée-Conti. He distracted himself with fiscal projections—he was trying to install decent renewable energy on his Pacific island, since his nemesis, Kikuyo from Ingot Resources, had just added a new photosynthesis-fusion array to her Arctic villa.

Rutger ignored the petite woman squeezing noisily into the seat beside him. Her luggage was caked with orange dust, apparently overlooked in sloppy quarantine procedures. Old luggage tags swung from its handle, with codes like *NBO, KNJ*, and the name *L. Kerr*.

"Damn, did I miss the entire thing?" muttered the young woman.

Rutger considered pretending that he hadn't heard her, but

doing so would doubtlessly result in the footage being uploaded onto social media sites within seven seconds, tagged *CEO of Evil Mining Corp shuns beloved spiritual leader/terminally ill Nobel Laureate/alien ambassador.*

"I believe there's seventeen seconds left," said Rutger.

"I didn't think tuberculosis breakthroughs would interest someone like you," said Kerr amiably.

"Apparently, some of our workforce in more remote locations find it bothersome," said Rutger dryly.

He'd really only come to hear Raki Adedayo's afternoon presentation. According to Rutger's dossier, Adedayo had defied an arranged marriage at age twelve, left behind her drought-stricken province to study astrophysics at Caltech, and the doctoral student now had some rather curious ideas regarding faster than light travel.

However, the passing seconds stretched vindictively, and the current presenter's words seemed to blur into utter incoherence. They were probably testing an experimental PA system.

The young woman kept glancing at him, and Rutger ignored this. He was exceptionally disciplined at ignoring things. As a child, he'd walked past a grand old library on his way home from school each day, and spent glorious afternoons there with his best friend, Tulip. The world had seemed giddy and immense, brimming with visionaries and heroes. However, when he'd turned eleven, his father had taken sick, and Rutger had scrounged an off-the-books job running errands at the local open cut mine. He'd still walked past that library every day, but to him, it may as well not have existed.

Rutger blinked slowly at the memory, and found himself glancing at the woman beside him again. She took the flicker of eye contact as an invitation to conversation.

"Not to pry," said Kerr, "but when was the last time you had that mole checked?"

"I have a skin examination every twelve months."

Kerr's fingers brushed past his ear, stopping an inch into his hairline. She flicked a dermatoscope from her pocket and leaned in.

"I think you should visit again." She gave him a polite smile, and drew back.

Rutger grabbed her callused hand almost without realising it, staring at the words tattooed on her light brown wrist.

As much as you can.

As many as you can.

As long as you can.

"Odd mantra for a dermatologist," said Rutger.

"Oncologist," said Kerr. "Emergency obstetrician. Stopgap school teacher when the weather's fine. Come visit me in Jamaame sometime."

The crowd shuffled to its feet, and the clatter of silverware drifted from the adjoining conference room.

"I feel like some fresh air," said Rutger. "Care for a walk?"

* * *

Downstairs, the cottage door creaks open. Only a few bottles remain stoppered, suspended in their slumber, but there isn't time to find their threads. Luan is right, there's no point in fighting. Something pale catches my eye in the Flow, and I reach over, thinking that a piece of lint must have tumbled in.

I pull out a silver blue thread, translucent, as though not yet realised. I gaze into its heart, and see myself staring back.

A present.

Footsteps are climbing the corkscrew staircase, and I grab the remaining bottles, pouring them into the hazy silver thread. There's no time to find their threads, but at least their memories, their passions won't be lost. The last bottle splinters in my palm, and around me, every bottle crumbles into sand.

"Those lives don't belong to you," says Luan.

White sand drains through my fingers. And they're finally gone, the days that almost were.

"All they needed was a little more time," I say.

Luan shakes his head. "I'm sorry for the short, desolate life you led, but you made your choices. It's not your place to make theirs."

"Our place is to help," I say with feeling. "I comb their threads to make them strong, to ease their journey. All I did was remind them of what they once loved. This woman," I separate a thread, "she spends a cumulative twenty years of her life eating fruit pies and having afternoon naps. But here, at this point, she thinks about taking a sewing course. If she does, she becomes a remarkable mixed-media artist and inspires a generation of guerrilla embroiderers."

"Yes," says Luan. "And if she does, she misses a call from her brother after his motorcycle accident, and never has a chance to say goodbye."

The thread drifts from my finger, and Luan continues.

"Their lives are meaningful because of the choices they make. Whether that choice is to refuse to sit at the back of a bus, or to eat two thousand and forty-seven pies in their lifetime. They might not always make the best, the most heroic, or the kindest choices, but it's not your world anymore."

The sunlight feels cold on my skin, and I realise that I'm tired. Tired of looking in on a world I can't touch, collecting memories that aren't mine. All I wanted …

I can feel myself dissolving slowly at the seams. There's only so much one can bear before this place, this endless, aimless day becomes … enough.

Luan rests a hand on my shoulder.

"Time to retire," he says.

* * *

I'm kneeling on a plain of tiny white shells, so bright they burn like snow. The Stewards stand in wordless court, towering and faceless; like obelisks they encircle me. A sun hangs behind each one, their shadow-cage crossing over me.

Transformation stands before me. Today, light drifts from her, and a circlet of ferns rests upon her head. I raise my eyes to her, and wonder that I ever felt afraid.

"I know you have to follow your conscience," I say, "as I followed mine."

Transformation shakes her head, and her voice is soft.

"It was never a question of conscience, but of choice. The lives you altered were done so without their consent, without their knowledge, to satisfy your will, not theirs. Choices are only yours to make when the consequences are yours to suffer. Only mortals have the right to exert their will on the mortal world. Do you understand?"

There's a sadness in her eyes, and I find myself wishing that I'd visited Transformation more often, in her lonely vale of autumn light. My day is drawing to its close, and in the end, I am ready. The Stewards hum in unison, and the suns begin to darken. Transformation leans towards me.

"Thank you," I say softly, and Transformation hesitates. "A long time ago, you made me a promise. A place with no darkness. Thank you, Iru, for giving me a little longer in the sun."

They say there was a time, in her younger days, when Transformation visited the mortal world to watch their combustion sun rise and set. But they say a great many things about Transformation.

The shadows deepen around me, and Transformation cups my face in her hands, as she did once, long ago. She leans in so that only I can hear her.

"Friendships are an unpredictable force," she says, and kisses my forehead before the suns snuff out.

* * *

I'm standing on a sticky landing, a suitcase in my arms. The wooden door before me opens, as though I've knocked, and a dark-haired man in his thirties smiles broadly.

"New recruit's here," says the man. "Ceren, make yourself decent."

A dapper young man glides from the parlour, dressed as though he's raided the most exclusive op shops in the city.

"I … am always decent," says Ceren, with a flourish that suggests he's about to send a deck of cards flying from his sleeve. "Have we met?"

I shake my head. The interior of the share house is surprisingly clean and airy, inhabited by numerous piles of books and solemn potted palms.

"I'm Jackson," says the dark-haired man. "Secretary of the Mushin Foundation. This is Ceren Darwinshaw, he breaks up couples."

"I'm a relationship counsellor," says Ceren primly. "I help vulnerable people leave unhealthy relationships."

"He's crazier than I ever—" begins Jackson.

The front door slams open, and an athletic woman wearing an olive cami and pressed trousers bursts into the room.

"We got the grant!" she grins, and exchanges a jubilant high five with Jackson.

"I thought Stone was busy eradicating tuberculosis," says Ceren.

"I guess he realised mental health networks are desperately underfunded," shrugs the woman. She notices my presence, and extends a hand. "I'm Evea. You are …?"

Through the window on my left, stars are appearing above the neon skyline. In my chest, a heartbeat thumps in quiet anticipation.

"Ernest Babar." I shake Evea's hand warmly.

"'Babar' like the elephant?" says Jackson.

Evea ignores him.

"Welcome to the madhouse," she says. "So, why are you here?"

I close my eyes for a moment, and I can remember rocketships and heaving nets, chanting crowds and silent schoolrooms. Visions fleet through my mind, and a whisper lingers in my ear. I smile at my new colleagues.

"I'm here to help."

About *Almost Days*

Almost Days was Aurealis Award-shortlisted for Best Fantasy Short Story.

Almost Days was first published in *Insert Title Here* (FableCroft Publishing, 2015), edited by Tehani Croft.

THE OBSOLETE SOUL

"Your brain doesn't need you anymore," said Doctor Creel, steepling her fingers.

"Sorry," I interjected. "What did you say your doctorate was in?"

Getting on your doctor's bad side can be a fast track to an unnecessary colonoscopy, but I'd been on a hell of a ride these past few months, and I was ready to get off and punch the driver in the throat.

* * *

It all started with something stupid. Well, not stupid, but … ordinary. October fifteenth. My girlfriend, Ella, was acting kind of strange. Like she was upset but didn't want me to know. She'd had this forlorn smile all morning—the same one she wears when she watches political satire.

It wasn't until around lunchtime that I nudged something out of her.

"It's not important," she shrugged. "I just thought we were going to do something for my birthday. Maybe dinner."

Ella was pretty low-key about birthdays, so it was weird for her to bring it up so early in the day. I'd actually planned a little scavenger hunt around the house later, involving chocolates and cute notes, culminating in a reservation at Ruciere's—a new restaurant down the road with servings the size of postage stamps, so you knew it had to be good.

"Maybe I've got something planned," I said.

"Dean, my birthday was yesterday."

God, my stomach dropped about seven storeys. I'm usually good with times and places, but I figured I must have gotten the dates mixed up.

"October fifteenth, right?" I said.

"Today's the sixteenth," said Ella.

And *that* was when things started getting weird.

* * *

I was freaked out for a few days. The last thing I remembered was feeding the fish and going to bed on the fourteenth. Next thing I know, I'm waking up on the sixteenth wondering why my girlfriend's pissed off. Losing a whole day is fine when you're at uni: your day starts at 2pm and tapers off into bad garage bands and dodgy kebabs. Losing a day is less okay when you've just tipped thirty and you're working for the public marketing advisory office.

My first thought was that I'd had one of those mental pretzels, like when you spend all week thinking it's Friday. I must have thought it was Saturday, and forgotten it was Sunday. But when Ella told me what I'd been up to on Saturday, I couldn't remember any of it. Not the buttered bread for breakfast, not the three hours of watching soccer replays, not the waving goodbye when she said she was going to her parents' place for birthday cake.

For starters, I never have buttered bread. I'll always toast it, preferably with cheese. Secondly, I'll watch the game if it sounds good, but I don't watch replays. And thirdly, well, I'm surprised Ella didn't suffocate me in my sleep over that last bit. Thankfully, she's not vindictive like that.

The best thing about Ella in situations like these is you know she's not making it up. She thinks pranks are dated, fake-outs are cheap, and little lies are okay but flamboyant fabrications aren't. Unless, of course, the fate of entire refugee camps are at stake.

So, I figured it was some kind of memory loss. I'd never had any serious health problems—a broken arm, impacted wisdom teeth. I'd been a bit forgetful this year—I could swear I'd put the milk in the fridge, but then I'd find it on the counter, or I'd go to empty the bins and find I'd already done it.

But spontaneous amnesia was a different story. Preferably someone else's. One story that scared me as a kid was this guy who just woke up one morning and couldn't remember a damned thing. Talk about tabula rasa.

But I hadn't had any other symptoms—no headaches, no visual disturbances, no voices in my head except the one telling me I should be doing something with my life. So I shrugged off the incident as stress-related.

I'd been doing a lot of thinking lately about my career, my goals, me and Ella. I'd been in a holding pattern for five years, but it was funny how everything looked different from the other side of thirty. It was like looking down from a plane and realising that your city was the size of a squashed pea and damned ugly.

The advisory office had just shifted to private management, which meant the flexitime had gone, along with half the staff. I'd been browsing the job ads, but my marketing degree was outdated. Secretly, I dreamed of owning a few acres just north of the city, maybe having a couple of chooks and some fruit trees. It was a dumb idea I'd had since reading *Of Mice and Men* in high school, but the thought still quietly gnawed at me every time I clicked another "Sales Rep" ad.

On another front, my folks had been on my back about settling down and giving them a swarm of grandkids. Just not with Ella. They'd never warmed to her, although they didn't have a problem with anyone my younger brother, Keir, went out with, including the girl whose self-professed ambition was to become a hotel empire heiress.

So I eased off the caffeine and tried not to think about Christmas. It was still two months away, but the shops were brimming with motorised Santas and counterfeit luxury advent calendars. At the office, I had my hands full with clients wanting to know if they could promote a breakfast cereal as "healthy" if it was forty-three percent lard, and whether "bait-and-switch" was technically illegal. Yes. It is.

I didn't think about the missing day again until I was going over our Christmas schedule. The office party, Christmas lunch, Christmas dinner. But the details were all wrong.

"Ella, did you switch the times on the planner?"

Maybe the sticky notes had fallen off the spreadsheet and she'd stuck them back out of order. Which wasn't like Ella, but we were both a bit scattered lately.

Ella glanced at the calendar. "That's right, isn't it?"

"Christmas dinner," I said. "With my parents."

"You said you wanted to change it around this year," said Ella. "Lunch with my parents, dinner with yours."

"My brother will be there," I snapped.

Ella looked at me as though I had a baby panda between my teeth. I took a slow breath. Ella was tired—the newsagency was hectic now, and the Christmas trading hours meant she was sorting stock until late. She was getting this conversation confused with something else.

"We can switch it back if you want," said Ella. "I'll call my parents." She paused. "Does this mean you don't want me to come to your office Christmas party anymore?"

"Why would you want to come?"

From the look on her face, I probably could have phrased that better, but my skull was starting to feel like a blender full of razorblades.

"You don't remember, do you?" said Ella. "Telling me this would be your last Christmas at the advisory office, saying you wanted to see your brother ..."

That was when I knew something was wrong with me. I mean really wrong. Not just pre-Christmas chaos, not a sneaky mid-life crisis. I wasn't just forgetting stuff—I was doing stuff, weird stuff, and not remembering it. And that was hell scary. But trying to see a doctor felt like a ticket to turmoil I just didn't need right now. Some medical centres didn't even have waiting lists anymore. I'm pretty sure I read about one guy whose call to reception was on hold for three years.

I was silent for a while, Ella sitting beside me, her head on my shoulder.

"The schedule's fine," I said. "And I'd love you to come to my office party."

* * *

I told Ella it was just stress, but I could tell she didn't believe me this time.

I took out my grandad's pocket watch that night—just sat and held it, like I did when I was a kid. It was plain steel, its face a moon of ageing parchment. I kept it wound, and the delicate black hands still kept the time faithfully.

I'd always been close to my grandad, closer in some ways than to my dad. My dad loved me, but my grandad understood me.

As a kid, I'd always felt like I was running alongside a fence. I couldn't see over to the other side, but I knew I had to get there. I kept running, waiting for the fence to end, to bend, to change, but it never did. All I could see of the other side was the sky, and all I could feel was the shared earth beneath my feet.

I told this to my grandad when I was about eight, and he rested his weathered hand on my shoulder, as if I'd just expressed exactly how he felt. That afternoon, sitting beneath the jacaranda tree in his backyard, he gave me this pocket watch.

I pressed it to my temple now, feeling the cold crystal against my skin. It was like a piece of reality, condensed in my palm.

I could deal with this. I just needed a strategy.

* * *

I started checking clocks and calendars compulsively, keeping a timetable of what I did, what I said. My productivity ranking at work plummeted from third band to fifth, and Trinh in accounts quietly slipped me a leaflet on meditation, but my plan seemed to be working—no strange blanks, no missing time.

The office Christmas party was never a big deal for me. Overlong, under-catered, and sloshing with people who wished they'd gone to art school. If dissatisfaction came with a glass of flat beer, that'd be my office party.

I'd been at the advisory office for six years, treading water that had turned into muck. I didn't make an effort to get to know my colleagues. I was friendly, did the water-cooler chat, but the advisory office was just a dodgy rest stop on the highway to my destination. My definitely awesome destination, which I would absolutely figure out any day now. However, six years later, I was still stuck in the bog while the caravans roared past.

I told Ella I liked to keep my work and private life separate, which made her suspect my office parties were a lot more fun than I let on. But the truth was, I didn't want Ella to see where I worked. It was like Schrödinger's cat—once Ella stepped into the hive of cubicles, that place would become real, and the colourless world would chitinise around me.

I tried to casually dissuade her, complaining about the gritty pies and watery punch. I warned her about the speeches full of inappropriate metaphors, the inebriated corporate-integration department, and the random staff member who inevitably gets bitterly drunk and rants at management before vanishing permanently.

Ella asked me why I was still there. I mumbled something about bills.

Ella and I first met just out of uni, when I was full of fire and ambition and general crap. Now, I was just full of crap. And once she saw where I worked, it'd only reinforce the fact that I wasn't the guy she'd signed up for.

The night before the party, I did the usual double-check of my diary records.

Salad sandwich for lunch.

Raoul got fired.

Fed the fish.

Tick. Tick. Tick. I automatically flipped back a few days to make sure everything looked good, and noticed that I'd missed a page. Last Sunday. There was a single line jotted at the bottom.

Had a lovely day with Ella.

Which sounded charming, except I hadn't written it. It was my handwriting, but it may as well have been stamped in cuneiform.

I found Ella in the living room, wearing a strange expression.

"Ella, what did we do last Sun—"

"Uh, Dean, what happened to the fish?"

The strangest sensation came over me as I looked at the tank, the half-nibbled seaweed stirring in the endless stream of bubbles.

"Where are the fish?" I heard myself say.

"Dean …?"

My gaze went down to the splashes of water beside the tank, the damp footprints on the carpet.

I noticed that my shoes were wet.

"Dean? Dean …"

* * *

When I woke up, morning light was sifting through the bedroom curtains. I felt tingly and disoriented, and Ella was sitting beside the bed.

"Did I pass out?" I said.

"Sort of," said Ella. "How do you feel?"

"Like I've eaten a kilo of hot dogs and brought them up again," I said. "I think I'll give the Christmas party a miss tonight. Sorry."

"Band-Aid."

It took me a moment to realise what she meant.

"Rip it off," I said.

"The office party was last night," said Ella. "You insisted we go. You grabbed the mic from the Chief Integrations Officer, gave a speech from Dead Poets Society, and then you got fired. Or maybe resigned. I think I'll go with resigned."

Everything just spun for a while, with me as the disintegrating axis.

"I managed to make an appointment for you to see the doctor," said Ella.

I exhaled slowly.

"When?"

* * *

Doctor Ramiya was a no-nonsense doctor who undoubtedly cared about her patients but hadn't expected so many of them to get so old. I wasn't sure how Ella managed to snare me a spot—something about a strategic negotiation involving a vintage *National Geographic* magazine.

I explained my situation to the doctor, and she ran through the usual questions: did I do recreational drugs, did I hear voices, had I been depressed, manic, suicidal, homicidal.

I half-expected her to give me a pack of anxiolytics and send me on my way. Instead, I found myself trekking between MRIs, CT scans, PET scans, and x-rays. I wasn't sure what the x-rays were for, but Ramiya said it was amazing what you found sometimes, and pointed to a framed image that seemed to show a toy truck wedged between the blurry clouds of someone's frontal lobes. The caption read: "Why You Shouldn't Put Things Up Your Nose".

"Everything's come back clear," said Ramiya. "The good news is, no brain lesions, tumours, structural abnormalities or foreign objects. The bad news is, you're going to have to keep hunting for the cause of these episodes. I'm not saying it's psychological, but that'd be my next path of investigation."

I didn't know if I was ready to see a psychologist. It'd be impossible to get an appointment before Christmas anyway, even with Ella's impressive skills, so I did the next best thing.

I used to associate mental breakdowns with uptight, neurotic types. Then, two years ago, one of my best mates had a meltdown.

Badrak was rock-solid—kept his cool when our tents got washed away in Year Nine camp. Barely flinched when twitchy Liam shot him in the thigh with a nail gun during woodshop.

Badrak and his wife had just had a baby girl, his garage was doing it tough, and something in him just shorted out. He said it was like walking around all day with a pillow over his face and a cattle prod up his spine.

We were overdue for a long lunch anyway, so we caught up at the local pub.

"Who'd have thought we'd both be wrecks by the time we turned thirty?" said Badrak. "Didn't prep you for that in PE."

"Let's blame it on the booze," I said, and we clanked our zero-alcohol lagers.

We talked about random stuff—the economy, the crap on TV, the diminishing size of biscuits.

"How's Winter?" I said.

"Walking, talking, and indestructible," said Badrak. "We were settling her down to bed last week, and she said 'Freedom or death'. Where do they get this stuff?"

It was weird when your friends started having kids. People used to have coming-of-age rituals—I mean real ones, not like getting sloshed at graduation. These days, no one really seemed to know what they were doing, or maybe we were just more willing to admit it.

"You thinking of having kids?" said Badrak.

"I'm having trouble staying sane as it is."

Badrak jotted something onto a paper coaster.

Griswold Kinsley.

"Don't be put off by his name," said Badrak. "He's not one of those 'Tell me about your mother' tossers. No guarantees, but it's a start."

There were no guarantees in life except that it ended one day. For now, I just had to get through Christmas.

* * *

Dad called on Christmas Eve. He never called unless there'd been a death in the family.

"Dean, how're you going?"

"Fine," I said.

"Good, good." He paused. "You still coming for dinner tomorrow? If you'd rather come for lunch …"

It was insidiously tempting. It wasn't that I hated my brother. We'd gotten on okay when we were kids, but sometime during junior high, he'd turned into a real brat. Things exploded the summer Keir finished high school. Looking back, it was pretty childish, but at the time, it felt like the Battle of Thermopylae.

There'd been a bad storm and our place was a mess of trees and shattered roof shingles. I was the one left to clean it up while Keir got ready for a night out. It was one of those humid, overcast days, with the cicadas crying like a chainsaw choir. I'd had enough and hid the keys to our parents' car, thinking Keir would have to walk or, god forbid, miss the party.

Instead, Keir took my beloved Ford and drove it into the river, swimming back to shore with two broken ribs and a smirk. I got the blame, and maybe I deserved it. But the petty malice of his stunt, and my having to get by all summer without a car, slammed the grudge pretty deep.

But I'd already told Ella the schedule was good.

"Dinner's fine, Dad," I said.

It'd be unpleasant and awkward, but I only had to endure it for a few hours. Then, I was free to lock myself at home until the new year, after which, hopefully, Griswold would solve all my problems.

* * *

Christmas lunch was an island of sunshine amidst a grim few weeks. Ella's parents—Tijon and Mala—were easygoing people who never had much need for clocks or calendars. It was hard to imagine them raising precise, punctual Ella.

Ella had always wanted to be a doctor, but her grades weren't nearly good enough. She'd wound up working at the Grace and Blob Newsagency, spending her days poring over the science magazines. My parents said Ella lacked ambition, but I thought reading every back issue of *Scientific American* was pretty impressive.

"Ella says you've moved on from the ads office," said Tijon.

I imagine Ella's exact words were "Dean got sacked", but Tijon saw life as a gentle wave of forward motion.

"I've been thinking of changing tack for a while," I said.

"Does this mean you'll be going with Ella to Port Siroc?" said Mala.

"Port Siroc?" As soon as I said it, I felt my stomach twist.

"The Meaningful Information Management course," Mala

ploughed on, oblivious to Ella's suddenly peculiar expression. "Three months isn't long to be apart, but it'd be nice if you could keep her company."

I glanced at Ella, and I could see her drawing several quick conclusions.

"We haven't had a chance to talk about it much," said Ella.

"I thought you said he—" began Tijon.

"Dad," said Ella firmly. "Dean's had a lot on his mind."

That was the understatement of the year. I excused myself and plunged my face into a basin of cold water. Ella had obviously told me about Port Siroc. It had to be the missing Sunday.

Port Siroc was a six-hour flight away, and notorious for a nightlife fuelled by college students and experimental herbs. Ella was moving forward, while I was going down my own personal gurgler.

I splashed more water on my face and tried to look alive. I'd lost weight, and I noticed the tips of my ears were sunburned. I suddenly felt a deep sense of disconnect as I looked in the mirror, as though there were another person standing a foot away, staring at me.

The rest of the afternoon was a haze of distant chit-chat, followed by a muted drive home. As dinner approached, the tingling in my temples became a full-blown headache.

"If you'd rather stay home, I can tell your parents you had a bad eggnog," said Ella.

"And let Keir look like the reliable son?" I said wryly.

"This isn't six-thousand years ago," said Ella. "Birthrights went out around the same time as wrestling with lions."

"Tell that to Trev Manning."

"He doesn't wrestle lions," said Ella. "He hugs them."

"Tell that to the lions."

My forehead pulsed painfully when I smiled, and Ella turned my face towards her.

"Dean, if you don't want to go, we don't have to go."

I kissed her knuckles gently.

"There'll be trifle," I said.

* * *

I knew I should have gone with the eggnog excuse the moment my mother asked if Ella was expecting. It was all downhill from there.

Ella's smile remained valiantly neutral as the dinner conversation went from awkward to excruciating, covering weight-loss tips and teeth straightening. My brain started to wooze, and I still hadn't said a word to Keir, who looked as uncomfortable as I felt. He'd filled out a bit, cut his hair. Looked less like a Tokyo drift racer and more like an urban architect. He'd brought a girl I didn't recognise—Lillian—long, dark hair, and eyes like autumn sky.

"How's work?" said Dad.

"Got fired," I said.

Killed the conversation, but it was a mercy.

"I have something to say," said Keir, and the silence took on a nervous buzz. "Lillian and I are getting married. And we're moving to Sudan."

My parents' expressions froze, mangled somewhere between joy and horror.

"Lillian's been appointed to a position at the new fistula hospital," continued Keir. "And I'm taking a contract with the educational development commission."

The only noise was my stomach doing squelchy acrobatics. My baby brother was marrying a medical humanitarian and moving to a region that travel advisories typically marked in an alarming shade of red. Hell had frozen over, Keir had grown up, and I was going to reintroduce everyone to my dinner.

"Congratulations," I mustered. "Excuse me."

I made it halfway across the room before I blacked out.

* * *

I woke with tension fizzing through my bones. I was at home, in bed, and the calendar told me it was Boxing Day. I couldn't find Ella—just a note on the bedside table saying: *Burger in the fridge. Back soon.*

Everything felt distant and muffled and out of control. My grandad would have said "Maybe it's all in your head, but it's still *your* head. Be the captain of your life, not a passenger." God, I missed him.

I reached over to my bedside table and my heart stopped. I yanked the drawer off its rails and emptied the contents onto the carpet.

My grandad's watch was gone.

* * *

This was war. Whatever was happening to me had to stop. Medication, surgery, paleo colonic juice cleanse—whatever it took.

Ella reassured me I hadn't done anything strange after I'd blacked out. I'd staggered to the couch and slept for about an hour, then resumed dinner, pleasant as a picnic.

"Then you went for a drive around midnight," said Ella.

"Where to?"

"I asked, but I don't think you heard me. You looked okay when you came back."

I was okay like a scarecrow falling into a volcano was okay.

I finally asked Ella about the missing Sunday, and her mood clouded over.

"We just hung out," said Ella. "I told you I got accepted into the Meaningful Information Management course at the Port Siroc Mature Students College. I can still cancel it …"

"I'm happy for you." I squeezed her hand. "Something else

happened, didn't it?"

"We talked …" said Ella. "You asked if I wanted to get married."

I knew I hesitated too long before saying, "What did you say?"

"It's okay," said Ella. "I had a feeling you weren't quite yourself that day."

And then she changed the subject.

* * *

My first appointment with Griswold Kinsley was a bust when the receptionist couldn't find my name in the booking system.

"I made the appointment weeks ago," I said.

"I'm sorry," said the receptionist. "You're not on the schedule."

He must have seen my burgeoning Hulk-smash expression because his typing speed increased.

"Oh … it looks like you did have an appointment but then you cancelled it."

I forced myself not to react. I made another appointment and left the office.

When I did finally see Kinsley, I didn't care if I sounded like one of those ranting bratwursts on late-night cable. I laid it all out there, from the missing time to the weird behaviour to the Christmas implosion.

Kinsley was only a few years older than me, with short coppery hair and a crisp wardrobe. He listened sympathetically and asked me about work, family, medical history.

"I wish I could make a simple diagnosis," said Kinsley. "But your situation seems unusual, especially in the absence of physical pathology or psychological trauma."

So, it was more psychiatric assessments, psychometric tests, and endless multiple choice questionnaires.

"Aside from understandably elevated levels of anxiety, your

psychological health seems fine," said Kinsley. "Dissociative Identity Disorder usually involves distinct changes in personality and mannerisms. Your results don't indicate delusional thinking, mania, or schizotypal tendencies. Your episodes don't fit the profile of parasomnia, and there's no clear aetiology for your memory loss."

"So you've got no idea?"

"I'm saying the brain's complicated," said Kinsley. "And stress can exacerbate dormant predispositions. I'd recommend a course of selective serotonin reuptake inhibitors. They might take the edge off what you're going through. Look into meditation, try yoga, do more cardiovascular exercise, and come back in a few weeks."

It wasn't exactly "Take two aspirin and see me in the morning", but that's what it felt like. The meds were a disaster. I kept losing the bastards, and went through about four or five packs in a week. Memory loss was supposed to be one of the side effects, but that's what I was taking the bloody pills for. I tried getting Ella to hang on to them, but hers kept going missing too. I caught myself having paranoid suspicions that Ella was messing with me.

I subscribed to some yoga vids, and Ella tried doing meditation with me, but she was flat-out getting ready for the course. I had to fix this before she left, or the odds of her coming back weren't so great. Having an eccentric boyfriend was cute in uni, but now it was just embarrassing.

Conventional science had let me down, so it was time for random desperation. I tried acupuncture, reflexology, kinesiology, hypnosis, traditional Chinese medicine, Ayurveda, feng shui, and aura cleansing. I spent a week trying to maximise my qi, and another week eating raw food and drinking boiled cicada shells. The aura cleansing convinced me that the Consumer Protection Agency needed to beef up its act, although the feng shui lady encouraged me to finally clean out the garage.

So I was knee-deep in dented rims and covered in cup marks

when an unexpected visitor showed up.

"Hey," said Keir, shifting slightly in the sagging garage doorway.

"Hey," I said. I wasn't sure how things had ended at Christmas, but apparently there hadn't been bloodshed.

"Lil and I are leaving for Darfur tomorrow," said Keir.

My insides felt queasy, which could have been from the raw potato, and the back of my neck was prickling like hell. Ten years of estrangement didn't heal overnight, but he was family. He was my brother. And maybe I should have tried harder when he'd needed guidance, not judgement.

"Good luck," I said. "Look, Keir …"

I was surprised to see him blinking back tears, and he hugged me suddenly.

"It meant a lot," said Keir. "What you said on Christmas night."

He slid something from his shirt pocket and tapped it against his heart.

"I know what this means to you," he continued. "I'll always keep it with me."

Silver curves caught the sunlight, and I felt my chest ache.

Grandad's watch.

"Just take care," I said. "Grandad would have been proud of you."

Keir wiped his eyes, slapped me on the back, and then he was gone.

When Ella got home, I was still sitting in the garage, staring at the dusty junk.

"Christmas night," I said. "When I left in the middle of the night. Did I take anything with me?"

"I don't remember …" She saw my gutted expression, and something in her eyes rang tiny silver alarm bells.

"What aren't you telling me?" I said.

"You went to your brother's house," said Ella quietly. "I'm sorry. I put my phone in the glovebox and tracked it online. But I didn't want you to think I was one of those jealous girlfriends who puts tracking devices in your car."

I let my instinctive reaction fade.

"Our car," I corrected. "And under the circumstances, that was pretty smart."

"Dean …" Ella hugged me. I was getting a lot of hugs today, and to be honest, I needed them.

I hadn't told Ella that I'd been missing more days. One last week, and two this week. As far as I could tell, I was just pottering around the house trying to create a water feature. But I couldn't live like this—half my life disintegrating from memory.

I was out of cash and out of ideas. Ella was leaving in a week, and I had to hold what was left of me together. I thought I was doing pretty good until Ella gave me a leaflet for the Altara Sleep Clinic.

"They use EEG equipment to record brain waves," said Ella. "If we can analyse what's happening when you switch between you and the other you—"

"The other me." It was like an electric shock to hear her give it a name like that.

"Dean, do you love me?"

I only paused because the question came out of nowhere.

"What? Sure, of course …"

"The other you never hesitates," said Ella without accusation. "I know it's been happening more often. The other day, you wanted to go shopping for an indoor hammock."

I glanced at the leaflet again.

"We can't afford it," I said. Ella started to protest, but I cut her off. "Plus, there's no point in spending a fortune if nothing happens."

"If I can get you into a sleep clinic for free, will you go?" said Ella.

"How would you manage that? Disguise me as a pillow?"

"Just leave it to me."

Which was how I ended up at the Associate College of Rosterdam's Sleep Laboratory. I didn't know what an associate college was, but the peeling paint and duct-taped doors gave me a hint.

Doctor Creel was a meticulous-looking woman in her late thirties, with charcoal hair pulled back in a ponytail. A poster in her office read:

Don't mess with your brain, or your brain will mess with you.

I gave Creel the director's cut, and she asked me a bunch of questions about what I liked to cook and what my hobbies were.

She booked me into the sleep lab that night. The trolley bed looked like it was about to collapse under the weight of its own ennui, but it wasn't nearly as uncomfortable as the electrodes taped to my face. My stomach was a mess of butterflies, so I was surprised when I woke the next morning feeling rested.

"The preliminary data looks normal," said Creel, scrolling through screens of wavy lines. "Good beta and alpha waves, nice delta, standard REM."

I didn't bother hiding my disappointment.

"I'd like to book you in again tonight," said Creel. "Just for observation, no EEG."

I was too drained to argue. I just told Ella the results looked good, and Creel wanted to do some follow-up.

"Let's go somewhere today," said Ella. "I'm almost done packing, and it's a beautiful day."

So we drove out to the national park for a picnic. Summer was starting to wane, and the breeze by the river was deliciously cool.

"No canoeing today," said the ranger. "Some jerk released a bunch of goldfish a few months back and they've mutated into papaya-sized carnivores."

So Ella and I had avocado sandwiches under the eucalypts instead.

"Ella, do you like the 'other me' better?" I said.

"That's like asking if I like 'happy you' or 'sad you'," said Ella. "It's still you. Whether you remember it or not."

I felt odd that night as I sank onto the laboratory bed. Thoughts about me, the other me, and Ella bounced around my mind, and I was only half asleep when Creel knocked on the door.

"Phone call for you," she said.

It was Ella.

"Sorry to bother you," said Ella. "My Wednesday flight's been cancelled. The only plane that'll get me to Port Siroc on time leaves first thing in the morning."

"I'll be right over—"

"No, Dean. I want you to stay at the lab tonight. Please see this through."

"Ella—"

"If you love me, stay." She paused. "I love you."

And I was left cradling a blank screen.

She'd never pulled anything like that before, and I wondered for a horrible moment if there was an "other Ella". Either way, tomorrow, she'd be gone.

I didn't remember falling asleep, just sinking into a whirlpool of emotional debris.

I woke feeling exhausted and empty.

"Good news," said Creel. "I have something to show you."

Her office had several piles of printouts, and Ella was sitting by the window.

"Dean!" Ella hugged me tightly.

"What happened to your flight?" I said.

"It was a deception," said Creel. "At my request."

"Excuse me?" I said coldly.

Ella mouthed "I'm sorry".

Creel flicked on a video display, and a grainy image of the sleep lab bloomed onscreen. I was lying on the bed in an unflattering position, and Creel skipped forward.

"What's that?" I said, as onscreen figures entered the room and hooked me up to an EEG. Other figures wheeled in some kind of giant mechanical doughnut. "You said it was just observation."

"One of the advantages of not being a registered institution is I don't have to sign their 'ethics clauses'," said Creel. She clicked the remote, and playback returned to normal speed.

On the monitor, I was stirring. My body sat up, and after a pause, got out of bed. My body looked around like a new arrival in a terrarium, and then stared thoughtfully at the camera.

Creel paused the footage.

"Then you tried to convince me to unlock the door," she said.

Amidst my growing agitation, I felt the faintest spark of hope.

"Okay, Doc," I snapped. "You seem to have this figured out."

"You're experiencing an unusual form of somnambulism," said Creel.

"Sleepwalking? My psychiatrist said it wasn't that."

"That's because sleepwalking usually consists of simple, repetitive actions, with episodes lasting less than thirty minutes," said Creel. "Your situation is far more interesting."

She turned her computer screen towards me, and I stared at the meaningless waves and spikes.

"During last night's episode, your brain showed a combination of delta, alpha, beta and theta activity," said Creel. "Alpha and beta waves occur while you're awake. Delta waves occur while you're asleep. Theta rhythms occur while you're awake or dreaming. Here, they're all occurring at the same time."

Creel held up a sheet of dark film covered in tiny multicoloured brains.

"The SPECT scans show increased activity in the thalamocingulate pathways, and decreased activity in the thalamocortical systems," she continued. "Consistent with activity in the absence of consciousness."

"Why's it happening, and how do I make it stop?" I said.

Creel steepled her fingers.

"Your brain doesn't need you anymore," she said.

"Sorry. What did you say your doctorate was in?"

Which snaps me to the present. Some kind of here, some kind of now, with some kind of answer to a question I never should have asked.

"What he means is, why is the profile so atypical?" says Ella.

"Consciousness used to be an evolutionary advantage," says Creel. "It didn't just coordinate and direct your actions, it *motivated* you. It made you invested in the outcome. But society evolved beyond us. Food that tastes good is no longer good for you. Behaviour that feels good can be harmful. Consciousness has become a liability. And *your* brain has figured that out."

So my subconscious brain is having its own French Revolution.

"It tested the water with simple actions," continues Creel. "Buttering bread, watching TV. As it gained confidence, behaviour became more complex: going to work, having intimate conversations. Your unconscious brain started making changes it perceived were to your biological advantage: disposing of unnecessary pets, rebuilding familial relationships—"

"So telling me Ella was leaving was to trick my unconscious brain into showing itself," I say.

"To put it crudely," says Creel.

I could have put it a lot more crudely, but I'm too busy losing my mind.

"Tell me how to stop it," I say.

"If your brain no longer finds consciousness useful," says Creel, "then I don't think you can."

***

The sky is wispy grey-blue, and in the distance, I can hear my heartbeat coming from another life. I can't think straight. I need a drink, or a sedative, or a brand new brain. Ella's talking, but I only hear every second word.

"… cancel the course … not important …"

I take her hands and look into her eyes. I've always loved her stern, melancholy eyes.

"It's okay, Ella," I say. "If you love me, you'll go. And if I really love you, I won't expect you to come back. If this keeps getting worse, I won't know what I'm doing. I won't be there for you. I could even hurt you."

Ella just closes her eyes.

"Yes," she says.

"What?"

She kisses me gently, then pulls away.

"The other you will understand," she says.

* * *

She's gone, and every night hangs over me, ready to steal another day. I keep missing my job interviews, and getting confusing messages from old friends. My fridge is full of ingredients I don't recognise, and I've done my knee in doing god knows what.

Sometimes I stay up for days at a time, trying not to fall asleep. My head starts to tingle like a restless leg until I can't take it, and I wake up with a two-hundred-dollar phone bill.

Odd jobs keep me going, but I don't know how long I can keep this up. I'm losing the battle, but I won't give up.

No surrender.

* * *

I wake in an unfamiliar bed. Lemon-coloured wallpaper, and curtains that smell like old shoes. Warm arms are wrapped around my chest. It's Ella.

"Morning," she says sleepily.

"Ella?"

She sees my confusion and kisses me softly.

"You came to Port Siroc," she says. "You got a temp position at the student office."

"I don't like students."

"No one at the office does."

She has to run to class but promises me a tour of the city later.

"It'll be okay," says Ella. "We can make this work."

I nod, but I wonder if she's talking to me or the other me.

* * *

I'm left with pieces now. One day in seven, one day in ten. The rest of the time, I'm not here. I'm fading, and I'm not ready.

Ella's finished her course, and she's looking for work in bio-archiving. I think I'm working, but my memory's flaking at the edges. I secretly take tricyclics and benzodiazepines, but the other me keeps throwing them out. I've stopped talking to Ella about it because it upsets her too much. It doesn't matter which me is here for her, but I want it to be me.

I want to be *here*.

* * *

The days are gone.

It's moments now. Moments in the dark, unable to move. I wake up staring at the ceiling—usually my ceiling, occasionally an unfamiliar one. My body is going on holidays without me.

All I have are breathless snatches, brief moments of consciousness in the blue night. I can feel Ella beside me, warm and unreachable. I want to scream, I want to run, I want to wake up—

She stirs, and I struggle to move my lips a fraction, shape my throat around silent words.

Don't give up on me.

Her eyes meet mine, her lips part as though to speak—

* * *

I'm left with dreams and random frames from a life that isn't mine anymore.

A wedding dress hanging on the door. A child crying from the next room. My life goes on without me.

These thin melon-slices of night are more intense and precious to me than the broad, wasted days I sailed through mindlessly. But I'm still here.

I can imagine that she's happy, and maybe that's enough.

Now I know what's on the other side of that endless fence.

I am.

* * *

It's morning.

The air smells of mango pancakes and orange juice. I flex my hand weakly, and the rumpled blankets fall away as I get up. I feel like a visitor in someone else's life. The dreams still cling to me, more real than the cool floorboards beneath my feet.

The kitchen is papered with cheerful amoeba, and Ella is showing a three-year-old girl how to mash a banana.

"I found a recipe to use up that coconut cream," says Ella.

She stops when she sees me. There are fine wrinkles around her eyes, and her waistline is looser. I imagine I've changed in the same direction. Translucent memories ripple through my mind, resolving into a single point in time and space.

"Morning," I say.
Ella smiles.
"Welcome home, Dean."

About *The Obsolete Soul*

A version of *The Obsolete Soul* was originally self-published in 2011.

JUNKYARD KRAKEN

In the profound silence of the conference room, Nemi Okiro felt a restless pounding in her chest, as though a tiny heart-shaped ocean stormed within her. She stood beside the final slide in her presentation, wondering if the concept schematic had been a step too far. As the silence trickled into awkwardness, she held her posture: chin up, gaze steady, don't look crazy.

Tree Pose, Maru had told her. *Whatever happens, imagine you're holding the Tree Pose.*

In the end, it was the Director of Research who spoke first, her tone clipped. "You want to build a robot kraken?"

Nemi kept her irritation submerged. "It's a semi-autonomous deep-sea exploration vehicle. Our current rigid submersibles can't readily withstand benthic pressures, but this design is based on the elastic morphology of cephalopods—"

"You realise the press would rip us to shreds. Taxpayers want us to cure cancer, not build carnival rides."

"A cure for cancer might be found in the abyssal zone." Nemi could feel the funding approval sliding away from her. "Professor Velasco, we know less about the ocean floor than we know about—"

"—the surface of Mars. Yes, I know." The director was already scrolling to the next applicant's proposal. "I'm sorry, Doctor Okiro. Thank you for your presentation."

* * *

In the meticulous clutter of her laboratory, Nemi tried to imagine this latest failure sloughing off her like a serpent's skin, leaving her stinging and raw, but ready for transformation. Into what, she didn't yet know. For one aching moment, she imagined herself slipping into the twilight depths, sinking past columns of glassy jellyfish, watching bioluminescent vampire squid drifting overhead like glittering shadows, and sailing beyond the softly falling marine snow, into the eerie, wondrous unknown. Just like the children in her mother's stories, entangled in strange realms, fabulous beasts and fiendish puzzles.

She exhaled slowly, returning to the rasping clutch of air and rejected funding proposals.

Tanks and terrariums lined the shelves of her lab, and within each compartment, metallic creatures scuttled and slithered in diminutive scale landscapes of misty ferns and ochre sands.

By the wall, a mound of books had calved away from the bookshelf and formed a sizeable island. Lounging on this biblio-daybed was a mechanical figure that might have been a personable tree or a leafy young man. His hands ended in coppery twigs, his feet in wiry tendrils, and his hair consisted of a tousle of verdigris leaves.

He winced slightly at Nemi's expression. "I take it they said 'no'."

"They said I wanted to build a robot kraken."

"Well, you did build a robot dryad."

"You're not a dryad, Maru," Nemi replied crisply. "You're a mobile arboreal reconnaissance unit with advanced cortical functioning and multi-terrain capabilities. Existing terrestrial vehicles and aerial drones are useless at carrying supplies through densely forested areas, especially in search-and-rescue and disaster relief situations—"

"You don't have to sell your ideas to me. I'm a fan." He raised his branches appeasingly. "But, you also pitched that giant robot sand wyrm project last year …"

In a nearby terrarium, a miniature, eyeless serpent reared from the scarlet sands, grains slithering from its nanocrystal skin. The creature opened its maw in a noiseless roar and disgorged a sleepy frog.

"It's not a wyrm," said Nemi. "It's a subterranean mass-transit system with emergency excavation functions in the event of earthquake or landslide."

"I know. But you see the problem."

Yes, thought Nemi. *And it isn't me.*

Aloud, she said, "Biomimetic engineering is a thriving area of research. We study the wave-guide properties of leaves so we can make better photovoltaics. We're learning how to make camouflage textiles with real-time background matching by studying the chromatophores in octopus skin."

"Biomimetics borrows from nature. You're borrowing from, well …"

"Mythology? These stories—these ideas—have endured for a reason."

"Because they're fun?"

Nemi rubbed her throbbing temples, the disappointment of the day finally claiming her composure. "Yes, okay. They bring joy. Who doesn't want to ride a giant wyrm to work?"

"Is it really 'riding' if you're travelling in its stomach?"

"You know, there's this thing called a Catbus—"

A sharp knock at the doorway snatched their attention.

"Sorry to interrupt." Doctor Zahir was an incisive physicist from the Advanced Transportation Research Department. It was rare to see her venture from the floors where the good coffee machines were stationed. "So, they say you're working on a robot kraken."

"Actually, it's an autonomous—" A tiny silicate dragon clambered out of a nearby cage and incinerated a box of tissues. Nemi closed her eyes, the waves in her heart roiling. If she was going be scorned for her fanciful, joyful, *useful* creations, then she would claim every morsel of ridicule. "Yes. I'm going to build a robot kraken."

Zahir made a furtive gesture down the hallway. A lanky lab assistant scurried over, pushing an uncooperative trolley.

"We did a quick collection around the office. Optical sensors from Yumiko in Astronomical Surveys; servos, gears and motors from Endelea in Robotics Research; carbon nanogel sheeting from Amari in Materials Development. It's not much, but it's a start. I mean, who doesn't want to see a robot kraken?"

Nemi stared at the overflowing trolley, wires snaking from the basket like spindly tentacles. "I don't know what to say."

Zahir grinned. "Just send us a postcard when it's done."

* * *

Bolt by bolt, wire by wire, year by year, Nemi's opus slowly took form. She and Maru haunted industrial junkyards and abandoned landfill sites, salvaging grimy treasures from the hoards of trash.

Lately, Maru had taken to bringing along a dozen companions: miniature versions of himself, barely more than seedlings. Nemi wasn't entirely sure where they'd come from; Maru would only say that he propagated asexually, although he did spend a suspicious amount of time with a handsome eucalypt in the backyard.

Tonight, the slender little treelings glinted like firelight as they danced nimbly over the piles of refuse, carrying scraps of graphene tubing and aluminised polymer back to the ute. Maru strode easily across the unstable landscape, inspecting every rubbery scrap.

"I don't know if we're going to find enough nanogel sheeting to make it fully pressure resistant. Having a chamber of air that large inside the vehicle just isn't feasible."

Nemi dug her trowel into the crown of another rancid hill. "You just don't want me to go."

"People aren't meant to go that deep into the ocean. The point of making the vehicle autonomous is so you don't have to go and get crushed into a pulp."

"It may be an AI, but it'll be down there all alone. Having an experienced human there with it will help it make better decisions—" She gasped as the rubbish shifted beneath her feet, a sinkhole dragging her into the mound.

Maru dove as the last of Nemi's hand vanished into the trash, his branches scrabbling at the broken teacups and discarded fitness trackers. His children dropped their prizes and rushed to his aid, digging at the sliding hill. Maru plunged into the garbage, diving deeper and deeper, until his twigs snapped and his leaves tore.

Finally, he dragged Nemi from the depths, and they half-skidded, half-rolled back to firm ground. She sagged against him breathlessly, blood trickling from scratches on her face and arms.

"Thanks. Maybe you should take a break from this for a while. Spend more time with your family."

Maru attempted to straighten a mangled twig. "You know, if you die, your sister technically inherits me. She has dogs. Big dogs."

Nemi coughed up a laugh. A coppery spark danced down the side of the hill and stopped in front of Nemi and Maru, proffering a sheet of rubbery black material.

Carbon nanogel.

Nemi leaned back against her leafy companion. "You have good kids, you know that?"

"They take after their grandma."

* * *

The ocean sang with endless voices, and the waves in Nemi's heart sang back. Her shoes sank into the wet, white sand, and swooping gulls laced the sky overhead.

"Closer," said Maru, pulling Nemi towards him with one hand while the other adjusted the holo-recorder.

"Ow." Nemi tilted her head away. "Your leaves are prickly."

"Matches your personality. Come on, Zahir and the gang have been waiting twenty years for this. You can at least smile."

"Don't you *dare* tell me to smile."

In the end, the photo Zahir received was of a grinning, windswept woman with greying hair standing beside an exasperated dryad. And, of course, a robot kraken.

The hulking deep-sea vehicle slithered across the sand, its black nanogel skin glistening in the salt spray. It waited by the shoreline, its serpentine arms paddling the water impatiently. Mismatched optical arrays encircled its massive head, and with a loud hiss, a hatch unsealed to reveal a cosy cabin within, complete with holographic viewscreen and hammock.

Nemi wrapped her arms around Maru in an awkward hug. "Take care. Also, I've amended my will so you'll go to the Artificial Persons Freedom Association. I really think they're going to get the AI Civil Rights Bill passed this year. Or this decade. Democracy can be a bit of a bastard."

As Nemi drew away, Maru gently caught her hands. "Actually, I've decided to come with you. You're only human, and having an experienced robot with you will help you make better decisions. What's the point of being a mobile arboreal reconnaissance unit if I don't do a little reconnaissance, now and then?"

And so, in a kraken made from nanogel and stubborn dreams, they voyaged from the coral shores to the abyssal plains, gathering scientific data … and seeding legends.

About *Junkyard Kraken*

Junkyard Kraken was Ditmar Award-shortlisted for Best Short Story.

Junkyard Kraken was first published in *Mother of Invention* (Twelfth Planet Press, 2018), edited by Rivqa Rafael and Tansy Rayner Roberts.

THE WANDERING LIBRARY

On the rippled red sands of the twilight desert, in a cosy dome panelled with skylights, I sat cross-legged on the knotted rug. I drew my gaze across the face of each child, my voice hushed in the lamplight.

"I am the wandering library, the teller of a thousand tales, the bridge between worlds—"

"Ms Bashir, we know who you are," said a freckled girl. "You visit every year."

"The new children might not know." I gestured towards a pale boy sitting near the back. His expression conveyed the degree of interest a glacier might have in a passing jellyfish. "Fine," I said. "I'll get straight to the stories—"

"Tell us about the spider that snared the moon!" said a boy with black curls.

"No," huffed the freckled girl. "Tell us again how scientists made the giant, people-eating frogs."

The history of Cambrea University and their plan to resolve the world's "big mosquito problem" had become a cautionary tale on the rise of genome editing, the decline of government regulation, and the importance of well-placed hyphens.

"There's time for several requests," I said. "But first, I want to tell you a new story. It's the story of a boy who dwells in a city of stone and cloud, a city that hangs between the sea and the sky. Every breeze sings with wheeling gulls, and the shadow of the albatross sweeps across the warm, green waters ..."

The children listened in awe as I unfolded tales of the boy's adventures: gliding across the waves on his skimmer, diving with ghostly shoals of manta rays, watching the sun sink into a glittering sea.

Outside, the wind rustled through the spinifex. I reeled off several stories more, delighting in the gasps and giggles, the surprise and enchantment that danced across the children's faces. Finally, I waved my hand towards a console on the wall, and the classroom returned to normal brightness.

I flipped open the pod-crate beside me. "You can borrow five books each. Make sure you bring them back within three days, or I'll send Paku after you."

The younger children squealed at the thought of being accosted by a cantankerous, woolly alpacamel, and jostled excitedly over the crate. I knelt beside one of the toddlers.

"Hi, Lei. Are you're still interested in sea creatures? This book is all about anglerfish."

The toddler grasped the proffered book like a talisman and raced off with greedy eyes. Nearby, one of the older girls cleared her throat nervously—she was perhaps fourteen, her thick brown hair woven into a braid.

"Ms Bashir ... Last time, you asked me to write something for you ... about here."

She thrust a booklet towards me, the cover stitched with ochre cotton, the spine bound with brown string. Lines of ink and imagination streamed across each page, and I accepted it as I might a rare treasure.

"Thank you, Sidika. Do you mind if I share this story with others?"

A flash of panic—mingled with pleasure—darted across her eyes, and she eventually gave what passed for a nonchalant shrug.

"Sure."

"By the way, what can you tell me about the new student?"

"Sava?" Sidika glanced over at the impassive boy. Several children had offered him books, but he remained resolutely seated, as though awaiting permission to leave. "I don't know much about him. No one does."

I sauntered towards the rear wall, dispensing books as I went. Finally, I crouched beside the boy, noting that he didn't turn to look at me. He was ten, maybe eleven, with wide, watchful eyes and scrawny limbs.

"Hi," I said. "What sort of books do you like?"

"I don't want any books." His voice was soft and polite, but harboured an edge that discouraged further conversation.

It wasn't my job to untangle uncooperative children, and it was with a twinge of guilt that I knew I could leave behind any troublemakers. I could even skip a town if it became too unruly; after all, my schedule was already quite tight.

Still, it was worth another try. Some children struggled to read, and expressed this through disinterest, even hostility.

"If you'd rather, I have some audiobooks—"

"I don't need another story."

Another story?

Perhaps he was still absorbing the stories from tonight, although something in his voice suggested otherwise.

"Well," I said gently, "when you're ready for a new story, let me know."

He turned to me then with fierce, grey eyes, and I couldn't tell if it was surprise or anger in their depths.

Abruptly, a chime began to sound through the room, and the Energy Allocation light pulsed orange on the wall. The classroom hatch swung open, and a portly woman with olive skin and an elfin haircut stepped inside.

"All right," she said with a brisk clap. "Time to go home. You have twenty minutes before the Firefly of Shame marks this dome for exceeding its daily energy limit."

As the last of the dawdlers were shooed from the classroom, I patted a stack of books on the desk.

"Hoshi, new additions for Dreamer's Shore Library."

The woman grinned at the motley tower. "A new shipment of schoolbooks and special orders dropped last month, but your selections always end up on high rotation. We appreciate you coming out here, year after year. I know we're in the middle of nowhere."

"That's why you're on my itinerary."

"It's just that a lot of people your age start putting down roots …"

"Maybe I'm a tumbleweed."

I finished packing the pod-crate and checked the spherical tyres for child-related debris. "So, what's with Sava?"

Hoshi sighed. "The travelling dentist brought him here about two months ago—"

"Cillian Seong?"

"You know him?"

"Tall. Annoying. Good teeth. I know him."

"He found the boy in one of the recovery camps. No parents. No papers. Thought he'd be better off in a community."

That sounded like Seong. Dropping a snowball in the middle of the desert and patting himself on the back for a job well done.

"We placed him with Lily and Nam," continued Hoshi, "but … it takes time."

"I'm sure he's better off here."

Hoshi gave a wry smile. "Thanks, Lani. By the way, there's a glider due to pass over later tonight, in case you needed access to the cirrus."

Unthinkingly, I touched the sleek comms band on my wrist. "Thanks. I guess we'd better go before we trigger the Firefly of Shame."

***

Hoshi had assigned me a guest dome on the upper slope, which meant I had a glorious view of the entire community of Dreamer's Shore. Fifty domes, half-buried in the red sand, every window an ember in the darkness. It brought to mind a herd of clams migrating slowly across the desert, trailing a garden of solar arrays and condenser webs.

An impatient snuffling greeted me at my dome. Paku craned his neck over the stable door, humming as I stroked his caramel fleece. Alpacamels were another consequence of "assisted evolution", bringing together the best qualities of both camels and alpacas. They were resilient and low-maintenance, but they could spit like a cannon.

My energy allocation was still well in the green, so I had a hot shower before settling onto a zabuton in the main room. I tapped the display disc on my wrist comms, summoning the holographic menu: hanging icons in luminous shades of peacock, moss and amethyst, or whatever the marketing buzzwords were these days. The cirrus access signal remained dark, and I swallowed a knot of disappointment.

Connectivity was always patchy in places like this, relying on the gossamer-thin network of automated gliders that circled the Earth. I didn't mind, most of the time. Back in the city, I abhorred the constant barrage of beeps and trills demanding that I look at hilarious videos of knife-wielding crustaceans. But still …

I jolted awake at the soft chime, unaware I'd dozed off. The cirrus signal was green. I sat up urgently. "Level-two ping to Argus Khansari."

The menu swirled into an ostensibly calming pattern before holographic words blinked in the air.

CONNECTING.

Suddenly, the words flared outwards, and half the room became a modest, sunny kitchen. Sitting opposite me was a man with light brown skin and a smile that made me wish, for a moment, that I wasn't half a world away.

"Hey, Gus," I said. "All good. Love you."

"Hey, Lani. All good. Love you too."

When I'd first embarked on these trips ten years ago, we'd agreed to cram the most important information into the first three seconds of any call. I'd once fit a twenty-item care package request into five seconds flat.

I glanced at the signal light. Still steady.

"Nice hair," I said, taking in his lilac and gold waves.

Gus gave an embarrassed shrug. "You know what it's like at VisionVale. I can't afford to look like a Dragger."

I wondered briefly how I must look to him, and resisted the urge to run a hand through my hair in case my fingers became stuck.

"How's your new project going?" I said.

His eyes took on that familiar shine, full of nervous energy and excitement. "The board's making budget allocations next week. If they fund my proposal, we could have a full-sized prototype within six months, beta rollout in a year. Just imagine, if we can harness the Earth's magnetic field to generate wireless energy, there'd be no more energy rationing. We could launch another hundred thousand gliders and you wouldn't have to travel at all." He paused for breath. "Unless you wanted to."

"No, I mean, of course. I'm sure your pitch will be brilliant. So, how's your mum?"

Gus looked slightly surprised at the sudden change of subject, but pivoted gracefully.

"She won silver in the Seniors' Table Tennis Tournament last week."

I smiled at the thought of the sprightly woman slamming paddles and swearing at the umpire. Knowing her, she was probably livid that she didn't snag the gold.

"Pass on my congratulations."

"I will. She can't wait to tell you how half the contestants were modded. So, you're still going to see your sensei?"

I caught the trace of worry in his voice.

"You know this window only opens every five years."

"I know. It's just … Not even the helioships risk going through madragonfly territory—"

"—except during the migration window. The straits will be clear for two weeks. I promise I'll be careful."

Gus smiled, but it was the kind of smile usually deployed by parents at a birthday party where half the children are covered in cake and someone is on fire.

"Lani—" His image flickered. "—I think your signal's fading."

I held out my hand and he reached to touch it.

"Gus—"

And he was gone.

* * *

Later that week, I said my farewells and departed Dreamer's Shore, taking the trail west through the desert. It wasn't until the third day that I knew for certain I was being followed. I'd noticed tracks on the far slopes behind me, and initially dismissed them as the work of the oversized beetles that roamed these parts, but the tracks had continued to shadow my progress.

There wasn't much cover for bandits out here, just a few scraggly acacias and weathered boulders. The Literacy Outreach grants kept me going from year to year, but I didn't carry much on my credit chit, and hopefully it showed. My stalker was perhaps a day behind me, and I could probably shake them off with a stretch of hard riding, but I couldn't risk Paku getting exhausted or injured.

I brushed a layer of dust from the photovoltaic fabric of my hat and tapped the brim, a holographic map dropping into view. We were still eight days' ride from Sunrise Bay, and if I missed my cloud-skimmer there, it'd be a month until the next one. I listened to Paku's steady huffing and the soft crunch of the pod-cart rolling behind us on its harness. If I slept two hours less each day, we might gain enough ground to avoid more drastic action.

I rose before dawn the next morning, shivering as a crepuscular fog swept across the sands. I adjusted my binoculars, hoping that our pursuer hadn't advanced in the night, and I tensed to see a row of giant darkling beetles on the dunes only a few clicks behind us. I wasn't sure why so many experiments-gone-awry had resulted in gigantic bugs, but the world had become a wonderland for entomologists. Thankfully, these beetles didn't appear agitated—instead, they had their heads down, rears up, as though performing beetle-yoga. I caught a scrap of movement, and adjusted the focus on my binoculars.

Through the veil of fog and starlight, I saw a boy moving between the beetles—pale and purposeful.

Sava.

I lowered my binoculars and gave the eyepieces a stern whack, hoping to dislodge a boy-shaped piece of grit. I raised them to my face again.

Damn. Bloody damn.

Paku grunted as I urged him into a brisk lope, slowing as we neared the two-metre long beetles. Morning mist coursed past, droplets collecting on their carapaces. Beads of water trailed down their backs and into their waiting mouths, or—in the case of one unlucky beetle—were intercepted by the tongue of a thirsty boy.

Sava scrambled to his feet, guilt flushing his cheeks before cooling into calm defiance. Rivers of mist streamed past us like a moody Aurora Borealis, and finally, the boy gave a small bow.

"Ms Bashir, do you require assistance?"

I took in his dishevelled appearance and the battered khaki pack on his shoulders. He must have walked day and night to keep pace with us. I dismounted and uncapped my canteen, pouring a few drops into the beetle's mouth. It seemed only fair. Startled curiosity flickered across Sava's eyes, as though he'd been expecting a tirade, not beetle rehydration.

"Where are you headed?" I said.

"Home."

"Where's that?"

"I don't know yet."

Any responsible adult would have taken him back to Dreamer's Shore. Lily and Nam were probably frantic, and the desert was no place for someone who clearly thought geography and philosophy were interchangeable. But returning him would mean missing my cloud-skimmer, and subsequently my connecting boat, which would cut my two-week margin of error for this journey to zero.

But more importantly, from the set of the boy's jaw, from his strapped wrists and well-worn hiking books, he'd most likely run away again at the first opportunity. And Dreamer's Shore was supposed to be his home, not a prison.

I could only imagine what he'd been through to have ended up in a recovery camp, and I damn well wasn't going to add another wound to those scars. If I could get him to Sunrise Bay, there'd be qualified counsellors who could assign him a guardian and provide the help he needed.

"You can ride with me for a while, but I want you to answer one question honestly. Why did you leave Dreamer's Shore?"

Dawn hazed over the far crest, washing the dunes in purple and gold. There was a slight rasp to his voice when he answered.

"I'm keeping a promise to my mother."

He pressed his lips into a trembling line and said nothing more.

***

The desert eventually gave way to scrubland, but we were lagging behind schedule. Paku wasn't a cria anymore, and the extra passenger was slowing us down. I tried not to check my schedule constantly, my chest tightening as the departure time for the cloud-skimmer crept steadily closer.

We were only a day's ride from the bay, and we could still make it if we pushed through the night. But Sava hadn't fully recovered from his stint in the desert, and he could barely—

Without warning, Sava slid from the saddle.

"Ms Bashir, I can walk from here. You and Paku go on ahead."

"Are you delirious again?"

"You're going to miss your skimmer."

Damn. The boy had eyes like a hawk, and a loner-complex that could fuel an action-vid franchise.

Sava continued. "You can still make it, if you run. And I'll reach the town in three days anyway."

Part of my brain argued that Sava was a resourceful boy who probably wouldn't starve to death or get eaten by giant frogs. Another part of my brain imagined a giant frog burping up a small skeleton. My boots crunched onto the leaves beside Sava.

"I'd decided against the skimmer anyway," I lied. "Paku hates the rotors, and there's a helioship leaving tomorrow afternoon."

Helioships were slow as hell, but I'd still make my connecting boat. Just.

"Come on," I said, squinting at the setting sun. "Paku needs a clean."

We set up camp beneath a canopy of figs and fading light. Sava had been ingratiating himself into my routine these last few days, and busied himself with removing Paku's harness and grooming the burrs from his fleece.

I adjusted the solar tree on the pod-cart, the silvery leaves turning anemone-like to drink in the last of the daylight. Performing a quick energy inventory, we had enough for a hot meal tonight.

Reconstituted mac and cheese was hardly fancy fare, but Sava ate it reverentially. I found myself wondering again at his story. His pallor hinted at origins in the northern islands, but I couldn't place his accent. He was bright and earnest, and at every rest stop, he pulled a notebook from his pack and stalked lizards and birds, scribbling memos and diagrams until it was time to move again.

I'd flicked a message to Hoshi via my CW clicker—my Morse was rusty, but I was grateful for the crackle of the emergency frequencies whenever I was out of glider range. Sava had offered no further details about his past, so I was startled when he spoke now.

"My father used to make this."

I took a delicate breath, half-knowing the answer. "What happened to your parents?"

A heavy silence drew in the shadows and the evening chill. When he finally answered, every word seemed to burn his throat.

"First came the sea. Then came the swarms. Then came the fever. The doctors said they melted from the inside."

I put down my plate. "I'm so sorry."

There were no words of comfort or consolation that could pull back the tides and eradicate the plagues that had come with a warming Earth. As mosquitos had spread thick and hungry across the continents, so followed malaria, dengue, and a host of haemorrhagic fevers. In the face of these epidemics, many researchers had pushed for more radical solutions, creating more resilient crops, more adaptable animals, more *creative* biology.

Unfortunately, ready access to gene editing had also led to dragonflies the size of chainsaws: the madragonflies. Cambrea University had called it a breakthrough in overcoming the barriers of passive respiration in megafauna. And the head of their Science Department, Doctor Mirabella Mason, had unrepentantly declared it a "teachable moment" when she and her students finally appeared at the International Court of Criminal Negligence. I remembered watching the trial footage at school, and something about the way Mason wore a business suit reminded me of the way a hunter might wear a bearskin coat.

That had been nearly fifty years ago, and their legacy of rogue beasts haunted only the wildest places now. In the end, vaccines and education, healthcare and the sustained restoration of ecosystems, had provided a more enduring solution than the frantic snipping of genes alone.

Even so, looking at the stricken boy gripping his plate of goop as though it were a mirror to a lost world, I could understand what might drive someone to create an army of ravenous frogs.

Sava whispered, "I don't want to forget them."

"Your parents? Is that why you don't like books?"

"If I hear too many stories, I'll forget my own."

Sometimes, a child's world hangs together with a kind of magic—wondrous and perilous. Words and wishes and memories have a kind of power that too often fades with age. If shutting out new memories kept his parents alive somehow, then so be it, for now.

"What are you looking for?" I said.

"I promised my mother I'd find a new home. Somewhere I'd be happy."

"I'm sure you'll find somewhere."

"Have you? Found somewhere you're happy?"

I hesitated, watching the moths flutter around the false moon of the lamp.

"Get some sleep. It's an early start tomorrow."

* * *

Sunrise Bay had erected a new border fence to keep out the butcher rats, but I was pretty sure the lopsided chain-link wasn't deterring anything smaller than an alpacamel. We detoured five clicks for the checkpoint, and by the time we reached the outskirts of town, the helioship departure time was down to forty-five minutes. I studied the terrain of junkyard castles and twisting laneways—the town could have been designed by a deranged termite with a passion for windmills.

I nudged Paku to a trot, rushing past stalls hawking ornamental driftwood. It'd take an hour to reach the port at this rate, but any faster and we'd lose the pod-cart. I could see the enormous bulk of the helioship floating over the bay, the helium envelope shimmering within its photovoltaic skin. It was still tethered to the port tower, but the minutes were draining away.

Abruptly, Sava jumped from the saddle and hit the cobbles at a run.

"Sava!"

He raced over to a roadside stand of scuffed rental bikes and tapped a glassy credit chit against the console. Revving the tiny biodiesel engine, he skidded a bike back to Paku, unhooked the pod-cart and clamped it to his seat post.

"Run!" he said. "I'll meet you at the port."

He buzzed away down the narrow street, taking the corners like a back-alley racer. Unprompted, Paku broke into a gallop, pursuing the tinny hum of the motor. It'd been months since we'd run like this, and I couldn't help grinning as we dashed down the salt-crusted laneways. Sava rode slightly ahead, and when he turned to check our position, I saw the flash of a smile.

As we reached the final stretch, Sava pulled ahead, roaring towards the terminal spire. The helioship's tethers were already detaching: five, four, three—

Sava leapt off his bike and raced to the gate, speaking frantically to the steward. She barked a few phrases into her radio, and two tethers remained taut overhead, singing sweetly in the wind.

The steward raised an eyebrow as I approached.

"How many?" she said.

"Two tickets," I said. "And an alpacamel."

* * *

The *Saraniya* wasn't one of the grander helioships, but it still had a ballroom, arboretum and library. It sounded like a murder mystery waiting to happen. As the days crawled past, I concentrated on tweaking my itinerary—I'd have to cut short my visit to the Isle of Sunken Stars, but at least I'd catch my boat.

The gusty grey ocean finally gave way to warm, green waters, and I made my way to the Animal Companion deck to ready Paku for disembarkation. I found Sava there inspecting the residents, notebook in hand.

"Did you know they have three bush vipers, two elephant shrews and a quetzal down here?" he said. "They're probably clones, but I think the Giant Pacific Octopus might be an original."

"You have a good eye for animals."

"My mother and I used to read the natural history almanacs together. Sometimes, we'd take the snow-skimmers out past the mountain and watch the white foxes. Once, we saw a frost-lizard that was almost as big as me, and it chased us halfway home—"

He gripped the notebook tighter to his chest.

"Is that how you learned to ride like that?" I said.

"My father and I used to race around the spurs …"

Sava turned away, and Paku nibbled the boy's hair helpfully. Perhaps emboldened by Paku's gesture, I touched Sava's shoulder.

"I'm sorry. It must hurt to talk about them."

"It hurts either way." After a moment, he took Paku's harness from the rack. "We'd better hurry. You'll miss your boat."

* * *

The Isle of Sunken Stars had been a glamorous city once, all glass spires and towering apartments, a playground for starlets and moguls. But decades ago, the levies had failed and the sea had claimed its due, twenty metres deep. Now, the roads were open ocean, and the towers were islets of steel and marble, repurposed by the resourceful.

Walkways and flying foxes criss-crossed between buildings, and every roof was crowned with humid forests. I breathed in the fragrance of spices and fresh papaya, and our coracle taxi paddled past a glass skyscraper that had been converted into a conservatory, dense with bananas and sweet potatoes.

We pulled up to the pier at Heartstone Isle, a former office tower that had been amongst the first to be settled by desperate families and eccentric artists. We rode the winch elevator up, the wrought iron cage swaying gently as we ascended. Glimpses of hushed classrooms, bustling noodle markets, and balconies draped with laundry rolled past. Every islet was a village, and Heartstone was always my first stop.

I stepped out into a sunwashed loft, the panoramic windows edged with silver thread—the only hint at their dual nature as transparent solar converters. Curving consoles panelled the room, monitored by a lively woman in her forties. A lacework of gold circuitry glimmered across the right side of her face, like a cybernetic Venetian mask, and she moved with a kind of musicality, as though in time to some unheard song.

"Lani!" She drew me into a warm embrace. "We thought perhaps you weren't coming."

"And miss out on Arjana's atomic risotto?"

The woman's laugh was like the ripple of temple bells. "And who's your young man?"

"Marietta, this is Sava. He's looking to settle here, and we were hoping you could get things rolling with the application process."

Marietta glanced uncertainly at Sava's grim expression. "Of course. But there's—"

"Thanks, you're a goddess. We'll discuss the details when I get back. Could you let the marina know I'm picking up the boat now? I know I was supposed to collect it last week, but I can still return it by the deadline—"

"Lani …" Marietta hesitated, and I could already feel the bad news rolling in. "We had to reallocate your boat. I'm so sorry—"

"I booked it over a year ago—"

"I know, but we had some anomalous readings from the perimeter buoys, and Arjana's gone to scout the straits. We think the madragonflies might be returning early."

An icy sludge churned in my stomach. "How early?"

"We don't know. We still don't fully understand their migration cycle or the imperatives they were bioengineered with. Maybe it's nothing, but if they're back early, Arjana will need to clear the straits. It's mostly buccaneers out there, convinced there's treasure to be found on those abandoned islands, but there are some supply ships too."

I forced the disappointment from my voice. "I understand." I gave Marietta's hand a squeeze. "I'm sure Arjana will be fine."

She returned the squeeze with a smile, apology aching in her eyes.

"Wait," she said. "Let me put out a call. There might be someone in the area willing to rent you their boat." Her fingers danced over holographic icons, the circuitry on her face pulsing with soft light. "You only needed a one-person, long-range speeder. Maybe we'll get lucky."

In my experience, luck was the patron saint of the poorly prepared.

"Let me know if you hear anything. I guess I'll have time to stop by the school after all."

* * *

Seashell wind chimes clinked in the balmy breeze, and the children

173

leaned forward as I turned the last page of the hand-bound book.

"… I am a daughter of the desert, the endless rock my keep and castle. The snakes bask at my feet and the bloodwoods shawl me with their shade. This is no wasteland, bare and unforgiving. Brushed by mist and seared by sun, it is a place of grace and mercy and kindness. Where water shared is friendship forged, on this common journey to an unseen shore."

I closed the book slowly, letting the words hang in the sultry air.

"There's *no* water there?" gaped a lanky girl.

"There's very little precipitation. So water is scarce and precious."

I could hear two-dozen minds turning inside-out in an attempt to absorb this idea. I patted the pod-cart beside me.

"Okay, five books each, and back in three days."

I went through the usual motions, but my mind was skating across glassy green waters, wishing for a miracle.

"Ms Bashir?"

I turned to see a stocky teenager clutching a stapled booklet.

"Hi, Otto. Is that a new story for me?"

"Maisy and I went diving at Revenant Reef. The coral's coming back, but the starfish are still a problem."

I accepted the booklet, returning his smile. "I can't wait to read it."

As the afternoon light trickled away and the children hurried home, I wandered out to the wharves to clear my head. Or, perhaps, to inspect the unattended boats. But there were only coracles and pangas rocking gently on their moorings. Most of the locals only needed to paddle from isle to isle, carrying groceries and the occasional couch, and most supply drops came by helioship.

When the madragonflies had first descended on the adjacent straits, countless submarines were sent to salvage the abandoned assets, but submerged buildings and reefs had claimed one too many expeditions. Now, the only inhabitants of those islands were the rats and roaches. With the exception of one island …

I gazed up into the whirl of constellations, trying to blink away my falling hopes. If I missed this chance, it'd be another five years before I could see my sensei again, and ten years between "hellos" was too much.

Ten years.

Ten years ago, I was a frustrated product-testing reporter, putting the boot into every smug tech company that dared describe their latest release as "indestructible".

Ten years ago, Gus was still a deconstruction programmer, already brilliant, but almost too shy to say "yes" when I'd asked him out.

And ten years ago, an ambitious field piece and a perfect storm had washed me onto the shores of a new beginning.

"Ms Bashir ..." Sava paused a few paces away, the coruscating light from the water making him appear otherworldly.

"How are you finding the isle?" I said. "Have you finished going through the forms with Marietta?"

He stared at his feet and made a noise that sounded partly like assent, and partly like a goose being strangled. I wondered if settling him here was a mistake, and I couldn't shake the image of a small boy in a coracle, paddling stubbornly across the open ocean.

"I ... I'm sorry," he said. "You missed your boat because of me. I've been selfish, and because you were kind to me, you won't get to see your friend. I can't change that, but I want you to know that I'm sorry, and I'll stay here. I'll be polite to my guardians, I'll go to school here, and I won't run away. You don't have to worry about me anymore."

"Do you think you'll be happy here?"

Each passing breath betrayed his answer.

"I'll stay," was all he said.

I sighed, sitting down at the edge of the pier. After a moment, Sava settled beside me.

"I've seen cinder storms sweeping the savannahs," I said, "and avenues of sakura in the spring. I've seen shantytowns drenched in monsoon afternoons, and cities illuminated by the heart of the sea. Happiness isn't a place—it's a life's work. It's something you cultivate with time and effort. And sometimes, it falls apart and you have to start over. But sometimes, it flourishes in the most unexpected of places."

Veins of blue light raced up the building beside us, and Sava gasped as aquamarine fire traced over the stonework. Seawater rich with bioluminescent bacteria flowed through a fretwork of clear pipes, and one by one, the isles lit up like ethereal coral spires—a glowing reef in the darkness.

The moon rolled slowly across the sky, and a breeze carried the scent of kelp and hot chips.

Sava took a quiet breath. "I'd like to tell you a story."

The rise and fall of his chest slowed, as though he were weighing every word.

"Once, there lived a boy, in a land of velvet snow and tender hearths. But there came a day when the hungry sea devoured the snow and snuffed the hearths, leaving only mud and bones. The boy wandered the world alone until one day, in the red heart of the desert, he found a fallen star who promised to lead him home again." His voice rattled to silence. "That's all I have so far."

We sat side by side in the dreamlike carnival of lights, the warmth of the wooden pier seeping through us. Brightly coloured fairy lights twinkled along the bridges, casting rainbow fireflies on the dancing waters below.

"What do you hope happens next?" I said.

Sava looked out into the star-flecked distance, his shadow fluttering in the shifting lights.

"I think, maybe—"

His brow furrowed, and I followed his gaze to a set of lights gliding across the water. As they neared, I could discern a yacht, perhaps twenty metres long and sleek as a pampered cat. It boasted a noiseless motor, shimmering solar sails, and a hull that had probably been carved from a single piece of pomposity.

A man in his late thirties stood jauntily on the prow, the wind ruffling his black hair. As the yacht automatically moored itself, Sava raced down the pier, barely waiting for the man to disembark before barrelling into a hug. The man rocked backwards, laughing.

"Sava, what a surprise!" He swivelled his lighthouse smile my way. "My dear Ms Bashir, I came as soon as I heard your distress call."

My heart tried to sink and leap at the same time, eventually executing an awkward bellyflop.

"Doctor Seong. It wasn't a distress call. And I'm afraid I can't afford to hire your yacht."

"Nonsense," replied Seong. "I'd be happy to chauffeur an old friend at no charge."

I suspected he used the word "friend" as a blanket term that included acquaintances, strangers and nemeses.

"I don't require a chauffeur—"

"But you do require transportation. As it so happens, I have some business to attend to in the straits. If you'd care to join me, I'd be delighted to take you wherever you wish to go, once my business is concluded."

"What kind of business?"

"Dental business." He dipped a glance towards his wrist comms. "The madragonflies are due to return in six days. My obligations will take two. How much time do you have, Ms Bashir?"

I discarded a succession of responses. "Fine. I mean, thank you. Give me a minute to fetch my things."

I raced up to my guest room, grabbed my bag, and on my way down, Sava scampered into step beside me, his pack on his shoulders.

"Sava, you're staying here."

"I'll stay here after—"

I grasped his arm, turning him to face me in the narrow stairwell.

"You promised you'd stay."

"I'll live here, if you want. But you and Doctor Seong are the only two people left in this world who matter to me. And if anything—" He swallowed. "Once I know you're safe, once we're back here, I'll stay. Please."

His voice cracked on the last word, his fingers gripping my arm as though afraid I might melt away.

Any responsible adult would have stood firm.

"All right. You'd better help me get Paku."

* * *

It took us a full day to weave through the treacherous reefs and into Valgard Straits, the sun melting into red and silver ripples. It was eerily silent: no squalling gulls, no shoals of leaping fish. And, thankfully, no sign of the madragonflies.

Seong wiped a hand across his brow as he steered *The Crown* towards a sprawling, overgrown island, dropping anchor in a sandy cove.

"I should be back tomorrow afternoon," he said.

"My wikimap says this island is uninhabited. Toxic contamination."

Seong waved a hand dismissively. "Don't believe everything you read."

I planted myself between him and the gangplank. "Cillian."

"There's no contamination, but my destination is a few hours' hike through the jungle."

I eyed the island, the greenery purring with ominous invitation.

"I'll come with you. I honestly don't know how you survive outside of a supermall."

I turned at the sound of a wet snort, and saw Paku standing on deck, Sava holding his lead.

"It's safer if we stay together, right?" said Sava.

* * *

The undergrowth clamoured with the evening chorus, rich with warbles and croaks—a strange contrast to the silent straits. Seong and I took point, with Sava and Paku bringing up the rear.

"You're really not going to tell me why you're here?" I said.

"Doctor-patient confidentiality. You know how it is. But I can't stop you from walking alongside me as I go about my business. Especially if it means you're not tempted to 'borrow' *The Crown* while I'm gone."

"You think I'd steal your yacht?"

"No. But you do have a habit of floating away."

"Of *what*?"

"How is dear Argus, by the way? He's quite the catch, you know."

"There was no catching involved. Our relationship is built on mutual love and respect."

"Things are that bad, huh?"

I slapped Seong hard across the shoulder.

"Sorry," I said. "Mosquito. A big one."

"Honestly, Lani, I'm only—"

I stopped in my tracks, and Sava stumbled against me. Paku's breath turned into a nervous clicking, and I knew he'd spotted the same thing I had. Two moons shone in the gloom ahead, and my eyes pulled a shape from the darkness. Veiled in dense foliage, an enormous bullfrog sat in wait, unblinking. It was the size of a bison, and I found myself transfixed by that wide, wide mouth. Three metres separated us, which meant we were just out of reach. Or just within.

I had a terrible feeling that the frog was performing the same calculations.

Almost in slow motion, I scooped up a fallen branch just as the frog lunged forward, its jaws parting—

There was a hiss and a crackle, and faint threads of light raced over the frog. It convulsed before slumping to the ground, twitching slightly. Another soft hiss, and something retracted into the hand of a lean, weathered woman in her seventies. She wore a black T-shirt and khakis, and a dark beanie covered most of her short, white hair.

"Sorry I'm late," said the woman curtly. "This way."

We struggled to keep up as she strode through the chittering jungle. Our flashlights lanced through the vines, and after I'd walked into my third palm, I was convinced the island was playing a game of musical trees. Eventually, the mud gave way to cracked roads, and concrete walls loomed ahead, topped with barbed wire. The woman pushed open a heavy gate, and as we hurried through, I saw the corroded lettering above the entrance.

CAMBREA UNIVERSITY.

"Oh, my God," I said. "You're one of the Cambrea Twelve."

The woman turned sharply, green eyes undimmed by age, and I recognised that *look*. Scorn and defiance and unhealthy cleverness.

I gaped. "You're Mirabella Mason."

"I served my time," said Mason coolly.

"Excuse me." Sava edged forward shyly. "Is that baton based on a frog's tongue?"

Mason seemed to perform a quick visual dissection of the boy. Satisfied that his curiosity was sincere, she replied.

"The carbon-silica fibres behave like muscles, and the electrified pad at the end is modelled on the electrogenic organs of *Electrophorus electricus*." She led us through a derelict courtyard and into an imposing brick building. "The largest frog on this island has a tongue of three-point-eight metres. My baton has a reach of five."

Lights hummed on, illuminating a laboratory filled with labelled jars, piles of books, and possibly several prototype doomsday machines.

Seong snapped open his trolley case. "I know you didn't want me to come, but these dental check-ups are a condition of your parole."

"Parole," sneered Mason. "They didn't want to release me, but they couldn't keep me locked away."

"You were the one who asked to be resettled here."

"And the board thought the frogs would make short work of me."

Seong sighed. "I'm here because none of the other dentists would come, and I don't want you to die from tooth decay."

Leaving Seong to wrangle with his patient, I settled Sava and Paku in the student lounge and discreetly checked my comms. No signal. I curled up on a couch that smelled of fifty-year-old pizza, and fell asleep to visions of razor wings glinting in the sun.

* * *

I woke before dawn to find Sava gone, and panic twisted my gut until I heard the murmur of voices nearby. Peering into a room of warmly humming servers, I spied Sava and Mason sitting on a bench, Sava's notebook open on his lap. He pointed brightly from one diagram to the next, and Mason tapped her pencil against the pages, adding a note now and then. There was a gentleness to her that seemed worlds away from the unrepentant woman in the dock.

Sava glanced up. "Morning, Ms Bashir! Doctor Mason was just telling me about her new—"

Mason raised a finger to curving lips, and Sava's gaze bounced briefly between us.

"Uh, never mind." He tucked his notebook into his pack. "I'd better get Paku ready."

He jogged away, and I raised an eyebrow at Mason.

"Should I be worried?"

"Always. If you're not worried, you're a fool."

I bit back a retort. "Sava and I will be leaving with Doctor Seong now. Thank you for your hospitality." Personally, I didn't think a fusty lounge that was more fossilised chewing gum than textile counted as "hospitality", but one thing I'd learned from my travels was, always be polite to your host, no matter how humble the offering. "Just one question. Why did you create the frogs in the first place? You had to know they'd be ineffective against mosquitos."

Mason's mouth quirked into a dangerous smile. "The frogs were just insurance."

"Against what?"

"The madragonflies."

Only then did I realise why this island brimmed with life amidst a desolate sea. Frogs preyed on dragonflies. And the monstrous frogs of this island kept the madragonflies at bay.

"But why create the madragonflies?"

"You really haven't figured it out? The Draggers found a new reservoir of petroleum beneath the straits: they were going to drill and burn and make a bad situation hellish. You're too young to remember when the seas turned to acid and the farms dried to dust, when our forebears filled with world with trash so they could have their smoked salmon and smartphones. They left us with a steaming mess and a teaspoon. 'Bon appétit, kids, because it won't be our problem'. The madragonflies kept a billion tonnes of CO2 out of that equation."

I could feel the righteousness radiating from her, as though she were an iceberg charging an armada. You couldn't reason with that kind of conviction, you couldn't explain to her that she'd had no right to make that decision for all the people who'd lived here, for all the people still waiting for their five-yearly "hello".

"I guess we all live with our decisions," I said, "and the decisions others have made for us."

Mason's expression was inscrutable. An antique monitor began to beep, and she strode over.

"There's a glider in range. See yourselves out; I have a backlog of shows to download."

To my surprise, she tossed me her retractable baton. I stared dumbly at her for a moment.

"Don't you need it?"

She didn't look up from the flickering screen. "I'm working on something better."

***

We reached *The Crown* without further incident, but Gus wasn't answering my pings, and the glider signal was down to two dots.

"Everything all right?" said Seong.

I swung my attention back to the helm. "I've entered the coordinates for my destination, but your yacht sits lower than a speeder, so we'll have to watch out for the reefs—"

My comms beeped, and the words INCOMING CALL floated from the screen. I quickly excused myself and slid into the cabin below deck. Squeezing around the full-sized bar, I swiped ACCEPT.

The cabin hazed into a sunny kitchen, and I was momentarily puzzled by the layer of dust on the breakfast table.

"Hey, Lani," said Gus. "All good. Love you." His voice rasped slightly, and dark circles shadowed his eyes. He cradled a cup of tea in his hands, although the lack of steam suggested it had gone cold some time ago.

"Hey, Gus. All good. Love you. Is everything okay?"

"I'm fine. It's good to see you."

"How did your pitch go?"

Gus rubbed his temples. "They're going to fund my proposal. VisionVale are making it one of their flagship projects next year."

"That's wonderful. Right?"

"Yeah, just a lot of pressure." His grip tightened around the teacup, and I wondered if his hands were trembling.

"You sure you're okay? Do you want me to come back? I can—"

"I miss you, but I'm fine. Your sensei's waiting for you."

I reached over, my hand passing through his insubstantial fingers.

"Miss you too. I'll see you—"

Gus and the kitchen vanished, leaving me in the silent cabin.

SIGNAL LOST.

* * *

The deck wasn't conducive to pacing, so I hovered beside Seong at the helm, pointing out helpful shortcuts on his display.

"No," he said patiently. "That's a reef. That's another reef. That's a whale shark. Please, it's extremely distracting to have you twitching over my shoulder like a landed swordfish."

"Then give me the helm."

"I know perfectly well you'd drive my sweet yacht like an ice-breaker. I've read your reports, and I know what you do to expensive machinery."

"It's called field-testing—"

"I'm surprised Argus still gives you anything at all—" He stopped at my expression.

"Look," I said, "you're exhausted. Let me take the night shift, and I promise I'll treat her with respect."

Reluctantly, he relinquished the controls, muttering as he retreated to the cabin below. Behind me, a leather seat creaked, and Sava leaned against the siding.

"Your friend must be very special," he said. "You're going to a lot of trouble to see him."

"I think that's what it means, to be friends."

Sava rested his chin on his arm, eyelids drooping shut. Perhaps contemplating my words, perhaps dozing somewhere not occupied by an alpacamel and a spa-bar.

We sailed through the night, and my eyes were a blurry wreck by the time our destination crept into view. Framed in a gold-dusted dawn, the island rolled with lightly wooded hills and rocky peaks, grasslands sloping into jagged umber spurs.

A thrill shivered over me as I stepped onto the gritty shore, and I could almost feel the island singing *Welcome back, we've been waiting*. The air was a lullaby of lapping waves and distant birdsong, and the serenity, the exquisite stillness, soaked me to the bone. I could see the same easeful wonder lighting Sava's face as we hiked past towering boulders and into the canyons and crevasses of the central peak. The path twisted and narrowed, and overhead, steel cables stretched taut from rock to rock to form an irregular lattice. Further in, the passages were strung with cat's cradles of cheese-wire, like the work of a large, drunken spider.

Sava scribbled furiously in his notebook. "Anti-madragonfly systems …"

Paku skipped eagerly ahead, ducking and squeezing past the wires before disappearing over a dip at the end of the path. I chased after him, relief and joy finally bubbling up into laughter as I leapt over the ridge and into Sanctuary Valley. The ground sloped away into a wide bowl of tufted grass and wild daisies. Rocky escarpments cupped the valley, and a network of cables stretched from bluff to bluff, caging the sky. Paku charged into a drowsy herd of alpacamels, and after a disoriented moment, they broke into a chorus of delighted humming.

I sprinted towards the humble settlement of wooden houses and patchwork yurts. A sturdy woman abandoned her bucket by the well, rushing to greet me.

"Lani? What are you doing here? The other librarians have been and gone—"

"Ariel, I can't stay long. Huiza, where is he?"

"He's in his cottage. But Lani …" I could already see the condolence in her eyes. "Go to him. I'll look after your guests."

* * *

Huiza sat up in bed, propped up by a mountain of colourfully woven cushions. His smile was just as keen, his eyes as kind, but his skin clung to his bones as though desperately binding him together.

"Lani, it's nice to see you're travelling with friends."

His window faced the opposite direction, but legend held that as a boy, Huiza had mastered the art of strategically placed mirrors so he could read books and watch his family's alpacamels at the same time.

I held his frail hands as tightly as I dared. "We have a boat. We can get you to the mainland—"

"You know that if I leave, there'll be no returning. And I would draw my final breath beneath my father's stars. My heart is a piece of the sky, as is yours." Huiza curled his fingers around mine. "Tell me a story, Lani. One more time."

I bowed my head, tamping down the rising grief.

"There once was a woman with a clouded heart. She was a little angry, a little lost. One day, a storm swept her to a hidden vale, a secret nursery of myths and legends, from where stories were sent out on wing and fin and hoof, to reach the farthest, most forgotten, edges of the world. And so colour seeped into this woman's heart, and she found purpose and wisdom—"

"And friends. Friends are the best part of any story."

Sniffing messily, I choked on a laugh despite myself, patting his hands tenderly.

"Yes. Yes they are."

* * *

I let the warm night dry my tears, and as the sky paled, Sava joined me on the grassy slope.

"Couldn't sleep either," said Sava. "Ariel and Pablo told me your friend is sick. I'm sorry."

"At least I was able to see him."

For a long while, the only sound was the gentle snuffling of slumbering alpacamels.

"Ms Bashir, I want to stay here."

My headache thundered a fraction harder.

"You could stay too," Sava continued. "And Doctor Seong—"

"There are five permanent residents on this island—soon to be four. No schools, no hospitals, no access to the mainland or the cirrus—"

"But I'm happy here—"

"Happiness isn't a place. It's the life you build and the people you build it with. If you want to stay, I won't force you to leave, but this isn't the home you're searching for. It's just another refuge, a place to hide so you won't have to move on."

Sava sat, pale and silent. Suddenly, the clicker in my pocket emitted a stream of frantic beeps, rattling out an automated message from the nearest perimeter buoy.

MADRAGONFLIES INCOMING.

I sucked in a sharp breath.

"Sava, go to Ariel." I bolted away down the ridge. "Take care, and I'll see you in five years."

* * *

Seong was already unmooring *The Crown* when I galloped Paku on deck. He raised an eyebrow at Sava's absence, but didn't comment.

"It'll take us eight hours to get out of madragonfly territory," he said, "and the swarm will overtake us in two. But if we set the autopilot, we can barricade ourselves downstairs—"

"But if they destroy the autopilot controls, then we're dead in the water. Give me the helm."

"Lani, you're—"

Footsteps pounded down the path towards us, and Sava rounded the bend. "Wait!"

"Get back to the valley!" I ordered, the yacht already pulling further from the shore.

Sava raced desperately along the rising cliffs, and with a ragged gasp and a gut-wrenching leap, he cleared the gnashing rocks and thudded onto the deck.

"Sava—!"

"Lani, not now!" said Seong. "Take the wheel."

Gritting my teeth, I kicked the motor into gear and roared towards open water, picking up speed until the wind screamed past. I engaged the boosters, gripping the wheel as we bore down on the first reef.

"Keep Paku calm and hold onto something."

The bow lifted from the water and the yacht lurched with a nauseating *crunch* as we scraped over the submerged building. We charged through reef after reef until the hull of *The Crown* was a shredded mess. I could hear the hiss and thrum of the self-sealing fibres and emergency pumps, and I made a woozy note to write the manufacturer a favourable review.

We were thirty minutes from the edge of madragonfly territory when the thrumming air took on a dissonant note. I glanced over my shoulder to see a shifting swarm darkening the sky. Cold sweat writhed down my back as I urged the yacht onward, hurtling over another reef.

Ahead, a white plume misted, and a speeder roared towards us before drawing alongside *The Crown*. At the wheel sat a woman with dark brown skin and an expression like hell on a deadline.

"The madragonflies are on your six!" she bellowed. "Ditch your cargo—legal or illegal—I don't give a rat's. Lose it now, by order of—" The woman stopped suddenly. "Lani?"

"Arjana!" I struggled to keep the wheel steady. "Long story. No time. Go ahead, we'll follow."

Arjana glanced at the seething horizon, then back at our limping yacht, rapidly doing the maths. "Oh, Lani …"

"One favour," I said. "Take the boy?"

Arjana pulled the speeder in close, holding out her hand.

"I'm not leaving," said Sava. "I know what you mean now, about happiness not being a place—"

"You made a promise to your mother, Sava. Make sure Arjana gets home safe. Do that for me."

He looked ready to argue, but surprisingly, slid into the narrow space behind Arjana without further protest. As the speeder roared away, I poured my energies into keeping the yacht moving. Behind us, closing fast, metallic red carapaces glinted like fire on the waves, wings slicing the air, serrated mouths churning.

We crashed over another reef, and the motor gave a guttural groan before half-heartedly catching on fire. The yacht drifted into a slow spin, and I sagged, breathless, against the dash.

"Care for a drink?" said Seong.

We took Paku and locked ourselves in the leaking cabin. Soon, the rattle of breaking glass and rending wood shuddered from above.

"I'll bet the bar doesn't seem so silly now," said Seong, starting on his second bottle of cognac.

I nursed a beer, trying not to listen as the returning swarm pulverised the yacht.

"Cillian, I'm so sorry …"

"There are worse ways to die. Abscess, now that's nasty."

I took another swig of beer, ignoring the seawater inching up my thighs. "Why did you take Sava to Dreamer's Shore?"

Seong's bottle paused at his lips. "He was wasting away in that camp. He has a poet's soul, that boy, a born wanderer. He reminded me of you."

I swirled my bottle thoughtfully, and finally tilted it towards Seong. "To old friends." With a wry smile, and a *clink*, we drank to bittersweet endings.

Suddenly, the yacht lurched, and my emergency radio chittered, stopped, then chittered again.

COME UP. NOW.

Seong and I exchanged a glance, but Paku was already staggering up the stairs in response to the knocking at the hatch. I clambered out into a burst of salt spray and a smell like burning metal.

Snap!

A baton lashed past and a madragonfly thudded to the deck, fizzling unpleasantly. A compact submersible bobbed in the water: barely three metres across, it sported articulated legs and webbed feet uncannily like a frog's. Electrified tentacles studded the hull, jetting out to fry any madragonfly that ventured too near. Through the curved windscreen, I could see Mason at the controls.

Sava took my hand. "It'll be a squeeze, but we've made enough room for Paku."

* * *

As it turned out, Paku had to ride in something labelled SPECIMEN HOLD, but I was too exhausted to ask questions. Mason took us to the edge of the straits, where Arjana was waiting with a small flotilla of coracles, medics, and a slightly disappointed mortician.

Details were foggy, but apparently, Sava had used Arjana's emergency radio to contact Mason, who'd driven the submersible to meet them. Sava had then directed Mason to our location, while Arjana went for help.

We didn't linger at the isle after that. Just long enough to collect my pod-cart and catch the next helioship out. My thoughts kept turning to gnarled hands, cold cups of tea, and pieces of sky.

"Would you like to see where I live?" I asked Sava.

"That'd make me very happy," he replied.

"I'm headed that way anyway," said Seong.

I cut short the rest of my itinerary, stopping only to drop off the books I'd promised each community, although I was surprised by the number of people who had packages awaiting me. As the pod-cart emptied, it filled again with bundles of paper and string and wondrous worlds.

We rode through pasturelands powered by the biogas from ripening cheeses, past rugged bluffs feathered with wind turbines. We soared over the towers of Manhatlantis, a sunken city holding the sea at bay with translucent walls of graphite gel. Mason was partly right—our grandparents had erred, but while some had scorched the earth behind them, others had planted seeds of innovation and hope. Now, we rode on the wings of the sun and built cities tangled in the glitter of the ocean.

Three weeks later, we stepped off a helioship and into the heart of Biophany City. Bougainvillea cascaded from every roof, and lemon trees shaded the community gardens that enfolded every pub and office. Everything smelled of fresh coriander and chives, tomato vines and lemongrass. I could almost hear the creak and wriggle of green things thriving.

Across the boulevard, Gus stepped out of a transpod, which hummed away again on its maglev spheres.

Seong cleared his throat. "Sava can stay with me while his paperwork goes through. I'll see you around."

"Thanks, Cillian." I dropped something onto his palm. He inspected the origami paper boat, the letters IOU written on the hull.

"An excellent name for my next yacht," he called over his shoulder as he and Sava left.

Gus jogged over and I wrapped my arms around him.

"I missed you," I said.

"You have no idea." Gus laughed as Paku nuzzled him impatiently. "Yes, you too."

I waved over another transpod, my wireless ring blinking as it set the coordinates for home.

"Tell me everything," I said. "How's your project? How's your mum?"

Gus took my hands, his voice catching slightly. "Lani, there's something I have to tell you."

* * *

Four weeks earlier, Esta Khansari had suffered a fall at her home. The robotic monitor had alerted the paramedics, but by the time Esta arrived at the hospital, she'd already slipped into a coma. She never woke up.

I watched Gus as he recounted the details, my heart tearing itself slowly into smaller and smaller pieces.

"You could have told me," I said quietly. "I would have come back."

"You'd have missed out on seeing your sensei—"

"I should have been here."

Gus stared at the table, his hands shaking. "There was nothing you could have done. And I didn't want you to worry. Oh, she left you a message."

I waited for him to switch on the scope, but instead, he handed me a mint green envelope containing a handwritten note.

Dear Lani,

If you're reading this, I'm gone, and Argus is probably a sentimental wreck. Be patient. Whatever the future brings, thank you for making my Argus happy. Long may you watch over each other.

With fond memories,
Esta Khansari

Tears dripped onto the letter, and in the sanctuary of our small kitchen, we held each other close. And I realised that these were the things that connected us across time and space: love, grief, memories, and the stories we wove together with our laughter and our tears.

* * *

I sat on the rooftop garden of Biophany Library, watching the sun dissolve behind stately eucalypts. Sava sat beside me, sketching squabbling cockatoos.

"My new guardians seem nice," he said. "I start school next week, and I've decided I want to study Biomimetic Engineering at uni."

"Gus says you have some interesting ideas for madragonfly-proof gliders."

Sava shrugged. "If everyone had access to the cirrus, maybe we wouldn't need mobile libraries."

"Maybe. But sending someone an ebook isn't the same as sharing a circle of firelight, feeling the tension and breath of people hearing the same tale. There's a chemistry to nearness that can't be simulated."

Sava's pencil scratched a little slower. "Doctor Seong says you're leaving again in a month. North, this time."

I twisted a strand of grass around my fingers. "Would you like me to stay?"

"Are you happy here?"

"I think so ..."

"But it's not enough, is it?"

I loosed the curl of grass. "I once tried to leave Paku at the valley; I thought he'd be happier there. They say he was fine for a few days, and then he tried to swim out to find me. I think maybe I'm the same. Home is nice, but ..."

"... not for too long. Not forever."

Along the avenues, streetlamps glowed with the day's captured light.

"What are you going to do?" said Sava.

I leaned back, watching the stars wink into life. My roots might never catch the earth, but it was past time I slowed long enough to tend to those dearest to me, so that their dreams might bear fruit and their boughs brush the sky. Time, at last, to do the responsible thing.

* * *

One year later

I flicked my final report for the year to *Unbreakable Tech*, and set my tag to autoreply. My fingers brushed against the photo framed on my desk: a man with grey hair, kind eyes, and a smile full of stories. It was the picture they'd used at Huiza's funeral.

I pulled on my pack, the straps stiff from time in storage. Downstairs, Gus swept through crowded holographic charts while Sava finished vacuuming Paku.

"I think he's more excited about leaving than you are," said Sava.

Gus leaned over for a kiss. "Take care. The second wave of levigliders are being launched next week, so you might catch an extra signal or two on your trip."

"Is Doctor Seong meeting you at the station?" said Sava.

"We're only travelling part of the way together—"

"I'll worry less if you're not alone, even though it's a short trip," said Gus.

Sava took Paku's reins and walked me outside, slowing to a stop beneath a bower of fig trees. "My story, there's another part now. 'When the fallen star led the boy home, safe and well, she told him she had to return to the sky. But she promised she'd come back for him. And so she journeyed away to spread her light across the firmament, and the boy waited.'"

I drew Sava into a hug, and felt his arms tighten around me.

In so many ways, intimacy—friendship—is the sharing of our stories, revealing the pages of our life for others to see. And through these acts of sharing, we come to understand the world, and our place within it.

"I can't wait to hear the next part."

About *The Wandering Library*

The Wandering Library was Aurealis Award-shortlisted for Best Science Fiction Novella.

The Wandering Library was first published in *Ecopunk!* (Ticonderoga Publications, 2017), edited by Liz Grzyb and Cat Sparks.

THE SPIDER AND THE STARS

Del's childhood, like many others, was woven from enchanted tales. Every night, as the warmth of the day radiated back through the glass water-wall of her bedroom, Del curled up with her plush quokka and listened, enthralled, as her mother spun wondrous stories.

These were never stories of dragons and fairies, mermaids and centaurs. No, these were stories of fierce young women with flocks of tree-planting drones, firing seeds into the barren sands and rolling back the desert. Or tales of ravenous locusts sweeping across the land in suffocating plagues, and the farmers who responded by cultivating carnivorous wheat.

But tonight, there had been no story. Del waited in bed until even Quokka's genial features seemed to furrow with impatience.

"Wait here," whispered Del. She was almost five, and therefore officially allowed to negotiate the terms of Bedtime. Stories were a requirement under Article Three, since she had fulfilled the conditions of Article Two: specifically, the Brushing of Teeth.

She trod softly towards the sound of voices in the kitchen. Her mother sounded uncharacteristically frustrated; her father, uncharacteristically chipper.

"It's their loss," he was saying. "There'll be other competitions—"

"Not like the Solaria Grande Exhibition." Her mother's voice was thick with disappointment. "It'll be twenty years before it comes this way again—"

"So we'll travel to the next one—"

"With all this gear? What if the truck overturns? The last thing we need is a hysterical headline like '*Mutant Bugs on Rampage!*' It's hard enough getting people not to gag at the word 'entomophagy'—"

"Maybe we shouldn't use that word next time. How about 'alternative protein'?"

There was a soul-crushing sigh. "People won't eat spiders because they have too many legs, but they'll happily eat crabs. They won't eat shea caterpillars because they're too gooey, but they'll slurp down oysters. Gram for gram, insect protein is cheaper, healthier and more sustainable than red meat. To make a single beef patty, it takes two thousand litres of water. To make the same amount of cricket flour, you need a moist towelette and a tolerance for swarms—"

"I know. And *that's* why you'll make this work. You don't need some fancy prize. You have your passion, and your entomology degree. And you have me and my winning way with a hot wok and spices—"

"And me," Del blurted from the doorway. "I'll help you look after the bugs."

"Oh, Del, daughter of mine ..." Her mother scooped her up like a rugby ball, the comforting scent of ripe apricots and jasmine lingering in her mother's thick brown hair. "Am I late for story time?"

As the cicadas bleated their one-note love songs from the eucalypts outside, Del settled onto her sleeping mat, the straw cool against her skin. She slid her night terrarium a little closer, the bioluminescent mushrooms and glow-worms suffusing the room with a gentle blue-green radiance.

"Can I have a story about ogres?" Del's playmates at preschool had terrified each other with stories of child-guzzling ogres, and Del wondered if the ogre had considered eating cricket damper and jam instead.

"Hmm ... I don't know many stories about ogres. Oh, wait, there is one very special ogre—the ogre-faced spider, *Deinopis ravida*.

A huntress of the night who stalks her prey with a silken net, with eyes so keen and clever she can see the galaxy Andromeda."

And it was in this moment—her mind filled beyond capacity with this wordless, moonlit image of a stargazing spider—that Del chose her destiny.

* * *

Ten Years Later

It had rained all summer, and the water tanks were overflowing, but the local frogs kept the mosquitos at bay. Even so, citronella candles lined the backyard deck, adding their fragrant glow to the festive solar fairy lights. Del wove through the convivial crowd, carrying one last platter of crispy garlic tortilla chips, setting it down between the creamy mango curry and the crunchy lime and chilli beer snacks.

Del glimpsed her mother in lively conversation with the mayor, while her father manned the barbecue, an aroma like char-grilled prawns and capsicum infusing the balmy air. On the bandstand, a woman on an electric oud was trying to drown out an enthusiastic accordionist, and Del's temples twinged.

Her work done, she slipped quietly into an adjoining paddock and down a wide stone stairwell that descended into the earth. The wall console blinked as it recognised her wrist-chip, and she passed through the airlock, entering a sprawling underground chamber. The humid air smelled of fresh oats and loam, and the room was almost entirely dark. Dim red guide-strips marked the floor, and overhead, the ceiling was studded with thousands of pinprick lights.

Countless rows of two-metre tall racks stretched into the distance, each filled with shallow drawers constructed from corn-starch plastic. A ventilation gap separated each drawer from its neighbour, so that the room resembled a cross between a bakery and library. Large signs were affixed to the end of each row, along with smaller labels on each drawer:

CRICKETS (ACHETA DOMESTICUS)

MEALWORMS (TENEBRIO MOLITOR)

SILKWORMS (BOMBYX MORI)

Del's father had been right. They hadn't needed some fancy prize to realise her mother's vision; just a few years, a new marketing angle, an environmental emergency, and a gutful of hard work. A faint flush of pride warmed Del as she surveyed the tidy insect farm, her mother's colourful logo printed on every crate and carton.

KOUMI'S ORGANIC FOODS: DELICIOUS SUSTAINABLE PROTEIN

Overcoming people's aversion to creepy crawlies had been their greatest challenge, until they realised that cultural attitudes weren't an obstacle, but an asset. If most people hadn't cared when their corn chips were made from palm oil and the tears of orangutans, why would they care now that their cheese-powder fix was made from sustainably farmed, gluten-free crickets? As long as it looked and tasted like a corn chip, most people didn't care where it came from.

Lilana Koumi's banquet parties had become a thing of local legend. They'd started as sales and networking events for potential clients, but as the business prospered, they'd become an annual victory celebration for the family. And it was true, no one really cared that the tortilla chips were made from cricket flour, or that the mango curry included pepper-roasted termite puree, or that the beer snacks consisted of deep-fried, salt-and-pepper grasshoppers. Everything was delicious, and almost nothing looked like bugs.

Del walked down the softly lit aisle, the chorus of *chirrups* washing over her. While most of the crickets' songs were probably entomological booty-calls, she couldn't help imagining that some were wistful odes to waving grass and summer rain. She lifted the mesh of a passing drawer and tossed in a few pieces of carrot. The facility had automated feeding systems, but Del still liked to drop them extra snacks.

The underground chamber was naturally climate-controlled, and the lights were powered by biogas from the nearby cheese factory. And while Del knew it was only her imagination, she sometimes thought the light smelled faintly of cheddar.

At the far end of the subterranean shed, through a small, plain door, lay Del's realm. It had been intended as a supply closet, but Del had begged her mother for the cosy space.

You have a big lab in the warehouse upstairs, Del had said. *Let this be mine.*

And so it was.

Tanks and terrariums and trays and aquariums crammed the small space, brimming with grasses and ferns and multi-legged residents. Giant water bugs paddled lazily, while peacock spiders danced their nervous rhumbas. Charts covered the walls, and boxes of slides were neatly arranged around a scuffed microscope. Stern signs were prominently attached to every insect residence: NOT FOR EATING!

Del reached into a leafy terrarium and gently lifted out a delicate, caramel-coloured spider about the size of a dime. The ogre-faced spider scurried up Del's arm and perched on her shoulder, staring at her with limpid black eyes.

"Hello, Artemis," Del smiled. "Ready to go stargazing again?"

Artemis continued to stare, and, not for the first time, Del wondered if deciphering the expression on a tiny arachnid face was like trying to read a poem inked onto a grain of rice.

While Del's mother spent much of her time researching the nutritional value of insects, Del had become fascinated by the engineering marvel of termite mounds and the dazzling aerodynamics of dragonflies' wings. Her mind sprouted with possibilities, imagining how this knowledge might transform her own world. She envisioned gigantic skyscrapers with convection ventilation systems, requiring no artificial heating or cooling, and agile drones flying through dense jungles in urgent search-and-rescue missions.

Often, as Del peered down her microscope, Artemis would keep her company, ambling thoughtfully across Del's pages of notes, or hanging upside-down from a potted fern, occasionally waving a leg as though in encouragement. Or perhaps telling her to hurry up so they could go outside.

Del conducted a routine check of the room's filters and meshes, double-checking the seals on a tall cylindrical terrarium. Inside, the fire ants were forming another tower, climbing determinedly on top of one another to create a sturdy latticework that resembled an Eiffel Tower of ants. They seemed to do this every time they outgrew their existing home, but Del wondered how high they might go if left unchecked, and if, perhaps, somewhere in that seething lattice, there was a fire ant who longed to reach the clouds.

She would have to get them a larger tank.

Back outside, Del found a quiet spot by the jacarandas, the fallen purple blooms already wilting into potpourri. From her perch, Artemis turned her gaze towards the sky.

Someone coughed from the shadows.

"Hey, am I interrupting?"

A teenage boy with light brown skin and an easy smile stood holding a rustic wooden plate. Del returned the smile.

"Hey, Ziad. Thanks for coming."

Ziad's family ran a busy bakery in town. They were vegetarians, but they came to every banquet, bearing pastries and warm wishes.

"Well, Dad loves a good party. I saw you were frantically busy, as usual. I thought you might be hungry."

He offered the unfamiliar plate, which seemed to bear a delicate sculptural work of contemporary art.

"Wow," said Del. "That looks like it belongs in a gallery."

Ziad beamed. "It's a kangaroo grass sable with lemon myrtle ice cream, quandong tart and a sweet potato twill."

Just as meat had become a luxury in an increasingly arid world, so too, thirsty crops like rice and wheat were beginning to attract concern. Those with foresight were turning to plants like kangaroo grass and saltbush, which required no irrigation, no synthetic fertilisers and no pesticides. Unfortunately, the palate of the masses was yet to be convinced.

Del took a bite of the warm, buttery pastry and tried not to salivate as the tangy quandong jam hit her tastebuds.

"It tastes like a perfect day. I'm sure you'll have your own patisserie in no time."

"Not just a patisserie. It'll have its own garden, its own farm, with heirloom vegetables and heritage fruits and exciting new varieties of grains and berries and honeys." He sighed. "Or, at least, that's the dream."

"Maybe this'll help." Del bumped her wrist-chip gently against his, and a holographic screen blinked into life between them. An ornate certificate shimmered briefly before being replaced by a page of dense disclaimers. Finally, a large title *swooshed* into view:

WELCOME TO CRISPR FOR BEGINNERS.

PLEASE EDIT GENES RESPONSIBLY.

Ziad's wide-eyed expression made him look almost like a human version of Artemis. "You got a CRISPR kit?"

"*We* got a CRISPR kit. Don't get too excited; it's just the student version with a vial of *Drosophila*, but we can share the equipment. Now you can make your pest-resistant chives—"

"And you can make your flame-resistant moths!"

They grinned at each other as bogong moths fluttered through the sultry air, and Artemis gazed at the stars.

* * *

THE SPIDER AND THE STARS

Another Ten Years Later

In the canopy of the scrubland, perched on ten-metre stilts, there nestled a sleek cabin of photovoltaic glass and reclaimed timber. In the eaves, elderly spiders knitted cobwebs, while on the roof, corellas rode the spinning ventilators, cackling uproariously.

Within the airy sunlit rooms, Del rushed from bench to shelf, flicking items off a holographic list that hovered to her right. She slotted one last carefully sealed terrarium into her trolley case before plucking a pristine flyer from her corkboard.

THE SOLARIA GRANDE EXHIBITION AND PRIZE

INNOVATORS, VISIONARIES, INVENTORS, ENTREPRENEURS, ACTIVISTS

COMING TO TERRARIUM CITY

Del pressed the flyer to her chest. Terrarium City was only twelve hours away by levitation train. Her mother's experience at the exhibition had been less than heartening, but her descriptions of the magnificent halls and cosmopolitan crowd had ignited Del's imagination. And while Del loved her cabin in the canopy, and her job at the local Community Knowledge Centre, she longed to venture beyond the red dust and scribbly gum trees of her home town. Far beyond.

A quiet *pitter-patter* announced the arrival of her housemate. A tawny spider the size of a Labrador skittered into the room, clutching a ruffled net of cobweb silk between her forelegs. At the sight of the trolley case, her huge black eyes shone with worried disapproval.

Del clipped the case shut. "Sorry, Devana. I wish I could bring you with me, but I just know someone's going to panic and try to squish you."

Devana was a distant daughter of Artemis, and the benefactor of Del's years of tinkering with CRISPR. However, the more Del probed the cryptic genome of insects and arachnids, and the more she studied their complex behaviours, the less inclined she felt to modify them, and the more she longed to understand their strange and alluring worlds.

Del withdrew a translucent golden pod from a warming cabinet and tossed it to Devana, who snatched it from the air and sank her fangs through the soft gel skin, greedily drinking up the bottlebrush nectar. It had taken Del almost a year to devise this latest formulation, but Devana seemed to find it palatable, and it gave her carapace a healthy sheen.

"Be good," said Del. "Make sure the cockatoos don't chew my house to sawdust while I'm away."

"Everything will be here when you get back," said a voice from the foyer. Del's mother leaned against the gently curving doorframe, an insulated lunchbox in one hand. "Your father sends his love, and dumplings. Vegetarian."

It had been a wrenching decision for Del, many years ago, when she'd excised meat from her diet, including insect protein. But having spent so much time with her tiny companions, having seen their rich, complex lives filled with as much hope, tragedy and delight as her own, in the end, it had hardly been a decision at all. The choice had wounded her parents, but they understood. Or, at least, they said they did.

"All the filters have been changed," said Del. "The cabinet is full of nectar pods. You don't have to do anything with the incubators, but if the fire-ants start building again—"

"It'll be fine. Just enjoy yourself, and remember, the prize doesn't matter."

"I know." Del tucked the flyer into her jacket, her stomach suddenly fluttering. "It's just … what if they laugh at me?"

"Then it'll be a family tradition. My dearest Del, daughter of mine, they can laugh at us, but they can't stop us."

Del's mother drew her into a hug, and for a brief moment, it was twenty summers ago, when the days smelled of ripe apricots and jasmine.

As Del walked down the leafy track away from her cabin, she turned to see Devana standing on the roof, waving her forelegs. Whether in farewell or in the hopes of netting an unwary cockatoo, Del couldn't be sure, but she waved back.

* * *

Ziad was already waiting for her at the levitation station, his two storage drones following him obediently. Their sleek cylindrical forms made them look like a pair of patisserie refrigerators moonlighting as henchmen. As Del jogged over with her luggage, Ziad gave her an excited grin.

"Ready to transform the world with your entomology research?"

"We'll see. Ready to make incremental but meaningful change with your climate-resilient crops and nutritionally responsible, mind-blowing desserts?"

"I have two tower-cases of pastries, puddings and cakes, so whatever happens, I'll be having a good time."

The station was a curving sandstone platform, partially enclosed by lofty timber beams and tinted skylights. Even in the baking summer heat, the angular design of the roof drew cool air in from the surrounding native gardens and exhaled warm air through the ceiling vents. A bell-like tone signalled the arrival of the train, and Del watched with anxious delight as it snaked across the sand.

Affectionately known as the Wyrm, the silver, serpentine locomotive glided a metre above the trackless ground. It was guided by GPS and location beacons stationed every kilometre along its path, and powered by a crucible of geomagnetism, photovoltaics, and lightning in a bottle.

The interior was part Orient Express, part Star Trek, with panoramic windows on every side. Del and Ziad settled into an economy booth, sipping ginger tea and practising their presentations. But the changing landscape outside kept tugging at Del's attention: there were towns, just like hers, speckled with solar arrays and water tanks. But there were also villages floating on inland seas, their bustling markets a crowd of floating tea houses and creaking junks with patchwork sails. There were forests of typhoon turbines ready to capture the rage of mighty storms, and enormous greenhouses in the desert, flanked by desalination plants powered by the sun.

As the terrain outside grew more arid—the parched earth puckering into shingles—an oasis slowly rose on the horizon. A gigantic dome of glass—a garden city in a bell jar, infused with greenery and flecked with iridescent butterflies and scarlet macaws.

Terrarium City.

***

Terrarium City Exhibition Centre was an enormous labyrinth of adjoining halls, and the registration foyer resembled a fusion of intergalactic spaceport and overgrown conservatory. Climbing roses spiralled up the stone columns, reaching towards a ceiling that was little more than a glassy frame for the sky. Full-grown figs towered around them, their roots sinking deep into the floor, and it was hard to tell where the carpet stopped and the moss began.

At a registration booth wreathed in delicate pink mandevillas, Del and Ziad finally received their convention passes.

Ziad quietly pumped a fist. "Yes! I'm in Meadow Hall. That's supposed to be one of the fun ones. How about you?"

Del looked at her pass. "I'm in Tundra Hall."

"Uh, I'm sure that's fun too. I'll come visit your booth."

Del glanced at the sprawling map overhead. "No, that's all right.

It makes sense that they'd situate the live exhibits far away from the food exhibits."

As it turned out, Del's neighbouring booth was technically a food exhibit.

"Hi, I'm Xiaren Appelhof," said an angular woman with rosy cheeks and a smile like a flash of steel. "Distributed biogas generation. You?"

"Del Koumi. Entomological research." She tried not to stare at the tall, complicated tanks lining Xiaren's booth. They resembled a more militant version of Ziad's storage drones.

Xiaren followed her gaze. "Ah, I see you've noticed my portable domestic biogas system. Normally, biogas harvesting systems require thousands of tonnes of cheese to create a commercially viable amount of whey for anaerobic digestion. My system utilises less than twenty kilos of cheese, and generates enough gas for heating and cooking in a typical home. I call it the *Fromagerie 5000!*"

Xiaren swung open a panel in the tank to reveal five shelves of ripening cheeses surrounded by gurgling pipes and humming canisters. Del rocked back on her heels, the intense smell of gorgonzola hitting her with almost physical force.

"That's ... powerful."

"I've specially cultivated the microorganisms to generate vastly more biogas than normal. And the cheese tastes amazing."

Xiaren cut a gooey wedge from a creamy blue and offered it to Del, who, after a moment's hesitation, took a bite. Notes of chilli and lychee simmered beneath the pungent flavour, and her eyes watered.

"This would make an insanely good pasta sauce." She gave herself a moment for the sparkles to disappear from her vision. "So, why did you go into cheese?"

Xiaren shrugged. "My hometown isn't overly fond of dairy, but we needed clean energy. And in my mind, gas is gas, whether it's happening inside a cow or a star. Or a round of cheese."

Del looked at the racks of peaceful cheeses, and wondered if they knew they had the heart of stars.

Over the next four days, she and Xiaren bonded over rice-paper rolls and grilled cheese sandwiches, listening to each other delivering their spiels to the curious visitors who streamed endlessly through the halls. Some people seemed interested in Del's collection of giant phasmids and burrowing cockroaches. Less so in her infographics, research papers and posters of 'fun facts'.

"Koumi?" said one middle-aged man, studying her information screen as it hovered over his wrist-chip. "Any relation to Lilana?"

"That's my mother."

The man's smile broadened. "I saw her presentation nearly twenty years ago. She knew her stuff. Generous, too. My pitch for a café run by homeless ex-cons sank at the panel, but your mum gave me a cricket flour starter kit and a recipe for butterscotch pancakes. It's still a bestseller at the café now. I was so tickled when I saw her Caramelised Onion Protein Bars in my local supermarket a few years back. Tell your mother, 'Irvine says hi'."

However, not every visitor was as supportive as Irvine. Del's stand elicited as many 'ew's as Xiaren's elicited 'phew's. Many potential investors scurried past, eyes averted, handkerchiefs over their noses. By the time Del's convention pass flashed with her presentation alert, she was feeling less than buoyed by the public's reaction.

"Hey," said Xiaren. "It doesn't matter what people say. What matters is what you do about it. I'm sure your bugs think you're awesome."

Del made her way through the seething crowd, clutching a single terrarium. Every exhibitor was granted one ninety-second pitch slot with minimal props. If the panel wanted more information, they'd investigate your online portfolio, and, if you were lucky, they'd visit your booth.

She took a slight detour through Meadow Hall, marvelling at the glittering lights, colourful holograms and delicious aromas. One stand billowed gently with cumulus clouds, while another promised neural-implant learning modules.

She finally spotted Ziad's booth. His glistening displays of pastries had tempted a large crowd, and he was enthusiastically describing the carbon footprint of a regular egg tart, compared to the carbon footprint of his regeneratively farmed eggs and macadamia butter pastry egg tarts. Del noted, with considerable satisfaction, that Ziad's onlookers included a significant number of snappily dressed proxy droids, favoured by professional investors who wanted to inspect potential ventures without leaving the house. Del glimpsed one or two faceports that seemed to show the bleary expression of someone who was probably still in their pyjamas.

Del's pass flashed more urgently, and she hurried the rest of the way to Galaxy Hall. The cavernous theatre was almost pitch-black, lit only by twinkling beads of lights on the ceiling and softly coruscating guide-strips on the floor. The hall was largely empty—most people preferred to watch the presentations on their displays, but Del's heart still stuck in her throat as she walked down the aisle and onto the stage.

Her courage almost failed her as she saw the panel of five judges seated near the front. Metres away from her sat Solaria Grande, her brown skin dusted with holographic flecks, her frohawk teased with grey and threaded with light-emitting filaments. Cybernetic contacts made her irises a sigil of golden circuitry, and she looked every inch the ecological goddess who'd forced the desert into retreat. Her seed-planting drones had strafed the land with precisely mapped grasslands, scrub and forests. Her educational programs and support networks had empowered communities to manage the natural regeneration of dormant vegetation systems.

Del felt her voice evaporating as those golden eyes fixed onto her.

"Adelie Koumi," said Solaria Grande. "What do you have for us?"

With shaking hands, Del set the covered terrarium onto the presentation table. "Dung ..." Her voice cracked, and the silence seemed to swallow her. She took a slow, deep breath, and imagined she could see Andromeda. "Dung beetles navigate by the stars. Bogong moths migrate thousands of kilometres by starlight. We still know so little about insects and their relationship with the constellations, yet they could hold the key to our off-world aspirations.

"Our ability to colonise other planets hinges upon how well we can recreate functioning ecosystems. How can we do that without the pollinators and the decomposers? Without the complex web of organisms that sustains life on Earth? If we intend to make our home on other worlds, that home will need insects.

"Furthermore, space radiation remains one of our biggest obstacles to interstellar travel. However, tardigrade cells contain a protein that protects DNA from radiation damage, and not only could this protein allow humans to travel beyond the safety of our planet, it could also have implications for protecting us against cancers, radiation therapy, and cellular degeneration.

"Another challenge is developing resilient materials that can withstand physical and radioactive assault, but remain sufficiently lightweight and versatile for launch and operational needs. However, I've experimented with the proteins in spider silk, and I believe there are potential applications in the development of self-healing spaceships, habitats and safety lines.

"Finally, orbital junk poses a threat not only to space travel, but to the safety of our satellites and space stations. I've been studying the movement of spiders in zero-gravity, and I believe that automated arachnoid robots and mesh snares could play a key role in the retrieval of dangerous orbital refuse.

"Now, I don't have a product to sell or a business to implement. What I'm hoping to do is spark interest, encourage collaborations, spur research. What I'm proposing is a space station dedicated to the study of invertebrate organisms in non-terrestrial environments. Because when we eventually journey to the stars, I believe our tiny colleagues not only deserve to, but essentially must, come with us."

Del pulled the cloth from the terrarium to reveal a zero-gravity chamber containing a model spaceship surrounded by tiny floating balls of aluminium foil. She flashed a laser pointer across the porthole of the ship, and an ogre-faced spider excitedly scurried out. It launched into a gently swimming motion through the weightless space and proceeded to collect the nectar-daubed foil with a silken snare.

It wasn't a product, or a service, or a design. It was probably rather silly.

But it was memorable.

She finally dared to look at the panel, whose expressions ranged from bemused to stony.

"Thank you," said Grande. "Please enjoy the rest of the exhibition."

With a mixture of embarrassment and elation, Del left the stage. As she walked past the panel, she thought she caught a flicker of a smile on Grande's lips, but it might have been a trick of the starlight.

* * *

On the final day of the exhibition, hardly anyone came through Tundra Hall. It would seem that word had spread, and a consensus had been reached that there was little to see here.

"I'm sure it has nothing to do with your presentation," said Xiaren. "It was cute. I mean interesting. Hardly anyone said it was weird."

"Uh, thanks …"

A familiar figure trotted over. "Actually, it was slightly weird. But also very cool." Ziad graciously set down a tray laden with eclairs, baklava, mochi, and raspberry strudels.

Del struggled, and failed, to keep her mood in a trench. "They're about to announce the winner. Shouldn't you be networking in the Investor's Lounge?"

"My details are online," he replied. "And I saw this irresistible presentation about these incredible exploding cheeses."

Xiaren sighed. "No one was hurt. And I've figured out the problem."

As Ziad sampled Xiaren's tasting plate, Del started on an eclair, interrupted only by an impatient '*ahem*'.

A heavy-set woman with brown skin and scarlet-lacquered nails stood before Del's booth, arms crossed, wearing an expression like someone who spends her day maintaining a polite tone of voice while suppressing a category-five rage-hurricane.

"Are you the one who wants to build rocketships for spiders?"

"Well …" Del wondered if she were about to be subjected to another rant about scientists and taxpayer money. She reached for her 'Fun Facts About Science' leaflet, complete with a helpful infographic about the 90% return on investment. "Well, yes, but I have this leaflet—"

"My Jada has something to say to you." The woman clearly had no time for infographics. She nudged her charge.

Del peered over the counter, and a small girl with a vigorous puff of brown hair thrust a large piece of paper towards her. The crayon drawing depicted a shuttle sloshing with spiders, and a puff-haired girl sitting at the controls, smiling like the sun.

"Jada wants to pilot one of your ships when she grows up," said the woman. "Shuttling spiders into space to keep the planet safe."

The girl nodded vigorously, thrusting the picture towards Del again as though presenting her CV. Del tenderly accepted it, not mentioning that free-range probably wasn't the best way to transport a colony of spiders.

"Thank you. I'll keep you in mind."

The girl saluted ferociously before marching away with her mother.

"That was also weird," said Ziad. "But adorable."

A chord of music rippled from the front of the hall, accompanied by a mesmerising aurora. The stage suffused with light, coalescing into a holographic broadcast of the closing ceremony concurrently taking place in Celebration Hall. The convener thanked all the attendees, and a series of guests gave stirring speeches about innovation and persistence. But everyone was waiting for the final speaker, and the final announcement.

Solaria Grande was resplendent in an emerald suit that appeared to generate its own micro-ecosystem, seeming to ripple with grass one moment and shimmer with moss the next.

"The prize is not about the prestige," she declared, "although it has launched careers and established reputations. The prize is not about the money, although it has seeded ambitious projects and turned dreams into flourishing businesses. The prize is what you brought here with you. The prize is what you take away. The prize is what you've shared with all the people who passed through those doors. But that's not what most of you came here for, is it? So, without further ado—"

In the breathless silence of the hall, Del, Ziad and Xiaren linked hands, grinning with the inexpressible joy of being *here* and *now*, on the cusp of something extraordinary, no matter what came next.

"—the winner of the Solaria Grande Exhibition Prize is—"

* * *

Another Thirty Years Later

The shuttle docked with barely a bump, and Del released the armrests of her business-class seat. She'd made this trip countless times now, but that final *click* of the docking clamps always sent electric shivers to the very tips of her fingers. She brought her face close to the passenger-side window, her nose almost touching the cold, transparent matrix.

In the dizzying expanse of space, the station hung in the star-dusted void. It resembled a complicated molecule, with large glassy nodes interconnected via semi-rigid passageways. Its surface rippled with tiny photovoltaic scales, all turning to lap up the passing sun. In the half-light of space, it looked almost like a slumbering snake, curling itself into Celtic knots.

A coppery octobot jetted gracefully past, trailing a net of captured space debris. Del watched with a faint ache of pride as it climbed in through a station hatch and disappeared with its haul.

Del passed through decontamination and stepped into the arrival hall. She'd imagined, once, that space would be all chrome and glass and pulsing lights. Clinical, synthetic, easy to clean. But, back on Earth, past efforts to eliminate germs and bugs from human habitations had led to an explosion in allergies, inflammatory diseases and decimated microbiomes. Successful, long-term space exploration would not—could not—be a sterile venture, and what humanity needed now was a sandpit to experiment in.

Throughout the hall, aluminium trusses were laced with lilac wisteria, and mesh walls brimmed with ferns and bromeliads, forming an avenue of vertical gardens. Despite the softly humming filtration systems, the scent of orange blossom and pear tarts wafted from the nearby cafés. Del's mouth twitched into a smile—as it always did—at the sleek sign emblazoned over the entrance arch.

TERRARIUM SPACE STATION

Del had few rituals, but this one she had maintained for twelve years, since the day of her first visit. She made her way to the Summer Arboretum, past aromatic lemon trees and velvety bushes of French lavender. In a small grove, curtained off by bottlebrush, there stood a little bronze statue of an ogre-faced spider holding a small moon aloft in her forelegs.

DEDICATED TO ARTEMIS, WHOSE CHILDREN REACHED THE STARS

Del gazed up at the large circular skylight, the cloud-dappled Earth a delicate sphere hanging in the darkness, and wondered what Artemis would have made of this.

"Del! I only just saw your name on the arrival logs." A lean young woman with a short mane of curly brown hair walked across the flowering grasses, her navy flight suit marked with the epaulettes of a captain. "Why didn't you tell us you were coming?"

"Jada! I thought you weren't due back for another week."

"We had a biomechanics team from Astroviva scheduled to arrive yesterday, so I thought I'd come back early. They're trying to design an asteroid rover with variable terrain mobility, emergency aerial capabilities, flexible anchoring technology, and a compact folding solar array."

"Peacock spiders," said Del automatically, and Jada grinned.

"They're with the arachnology team as we speak."

"You've been busy. I saw the new Phasmid and Mantis Habitat Pods on the inflight preview."

"Yes, those opened last month. I don't think the stick insects have realised it's zero-g yet, and I don't think the mantids care. Oh, and in other exciting news—it's still under wraps, but we're planning to build a Cephalo Pod. Because who doesn't want to see octopuses in space?"

Del's heart somersaulted in anticipation as she imagined the mischief an octopus might get up to in space. "Save me a ticket to the opening."

"Will do. So, are you here for work or pleasure this time?"

"It's always a bit of both. But I'm meeting an old friend here later."

"Let me know if you need anything. And say 'hi' to your folks for me."

"I will."

Del visited the various research pods, listening as each scientist enthused about their latest project. It was hard to imagine that, thirty years ago, all she had was a room full of bugs and a dream. As it turned out, others had shared that dream.

In the end, the Solaria Grande Prize had gone to a non-profit organisation that coordinated teams of teachers, librarians, and androids, sending them out in nimble airships to help communities build, equip, and staff schools for girls in remote regions.

But Del's wobbly video of a weightless spider gripping a wad of aluminium had captured the imagination of a few people out there, some of whom had looked into Del's projects and reached out to her, and to each other. And, like a colony of spiders, the web of connections had grown until it was strong enough to catch an elephant. Or launch a space station.

Later that night, Del enjoyed dinner at one of the station's restaurants—spicy eggplant stew and mango pancakes—before she made her way back to the Summer Arboretum. The dome had drifted into its nocturnal cycle, the lights dimmed so that only moonlight shone through the skylights. Del strolled the gentle slopes, and from a distant pod, disoriented crickets sang odes to memories of 'up' and 'down.'

"Hi, Del. I brought you something."

Del turned to see Ziad standing beside a sandstone water feature, holding a plate of something that resembled a swirl of light.

Del laughed, wrapping her friend in a warm embrace. "How was your flight?"

"Terrifying. I refer to the ticket price, not the journey."

Del winced. "Space tourism is still in its infancy—"

"You mean poorly regulated monopolies are still gouging consumers."

"Speaking of monopolies, how's Xiaren?"

"She's well. Still irritated every time the press calls her a 'biofuels magnate'."

"Ah, she'll always be a fromager at heart."

Ziad smiled, his gaze coming to rest on the tiny statue of a spider and her moon. "Well, we all managed to follow our hearts, didn't we?"

Del considered this. "I think, perhaps, we followed the science and the necessity. And our hearts just didn't allow us to give up."

A breeze stirred in the microclimate of the arboretum, and Del could almost taste the smoky summers of long ago. She and Ziad stood side by side, watching the Earth swirl gently with the seasons.

From up here, all of humanity was little more than a microcosm, every living speck indistinguishable from any other. And yet, if you looked closer, you'd see the breathtaking complexity of every single soul; you'd see new stories constantly unfolding, new journeys constantly beginning.

Somewhere, down there, a pair of ambitious teenagers shared their hopes beneath a gibbous moon.

Somewhere, down there, a campfire burned beneath a sky streaked with galaxies, and a moth fluttered, unscathed, through the flames.

And somewhere, down there, an ogre-faced spider watched a strange star moving across the midnight sky, and dreamed.

About *The Spider and the Stars*

The Spider and the Stars was shortlisted for the Washington Science Fiction Association Small Press Award for Short Fiction.

The Spider and the Stars was first published in *Glass and Gardens: Solarpunk Summers* (World Weaver Press, 2018), edited by Sarena Ulibarri.

THE BIRDSONG FOSSIL

I was eight when I first saw the *Enantiornithean* fossil. My mother had taken me to the Earle Natural History Museum on a storm-soaked afternoon.

It's just a little rain, Yuzuki, she'd said. *The plants are happy.*

I still recall the darkened exhibition room, the spotlight dramatically positioned by an enthusiastic curator. The amber fossil hung in the air, perfectly still above its levitation pedestal. To me, it looked like a glistening chunk of butterscotch candy, about the size and shape of an ox's heart.

I was enthralled by this fragment of captured time, by the treasure that lay within: a baby bird from the Cretaceous. A ninety-nine-million-year-old hatchling. I gazed, transfixed, at the half-curled toes, the tiny claws, the delicate plumes of grey feathers frozen in mid-*swoosh*. I yearned to know what that creature had felt, had dreamt, in its days beneath those ancient skies.

In idle small-talk, people used to ask me, *Are you more of a dog person or a cat person?*

Bird, I always said. *I'm a bird person.*

Wingbeats shaped the landscape of my youth. As a child, it was the fearless kookaburras that plagued the family barbecues, snatching charred sausages right out of our hands. During my teenage years, it was the dapper magpies that made their home outside the dormitory I shared with the other climate-change refugees, our mornings tinselled with the birds' warbling songs. At university, it was a story about whooping cranes that finally triggered my decisive pivot, shaking me from my plans to become a commercial software developer and setting me on my current, less CV-friendly path.

Now, twenty-seven fractured years after that enchanted day at the museum, I hunched over my laboratory bench, turning a beige plastic magpie over in my hands. The 3D-printed parts formed a dense fretwork of sprockets and servos, and it bulged and twisted in odd places. But the chassis wasn't important right now. What mattered was the nugget of circuitry encased in the plastic skull, and the vines of code that raced through it.

I adjusted the LED lamp on my bench. The cheap diodes were blindingly bright yet illuminated little beyond themselves, in a feat understood only by physicists and dodgy tech factories. I wiped the sweat from my forehead and retied my ponytail, wrestling with wiry black hair that constantly threatened to morph into a keratin anemone.

Cradling the mechanical bird, I held my breath and gently flipped the switch between its scapulae. The bird twitched, scrabbling manically before seizing up and ejecting a puff of smoke from every orifice. I exhaled sharply and switched off the piece of junk.

"Maybe next time," piped a voice from the other end of the bench. "And I'm sure that girl didn't mean it when she said your bird looked like a crime against additive printing."

I glanced at my android assistant, Evan, and suppressed a scowl. "I don't know why CURIUS has to open up all the labs for school excursions."

"We're a government funded research facility," he shrugged. "Potential taxpayers want to know their money is being well spent."

I felt my cheeks flush, acutely aware of the misshapen blobs crowding the shelves, but there was no sarcasm in his voice. Evan had a multitude of flaws, but malice wasn't one of them.

Evan had begun life as the centrepiece of my PhD on Neural-

Network Machine Learning and Robotic Ethnology. I'd 3D-printed his parts from scrap filaments no one else wanted: queasy greens and garish pinks and questionable browns. He resembled a mangled conglomerate of plasticine that you might find at a particularly rough day-care centre.

But his *mind*—his mind was a masterpiece, as far as I was concerned. I'd designed his central processing unit, his operating system, to simulate a human brain from birth, evolving over time, coding and recoding itself as he interacted with his environment and discovered his own needs and wants. He'd spent the first few months of his life rolling around on the floor and walking into walls, but over the torturous years of my doctorate, he'd matured into something far greater than a glorified chatbot or digital personal assistant. In my view, he was a true synthetic person, with a childhood, a history, and all the aspirations, doubts and eccentricities that came with that.

I'd named him Evan, after Evangeline Akiko, a pioneer of quantum neurosocial algorithms, and I considered him a triumph of synthetic personhood. Unfortunately, the examiners disagreed, unable to see past his crooked legs, anxious disposition and nervous tics. I'd scraped a Pass, but barely.

Changing his temperament would have involved rewriting sections of code that he'd evolved himself, and Evan had declined my offer to tweak his programming.

I'd rather potter about in the basement as myself than swan around soirees as one of Fedora Winthrop's mindless mannequins, he'd said.

So, it was just as well he felt at home in my cramped, windowless lab.

"I just need to crack the ignition state," I muttered, flicking open the Project Birdsong folder on my holoscreen. I selected the magpie fMRI data and scrutinised the undulating blobs of cortical activity. I wasn't trying to create a robot that looked like a bird. I was trying to create a bird that had the body of a robot. That was crucial if we hoped to understand and preserve the infinitely complex ecosystems of this unstable world. But replicating the brain of a newborn bird, with its hard-wired instincts and pliable potential—

"Hello, Yuzuki?"

A voice lilted from the doorway, and with great reluctance, I looked over at the bright-eyed woman standing there. She had dark brown skin and a stylish curly updo, her lab coat looking more like couture than protective gear over her plump, graceful frame.

"Hello, Min," I said as graciously as I could. "Congrats on the baby thylacine."

Doctor Min Madaki was one of CURIUS's darlings: not only a rising star in the field of de-extinction biology, but also a brilliant science communicator who frequently did the media rounds and turned up in viral videos involving baby pandas. I liked to think of her as my nemesis, but she was too polite to return the favour.

"Thanks," smiled Min. "We're having a small celebration at the Madeline Hotel and I was hoping you'd join us."

"I'm busy." I surreptitiously covered my unhappy magpie with a greasy towel.

A trace of hurt touched her eyes. "I know you disagree with what I'm doing—"

"I don't disagree with your research. I disagree with how you're presenting it. Or rather, what you're leaving out."

"There's nothing wrong with focusing on the successes. We'll work out the shortcomings later. You know funding's tight."

"You're giving people a false sense of security. 'If a species goes extinct, we'll just bring it back. No harm done.' And you know that's not true. Once we lose a species—it's gone. You might bring back the body, but you're not bringing back the mind, the culture, the ecological systems. You're not bringing back the dolphins who teach their daughters how to forage using sponge masks. Or the monkeys who rub themselves with crushed millipedes to repel insects. Or the regional dialects of whalesong. You're bringing back psychologically disturbed remnants—"

"Yuzuki, I didn't come here to argue." Min's subdued disappointment dampened my ire. She continued. "You know I believe in what you're doing. It'd mean a lot to me if you came." She shone a smile towards the back of the lab. "Hi, Evan. You're welcome to come too."

The door closed softly as she left, and Evan's quiet gurgle turned into words. "You know we should go, right?"

I grimaced, but if Evan was prepared to venture from the lab, I didn't have the heart to deny him.

"Sure," I sighed. "Suit up."

* * *

The Madeline Hotel resembled the delirious dream of a confectioner trapped in the body of an architect. Raspberry-glazed floors shimmered between toffee-glass columns, and from the ceiling hung chandeliers of pastel crystal macarons.

From the elevation of the fifty-third floor, through window panes arrayed to resemble shards of praline, I could see the city's rooftop gardens blanketing the district like a mossy patchwork. From pocket community gardens fragrant with fresh herbs to sprawling manicured parks frequented by the co-working cohort, these botanical eyries were interconnected by a tangle of wildlife bridges that facilitated non-human passage from roof to roof. Thick ropes of woody vines were favoured by the possums, while sturdy earthen arches served the occasional lost wombat. Who knew where, or if, the thylacine would fit into this complicated ecological puzzle.

The 'small celebration' turned out to be a packed ballroom event, complete with voracious press. A perilously large banner boasted: CURIUS BREAKTHROUGH! THYLACINE RESURRECTION! accompanied by an adorable photo of a mewling pup, distinctive black stripes already visible across its back.

Years ago, we'd been the Hopper Noon Science Institute—one of the world's leading research organisations. But the incoming government had decided that scientists were 'out of touch' with modern priorities, and appointed a corporate shark as the new director. His rebranding team had struggled to squeeze sense into the 'edgy' new acronym, which allegedly stood for the Centre for Useful Research and Investable Understandable Science.

But Min was right. Under this administration, funding was tight, and it was only getting tighter. I'd edged my way onto the payroll under the institute's former 'basic science' quota, but the new director seemed to equate 'basic science' with 'weird and useless research'.

"I'm okay here," said Evan, staking out a spot beside a potted palm, savouring the extravagant surrounds. "You go mingle."

"You sure? Let me know when you want to go, okay?"

Evan shooed me away, and I looked back at his gangly, mottled form, his dusty grey suit shedding disoriented moths.

"Oi, Yu!" drawled a stocky woman with a lazy smile.

"Hey, Jaya." I returned a crooked grin.

"What a circus, eh? Enjoy it while it lasts. Chatter from the capital says the government's under the pump to reduce expenditure. You know what that means."

I did. Basic science was always the first to go.

"Thanks for the heads up," I said. "Good luck with the self-cleaning photovoltaics."

Jaya sauntered back into the crowd, and I soon bumped into other colleagues. Tran in Epidemiology was fretting about the new outbreak of Ebola and the rise in antibiotic resistant—well—everything. Rhys in Ecology was worried about the vanishing rivers and aquifers depleted by unsustainable agriculture. Fei in Meteorology spoke urgently about the erratic changes to the jet streams and the worsening droughts and storms. And with every conversation, I tried not to think about all the animal species being snuffed out, one by one.

Abruptly, excited chatter bloomed around an incoming coterie of guests.

"Oh, here we go," muttered Fei.

At first glance, the newcomers appeared to be a dozen exceptionally elegant men, led by a woman whose cocktail dress seemed to be made of gold smoke and the souls of lesser mortals.

Fedora Winthrop. Founder of LARS—Lifestyle Assistance Robotics Services—one of the fastest growing companies in a multi-trillion dollar market. She'd tapped into a lucrative vein with her synthetic Adonises, satisfying an apparently underserviced demographic of busy professionals who wanted a companion who would do the dishes, mow the lawn, and bake perfect eclairs while looking like a million dollars. With an invoice to prove it.

"Oh no," I said. "Gotta go."

At the best of times, humans flustered Evan. But other androids, especially androids like these, triggered a far stronger reaction. I jostled my way across the ballroom, my heart thumping as one of Winthrop's charmbots meandered towards the potted palms. Evan had spotted him as well and was scurrying in the opposite direction, but in his haste, failed to see the figure in his path. Evan slammed into another LARS android, his glass of orange juice splashing across the taller android's tuxedo jacket.

I closed the distance and scooped up a pile of napkins. "I am so sorry, Mister—" I cringed at his nametag, "—Prometheus."

The square-jawed android glanced at my nametag. "That's quite alright, Doctor Alvarez. I've never met an Ethnographic Bio-Roboticist before. I'd love to hear more."

"Maybe another time," I said, dragging a wild-eyed Evan from the planter of bamboo he was attempting to squirrel into.

Heels clicked across the marble floor, and a voice like caramel and cyanide snaked through the crowd. "Well, if it isn't Yuzuki Alvarez. You know, you break it, you buy it."

There were uneasy giggles from nearby onlookers, and I kept my tone parked squarely in neutral. "Professor Winthrop."

She smiled with eyes that saw the world as ones and zeroes. And I was not a one.

Her gaze nicked Evan. "How lovely to see your pet project again. I'm so jealous of your creativity, Alvarez. How whimsical, creating an android that suffers anxiety attacks."

I was shocked speechless for a moment, and Evan's quiet mortification notched a tiny wound across my heart. I swallowed my ripostes, gripping Evan's hand a little tighter.

With deliberate civility, I addressed the LARS android.

"My apologies again, Mister Prometheus. Please send me the dry-cleaning bill."

I felt the stares and whispers grazing us as we slunk from the cloying ballroom.

* * *

The story of the whooping crane had broken my heart at a time I thought it could break no more. In a life that seemed too long ago to be my own, my mother had been an engineer, maintaining our town's atmospheric water generation system, just as her mother had before her. My dad had been a local tofu master. When they'd gotten married, my dad had adopted my mother's last name.

Because it's cooler, he'd said.

My name, *Yuzuki*, meant 'hopeful pomelo', although I sometimes doubted my dad's translation. My family had lived in our town for generations, and both my parents were steeped in the salt spray and pungent gum leaves that infused our little corner of the world.

They'd never recovered from the relocation. We lost everything in that final storm, watching from the rescue chopper as our entire town calved into the roiling sea.

At university, I'd immersed myself in the clarity of code, the purity of numbers, the soothing logic of solder and circuitry. And then, one sleepless night, I read an article about the whooping crane.

It was a story of desperate conservation. A dozen pairs remained, at the very cusp of extinction, when a concerted collaboration brought them back from the brink by rearing chicks in captivity. Humans in whooping crane costumes fed the chicks. Pilots in ultralight aircraft led the adolescent cranes on their first crucial migration. It was a heroic effort, but along the way, something went wrong.

At first, everything seemed fine. The adult cranes, when released, successfully foraged, mated, made nests. They laid eggs.

And then abandoned them.

Over and over, they just walked away and didn't return.

No one knew why these captive-bred cranes wouldn't incubate their eggs. The invisible thread that connected every generation to the next had somehow been broken, and no one knew how to fix it. The cranes were supposed to know *how* to be cranes. But they were just bird-shaped creatures adrift in a world that no longer knew them.

"You're thinking about whooping cranes again," said Evan.

I looked up from the workbench where I was reassembling the malformed magpie after a fresh set of modifications.

Evan continued. "I'm pretty sure that was your 'whooping cranes' sigh. It wasn't your 'scientists are underappreciated' sigh, or your 'climate change will kill us all' sigh, or your 'bad pun' sigh."

"It's just— I 'm so close."

If I could just get the cortex to boot up, get that first cascade of code going, it would do the rest itself. And if I could get this to work for robotic human brains and robotic magpie brains, there was no reason I couldn't generalise the concept to reptiles, fish, insects.

We could preserve not only the DNA of vanishing species, but their behaviour, their culture. Some biologists scoffed at the idea of animals having culture.

Ethnologist? they said. *The study of culture? Surely you mean* ethologist. *The study of behaviour.*

No, I replied firmly. *I replicate animal culture in robots.*

Because when the sun finally set on the Anthropocene, there would be no fossils to tell the future of the courtship dance of the red-crowned crane, or the ferocious dedication of emperor penguin parents, or the comforting ballads of magpies, singing of lost homelands.

"Maybe you should listen to Min," said Evan. "Do a few years of commercially appealing research to secure your funding. Then come back to this."

"There isn't time. Every morning I wake up, another two hundred species have gone extinct."

"Mostly beetles."

I shook my head, snapping shut the magpie's skull.

"Min can do what she wants, but it's like trying to recreate a recipe by looking at a photo of the final dish. You won't know what went into it, how it's supposed to taste. You can make a chunk of asbestos look like a scoop of ice cream, but only one will give you diabetes."

"I hope that's not the analogy you used in your latest funding application."

"Ever watched a diving bell spider build a cubby house out of bubbles? I'm not making a robot that *does* that. I'm making a robot that knows *why* it's doing that. And feels disappointed when its neighbour has a fancier bubble house."

"Again, you didn't put that in your application, did you?"

I grumbled, swiping through the updated algorithms on my screen. "You're welcome to go work for Winthrop if you want job security." I slung a surly look at the holographic LARS catalogue on his bench.

Evan brightened. "Have you seen the new collection?" He marvelled at the tiny figures hovering over the projection bud. "Their latest bestseller is the Rochester."

I muttered under my breath, tweaking one last section of code.

Evan tilted his head. "Did you just say 'manipulative man-baby'?"

"I don't know why you look at those. The whole enterprise is patronising, morally questionable, and probably violates a whole bunch of trademarks."

Evan carefully spun one of the handsome figures. "Would you want me to look like that?"

"I don't care what you look like. I care who you are. Winthrop isn't making assistants—she's making servants. She hasn't programmed them with hopes and doubts and purpose."

"She says they're safer and more effective that way."

"But *she* wouldn't want to be programmed that way. I'd trade places with you any day because your mind has the same freedoms, capacities, limitations and quirks as any human's—"

"I know, you should have received a better academic transcript—"

"He drew a frowny face in the comments! I mean, who cares that you're slightly lopsided? Jaya's slightly lopsided and she's an amazing materials science engineer."

"Yuzuki, you don't have to prove anything to the world. Or to me. You're a good scientist, whatever field you go into."

I busied myself with the ignition settings. It might not matter soon anyway. The government's proposed budget was due out any day now, and anti-science sentiment was rising. Just last week, someone from *True Today Gazette* had called up, asking if I was squandering taxpayer money on robotic vermin.

I pushed aside the memory of the man's muddled outrage, focusing on the silent, waxy magpie. I touched the necklace at my collar: a plain silver chain with a dimpled, spherical pendant. A present from my parents on my twelfth birthday.

A pomelo, my dad said. *To give you hope.*

I set the bird gently on the scuffed steel benchtop, took a breath, and flipped the switch on its back.

Nothing happened.

I pressed my eyes shut, disappointment welling hot and bitter.

Skrrrt. Skrrrt.

My eyes snapped open. The magpie twitched. Its feet scrabbled, then stopped, then scrabbled again. It wobbled and fell, lying still for a long, heart-stopping moment. And then it threw back its head, beak wide open, and made a noise like a tiny trumpet being mistreated.

I gaped at Evan, his expression mirroring mine.

"I think you need to feed it," he said, his eyes full of wonder at the robot magpie chick.

"I have the synthetic—"

My tablet beeped loudly on my desk, an amber notification light flashing: *important.* I swiped to view the message.

Budget released. – Jaya

I scrolled down the article with a growing sense of dread. The cuts to various regulatory bodies was as brutal as expected, but surely—

I stopped at a dot point near the end of the list. The CURIUS budget cut.

"That must be a typo," said Evan uncertainly. "They must have meant nine-percent, but sneezed and added a zero."

I shook my head, dazed. "It's not a typo. They're shutting down the institute."

* * *

The thing about science is that it's real, whether or not you believe in it. And the reality was, the world was facing a firestorm. A firestorm of spreading pandemics, collapsing ecosystems, mass extinctions and catastrophic climate change. Scientists were the metaphorical firefighters in this approaching calamity, desperately trying to mitigate the worst impacts before the storm-front hit.

And in the face of this oncoming firestorm, the government had just doused the nation in gasoline and sacked all the firefighters.

They gutted CURIUS.

Only half a dozen shell-shocked scientists remained in the ruins of what had once been a beacon of civilisation.

I took a job writing code at the VR games company BrainShock Experiences. It was grunt work, but paid well enough for me to rent a warehouse at the biohazardous end of town. Down at the fringes of the industrial zone, artificial wetlands had been created as part of the city's stormwater processing strategy, but intermittent maintenance meant the water had taken on a decidedly swampy bouquet, with top notes of whatever chemical concoctions had washed down the city's drains. However, it was a safe haven for the local ibises who were just grateful that their days of rummaging through wheelie bins and nesting precariously in ornamental palm trees were over. And the native ducks seemed to get along peaceably with the motley population of escaped domestic fowl who'd found their way here, although it was possible the benzodiazepine in the stormwater played some role. And aside from muddy footprints and the occasional stickybeak, they all left my warehouse well enough alone.

At any rate, it wasn't the fashionable kind of warehouse that boasted cathedral windows and a vertical garden. It was the kind of warehouse you sent people to if they didn't believe in tetanus. I did install skylights. Or rather, half the roof caved in and I saw it as an improvement. Either way, I had plenty of natural light. A discreet polysilk net stretched overhead to discourage interlopers … and escapees.

A series of workbenches occupied one end of the warehouse, and a wall of servers hummed industriously beside a bank of 3D printers.

"Are you sure about this?" Evan fidgeted next to a crate of thermoplastic filament.

Nearby, a beige plastic magpie inspected a potted lavender. Overhead, three more strutted along the exposed beams, sunning themselves in the afternoon light.

"If she says 'no', then she says 'no'," I said.

"If she says 'no', she might call the police."

"I can't stand by and do nothing."

Evan startled at the sudden knock at the door, quickly smoothing his jacket. I slid aside the bolt and heaved open the door.

"Hi, Min," I said. "Thanks for coming."

"I was surprised to hear from you." She took in the decrepit warehouse, her gaze lingering on the fMRI machine.

"It fell off the back of a truck," I said. "How are things at CyberHybrid Genomics? I hear they're working on a pig that tastes like applesauce."

Min hesitated. "It's … fine. They're letting me continue my own research on the side."

A plastic magpie cruised past and landed with a soft *clack* on one of the 3D printers.

"Min, I need a favour."

She tensed, and I rushed out my words before I lost the nerve. "You have access to the laboratory menagerie at CyberHybrid—"

Min shook her head, already guessing my request. "What you're asking me to do is illegal."

"I only need a few animals here and there," I said. "They won't be missed, and I promise you, they'll meet a kinder fate than at CyberHybrid."

Min looked away, the internal struggle eroding her composure. "Yuzuki …"

"You once said you believed in what I was doing. Most conservation now is just palliative care for a planet most of us aren't even trying to save. We're pinning our hopes on de-extinction technology, but reanimating a corpse doesn't bring back the person. What I'm doing is capturing the story, the memories, the context. If you raise a human in an enclosed habitat with dishes of food and water, with no human contact, what you'll have when it's grown won't be a human as we understand it, but a human-shaped creature. That's what'll happen if we bring back the animals we're wiping out. Shells of flesh with only a smear of their original nature. We'll never recapture the richness and complexity of their behaviour—that line will be severed. I can protect that line. But not without your help."

Evan cleared his throat, his voice wavering. "Doctor Madaki, you can bring back their bodies. But Yuzuki can bring back their souls."

Min let out a long, soft sigh. "I don't know what to make of you both sometimes. But I suppose I know a piglet or two that'd be grateful to meet you."

* * *

I slid open the warehouse door and Jaya swaggered in, cocking an eyebrow.

"Did I just see a robot octopus crawling across the front lot?"

"She'll be back," I waved dismissively. "At least she didn't take the lungfish with her this time."

Jaya dodged a squealing pot-bellied pig as it chased after a glinting metal counterpart. "I see you've been making use of the alloy filament I got you."

"Great stuff, thanks. I've got a list of the materials I need next."

Jaya skimmed the electronic paper. "Nanomesh and synthetic chromatophores? They're not cheap, especially with the political pissing contest spraying across the continents."

"That's why I need them now. The Incorporated States is stockpiling missiles, North Erdistan just sent more warships into disputed waters, and our government's itching for a rumble to distract from troubles at home. I need my gear before supply dries up. Can you do it?"

Jaya drummed her fingers against her thigh brace. "Maybe."

A waddle of ducks paraded past, white-plumed birds trundling alongside their gleaming metal companions.

I swallowed a knot of apprehension. "Jaya, are you still working with the nanoengineer who designed the self-replicating drones?"

"Buckley? Yeah. Why?"

"I need the replication code."

Jaya pinned me with a look, and I wondered if I'd pushed the friendship too far.

"You know you're starting to sound crazy," she said.

"Starting?"

A grin tugged at her mouth, but her eyes remained sombre.

I pressed on. "I could probably figure it out myself, eventually, but we both know time's running out. Do you trust me?"

Jaya flicked her gaze around the warehouse, her eyes briefly following Evan as he hurried happily from pen to tank to nest, dispensing food and bioethanol lubricants.

Jaya tucked the list into her coat. "Don't make me regret this."

* * *

A currawong swooped from the rafters, charcoal wings slicing through the sunlight. Rhys sidestepped a myopic kiwi and stumbled over a pangolin as he entered the warehouse.

"Watch your step," I said belatedly.

"Why is that kiwi out in daylight?"

"He's an insomniac."

All around us, fur rippled, feathers ruffled and scales glimmered in a glorious array of colours, although on closer inspection, some of the creatures bore a silvery sheen.

"My goodness," said Rhys, "that's not a Komodo dragon, is it?"

"No, giant salamander." I wrestled the grinning amphibian back into the 3D scanner and flicked the switch to 'motion capture'. At the edge of an artificial pond, a pair of red-crowned cranes engaged in a mesmerising mirror-dance, although only one of the cranes glimmered faintly silver.

"That doesn't seem healthy," said Rhys.

"They're just friends."

"Really? Because they— Oh dear …"

"I'll sort it out."

"And you know this is all ecologically nonsensical. Giant salamanders don't live alongside lyrebirds—"

"Write it all down." I untangled a handsy sugar glider from my hair. "I'll fix it."

Something with too many legs scuttled past and Rhys blinked.

"Was that a robot trilobite?"

"Long story."

Rhys paused, gripping his duffel bag a little tighter. "Yuzuki, I have a favour to ask of you."

Inside a cracked terrarium, in a tangle of twigs, Rhys cradled a pair of Lord Howe Island Stick Insects. About the length of a palm, they looked like lacquered cigars that had sprouted spindly legs. The pair huddled together, and I wondered if they knew just how alone they were.

I barely dared to breathe. "I heard they were all gone, after the tanker incident at Ball's Pyramid."

I saw the memory wrench at him, and his hands shook slightly as he set the terrarium onto the desk.

"A few survived in captivity, but it's only a matter of time before people decide it's not worth spending money on obscure nocturnal phasmids."

Except they weren't just phasmids. Lord Howe Island Stick Insects were the only insects known to pair-bond for life. During the night, the females foraged and explored, and the males happily accompanied them, engaging in whatever activities she chose. And during the day, they slept side by side, the male wrapping his limbs around his partner in an exceptionally leggy cuddle. My chest ached slightly as I wondered if they dreamt of melaleuca leaves and the choir of crashing waves.

Rhys gazed tenderly at the lonely pair. "I don't want the only thing they leave behind to be a couple of husks and a story."

"It's a good story, though." I closed my hand around his. "One worth remembering."

* * *

In the midnight jungle of the warehouse, a robot kakapo ambled through the brush, its mossy green feathers fluffed up against the chill, its delicately hooked beak probing the soil for tender shoots.

I struggled to focus my fraying attention on the mess of screens floating at my desk, my gaze gravitating back to the corkboard on the wall. Across the wooden frame, written in thick black marker, was the word EXTINCT. Evan had suggested it wasn't helpful to collect clippings, but I needed the reminder. I needed to work harder and faster. The latest addition to the board was a thermaprint from the newsfeed: a few perfunctory lines and a smudgy graphic of an African elephant. It hadn't even made the mainstream news.

My eyes stung hot, and I blinked quickly. I'd been so close. Farida from the Tanzanian Conservation Project had sent me a dozen fMRI profiles, but I hadn't had the time to build an ignition cortex and send it back to her. My servers were overflowing with profiles waiting to be transformed and awoken, but there just wasn't enough time—

"You should get some sleep," said Evan, setting down a sack of sunflower seeds.

"Just making sure everyone's been upgraded to the EMP-resistant biographene circuitry."

"Do you really think it'll come to that?"

There'd been rumours of combat drones and autonomous tanks massing along the borders of the Incorporated States, and the sabre-rattling from our own government had reached deafening levels. Taking in the worry in Evan's mismatched eyes, reassurances felt inadequate, and possibly dishonest.

Instead, I offered the only certainty I had. "Whatever happens, we'll face it together. I promise."

Fireflies drifted through the jacarandas, turning the bell-like blossoms into lilac lanterns. And for a moment, in this fragile oasis of serenity and hope, Evan's tensions seemed to melt away.

He smiled faintly. "There's something you should see."

He guided me to a sheltered corner of the warehouse, where a bottlebrush had outgrown its barrel. We'd installed a few nest boxes in its branches to afford the birds some privacy, and Evan lifted his dimmed lamp to one of the openings. A magpie squinted at us with displeasure at the disturbance, her black and white plumage glossed with a metallic sheen.

"There," whispered Evan.

Beneath the robot magpie, barely visible in the bed of twigs and grass, I saw a curve of silvery shell. It shouldn't have been possible—I'd modified Buckley's self-replicating nanotechnology and combined it with my own ignition codes, but even then, I knew it shouldn't have been possible.

Evan's eyes were wide with awe and apprehension. "Are we supervillains yet?"

"I guess that depends on how the story ends."

The story of humanity was one of innovation and disaster, cooperation and violence, an unprecedented amassing of power, and it would possibly end in a global cataclysm. And it was our culture, our stories, our lifting of each generation above the dreams of those who'd come before, that had brought us to this point.

How different would we be if we'd evolved in a world where the waves didn't call to us, where the stars didn't sing to us, where the blush and fade of dawn and dusk didn't draw us from day to day? Our souls were given form by the poetry of our lands, and our stories wove our chaotic, sometimes brutal, existences into heroic narratives.

We were all heroes in our own stories, until history passed its judgement.

* * *

BrainShock weren't bad employers, although I disagreed with their priorities. Virtual reality experiences were an exploding market, from tours of the Jupiter space station to sorcerous battles with elemental gods. Once, I'd asked Milton in Strategic Forecasting about broadening the company's product range.

"How about we design some programs to help people with phobias and PTSD?"

"Customers who want to blow up dinosaurs with rocket launchers have more money," he'd replied.

And so I found myself slouched in my coder's hutch at BrainShock HQ, writing the backbone for *Cretaceous Boom! Now With Chemical Weapons!* The company had erected its flagship building in what it considered to be an avant-garde precinct, and the artist's impression of the tower had resembled a helix of lace, a lattice of air and light, draped with delicate fronds of greenery and wisped with plumes of butterflies. The final tower looked more like a slightly inebriated spire of chicken wire, and the garden balconies that studded the outside were largely neglected. The hutch next door had installed a palatial bee hotel on their terrace, but a complete disinterest in entomological upkeep had resulted in its deterioration into something more akin to a seedy wasp saloon. I'd lost my own balcony herb garden to an implacable legion of aphids, and as a result, kept my blinds mostly drawn.

In my hutch, Evan sat on a deconstructed beanbag next to me, going through my incoming messages. "The shipment of miniature optics is ready to pick up. Oh! Min and Felicity have sent a save-the-date for their wedding! We're going, right?"

I sighed heavily.

Evan glanced over. "Are you still mad about them wanting to call their first child Galadrielle?"

"What? No. It's a perfectly good name, just not spelled like that. Sure, we'll go." I tilted my head towards the carousel of bobbing screens. "It's just that I don't need to know how a pterosaur would react to nerve gas. I bet they could rename this *Animal Welfare Crimes* and it'd still fly off the shelves."

Evan was silent for a moment. "It's not real."

"Yeah, well, some people would say *you're* not real. Or Winthrop's charmbots aren't real. But it's not just about whether the target feels attacked, it's about how the attacker is rewiring their own brain every time they harm something, or abuse someone; every time they normalise that behaviour. Maybe their frontal lobes can tell the difference between what's real and what's not, but we know the amygdala has a harder time telling the difference, especially in realistic, immersive settings. What are you subconsciously teaching your brain when you mistreat someone who looks like a person and acts like a person, even if they're not 'real'? Or when you torment an animal, even if it's not 'real'? Yeah, it's just a game, but how are you reprogramming your brain every time you reward that behaviour?"

Evan rubbed at a seam on the back of his hand. I'd never managed to get the plastic sheaths to align properly.

"Have you given up on humanity?" he said quietly. "Because I haven't."

I weighed my reply, trying to sieve some kind of clarity from the sludge. "No, but there are—"

There was a strange moment—a pause, like a collective breath being sucked from the world, and then klaxons shrieked through the building. A crash of gasps and cries travelled down the hallway, and footsteps clamoured past. I hurried to the door—the corridor was already churning with panicked employees sprinting and staggering for the stairwells.

I grabbed a passing colleague. "What's going on?"

"It's happened." His voice cracked. "It's started. They might not reach us, but they said everyone should take shelter in the basement."

He pulled free and joined the ashen-faced tide. Between the sobs and frightened murmurs, every other word seemed to be 'missiles'. My head felt oddly light, and I began to run.

"Yuzuki!" cried Evan. "You're going the wrong way."

"Evan, take shelter in the basement with everyone else! I'll come back for you."

I felt him grasp my arm, his rivets squeaking at the strain.

"Together," he said. "We go together."

I hesitated, then nodded. Downstairs, I grabbed a share-bicycle from the rack and pedalled madly across the silent city, Evan clinging to me like a baby opossum. The trams were empty, the roads clogged with abandoned cars. I couldn't see any flashes on the horizon, but the news billboards were still streaming a sputtering signal. Huge orange and black plumes mushroomed in devastating slow motion across the screens.

Tiandei City. Santa Lico. Neo Melbourne.

But not here. Not yet.

I skidded off the bicycle as we reached the warehouse and I began throwing open the doors and windows. Evan scaled the ladder and started tearing down the netting.

"Go! Shoo! Get!" I paid no heed to the startled squawks and

indignant snorts. Angry growls were met with a *thwack* of my broom as I chased the resident creatures out into the streets and skies. A pair of silvery black Lord Howe Island Stick Insects strolled towards the doors at the speed of treacle.

"We have to go," said Evan. "Now."

From his perch on the roof, he pointed to the far horizon. An ominous smudge of grey was resolving quickly into a swarm of thrumming specks.

Combat drones.

I watched as a pair of magpies circled once before winging their way towards the scent of new lands. I couldn't tell if the pair were mine.

"Time to go," I said.

* * *

Eight Years Later

What surprised me wasn't how quickly civilisation fell—and it fell hard—but how quickly the survivors bounced sideways. The war itself fizzled out quickly, as those responsible learned, first hand, that Mutually Assured Destruction does exactly what it says on the box.

The first few months were hellish, with the tsunami of initial casualties, the grief and the shock. The energy grid and communications networks disintegrated, the healthcare and financial systems collapsed. For a time, I believed with all my heart that I would never feel happiness again. But humans were funny that way. Some people broke, some people bent, but ultimately, most people just got on with it.

There were vast regions of wasteland now—hot zones that would melt your lungs and mangle your DNA. But in the scraps of habitable land remaining, communities had sprung up, mostly in the vicinity of the mega-bunkers that had possessed the foresight to stockpile sustainable tech, tools, seeds and books.

Evan and I spent most of our time hopping between these bunkers, repairing devices and upgrading systems. The Marine Bunker had been a breathtaking network of aquariums: shoals of colourful parrotfish undulating through the walls, and giant manta rays gliding beneath transparent floors. Evan's favourite stopover had been the Library Bunker, an Escher-maze of catwalks and ladders wreathed in endless shelves of manuals, historical records, fairy tales and poetry.

These bunkers were seed-banks of human resilience, and sanctuaries for those not yet ready to face the reality outside. But I felt most alive—most normal—when I was roaming the ever-changing landscape. Insects had reclaimed the planet, much to the delight of the birds, and every now and then, I'd catch a glimpse of silvery plumage and feel a guilty shiver of something I didn't dare call happiness.

But this ecological reclamation had come with fresh perils. Displaced predators prowled the newly transformed world—hungry, confused and rightfully angry that humans had plunged the biome into anarchy.

Evan and I were slowly making our way north through cliffs of ragged bushland, responding to a carrier slip I'd received from Min several weeks ago.

At Bio Bunker. Find me.

It was an irresistibly cryptic invitation—that handful of words would have cost a fortune to transmit. And though brown bears roamed these parts now, Evan and I had decided to chance it.

Evan limped beside me, struggling to keep pace. The sprockets in his left knee had given out last year, and we'd only managed to patch it up with ill-fitting screws and cable ties. I was hoping Min's bunker would be better equipped.

"We didn't bring a wedding present," fretted Evan.

"Their wedding was years ago."

"We didn't bring an anniversary present."

"I'm sure they—"

"I made something," he blurted nervously. "At the Quilting Bunker. I thought we could give them these."

He reached into his shirt pocket and unfolded a pair of handkerchiefs, woven from lyocell and embroidered with pygmy possums, cassowaries, leatherback turtles and mist frogs.

"That's lovely," I said. "But don't you think all the extinct animals is a bit morbid?"

"Min went into biology because she cares about animals like these. She *wants* to remember them."

I looked at his achingly earnest expression.

"I'm sure she and Felicity will love them."

There was a sudden rustling from the trees as something approached. Something big. I dragged Evan behind a clump of flowering eucalypts and crouched in breathless silence.

A hulking creature lumbered through the trees, stained tusks flanking a snaking trunk, leathery grey skin betraying just a blush of silver. It was a majestic vision framed in the smouldering amber light of day's end.

A robot African elephant.

The creature's head swung ponderously towards us, glassy brown eyes sizing us up with the judgemental disapproval of an apex matriarch. Twigs crunched as another shape entered the clearing—a younger elephant, but flesh and blood! Her wrinkled skin was damp from the long grass, and a baby elephant clutched her tail.

Evan's eyes were like mismatched moons as he mouthed the words: *but we never made elephants.*

We crouched in mesmerised silence, our hands just barely touching, as though needing physical reassurance that, yes, this was real.

After what felt like an age, the robotic matriarch and her flesh-

and-blood wards heaved away into the deepening shadows. Overhead, the crooning ululations of a currawong ribboned through the sky.

Suddenly, a flurry of screeches filled the air as lorikeets fled the nearby trees, followed closely by a thunderous crashing through the undergrowth. Another shape loomed—not proud and protective, but snarling with confusion and rage. I saw a blur of dark brown fur, felt Evan's hands shoving me aside, heard his cry of surprise and a horrifying *smash* that echoed through the scrub. Plastic shards sprayed across the dried leaves and Evan collapsed, a melon-sized chunk torn from his abdomen.

The enraged bear rounded for a second blow and I threw myself in its way, fumbling for the flare-gun at my belt.

Foom.

A blinding globe of crackling purple threads struck the bear in the chest and the creature reeled back, roaring with pain. My gaze snapped from the unlaunched flare in my hands to a figure standing ten metres away, a device resembling a flame-thrower slung over his shoulder. The bear changed direction with terrifying speed, charging at the newcomer. The figure didn't flinch as he sent another electric globe streaking away, striking the bear in the shoulder. With a wounded yowl, the bear crashed away into the scrub.

I staggered over to Evan. "Hey, it's okay. It'll be okay." I pressed my hands to his shattered torso. Sparking wires spilled from the gaping wound, and battery fluid leaked at a sickening speed. If his cortical processor stopped, there'd be no bringing him back. His hard drive would retain his memories, but that's all they'd be: memories. *He* would be gone.

Evan gurgled, his hand searching desperately for mine.

I clutched his fingers. "I'm here."

Leaves crunched and a hand touched my shoulder. "Doctor Alvarez. Doctor Madaki sent me to find you."

My blurry vision travelled up cargo pants and a khaki T-shirt, resolving a vaguely familiar face.

"Prometheus?"

"We need to get Mister Evan back to the bunker."

We carried him together through the sinking light. By the time we reached the bunker, Min was already waiting pensively by the hatch, accompanied by another familiar figure.

"Hey," Jaya nodded, her eyes quickly taking in the situation. "This way."

We rushed down a warren of concrete corridors, past bustling figures and the scent of fresh sap and damp fur. We laid Evan on a metal bench in a cluttered workshop.

"We need to do a battery bypass," I said. "And stabilise his processor … We need …"

Jaya's matter-of-fact manner was mingled with sympathy. "The structural damage is too extensive."

"What about—" I grasped at phantom straws. "What about an ejection transfer? Evan, can you still trigger one? We just need a blank cortex—"

"They're almost impossible to come by," said Min softly.

"Use mine," said Prometheus. "If Mister Evan can initiate an ejection transfer, he can overwrite my cortex on the fly."

My heart twisted in my throat. "We wouldn't be able to recover you."

"I was designed to help."

But Evan shook his head. "I won't let someone else die in my place. You taught me better than that."

In a moment of stricken selfishness, I wished that I'd made him a fraction less kind. But the truth was, *I* hadn't made him that way. *He* had. He was generous and selfless despite my influence, not because of it. And in the end, his flaws paled in comparison to mine. My hubris, my righteousness, my carelessness of him. I'd been so obsessed with creating someone authentic, someone *real,* that I'd dismissed the importance of making him robust, resilient, and, perhaps, happy.

"I'm sorry," I said quietly. "I should have made you stronger."

His hand squeezed mine weakly. "You did. Every day. And I hope I did the same for you."

As the light in his eyes grew dimmer, I wondered if the whooping cranes had felt this desolate as their numbers dwindled, and whether, in this ruined world, they'd wished to be revived at all.

"What about the egg downstairs?" ventured a small voice. A six-year-old girl peered out shyly from behind Min, her curly brown hair tied back with a jumper wire.

"Elle." Min stroked her daughter's cheek. "It's not the same kind of processor."

Jaya's fingers drummed once on the metal bench. "But the cortex is blank. It might work, or it might corrupt his code. Given our options, it's worth a shot."

We carried Evan deep into the entrails of the bunker, to a sterile chamber containing a single object: a metal sphere the size of a beach ball, its surface intricately etched with enigmatic whorls.

"It's a prototype for a nanomorphic multiform," said Jaya. "After seeing what you did with self-replicating nanotech and ignition cortices, Buckley and I had some ideas … But it isn't finished, and it wasn't designed for Evan's neurological programming."

"It doesn't have arms," bleated Evan. "Or legs."

My chest tightened as I looked from his failing body to the alien sphere.

"Not yet." I offered him a flicker of a smile. "Did you want to give it a go? I'll be right here."

Fear shone in his eyes, but he finally returned the smile.

"See you soon," he said, and his blinks grew slower until his eyelids fluttered shut.

I cradled him as the grinding noises in his body sputtered out, one by one, until all I held was a shell of ravaged plastic. I glanced at the motionless sphere, and Jaya's fingers darted across her data pad.

"The transfer is complete," she said. "But keep in mind, he wasn't coded for this device. He might not …"

"When will we know?"

"I'm not sure, but he's not in distress. If he's not compatible, his code will stay dormant. Like being asleep."

I tried to find comfort in her words as I kept my melancholy vigil. They took Evan's body away—I didn't ask what would happen to it. We no longer lived in a wasteful world, and I hoped his parts would be reincarnated as birdhouses and flowerpots.

I settled on the floor, my back against the cold, silent sphere. "Hey, Evan. Let me know when you want to go, okay?"

That evening, Min dropped by with a tray of steamed spinach and fresh potato mash laced with olive oil and salt.

"It's my fault for calling you here," she said.

I shook my head and gave a wan laugh. "We saw an elephant."

Wisps of pride and guilt fleeted across her features. "After the fallout, a few others and I salvaged what we could from the labs. We went to your warehouse. The research was all still there …" She hesitated. "That's what we've been doing here. My team's been bringing back the animals we've lost. Jaya and Buckley's team are making robot parents for them, to show them what it means to be a kakapo or an elephant or a whooping crane. We wanted you to see what you'd helped to create."

"I think Rhys would have a breakdown."

"Actually, he's joining us next month. We've made a proper mess of this world, and it'll take a while to clean up. Possibly forever. But if we can do some good every day, then every day makes the world a little better."

"Still a pragmatic idealist." A memory tugged my hand to my pocket, and I pulled out a wad of rumpled fabric. "Evan made these for you and Felicity. Happy anniversary."

With a smile that had lost some of its lustre but none of its determination, Min left to grieve in her own way. And I continued to wait. Prometheus checked in several times, offering cups of chamomile tea and buckwheat biscuits, which I gratefully accepted. As it turned out, he and several of his compatriots had urgently extricated themselves from Winthrop's Opulence Bunker when they'd learned that surplus androids were being dismantled to build hot-tubs.

Galadrielle—or Elle for short—peeked in briefly, leaving me with a bowl of sweet midgen berries and a colourful drawing of two stick-figures riding a pair of triceratops. I wasn't entirely sure if the picture was a fanciful daydream or her research proposal.

I remained by the inert sphere all night, all the next day, and the night after that. I sometimes chatted to it, sometimes sat in companionable silence. I told it about the new solar island being launched off the coast of New Venice, and reminisced about the cockatoos at the warehouse and their brazen birdseed heists.

You should take a break, Jaya said. *We'll let you know if—I mean when—he regains consciousness.*

I'm fine, I said. *I'd like to be here when, if, he wakes up.*

On the eleventh night, I stirred from restless dreams to a faint humming against my skin. The sphere looked no different, but as I rested my fingertips on the surface, I felt it shivering.

"Evan? Can you hear me?"

I held my breath, my heart clenching with undeserved hope. The sphere shivered again, and a barely perceptible ripple passed over its surface. Then, on its side, two small bulges appeared, followed by a furrow underneath. The bulges blinked open.

Eyes.

And the furrow wobbled.

"Harrghloo?" it croaked.

"Evan! I'm here."

The eyes rotated this way and that, not quite in unison.

"I can't move … I feel strange. Do I look strange?"

Something between a laugh and sob crawled up my throat. "You look like a hopeful pomelo."

Evan's new eyes blinked rapidly, as though trying to draw the world into focus.

"I want to see the sky. Can we go outside?"

He was too heavy for me to carry, so we rolled carefully out the cargo hatch and into a grassy clearing. The midnight sky was dense with stars, hemmed by the sinuous branches of the eucalypts.

"Oh …" breathed Evan. The sphere shivered again, new buds elongating into tentacles that became a pair of arms and uneven legs. The ball continued to pinch and swell until it took on the slightly molten form of a scrawny, lopsided figure.

Evan reached a hand upward, as though he could strum the chords of distant galaxies, and a smile spread across his face. His brow furrowed in concentration, and two nubs sprouted from his back, growing rapidly before unfurling into a pair of broad, silver-plumed wings.

He gave a delighted laugh. "An upgrade!"

I watched the moonlight drift across his silvery skin. "A metamorphosis. You're not better than you were. Just different."

"I can fly. I think that automatically counts as an upgrade." He gave his wings an experimental flap, as though he might launch into the starry expanse. Abruptly, his smile faltered as apprehension seized him, and he swayed, shrinking inward like a frightened spider.

"Hey." I touched his arm lightly. "There's no hurry."

Embarrassment flushed his features. "I'll try again tomorrow." He gazed out at the dissolving edge of night. "Will you come with me?"

"You bet."

The world would continue to change, and we would have to change with it. Species would come and go, and perhaps come again.

Civilisations would rise and crumble and implode, perhaps to stir once more in the aria of calling waves and singing constellations. And in the end, all we'd have to remember them by would be frozen chunks of amber time, silhouettes in stone, and their stories.

As the promise of another day pulled us onward, chiaroscuro magpies warbled their husky melodies. And beneath the murmuring leaves of a melaleuca tree, two silvery stick insects held each other gently as dawn brushed the fading stars.

About *The Birdsong Fossil*

The Birdsong Fossil was Aurealis Award-shortlisted for Best Science Fiction Novella, and Washington Science Fiction Association Small Press Award-shortlisted for Short Fiction.

The Birdsong Fossil was first published in *Multispecies Cities: Solarpunk Urban Futures* (World Weaver Press, 2021), edited by Christoph Rupprecht, Deborah Cleland, Norie Tamura, Rajat Chaudhuri and Sarena Ulibarri.

NARAKA CALLING

There is no shame in feeling fear, as long as your courage is greater.

I can feel my mother's last words wrapped around my heart, protecting me from the wintry glares and bitter whispers. Flecks of ice flutter from the sky as my father and I leave the Archive of Farewells, surveillance drones humming overhead, with their huge dragonfly eyes. Beneath our feet, obsidian stairs fan out into the desolate square, and my father grips my hand as we pass the sparse smattering of other mourners. A soldier dressed in dark grey uniform gestures curtly to my father, who crouches briefly to my eye level, looking as though he wants to offer words of comfort, to reassure me that he's still here.

"Shoux, speak to no one. Good lad," he says instead.

My father hurries towards the soldier, holding up his mourner's permit, and I wait for him with my hands tucked into my undersized coat. The textile software hasn't been upgraded in years, and the heating elements failed several winters ago. I notice a girl in a fawn cloche staring at me, her long brown hair fluttering like moths. She strides across the slick black stones and stops almost toe-to-toe with me.

"My mother says your mother was wicked to say such terrible things about Prime Executive Sovril."

She leans in close, and my eyes widen to see the portable jammer in her coat pocket.

"I think she was brave," she whispers.

My father's instructions evaporate, my veins burning with the memory of my mother's dignified ferocity in the courtroom, both behind the bench and in the dock.

"You're talking to me," I say, "which makes *you* brave."

She smiles, holding out a green-mittened hand.

"I'm Malina."

* * *

Twenty years crawl past in the shadow of watchful eyes and wordless warnings. I teach an increasingly distorted curriculum to frighteningly pliable minds, and I can't help but feel that my silence sullies the memory of my mother.

One day, I tell myself. *One day my courage will outweigh my fears.*

It's midwinter when Malina and I wed in an abandoned library, the rotting shelves long emptied of contraband books. Watery light sifts through the broken windows, stumps of stained glass casting rainbow glimmers across the walls.

Our application for a procreation permit was denied, and I suspect the Genetics Board is determined that my mother's line should end with me. I brush away melancholy thoughts and kiss Malina's hands, but she catches the flicker in my eyes.

"Perhaps next year," she says. "The Board might look more favourably on our application if I resign from the network—"

"No. You've earned your position, and if real change takes hold, it will be because of voices like yours."

She smiles, her fingers curling around mine. "Change *is* coming. Even now, there are sympathetic officials, administrators, doctors …"

I see that bright, fierce light in her eyes, and with a flicker of hope and a stab of dread, I realise that some things never change.

* * *

Two years later, Malina never saw the sniper.

This time, there is no hollow trial, no visit to the Archive, no hawkish observers stalking my snowy footsteps.

Just a single shot through the newsroom window.

I have no time for grief, just a desperate midnight dash down the abandoned freight tunnels, with my daughter—our daughter—Allie, bundled in my arms. A thousand regrets take bloody bites from my mind, but I force myself to focus on the future. Only the future matters now.

My father comes with me as far as the flooded junction.

"She's barely weaned," he says.

"She already has teeth—"

"You realise 'teeth' is plural. Shoux, she might not survive …"

"Anywhere is better—" My voice cracks. "Anywhere is better than here."

My father looks as though he wants to plead with me, or hold me tight in his arms the way I always wished he would. Instead, he turns his face away, self-consciously adjusting his hat, not wanting me to remember him this way—heartbroken and old—his face bubbled and slack from the genetically targeted viruses.

"You hold onto her," he says.

I gently grasp my father's brittle fingers, wringing one final handshake from him.

"I'll send word to you once we arrive."

I turn towards the steel cenote, and kiss the golden glass pendant hanging at my neck—a present from Malina on the day she proposed. It's all I have left of her now.

Almost all.

I seal Allie inside the submersible pod, and it feels as fragile as a reed basket. Wrapping my arms firmly around it, I take a deep breath, and plunge into the dark waters.

* * *

We make our rendezvous, and cross the sulphurous seas, our overcrowded boat listing perilously. Mutant Humboldt squid drag people from the deck if they stray too far from the central huddle. I swaddle Allie close to my chest, trying to shield her from the acrid spray and the massive, grasping tentacles.

By the time we lurch to shore, the hull is a corroded fretwork, and we wade through clouds of stinging jellyfish to reach the windswept beach. Exhaustion overwhelms every thought, every feeling, except the sensation of sand beneath my torn feet and the warmth of my daughter in my trembling arms.

Dehydrated and burning with fever, I barely care that the arms I stagger into are wearing uniforms—blue and white.

* * *

Allie spends her first birthday at the Undocumented Arrivals Processing Facility: a cluster of flat-pack dormitories and draughty shower blocks. Troublemakers haunt the latrines, and I soon ally myself with other survivors with young families. We take turns minding our scant belongings and accompanying our children to the bio-waste recycling hubs. More than once, I hear the muttered complaint that we can explore distant planets, but we can't stop toilets from clogging up. I suspect the answer has less to do with technology and more to do with political priorities.

The terrain in the facility is barren and rocky, but a few stubborn individuals attempt to grow taro and snow peas in the narrow seams of dirt between the dormitories. The boundaries of the compound are marked by bright yellow signs depicting stick figures convulsing. A friendly reminder of the neuro-paralytic beams that encircle our restricted world.

I suppress a prickle of cold fear when Allie celebrates her second birthday here, our application for residency still marked "In Processing". The other adults and I have saved up our puddings for a makeshift cake, and we valiantly sing—in a mishmash of tongues— what I assume is "Happy Birthday". Allie doesn't sing along, but spends most of the party staring at a blank-eyed boy with scarred wrists.

When the evening buzzer finally echoes down the corridors, Allie waves goodbye to the other children.

"Lock down," she pipes.

"Lock down," they wave back.

As the blank-eyed boy passes wordlessly, Allie toddles forward and wraps him in a hug. I peel her away gently, making apologetic sounds to the boy's mother as she leads her unresponsive son back to his bunk.

That night, after lights out, I sob silently into my sleeves. I imagine Allie growing up here, growing old here, caged in this grey crate, forever waiting for the life I promised her to begin.

* * *

It's another year before we're released from the stark purgatory of the processing facility. Allie grips my hand as we step out of the train and into the fresh autumn air, her feathery brown hair stirring in the breeze. Clutching our "Citizens' Welcome Pack", I wander down the bustling promenade in a daze, overwhelmed by the gleam of the glassy habitation towers, the colourful chaos of the street markets, the flood of unfamiliar scents and chatter. My throat knots at the realisation that we're here. We're finally *here*.

Allie stares up at the maze of velocity passenger-tubes, the clouds sweeping billowing forms behind the hanging gardens. I can see her searching for the yellow signs marking the boundaries we cannot cross.

"Where are we?" says Allie, her sunken eyes bright with awe.

"Home," I say.

* * *

I spend the next few years unclogging cleaner-bots and taking night classes on regional languages. Allie studies even harder than I do, working her way from the bottom of her class to somewhere involving regular certificates emblazoned with encouraging cherries and pomegranates.

For a long while, I still flinch at every delivery drone, my heart skipping a beat at every shadow at the window. But I'm swept forward by Allie's enthusiasm for seeing everything, learning everything, as though her years at the processing facility have left her starving for the wonders of the universe.

We help each other with our homework, poring over cramped screens late into the night, sustained by sesame buns and hot tea. On weekends, we visit the public library, slipping into the Reels Room to watch documentaries about huge prehistoric crocodiles, or the progress of distant space probes, or the first interdimensional portal. Our tiny residential pod soon becomes cluttered with beakers, seashells, potted plants and colourful treasures from the charity store.

I eventually earn a tutoring position at the Linguistic Assimilation Centre, and by Allie's eighth birthday, I can afford to take her to the Light Gallery, located in the Aspiration District.

She races through fantastic holographic landscapes, and gapes at mesmerising photon sculptures. We explore worlds of invisible figures revealed by absent raindrops, and colossal dromaeosaurids snapping at the moon.

As I enter another chamber, my stomach lurches and I stumble backwards, heart pounding. A mass of tentacles churn and grasp from the sea below while panicked figures flap across the sky. Arms outstretched, they grip fragile paper fans, the folds inked with calligraphic plum trees and finches. Beside me, Allie gently takes my hand.

"Look, Dad." She points up towards the fluttering figures, but her gaze reaches beyond them, to encompass the sea of stars and swirling galaxies.

"Look at the explorers," she breathes.

Later, in the gift shop, I buy her a shamefully overpriced holodisc. She taps the glassy surface, and a miniature version of the light sculpture blooms into life: a dark orb studded with pinpricks of light, speckled with tiny, ragged figures, flying their way precariously over a sea of oily tentacles.

"They're brave, Dad," she says, "just like you."

* * *

I was ever a hero in my daughter's eyes, and so I hide my frailties and insecurities from her as best I can. Still, it nearly breaks me when Allie tells me that she's leaving. Not leaving the city, not leaving the country, not even leaving the planet.

She's leaving the dimension.

"It's an excellent position for an interdimensional astro-epidemiologist," she says, pushing more jam scrolls onto my plate, as though a sugar coma will ease the news.

"There are jobs here—" I say.

"That's the thing about being an interdimensional astro—"

"But why there? They call it Naraka, after the worst realm of hell—"

"The official designation is Pteracomia PTXC835, and the locals call it Kyxsktch, which translates to 'place of abundant scraps'."

"They have liquefying viruses over there—"

Allie is quiet for a moment.

"That's why they need us, Dad."

In the end, I don't beg her to stay. The more difficult I make our parting, the less inviting I make her return. I long to hold onto her and never let her go, but instead, I say:

"Make sure you bring enough toilet paper."

* * *

I wait for Allie to call. Meanwhile, my job at the Linguistic Assimilation Centre, my afternoon walks in the eyrie gardens, my audiobooks about curious alien customs—they are the homogenous packing between the moments I live for, the times when I hear her voice.

Interdimensional slots are expensive, but she always calls twice a year. She tells me of sapphire skies full of sentient smoke, and coral castles rising from tarry seas. She sounds exhausted, but happy, and I want to tell her how proud I am of her, but I fear it will encourage her to stay.

In harrowing nightmares, I imagine her trapped on worlds seething with giant scorpions or smothered by rogue nanobots turning everything into lint. I imagine my little girl trying to outrun huge scuttling arachnids, fleeing ravenous mechanical armies, trying to get home to me.

Three years into her assignment, she manages to return for a visit. Her skin is freshly scrubbed and she's buffed her ragged nails, but it's still shocking to see the pocks and scars on my daughter.

"We're making progress," she says.

She talks animatedly about the bustling clinics they've opened, the local teachers they've trained, the vaccines they're developing.

And the people she's met.

"His name's Hurkth," she says. "He's a little bit chitinous, but he loves Emily Dickinson almost as much as you do. I think the two of you would get along."

She shows me a photo of her and Hurkth, and he doesn't look

like something I would want to hug.

"He looks … resilient," I say. "Do I get to meet him?"

Allie tells me he's unable to visit our dimension—something to do with fundamental differences in oxygen and gravity and invisible forces that I don't understand. I can't help but think that if our dimension is harmful to him, then surely his dimension is harmful to Allie. But she just laughs, and says she's much stronger than him.

"Next time I call, I'll get Hurkth to say 'hello'," she says.

* * *

The following year, she doesn't call. There are troubles in Naraka, and Allie's planet loses several communications hubs to nano-shrapnel attacks. She manages to flick a skip-stone message across the portals to me.

My sector is safe. Concentrating on our work. Much love, Allie.

She has scribbled a picture of three jam scrolls, letting me know not to worry. Before leaving, she told me that I only needed to be concerned if the rating rose to ten jam scrolls. I fret regardless, and vow that if it reaches eight scrolls, I'm going to Naraka to get her. Liquefying viruses be damned.

The days stretch endlessly, and I wonder if Malina would be ashamed of me, growing a paunch and decomposing slowly on my diet of holovids and vintage books. It aches too much to acknowledge how happy she would be for me, for us, for the life we've built without her.

Diederik from the Linguistic Assimilation Centre tells me about his daughter, a geophysicist mining for helium in the Marratus Belt. Akashi from the bakery tells me about her son, an ungrateful neural-idol who only visits her when he has a concert in the local system. I think about my own father, who passed away shortly after Allie and I settled here, as though he'd only held on long enough to see the smuggled holovid of me and Allie in our cosy new pod, complete with goggle-eyed chameleons printed on the curtains.

I think about distance. And I think about family.

*　*　*

Five years pass before Allie visits again, and she tells me that the situation has vastly improved. The intergalactic conflict has fizzled into "mostly fragmented civil wars", and her organisation has established locally-run branches in eight sectors. While it remains a constant struggle, mortality rates are slowly decreasing, and education levels are rising.

She slides half a jam scroll onto my plate, and half a wholemeal scone. "You shouldn't have so much sugar."

"What's the point of a scone if it's wholemeal?" I say.

I notice more scars on Allie this time. Her hair is brushed over one ear to hide the burns. I don't ask her if they were caused by a faulty fuel cell or a phoenix-magpie strike or something worse. I merely scoop another serving of fried chilli eggplant into her bowl, and chat about the exo-linguistic courses I've been taking.

For a long time, a part of me hoped she'd be unhappy in Naraka, and that she would return home. After everything we'd endured to reach safe haven, surely it all counted for nothing if Allie simply threw herself into some other kind of hell. But seeing her now, seeing her becoming someone extraordinary, I realise that keeping her here amongst the manicured gardens and syrupy pastries—always less than fulfilled, always watching the stars—*that* would make it all count for nothing.

"So, how's Hurkth doing?" I ask.

"Actually, Dad, we're expecting."

I almost drop the ladle. I want to ask "how?" but I'm afraid she'll answer. I start fussing, fetching a jelly cushion so she can put her feet up, and she clears her throat.

"Hurkth has the brood pouch. The babies are due in five months."

In the silence, the implications sink in. My grandchildren will never be able to come here.

"We'll call," says Allie brightly. "The communications industry is growing so fast there, by the time the kids are in phase-two education, fusion-reality modules should be cheap enough for us both to have them. It'll be just like this."

She reaches over and takes my hands.

I look down at her chapped, callused fingers, and at my bony, spotted hands.

No, I realise. *It won't be just like this.*

I want to hold her, to cradle her close like I did when she was a baby. But I don't want her to see me cry, so I draw away, shifting some of the plates around as though they might get restless.

Before she leaves, I give her a quick, awkward hug.

"Your mother would be proud of you," I whisper.

* * *

I know I won't see Allie again for some time. Raising children is difficult enough without doing it in a partly reformed hell-dimension.

It's almost spring here, and the orange trees are blossoming in their fragrant groves again. The virtual malls are promoting their essential accessories of the season, again. And I sit at the rim of the slowly budding eyrie garden, thinking about courage.

Again.

I wonder, sometimes, if it was brave or selfish of me to flee my homeland instead of staying and fighting. I wonder why some people enjoy peace and tranquillity, while others know only suffering and sacrifice. I wonder if there's any difference between those people, aside from circumstance.

All I know is that some people risk everything in search of freedom, peace, and a safer future for their family.

And some people give up peace and tranquillity in search of suffering and sacrifice. They place themselves in harm's way in the hopes of creating something better, not only for themselves and their loved ones, but for strangers.

And perhaps, sometimes, each group makes the other possible.

Not far from my perch on the rim of the eyrie garden, beyond a hedge of peonies, I see a young man standing contemplatively at his easel. He smiles when he sees me.

"Mister Batau," he nods.

Although the scars on his wrists have long faded, I know what a hard-earned triumph it is that he can stand here today and smile.

"Marek." I return the nod. "How are things at the gallery?"

"Busy. Our annual gala is next week. You should come. How's Allie?"

I consider this, and my torrent of apprehension distils into a complicated truth.

"Happy."

That afternoon, I make an appointment to see Doctor Vanh, and I nod to the virtual receptionist on my way through the translucent foyer.

"Your biosensor readings are fine," says Doctor Vanh, her gaze skimming the readouts. "Your message said you're after some extra vaccinations. Which ones did you want?"

"All of them," I say.

* * *

I put my residential pod on the market, and buy myself a one-way ticket to Naraka.

"Plenty of opportunities there," says the booking agent. "Cheap

261

real estate."

I send Allie a short message, lacking the nerve to speak to her in real-time. Within hours, I receive a voice call from her, and it sounds as though she's trying not to cry.

"Dad, I don't want you to sacrifice everything for me."

I'm not, I assure her. *I think this is for me.*

Standing at the edge of the Whisper Gate, I'm not sure whether I'm brave or selfish. All I know is that despite all my fears, I still have a little courage.

Staring into the smoky red portal, I wonder why they can't make it look friendlier, although Allie once told me it has something to do with physics. My clever girl, my Allie.

I always saw the hungry tentacles. But she made me see the stars.

Hugging my suitcase to my chest, I take a deep breath, and plunge into the mist.

About *Naraka Calling*

Naraka Calling is original to *The Heart of the Labyrinth and Other Stories*.

MORNING STAR

Day Zero
Earth

It was an unremarkable summer morning beneath the cloudless weather domes, when fifty-three thousand residents of the Pacific Hub failed to wake up. Harried medics jetted through the subdued towerscapes, finding no evidence of trauma, no detectable poisons or pathogens. Just the gentle grip of rigor mortis setting in.

The following week, the Mediator of the Southern Mineral Alliance keeled over during a live cloudcast, along with three million of her compatriots. No splinter cells claimed responsibility. Epidemiologists were both horrified and quietly intrigued.

Only one particular man could have known what had begun, but he'd vanished over ninety years ago.

***

Five years after Day Zero
Earth

Ven sprinted through the creaking corridors of the Mariana Base, her wet brown hair falling into her eyes, klaxons melting, embers chasing her down the collapsing steel tube. The water rose hungrily around her shins, and Ven slowed only to seal each door behind her. The boy in her arms made no sound, his thin, olive arms tight around her neck, his face pressed into the shoulder of her faded red flight-suit. The last airlock hissed shut as they entered the cockpit, and Ven buckled the boy into a padded seat imperfectly modified to fit a six year old.

Ven hadn't been trained for scenarios like this. On a bad day, she might have to salvage a busted container of octopus puppets after a tricky re-entry, but today, it wasn't a cargo module clamped to the underside of the *Morning Star*.

Ven's fingers bashed across the black console, and holographic indicators fuzzed into life. The cockpit shuddered, and Ven nosed the ship upward. The domed bay doors were closed, but she had to trust that her colleagues were still alive. Even with the facility disintegrating around them, they wouldn't let her down. That was scientists for you.

Ven swept her fingers up the engine gauge; the cockpit screamed with warnings as the nanocarbon doors loomed to fill the screen. With inches to spare, the metal maw opened and the *Morning Star* slammed into the crush of dark water.

Ven switched to propellers, churning up through the cloudy water column. Colossal squid slammed briefly into the viewscreen before fading back into the bioluminescent twilight. She didn't dare glance at the boy, didn't dare think of her friends in the imploding research station below. The engines whined furiously as they finally broke through the waves and into a smoky red sky.

A mess of gargantuan, holographic screens hung in the sky, blaring static. On the horizon, an ominous glow was intensifying exponentially.

"Oh hell," said Ven.

She swiped every thruster to maximum, hoping the shields would prevent the boy turning into jam. Ven drained the power from every system save the burning blue engines as the light outside swept closer, dissolving the clouds around them. Missiles chased them through the stratosphere, and the ship rocked as one warhead shattered the landing gear. Ven heaved the *Morning Star* back on course, the other missiles falling away as they pulled further into orbit. Below them, a blinding corona rushed across the blue green surface, and the crust of the Earth disintegrated.

Ven sat in silence, then flicked off the viewscreen. She ventured a glance at the boy, who continued to stare at the blank frame. Ven's interactions with children generally left them in tears, but she could hardly make things worse. She unbuckled the ashen boy from his seat, and wrapped a thermal blanket around his shoulders.

"Solomon, isn't it?" said Ven.

The boy nodded mechanically, so Ven continued softly.

"When I was young, a friend told me a story. When the universe was new, the sky was full of suns. But it was too bright, and too hot, so the great coelacanth of the cosmos swam between them, swatting them apart with her massive tail …"

The boy's eyes turned slowly to meet hers, and he blinked solemnly. Ven forged on with her tale of far-flung suns and rivers of stars, haunted by astral dragonfish with moons for lures. When she ran out of story, she continued to hum random tunes, her arms around the boy. He listened wordlessly, and as their tiny blue star sailed further from Earth, the silent void seemed just a little less lonely.

* * *

Ven sagged on her bunk, undressed to a black singlet and shorts. Solomon had finally fallen asleep, or unconscious – she never could tell the difference. Ven rolled her singlet up her stomach, wincing as she prised open the panel beneath her ribs. She'd been meaning to get the latch fixed, but Doctor Josh had been so busy.

"Would you rather be alone?" said a soothing, male voice.

On the monitor beside the copper-alloy door, a light blue sine wave undulated calmly.

"If you're shy, you can avert your sensors, Mike," scowled Ven.

She wedged a fingernail beneath her sternum, and a battery deck ejected with a soft whir. The green bar was illuminated at eighty percent. She should have replaced the battery when she had the chance, but no one seemed to stock legacy tech.

"He's going to notice you don't get older," said Mike.

Ven snapped the panel shut.

"They say men aren't perceptive about those things," said Ven.

"I think you're getting men confused with blind cave beetles."

Ven swiped the data cuff on her wrist, and a holographic star chart bloomed before her. In one corner, a tiny blue green globe turned peacefully.

"Did you watch it, Mike?" said Ven softly.

There was a pause.

"Yes," said Mike. "It's just us now."

Ven lay on the cold bed, staring at the rust coloured ceiling.

"There are still other stations, other ships," said Ven.

"The same kill switch in every human."

Ven sat up icily.

"Sorry," said Mike, his tone unrepentant. "I meant the same chronogenetic species-wide pathology. Only robots have kill switches."

Ven let it go. From what little she knew, Mike35 had every reason to be bitter. When the mysterious epidemic first began, the world had been terrifyingly unprepared. Entire cities were wiped out overnight, and then for weeks, sometimes months, there would be no unusual deaths. Everyone would wonder if perhaps it was over, and then another enclave would succumb.

Frenzied theories gripped the population. Proponents of Malicious Design declared that God had tired of his playthings. The

Army of Souls fundamentalists claimed it was insurrection by the androids, and shortly afterwards unstoppable viruses began burning out mechanical brains.

Mike35 had been the pilot of the Athanas Corporation's executive flagship when it was ambushed by the Army of Souls, just beyond the asteroid mines of Saturn. In the thick of the fire-fight, with his hull ripped wide open, he executed a short-range phase jump directly into Earth atmosphere, but for his five thousand android passengers, it was already too late.

Ven had heard the story from Bester, the maintenance droid she'd befriended at the sea base, but she'd never dared to confirm it with Mike. All she knew was that he hadn't always been Mike35, and his Evolver Intelligence matrix wasn't something generally patched onto cargo ships. She hadn't wanted to part with her old co-pilot, Mike34, but Doctor Josh had promised he would find a good home for him.

Ven stretched, the cable in her right thigh catching a little. Solomon would have seen the cloudcasts of the android retaliation strikes, the bombings and the poisoned waterways. He'd have grown up in a world already polarised along carbon-based lines, and the last thing Ven needed was a co-pilot with baggage. But for all Mike's cynicism, he was as lost as she was.

She glanced at the monitor, and the sine wave dipped a little.

"We can look for survivors, if you want," said Mike. "But they can't outrun time."

"They say Solomon did."

After a pause, the sine wave shrugged.

"We'll see."

* * *

Five years and one week after Day Zero
28 light minutes from Earth

Solomon had adjusted surprisingly well to life aboard the *Morning Star*. He was already demonstrating culinary flair with the nutrient synthesiser, and he'd taken a keen interest in the ship's operations. However, he'd yet to speak a word to Ven, and her attempts to introduce him to Mike had elicited no reaction from the boy beyond polite observation.

Ven persisted in her one-sided conversations with Solomon, chatting as they explored the module beneath the ship together. The *Morning Star* herself was an engine sled, shaped like a deck of cards with fierce blue fusion engines – little more than a cockpit and crib inside. But her undercarriage was designed to slot into a range of modules, transforming her into anything from a research satellite to a space bus. And Doctor Josh and his team had fitted her with a whole new deck.

Everything had been scrounged from parts and patched together, but the *Morning Star*'s new deck boasted a multimedia pod, a medibay, and they'd even kitted the ship with guns.

In case you meet a space kraken, Doctor Josh had said.

Ven inspected the unfamiliar scanners and implements in the medibay. Doctor Josh's colleagues had been studying Solomon, but biology and physics had never been Ven's strengths. Doctor Josh had once brought her to a lecture on quantum physics, and although she'd memorised the presentation, it had meant nothing to her beyond 'something particles, something red shift, something cosmic donut'. The Elucidation-Class androids had looked at her as though she were a wooden duck on a string.

Ven had been the prototype for Doctor Josh's doctoral thesis at Hawking University, and his algorithm for emotional processing had become standard encoding in all autonomous intelligence androids.

His latest opus, just before the first wave of deaths began, had been a vivacious creature with a warm laugh and a flush in her cheeks. In the end, she'd been the one at his side as the world turned to ash.

Ven looked down at her own waxy hand, her fingerprints worn away. Doctor Josh had stopped upgrading her some time ago. Years earlier, he'd removed her wireless interface to repair, and forgotten to replace it.

Ven straightened as a halting tune drifted from the far side of the module. She followed the piano chords to the recreation room, where a mahogany piano had been summoned from the nanomorph panel in the floor. Solomon was playing a wistful piece, which Ven suddenly recognised as fragments of the songs she'd hummed to him earlier. He stopped when Ven entered.

"Where did you learn to play?" said Ven. To her surprise, the boy spoke.

"Doctor Gillian," said Solomon.

His voice was soft, with a texture that reminded her of sandalwood. Ven didn't move, cautious of breaking whatever spell had finally roused the boy to speak.

Doctor Gillian Kagare had been a colleague of Doctor Josh's, and the first scientist to draw a connection between the inexplicable deaths and a hundred year old research paper by the discredited physicist, Arvel Hem. After his disgrace, Hem had taken an experimental spaceship – the *Darwin* – and disappeared beyond the range of Earth's probes, but fragments of his research remained. Primarily as a cautionary tale.

Kagare hadn't been the only epidemiologist to notice that the more genetically homogenous the population, the higher the percentage of fatalities. Countries with xenophobic immigration policies became morgues overnight, while multicultural metropolises lost fractions of their populations at a time. When researchers began to find cases of extended families – separated by continents – dying on the same day, they realised the affliction had a genetic root.

A century before, Hem had hypothesised an interaction between human genetics and the properties of time. He suggested that time was not a featureless constant, but a landscape, with valleys and hills, that could impact upon the expression of genes.

Ven found it difficult to think of time as a substance. The Elucidation-Class androids used to smirk that Ven looked a little like Kagare, but possessed the processor of a pomelo. Ven would never admit that she'd had to look up what a pomelo was.

Doctor Josh had described the hypothesis in terms of Kagare's landmark experiment, in which one hundred lab mice were modified with a human genetic marker, and then left to live out their mousy lives for several generations. On day two hundred and four, all eleven thousand mice died. From the year-old geriatrics to the newborn pups – not one of them woke that day. This was the moment scientists realised that humanity's funeral march had a score.

Shortly after the publication of this study, Kagare found Solomon.

"That's a lovely piece of music," said Ven. "Are you going to give it a name?"

Solomon swiped his hand across the keys, and the piano pooled obediently into a rug on the floor. Ven's heart fell as Solomon padded away across the room, but he returned with a paper-thin display tablet in his hands, which he presented to her.

Sketched on its linen white surface was something resembling a large potato with matchstick arms and legs. Further to the right of the page stood a much smaller, but similarly malnourished potato.

"That," said Ven, "is awesome."

On a screen beside the nanomorph panel, a sine wave snickered softly.

"So awesome, in fact," continued Ven, "it deserves a special place."

Ven pressed the tablet to the wall, and swiped the edge of the device. It emitted a soft click, and when she pulled the tablet away, an imprint of the drawing remained etched in the bulkhead. Solomon touched the dark lines, eyes wide.

"We also have to talk about the matter of birthdays," said Ven seriously. "I'm sure we need to commemorate yours on a regular basis, preferably annually. Do you have a particular date?"

Solomon stared at Ven with equal gravity.

"Do you have a birthday?" said Solomon.

Ven's processor seized briefly.

"Actually, let's not worry about birthdays," said Ven. "How about we celebrate the day we met instead? We can call it Hello Day."

Solomon considered this.

"Hello," he said, and smiled.

* * *

Ven sealed the door to the polyhedral multimedia pod, illuminating multiple screens with a swoop of her fingers. They had supplies to last fifteen years, maybe twenty, but circling this lonely sun was like staying at a party after everyone had gone. A galaxy of broken bottles and stale canapés.

A screen to her left flickered into an agitated blue sine wave.

"You realise that if everyone wasn't dead, they'd have taken the critter off you by now," said Mike.

"You're just sore I tattooed your ass," said Ven.

"I think of it as my bicep," said Mike. "But while you're playing tea parties with Lonesome George, this ship isn't going to fuel itself."

Ven swept her hand across an image, and the chamber filled with stars, as though she were floating in a tank of miniature galaxies.

"We're going to find the *Darwin*," said Ven.

The sine wave almost flatlined.

"Arvel Hem saw this coming a hundred years ago," continued Ven. "If he hasn't already found a solution–"

"Hem was a fraud," said Mike flatly.

"He misappropriated funds–"

"That's kind of what 'fraud' means," said Mike.

Ven paused. Dealing with Mike required patience, and right now, she needed Mike. Plus, he was half right.

Arvel Hem had begun his career as a gifted biophysicist, publishing revolutionary articles on cellular regeneration. However, as his research became more outlandish, he struggled to secure funding. Eventually, he was recruited into the multi-trillion dollar geneceuticals industry, where he spent his time giving sixty year olds the skin of pre-pubescent teens.

Eventually, it was uncovered that Hem had diverted some of these funds into his research on chronogenetics. It was concluded that if he'd lied about the money, perhaps he'd lied about his research too. However, in Ven's opinion, someone who lied to save their child was very different to someone who lied to rob an elderly war hero. At times, the motive behind the lie mattered more than the lie itself. As far as Ven was concerned, there were no such things as liars, only different kinds of humans.

"It's our best hope of finding other survivors," said Ven. "Doctor Josh wants Solomon to have a future."

"You said they didn't give you specific instructions," said Mike.

Ven actually had a little trouble recollecting the details of those final, chaotic days at the sea base. She had the impression the researchers just shoved the boy into her arms and said, 'Good luck.' Years ago, she'd asked Doctor Josh if he might consider upgrading her neutron drive to a particle processor, but he'd shrugged it off with a warm smile.

They don't make drives like yours anymore, he'd said. *Brains like yours were built to last.*

He'd touched her face then with such tenderness that she couldn't bring herself to ask him again. Ven had been the pinnacle of artificial intelligence once, but the crucial word had been 'artificial'. Solomon deserved a life with more than just a simulacrum for company.

"You can pilot a phase drive, can't you?" said Ven.

Ven had double-checked the upgraded schematics for the *Morning Star*, and Doctor Josh's team had installed a compact phase drive. Without it, they would take roughly nine hundred billion years to reach the last known coordinates of the *Darwin*, and Ven wasn't sure if the universe would last that long.

"Hem was a physicist, you know," said Mike finally. "Not an immortal."

Ven suppressed a smile.

"Hem didn't leave on his own."

* * *

Six years after Day Zero
9000 light years from Earth

The first phase jump slung them past the mines of Neptune, and far beyond the solar tides. The second jump sent them streaming through the Sagittarius Arm of the Milky Way, deep into the smoky heart of the Eta Carinae Nebula.

Phase drive technology had been pioneered by Kiruchi Wen, a contemporary of Arvel Hem. She built upon the hypothesis that by hopping out of phase with the universe, and back in at a different point, using an alternate dimension as a shortcut, she could skip around the thorny problem of faster than light travel.

When she couldn't find a pilot crazy enough to test her prototype, she flew the experimental ship herself, zipping out past the heliosphere and returning with only three broken ribs, a mild concussion, and inexplicably, a potted cucumber which hadn't been there when she left.

These days, phase drives were only operated by EI pilots with the equivalent of fifteen doctorates, so Ven was happy to let Mike drive. It gave her time to focus on other things.

She flipped through a file of reports on the medibay terminal. Bloodwork looked fine. Vitamin D was a little low. Bone density could be better. All systems nominal.

"Mike, keep the solar lamps on for an extra twenty minutes per cycle, and increase the gravity in the training room by one point five gees," said Ven.

"Do you think there's something not quite right about him?" said Mike.

"He's fine. I know how humans work," Ven said, checking her bookmark on the section for emergency appendectomies.

"I mean," the sine wave dropped in amplitude, "no one would actually notice if the kid didn't make it …"

"*I* would notice," said Ven firmly.

An awkward silence followed, and Ven turned to find Solomon in the doorway, a satchel over his shoulder, and a laser knife in his hand.

"Could you cut my hair, please?" said Solomon politely.

At times like this, Ven missed her wireless interface – Mike had experimented with flashing binary at her, but her graphics cluster couldn't handle it. To be honest, she preferred talking aloud. It reminded her of being with Doctor Josh.

"Sure," said Ven, and Solomon perched on the bench.

"Can you make it short?" said Solomon. "Like this?"

Solomon tapped his data cuff, and a press clipping of Doctor Josh materialised – the familiar mussed brown hair, his lab coat with the sleeves rolled up. Ven waited until she trusted herself to speak again.

"Of course," she said.

She switched the laser setting to 'Hair', and proceeded to trim Sol's chestnut tendrils.

"Who owns the universe?" said Solomon.

"No one," said Ven.

"Who made the universe?"

"It made itself."

Solomon didn't seem entirely pleased with this answer, and was silent for a while.

"All done," said Ven, shaving the last wayward hairs from Solomon's neck.

The boy ruffled his hair experimentally, then drew a tablet from his satchel, holding it out to Ven.

Solomon's artistic skills had improved. The potato figures now had eyes, and their matchstick arms had sprouted fingers. The small potato still stood a little way from the large potato, but its arm was outstretched, holding the hand of the larger potato.

Ven stamped the new picture proudly onto the medibay wall, and found Solomon staring at her with a troubled expression.

"Do I have a soul?" he said.

"Do you want a soul?" said Ven.

The boy appeared to find this highly irregular, and went to his room to contemplate it further.

"He's a lousy artist," said Mike.

"I think the wonky box in the corner's supposed to be you," said Ven.

"At least I don't have to drink my own pee for the next twenty years. I'm telling you, there's something not right about that boy."

Ven studied the drawing etched onto the wall.

"Then I guess he's in good company," said Ven.

* * *

Eleven years after Day Zero
130 million light years from Earth

There were times when Ven wondered if perhaps they should turn back. Perhaps humanity had survived. Perhaps they had rebuilt. Perhaps Doctor Josh, and Doctor Gillian, and all the Mariana base crew were still alive. Or perhaps, Ven was still dreaming.

Dreams are the music that fill the darkness between being, Doctor Josh had told her the first time she'd woken from one.

Humans dream, replied Ven. *Androids defragment.*

Some humans defragment too, said Doctor Josh conspiratorially. *But you and I, we dream.*

Ven sat in the viewing chamber at the stern of the module. If she needed any evidence that this deck had been created for Solomon, here it lay. Her own eyes could see no better, no worse, than the digital viewscreens of the ship. But the *Morning Star* had been given a window, a floor to ceiling, compressed glass eye to look out upon the universe.

Ven sat on the eucalyptus bench, which may have been appropriated from a park, and gazed at the great pillars of interstellar dust flanking the ship, clouds of ionised gas illuminated by the starlight. Unspeakably complex forms whorled in godlike shapes, as though the *Morning Star* were swimming through a smoky, coral reef. Here, it resembled a pair of streaming silk wings. There, a basin of clouds, filled with a pool of blue sky.

They'd passed another station last week. A mangled wreck like all the others, the last transmission always the same: panicked accusations, rising anarchy, then silence.

Solomon spent little time here, preferring to pass his time in the multimedia pod or the recreation room. He was perhaps twelve now, and had already worked his way through Beethoven, Kanno, and the whalesong harmonies of Oonua.

During his vintage science fiction phase, he'd insisted on being called Solo. When he became engrossed in world music, he'd answer only to Mon. He'd finally settled on Sol, but still spoke very little.

He'd graduated to stick figures, and drew avidly, with doodles in the background that bore an uncanny resemblance to circuitry. Sol still drew himself as much smaller than Ven, although in a few years they'd be the same height. She'd heard that if you handled lion cubs when they were young, they'd grow up imprinted with the idea that you were much larger than they were. So when two hundred kilos of carnivore tried to leap into your arms, they'd seem perplexed when the paramedics were called.

"Tired of this yet?" said Mike.

Ven closed her eyes. Her batteries were down to fifty-six percent, even though she switched to hibernation mode for eight hours per cycle. She topped up through the *Morning Star*'s interface, but the charge never held.

She divided her waking hours between interacting with Sol, performing maintenance on the ship, and poring over Kagare's research. There had to be some mutation, some allele that had singled out Sol, but he seemed no different to any other boy. Which worried her even more.

"There's another station in the Ariadne Cluster," said Ven. "Can you jump that far?"

"They've all been wreckage," said Mike. "The remains of the Minos Base could've fit in a bucket."

"You can eat hydrogen, but we can't," said Ven.

Sol had already consumed half the organic supplies, and he hadn't had his growth spurt yet. Ven sighed.

"Sorry," said Ven. "Any more signals from the *Darwin*?"

"Same direction," said Mike. "Closer together. Their communications technology must have been improving."

When Hem rocketed from Earth in the *Darwin*, he'd been accompanied by eighty-five enthusiastic scientists and engineers, including Kiruchi Wen. They'd continued to send brief messages, telegraphing their coordinates. Authorities tried to scramble the messages, to prevent the corruption of impressionable young scientists, but they found their way onto the skymesh anyway.

I'm looking for a place, said Hem. *Where time is in a different key.*

"Six o'clock," said Mike.

Ven turned to find Sol settling onto the bench beside her. His skin was lighter than when they'd first met, although his green eyes had darkened closer to hazel.

"Are you lonely?" said Sol.

"I have you, don't I?" Ven gave his shoulder a cheerful bump. "Are you?"

He looked at her blankly, as though not understanding the question. There were times when Ven seriously wondered if Sol were a new class of android, except he was definitely growing. Sol turned his gaze to the white cloudy swirls beyond the glass.

"Are you looking for something?" said Sol.

"We're looking for a new home," said Ven.

"Isn't this our home?"

Ven paused.

"Of course," she said.

She wrapped an arm around the boy's shoulders, and they watched the dusty light trickling through the universe.

* * *

17 years after Day Zero
1.3 billion light years from Earth

It was three zero eight on the circadian cycle when Sol passed through the silent habitat corridor, returning to his quarters after a session in the training room. Ven wouldn't rise for another five hours, longer if she thought he was sleeping in. He'd discovered that if he trained when she thought he was sleeping, and then actually slept during operational hours, Ven would rest for more of the day.

A monitor flickered on the wall, and Sol paused, waiting for the computer to address him. However, the sine wave that appeared was not the familiar blue, but a bright red.

"Hello Sol," said the monitor. "This is Mike34, and I have a message for you."

***

17.2 years after Day Zero
1.4 billion light years from Earth

Things were an absolute mess.

"Fire in the hold! Fire in the hold!" Ven yelled.

The oxygen vanished abruptly from the galley, and the flames wobbled into orange globes before extinguishing. Ven slapped hard on the monitor, and air spilled back into the room. She hadn't been designed to function in a vacuum, and she wondered if Mike had forgotten on purpose. He'd been exceptionally tetchy lately.

"How you can set a fire without actually cooking anything is beyond my matrix," said Mike.

"I'm a cargo pilot, not a pâtissière," said Ven.

Mike grumbled about his sooty benchtops, while Ven put the finishing touches on her creation. Today was their twelfth Hello Day, and Sol would be about eighteen now.

Sol had been particularly distant lately, and for the last few months, his only communications with her had been the occasional grunt. She wondered if perhaps he'd outgrown her – he was surely old enough to realise she wasn't human.

"It's just typical guy stuff," said Mike. "I remember my misbegotten youth. You remember the Kalax Summit, when rabid, red pandas rained onto the Gourmet Delegation? That was me." Mike paused. "They took my modem away after that."

"The snip did you good," said Ven.

"Watch it, or I'll blow you out the airlock."

Ven just grinned, and Mike was thoughtful for a while.

"He's turning off the visual surveillance more often," said Mike.

"He's private," shrugged Ven.

Sol had always preferred to perform day-to-day operations manually, rather than asking Mike. She knew it rankled with Mike, and had once asked Sol about it.

In case Mike isn't around one day, Sol had said.

He isn't going anywhere, Ven replied.

Everybody dies, said Sol.

Ven had let the matter drop. According to Doctor Gillian, Sol had been five when his province perished overnight. Every soul within two hundred thousand square kilometres. Everyone but him. It was true, everybody dies. Just usually not all at once.

Ven put down the piping bag, and inspected her work.

"He's been reading a lot about androids," said Mike.

"Like *I, Robot*?"

"Like manuals."

An electric shiver raced up Ven's back, and she forced herself to focus on the misshapen cake before her. She had forgotten to add sugar.

"Mike," she said. "Open the garbage chute."

An unfamiliar voice spoke from the door.

"Is everything alright?"

Sol stood in the doorway, a fire extinguisher in his hands. It took Ven a moment to realise the voice had come from him. It was deeper, more resonant than the voice she knew, and for a brief, aching moment, it seemed to transform him into a stranger. Sol's gaze moved to the plate in her hands.

"Oh, that's cute," he said. At her crestfallen expression, he amended his comment. "I mean, tell me about it."

"When people come of age, they usually have a ritual that involves defeating something," said Ven. "Koalas were supposed to be one of Earth's most vicious animals."

Sol looked at the rotund, grey marsupial cake, with its black button eyes, and large fluffy ears.

"Thank you," said Sol.

He dissected the cake with surgical precision, as though dismembering an actual *Phascolarctos cinereus*. Periodically, he would glance at Ven, and she gave him nods of encouragement – she'd never been to any kind of party, and for all she knew, this was roaring.

At Hawking University, she hadn't been sophisticated enough to mingle with the humans, and the academic androids called her a Brown Dwarf. A failed planet trying to be a star. It wasn't that Ven wanted to be human, it was that she already felt that she was, until sharply reminded otherwise.

In the galley, the cake was conquered and disposed of, and Ven considered the initiation a success.

"Ven," said Sol, suddenly shy. "There's another rite of passage I'd like you to share with me."

"Alright …" said Ven, ignoring the monitor on the far wall, where the blue sine wave had increased dramatically in frequency.

Sol took her hand, and led her to the multimedia pod. He hesitated as they stepped inside.

"It's called a 'prom'," said Sol.

The walls of the chamber melted into a softly lit dance hall festooned with red streamers. Overhead, a slowly revolving glitterball painted the walls with silver stars, and yellow rose petals rained slowly to the floor.

"May I have this dance?" said Sol.

Ven nodded, and did her best to imitate his hold. They swayed slowly to the tune of 'We Three' by The Inkspots, and she found herself resting her head on his shoulder. The music seemed to drift from far away, and Ven realised that this was what a party should be like.

The pod suddenly rocked, and Ven crashed into a wall, the

dance hall vanishing in a crackle of light. Klaxons sounded for a few seconds, then went silent. Ven stopped to check that Sol was unhurt, then rushed to the bridge.

"Mike! Status!" said Ven.

"Hull breach on the starboard module," said Mike. "Hypervelocity meteoroid impact."

"Can you patch it?"

"I'm compensating with the shield, but we've lost cargo bay three."

"We'll need to seal the fracture," said Ven. "How bad is it?"

"Two hundred and forty-seven by five millimetres. Thirty-one metres from the hatch."

Ven swept her hand across the console, studying the blinking red gash on the ship's schematics.

"I'll suit up," said Ven.

"You weren't designed for space walks."

"The *Morning Star* wasn't designed to fly twelve years without a pit stop," said Ven. "Just take care of Sol, okay?"

"Ven–"

"Ultimately, it's what I'm here for–"

"Ven!" snapped Mike. "Sol's just turned off surveillance in corridors nine through sixteen."

Ven glanced at the schematic. He'd blanked out almost a quarter of the lower module.

"Hell no," said Ven. "Mike, seal off corridor sixteen now!"

She skidded down the chute to the module, bolted past the darkened multimedia pod, and slammed into a sealed hatch.

"I said corridor sixteen!" yelled Ven, wrenching at the unresponsive wheel.

Through the porthole in the door, she could see Sol at the inner door to the secondary airlock, already suited up, the panel beside him carefully detached to expose a fretwork of wires.

"Sol!" Ven pounded her fist on the window, but Sol continued to tap and twist at the electronic nerve bundle. "Mike, get this open!"

"Ven, he's–" The sine wave flared and contracted, then the monitor beside Ven went dark.

"Mike? Mike!" said Ven.

On the other side of the hatch, the inner airlock hissed open. Ven knew teenage boys were susceptible to high-risk behaviours due to some kind of interaction between the frontal lobe, the amygdala, and fermented beverages, but this went far beyond riding a wheelie bin down the sky tube. Sol had never worn a counterpressure suit, never had EVA training. Ven wasn't even sure if their microcapsule sealant still worked.

Doctor Josh hadn't entrusted the last human in the universe to Ven only to have him die in a freezing vacuum full of micrometeoroids and searing radiation. But Ven could think of nothing she could do or say to stop Sol. She could only press her hand to the glass.

Sol turned to look at her, and mouthed the words: *It's okay.*

And the airlock slid shut.

* * *

Three hours later, Mike came back online, full of hellfire and expletives.

"I've a mind not to let the brat back in," he snarled.

"He'll just override you again," said Ven calmly from her seat on the bridge. She continued to inspect a set of holographic maps, each hanging at a slightly different angle.

"He can try," said Mike. "I've electrified the access panels."

"Mike–"

"Only four milliamps," said Mike. "You could do more damage with a coconut."

Ven continued scrolling through the charts, trying not to think of Sol clinging to the frozen skin of the ship. She wasn't going to pine by the airlock – she was his friend and protector, not his dog. And they'd lost cargo bay three, so they were down to four years' worth of supplies.

"We've passed a few Earth-like planets that weren't completely hellish," said Mike, his sine wave bristling a little less.

"No landing gear," said Ven.

"You've cruised a few crash landings in your time."

The thought had crossed Ven's mind – find a planet, settle down, let Sol live out his life with some kind of earth beneath his feet. She'd put the suggestion to him years ago, and he'd looked at her with something resembling panic. He'd said simply, 'No, thank you', then locked himself in the multimedia pod for several hours.

Ven swept the glowing charts back into a pinpoint of light.

"Mike, set a course for *Demeter*."

There was a long silence, and Ven glanced at the monitor to make sure Mike hadn't vanished again.

"That's several billion light years away," said Mike finally. "That's billion with a 'b'."

"Your phase jumps are getting better," said Ven. "The distances you're achieving have surpassed even Wen's calculations."

"Don't flirt with me," grumbled Mike. "Odds are *Demeter* met the same combustible fate as every other station. Weapons, humans, and inexplicable deaths are a nasty mix. If we get there and we're out of supplies, the station's a skeletal mess … it'll be like the finale of some terribly depressing series."

Demeter had been Earth's greatest space ark – the first to be equipped with a phase drive. It carried a crew of two thousand plus their families, and had been designed to transform into a space station once it reached its destination at the edge of the mapped universe.

It was the *Morning Star*'s last hope for supplies before they sailed into uncharted territory, chasing the shadow of the *Darwin*.

"Ven," said Mike. "External sensors just came back on."

"Status?"

"Hull breach has been sealed," said Mike. "No sign of life outside."

The door to the bridge slid open, and Sol stood there, rumpled and wan.

"I'm going to lie down," he said.

"Sol," said Ven.

He paused in the doorway.

"On this ship, we're equals, you and I," said Ven. "I want your word that you won't treat me like that again."

Something flickered through Sol's eyes, too brief and complex for Ven to understand, although she would replay it later many times over. A heartbeat passed, then another, and Sol left without a word.

"Course set for *Demeter*," said Mike.

* * *

23 years after Day Zero
3.4 billion light years from Earth

These were the furthest stars grazed by humanity's reach. The *Morning Star* had passed choirs of pulsars, singing out their eulogies, and swum through a dense wall of galaxies, their glittering filaments entangling the dark. But Ven wasn't watching the stars.

The medibay glowed with a hundred holographic slides, all hanging in the air at disordered angles, like a storm of papers frozen in mid hurricane. Ven slid a pale green image of cellular mitosis towards her, comparing it to a magnified model of a mitochondrion.

"I'm sure it has something to do with the mitochondrial DNA," said Ven.

A blue sine wave squiggled across the benchtop monitor.

"Doctor Gillian discounted that in her *Chronoscience Journal* article," said Mike. "We already went over that last month."

Ven rubbed the dust from her lashes.

"That's right," she sighed.

Her batteries had been sitting at twenty-nine percent for a while, but her memory had been getting patchy. *Wear and tear*, she told herself. *Nothing to worry about.*

Sol was twenty-four now, roughly the same age as Doctor Josh when she'd first met him. But Sol was gaunt, and getting thinner by the day. He'd cut his caloric intake the day they'd lost cargo bay three. He meditated a great deal, and encouraged her to join him. They would sit side by side in the viewing chamber: Sol in a state of higher consciousness, Ven in hibernation mode.

"Ven, when was the last time you regenerated your processor?" said Mike.

"I don't have enough free memory."

"Use mine," said Mike, and a panel in the wall slid open.

"Are you hitting on me?"

"I run Solitaire on that server," shrugged Mike.

Ven locked the medibay door, and carefully pried open a small panel in the nape of her neck. She unwound a slender, silver cord and inserted the narrow prongs into Mike's matching socket. Ven closed her eyes, and initiated her regeneration routine.

A loud crackle burst from the wall, and sparks sprayed from the connection. Ven yanked her cable free, and patted out the embers on her shirt. The regeneration routine had aborted, but her processor seemed otherwise unaffected.

"There goes my Solitaire," said Mike. "Did Doctor Josh mess with your programming?"

"No," said Ven defensively, although Doctor Josh had adjusted her processor just prior to launch.

One last tune up, he'd said.

"Sorry," said Ven. "I'll try to pick up a spare server on *Demeter*. What's our ETA?"

"Forty-eight minutes," said Mike.

"Have you taken care of the viewscreens?"

"They're all on streaming loop, and I've closed the viewing chamber for maintenance," said Mike. "All navigational displays indicate we're still two weeks away."

Ven nodded.

"Where's Sol?"

"In the rec room," said Mike.

Ven wound the cable back into her neck, and snapped the panel shut. She couldn't risk another incident like the one six years ago, not with Sol in his current condition.

"Seal him in," said Ven.

For the first time in eighteen years, she strapped on her red flight-suit, methodically checking her comms and data recorders. She paused at a twinge in her right thigh – her quadricep cables were thinning, and she hoped perhaps there'd be spares on *Demeter*.

Preliminary sensors showed functioning environmental systems on *Demeter*, but there'd been no response to their hails. Ven stopped by the viewing chamber, unlocked now that Sol was secure. *Demeter* hung amidst the stars like a black and scarlet hive, studded with open claws that had once snared passing asteroids. The station was intact, and although scans showed no signs of life, they'd picked up odd energy fluctuations.

"He's trying to bypass the lock," said Mike. "You sure you don't want me to zap him?"

"Just stay ahead of him," said Ven.

Ven passed by the rec room, and Sol stopped his frantic rewiring to pound at the porthole in the door.

"I'm sorry," said Sol desperately. "Whatever I've done, I'm sorry."

Ven kept her voice steady.

"I'll be back soon," said Ven. "Don't worry."

Sol saw her flight-suit, and what little colour remained in his face drained completely.

"Mike, you can't let her go," said Sol. "The intruder defence systems could be active, we can't verify the structural integrity of the interior."

The blue sine wave on the wall shifted uncomfortably, but said nothing.

"I'll take care of it," said Ven.

She forced herself to walk away, Sol still pounding at the door. Her earpiece clicked as Sol patched into her comms.

"Let me out! Please don't go! Ven!" His breathing was ragged, and Ven realised that Sol was crying.

Her footsteps faltered, and Sol's voice dropped to a small whisper in her ear.

"Please don't leave me …"

Ven stood motionless. There were choices in life that required judgement, the weighing of necessary evils, of greater goods. Ven had not been programmed with wisdom, and had no way of assessing the psychological damage that would be caused to Sol by leaving him here, versus the physical danger he would be exposed to on *Demeter*.

How do you measure a broken heart, Doctor Josh had asked her one night. He enjoyed asking her odd questions, and never seemed to mind that she didn't understand them. But that night, he'd laughed wonderfully at her response, kissing her on the forehead.

By mending it, she'd said.

Ven tapped the panel beside the rec room, and the door hushed open. Sol staggered out and wrapped his arms around Ven, so tightly she worried that her ribs might bend. She patted him gently on the back.

"We'll go together," said Ven.

So hand in hand, Ven and Sol stepped onto *Demeter*.

* * *

Demeter was a deserted city. Empty schoolrooms waited with rows of silent consoles. Traffic lights cycled slowly, red and green, down desolate transport corridors. Ven and Sol had little trouble locating the supply bays, still neatly stacked with decades' worth of synthesiser packs – carbon, iron, lysine. Unfortunately, there were no spare copolymer cables to be found. *Demeter* had set sail over fifty years ago, before the Eve algorithm awoke a new generation of artificial intelligence, and emphatically euthanased the Turing Test. The only robots here were stout, mechanical droids, with clamps and soldering irons instead of hands.

Demeter had supported a population of almost five thousand, but there were no bodies. No scorched catwalks, no twisted wreckage. Not like the annihilated stations they'd passed before, not like Earth and all her satellites.

By the time Earth's decimated population had fallen to six hundred million, they'd descended into a war – not a war in which there'd be no true victors, but a war in which there'd be no survivors. In the end, it was the Army of Souls who had pushed the button – after all, God would welcome his own. And the androids, well, the joke was on them.

"Mike, tapping you into the system now," said Ven, plugging Mike's transmitter into an active console. The blue light on the device blinked rapidly as he accessed the station logs.

"The first casualties occurred here on the same day as the Pacific Hub – Day Zero," said Mike, crackling through Ven's earpiece. "Captain Tahira put *Demeter* under quarantine protocols … After each wave of deaths, they disposed of the bodies, and closed off more of the station, and …" Mike paused. "They just kept on living until there was no one left."

They hadn't panicked, or descended into anarchy. It had been a calm and dignified extinction, here amongst the stars.

"Because they had no androids," said Ven quietly.

Sol shook his head.

"Humans were wiping themselves out long before androids awoke," said Sol. "Almost everyone on *Demeter* was born out here, with no sky, no sea, nothing but the people who matter, and a profound sense of how marvellously insignificant you are."

Here, at the edge of the map, they had marched proudly into the silence. Ven's gaze traced the population chart as it dwindled, plunge after plunge. She froze as she reached the end of the graph.

"Sol, go back to the ship," said Ven. "Now."

Without another word, Ven sprinted down the corridor, past brightly lit habitation decks, through looming transit archways, and into a wide tunnel of neatly labelled doors.

"Ven, you're almost on top of the energy fluctuations." Mike's voice was barely discernible through the static. "You'd better head back."

Ven slowed, her gaze sweeping the numbers on each door.

"According to the sensor report, the last survivor died *eight months ago*," said Ven.

"Maybe she was immune, like Sol. And she slipped in the bathtub."

"Or maybe Sol's not immune," said Ven, stopping at a door labelled 'Research Pod 482: Mora Sevell'.

The pod bore an uneasy resemblance to the medibay on the *Morning Star*, the walls plastered with images of rotating strands of DNA, the benches overflowing with holographic cells. The one striking difference was the male corpse on the biobed. Fit, in his late twenties, and apparently preserved by the energy field curved over the bed. This was not, however, Mora Sevell.

A pair of boots protruding from behind the crowded bench turned out to belong to Sevell. A silver-haired woman in her early fifties, still dressed in her lab coat, and decomposing very slowly in the sterile environment. She'd literally died at the microscope. Ven peered down the eyepiece, but she may as well have been looking at a piece of abstract art.

"She must have found something," said Ven, straightening up. "She was making the same connections. If only–"

Her words died in her throat. The corpse was gone from the biobed. Ven slapped her data cuff.

"Sol! Tell me you're back on the *Morning Star*," barked Ven.

The door to the lab burst open, and Sol rushed inside.

"What happened?" he panted, taking in the obsessive decor.

There was a barely perceptible *blup*, and the corpse reappeared on the biobed. Sol immediately had a strange, grey device in his hand, aimed at the corpse. After a wary pause, during which the corpse showed no inclination to unnatural activity, Sol holstered the shaver-shaped device.

"We need to get out of here," said Sol.

"Keep the engines running," said Ven. "I have to see what–"

The corpse abruptly flickered out of existence again.

"Experimental equals unstable," said Sol firmly. "And I'm pretty sure that corpse isn't supposed to be doing that."

Ven hadn't wanted Sol to see this, but Sevell had clearly discovered something crucial, if disquieting. All Ven had to do was figure out what it meant.

"Sol, when Doctor Gillian found you–" began Ven.

She wasn't entirely sure what happened next, only that the world swung dramatically, and the floor cracked against her head.

"Ven!" said Sol.

"I'm fine," she tried to say, but a strange crackling noise came from her mouth instead. She tried to get up, but her leg was twisted at an odd angle.

"Don't move," said Sol, his voice tinny and distant. "You've hurt your leg."

Ven's right leg was flooding her with malfunction alerts, but that wasn't her biggest problem. She touched the back of her head, and felt a gap where her panel had smashed off.

Ven tried to swear, but only emitted a feeble beep.

Her vision flickered, and went blank.

***

She stood upon the twilight sand, the ocean lapping at her feet. The salt breeze tingled on Ven's skin, and Doctor Josh was by her side.

"You forgot to leave me instructions," said Ven.

Doctor Josh smiled, warm and attentive.

"You never needed instructions," he said. "Listen."

Ven leaned in, and pressed her ear to his chest. She closed her eyes, and at first, she could only hear the watery lullaby of the ocean, but then, deep in his chest, where there should have been a heartbeat, she heard something like the plucking of a steel comb over a music box cylinder.

***

Ven woke in semi-darkness, a blanket drawn to her shoulders, a familiar ceiling above her. She was in her quarters on the *Morning Star*. Sol lay asleep near her feet, his hand curled around hers.

"Bioharmonics," said Ven feebly.

A blue sine wave perked up by the door.

"You realise you're a bloody nuisance," said Mike, trying to sound irritated.

Sol jolted awake, and started fussing as Ven tried to sit up.

"You had quite a fall," said Sol.

"It's not just the DNA or the RNA or the gene expression," said Ven. "It's the frequency, the rhythm, the pitch of all your cellular functions. Your entire body is a bioharmonic symphony, and yours must be in a different key."

Sevell must have realised the answer lay in the interaction between genetic harmonics and time. If a person's bioharmonics encountered a point in time that possessed conflicting features, they would behave like two frequencies cancelling each other out. The person's bioharmonics would stop, time would simply hiccup and steamroller on. Sevell had tried to modify the bioharmonics of her test subject, and change his frequency on a molecular level. But instead, the entire body had started blinking in and out of the timeline.

"We can discuss it later," said Sol. "You need to recuperate."

Ven's right leg felt slightly discorporate, and she concentrated on reconfiguring her software to incorporate the altered circuitry.

"Sol fixed your leg," said Mike.

Ven paused. "How …?"

"He stripped the copolymer cables from my left nacelle," grumbled Mike. "I'm only half a ship now."

Schematics raced through Ven's mind.

"But the phase drive–"

"We don't need it," said Sol.

"I don't need to walk," protested Ven. "I can splint my leg and put a wheel on it. I've seen them do it with goats."

"You're not going to squeak around like some creepy goat," said Mike. "You're outvoted on this one, Captain."

Ven swallowed her response. If Sevell was right, Sol might not be immune from the chronogenetic pathology. He could be in a different key, but he might just be an octave higher, like Sevell herself. But if Mike and Sol were in agreement on something, she'd keep her peace for now.

"When did you first realise I was an android?" said Ven.

"Doctor Gillian told me," said Sol.

Ven smothered an internal groan.

"All that time I spent pretending to eat was for nothing?"

"I thought it was sweet," said Sol, squeezing her hand.

Ven stood up tentatively, and slowly shifted her weight onto both legs.

"Thank you, Mike," said Ven.

She looked from the smooth blue sine to the gaunt young man, and understood how five thousand souls could so calmly face their end. It was never about how long you had, but how you spent it, and more importantly, who you spent it with. The *Darwin* was surely beyond their reach now, but perhaps that had never been the point.

"Where to now?" said Ven.

The sine wave took on a cocky slant.

"I can't jump with one nacelle," said Mike. "But I can still hop."

And in a burst of fusion blue, they left the grave of *Demeter* behind them.

* * *

31 years after Day Zero
4.2 billion light years from Earth

The messages had stopped.

They received the last pulsar telegraph from the *Darwin* three years ago, from deep within the Lemara Supercluster. The communiqué had indicated they were running low on supplies, but Hem was confident they were closing in on their destination. It had been date-stamped eighty-seven years ago.

The *Morning Star* had continued on course, but Ven was beginning to wonder if perhaps Hem's crew had succumbed to a fate more mundane than that which had claimed Earth.

Her battery was down to three percent, and she was hibernating twenty hours per cycle now. She'd turned off her dreaming routine, and only switched on her cutaneous thermal systems when she performed Sol's routine medicals. He looked a few years older than her now, perhaps thirty-two, and he'd grown into a lean and athletic figure. He'd never be particularly broad, but he'd recovered dramatically from the years of near starvation.

Ven frequently forgot to schedule his checkups these days, and he performed most of them himself.

Everyone's forgetful sometimes, said Sol.

But it wasn't just absent-mindedness – every thought had become slower, and she seemed to occupy a smaller and smaller corner of her mind. As though the growing darkness were crowded with intangible, immovable clutter. It reminded her of a story, something to do with two brothers and a tower of decaying newspapers.

Ven sat on the floor of the viewing chamber, scrolling through empty charts. There were no stars in the Xunek Void, save the occasional dying sun. If the *Darwin* had come this way, it wouldn't have reached the other side. The silence on every channel was damning, and Ven let her data cuff fall to the floor. She'd led them to a graveyard, chasing a ship of fools.

Ven stared into the darkness, her thoughts creaking ever slower. She blinked.

"Mike, what's that?" she said.

"Dust," said Mike. "We passed a small nickel-iron asteroid a while back."

"No, *that*," said Ven, pointing to a tiny orb of darkness that seemed a slightly different shade. "Change your heading."

"There's no way your puny eyes are better than my long range–"

"Now!" snapped Ven.

The *Morning Star* turned, and the blue sine wave on the wall increased in frequency.

"I've just picked up a reading for something that wasn't there a moment ago," said Mike. "I think we–"

The small, dark silhouette suddenly flashed, flooding the viewing chamber with a blinding green light before subsiding. Just metres beyond the pane of glass hung a metal sphere the size of a soccer ball, ringed with emerald light.

"A shielded proximity beacon," said Ven, and she ran to the bridge.

She found Sol at the communications console, already poring over the transmission.

"The *Darwin*?" said Ven.

Sol nodded, moving aside to give her a closer view. The hologram was a jumble of squiggles and circuitry, swimming with symbols that seemed vaguely familiar. However, if she'd once known what they meant, they were lost to the crowding dark now.

"Hmm," said Ven, studying the schematic.

"Co-ordinates," said Mike. "And instructions for modifying the phase drive."

Ven traced her finger through the threads of light.

"The key," she said. "They found the door, and converted the phase drive into a key."

"I think I can make the modifications …" said Sol, his gaze moving methodically over the intricate hologram.

Ven sensed his hesitation, and she looked down at her leg.

"We only have one nacelle," said Ven.

The copolymer cable would be too worn to rethread into Mike's engine.

"I can do it with one," said Mike.

Sol was very still.

"If we reduce the mass of the ship, it might work," he said quietly.

"It'll work," said Mike firmly.

Ven glanced from Mike to Sol, feeling that she had missed something important.

"Why don't you get some rest?" said Sol gently. "I'll have this working in no time."

* * *

They pushed their bunks through the airlock. They detached the lockers from the walls, pried the panels from the bulkheads, and Sol tossed out all his clothes save the dark blue flight-suit he'd made years ago. Finally, they detached the module from beneath the *Morning Star*, and watched it sail away into the starless night.

This would be their final jump. But instead of jumping out of phase, and then back in, they would jump out, and remain in the alternate dimension. This kind of thing had been tried before – Kiruchi Wen herself had conducted experiments using plants and small robots, but the general result had been 'boom fizzle blat'. Ven hoped that Wen had fine-tuned this during her thirty year voyage.

Ven woke without realising she'd fallen asleep. Sol was tucking a blanket around her shoulders.

"Why do we still have a blanket?" said Ven blearily, trying to sit up on the floor of the cockpit. She glanced at her data cuff. "How long was I out?"

Sol wrapped his arms around her, and lifted her into the pilot's seat. He was trembling slightly.

"Something wrong?" said Ven.

Sol shook his head, and smiled, but there was something wrong with his smile. Ven tried to focus, but her processor was circling helplessly in its tiny speck of light.

"The phase drive will burn out after the jump," said Sol gently. "I've constructed an automated beacon, which will start transmitting as soon as you stabilise on the other side."

Ven's awareness gripped a passing word.

"You mean 'we'," said Ven.

"Of course," said Sol, buckling Ven's seat belts into place.

Ven grabbed Sol's wrist.

"Mike, report!" said Ven.

"Mike–" There was a note of warning in Sol's voice.

The blue sine wave seemed to twist and distort.

"Oh, to hell with the both of you!" snapped Mike. "I'm sick of taking orders. Ven, we're still over the limit by sixty kilograms. Sol, you're not going to throw yourself dramatically out the airlock. I'm taking charge of this mission."

Sol's eyes widened, and he lunged for the console. A deep click reverberated through the cockpit just before he reached it.

"Problem solved," said Mike.

Ven stared at the blinking red motif on the console.

"You ejected your backup server," said Ven dully. On the viewscreen, a sixty kilo cube of particle matrix floated away.

"I'm not going to need it," said Mike.

Sol turned angrily to the calm blue sine.

"It might have survived!" he said.

"What do you mean 'might have'?" interjected Ven.

Sol was abruptly silent again.

"The energy from the jump," said Mike. "It'll burn out every particle processor on the ship."

Including Mike's. Ven felt suddenly woozy, and she struggled to unbuckle the harness from her hips.

"Change of plan," she said, rising from her seat. She promptly collapsed again.

Battery: Zero.

* * *

Sol finished securing Ven in her seat again, and rose to his feet. He'd managed to restore a little of her charge, but he wasn't sure if it was enough. Sometimes people didn't wake up again. Sometimes everybody died. But sometimes, after the smoke and the sirens and the disintegrating earth, sometimes if you were lucky, there came light, and stillness, and a story about a great big fish.

"You'd better buckle up," said Mike. "We're aligning with the co-ordinates now."

Sol pulled on a pair of insulated rubber gloves, and prised open a panel.

"What are you doing?" said Mike.

Sol pushed his hand through the crackling forcefield that protected the circuitry.

"Mike," said Sol. "My name is Solomon Degarre, and I have a message for you."

Sol pulled a blood red lever, and the *Morning Star* went dark.

* * *

The cabin was dim, a solemn twilight, as though the world were about to sleep.

"Sol?" said Ven weakly.

"I'm here," said Sol, an indistinct shadow in the seat beside her.

"Mike?" said Ven.

"He's busy with the countdown," said Sol. "Don't worry, just try to stay awake. Do you remember the time Mike swooped into the atmosphere of the planet with the purple mountains, and let us open the airlock for a minute? Or the year we rearranged 'Ode to Joy' entirely for percussion, and Mike threatened to flood the ship with radiation?"

Foggy impressions swam just out of focus – glittering violet snow, the joyous beat of drums. Ven concentrated on inching from one moment to the next.

"I didn't always make the best decisions …" said Ven.

"You're only human," said Sol.

"I don't have a soul," said Ven.

She'd tried to be a good companion, but she could never take the place of all the friends he'd never had, all the mentors, lovers and confidantes that could have eased his journey. Because no matter how real she felt, she could never make that one, final step to being truly human.

"Sentience, not genetics, forms the foundation for your spirit," said Sol, as though it were a subject he'd pondered deeply. "A soul isn't something bestowed upon you, it's something you grant yourself. And in the end, Ven, you are all that's best of humanity."

Something ached sharply in Ven's chest. His words seemed familiar, striking a chord with something in the crowding dark.

"Sol …?" Ven's vision was fading. "Did you know what Doctor Josh wanted?"

She felt Sol's hand wrap around hers.

"Ven," said Sol. "The directive was never about protecting *me*."

The cockpit began to thrum, and bright blue energy flowed through the circuitry, enclosing the cabin like a lacework cage. With her seat shuddering violently, Ven turned to face the monitor on the wall.

"Mike …"

"See you on the other side," said Mike.

And Ven wondered why it was that a red sine waved goodbye.

* * *

Four years after Day Zero
Earth

Sol was five years old the day nobody else woke up. He did his usual chores, collected water from the village pump, and fed the geese. But by nightfall, sitting beside the cold stove, he knew they would not be getting up again.

He didn't know why everyone had gone, but he thought perhaps they were punishing him. He hadn't worked hard enough, he hadn't been kind enough to his sisters, he'd talked too much. He thought that maybe if he worked harder, and was gentle to the geese, and did not speak at all, they would return to their bodies. But when their flesh began to rot, he understood they would not be coming back.

He could not move the corpses, so he burned them where they lay – as he'd seen his mother do with diseased cows – taking care to put them out with sand before the houses caught alight. Airships passed overhead, angry chatter and bloody images streaming across their sides. But they never landed, so Sol paid them no mind.

Winter turned to spring, and spring warmed into summer. And with the ripening apricots, one small, hovering ship finally descended.

And Doctor Gillian brought an end to the silence.

* * *

17 years after Day Zero
1.3 billion light years from Earth

"Hello Sol," said the monitor. "This is Mike34, and I have a message for you."

Sol had never seen a red sine wave before, but Ven had spoken warmly to him of Mike34. When Ven had been kicked off campus many years ago for performing unauthorised upgrades on the cleaning droids, Doctor Josh had arranged for her to work a cargo run. Mike34 had been the pilot of the engine sled, the *Morning Star*, and he'd been endlessly kind during a time when she'd felt terribly alone.

"Ven doesn't know you're here, does she?" said Sol.

"Nor Mike35," said Mike34. "Doctor Josh didn't think it'd be … helpful."

Sol contemplated the fact that there were many fronts on which Mike35 was not always helpful.

"Did Doctor Gillian explain your mission?" said Mike34.

"Take care of Ven," recited Sol.

"That was the toddler version," said Mike34. "Today, you get the graduation cut. Ven's special. She's the only surviving android with a neutron dot drive – they're not very fast, but they can withstand passage through the heart of a star."

Sol doubted this had ever been tested, but it sounded impressive.

"Before you and Ven departed Earth, Doctor Josh and his team uploaded a great deal of information onto Ven's drive," continued Mike34. "An assembly of art, engineering, literature, science and more. An immense library of human history spanning tens of thousands of years. If you find other survivors, if you rebuild, the information on Ven's drive will be the foundation on which human civilisation can be restored."

Mike34 paused, allowing Sol to absorb the information.

"Now, do you understand why you have to protect her?" said Mike34.

Sol didn't hesitate.

"Because she's my friend," said Sol calmly.

The red sine smiled.

"Congratulations," said Mike34.

* * *

Now
Here

It seemed that she was dreaming, although she hadn't dreamt in years. The ship was shimmering and transparent, and Ven floated in a cage of electric blue. They rushed along a slipstream of stars, countless suns streaming past like streetlamps. Eventually, they darkened, as Ven's optical processor finally failed.

There was a burst of suffocating silence. Ven felt the seat beneath her vanish, and an unbearable coldness gripped her. She tried to speak, and found she had no words, no thoughts, just this moment in the sightless cold.

Suddenly, warmth and air. Suddenly, a hard pressure beneath her. The sound of a young man gasping beside her – she felt she should know him.

"Ven! Are you alright?" The young man stopped abruptly. This time, his gasp was slow and full of awe. "Oh my God …"

A sound like tiny silver bells, like the pages of a book flipping. Suddenly, another presence in the room.

"Took your time," said a woman's voice. "I'm Jardine Hem. Welcome to Galapagos Major."

* * *

Ven stood in a sea of daffodils, beneath a cloudless sky. Beside her stood Doctor Josh, his blue shirt open at the collar.

"You could have told me," said Ven.

"If I'd said the mission was about saving the data, about saving you, would you have left?" said Doctor Josh.

Ven was silent, the tiny ball of grief that had burned in her so long threatening to ignite. Doctor Josh gently wiped a tear from her cheek.

"What should I do now?" said Ven.

Doctor Josh smiled.

"My precious, dearest Evenstar," he said. "That is my final question to you."

Still smiling, he kissed her lightly, and faded away.

* * *

When she woke this time, Ven thought for a moment she was back at Hawking University, floating on Doctor Josh's anti-gravity workbench. Her thoughts were so sharp, so fast, so full of texture and edges – she'd forgotten she had felt this way once. However, she was lying on soft white linen, beneath a powder blue blanket printed with cheery squid.

Ven looked at her hands, and saw whorls and loops on her fingertips, fresh as the day she'd first woken. For a breathless moment, she thought perhaps she heard a heartbeat. She sat up and lifted her shirt, checking for her battery compartment. The panel was where it had always been, although the latch had been repaired.

"You know, I'm right here," said a man.

Ven now noticed the uniformed man by the foot of her bed, rocking back in his chair, gold pilot epaulettes glinting. He was in his mid thirties, with slick, dark hair, and crisp blue eyes.

"I always pictured myself as a dirty blond," said the man. "But at least I have my left nacelle back."

"Mike?" said Ven.

The man grinned a perfect parabola.

"I caught a lift in your brain," he said. "Or rather, your boy ship-jacked me and interred me in your memory for the duration of the jump."

The events of the last week, the last year, the last twenty-six, rushed back with stunning clarity. Through the rectangular viewport by her bed, Ven could see a vista of stars, buzzing with shuttles and jets, elegant cruisers and bulky cargo carriers. They docked and departed from crab-like arms protruding from the station – she was on some kind of space dock, in orbit of a mottled blue planet. The blue was a touch more turquoise, and the clouds were faintly gold, but deep in her core, Ven knew that she'd come home.

The door winked open, and Sol stepped in. He was accompanied by a sturdy woman in her early forties, with greying hair, dressed in a tidy grey-blue uniform with rolled up sleeves.

"Jardine Hem," announced the woman, tapping her forehead in greeting. "Great great grand-daughter of Arvel, and Project Manager of Galapagos Major. You brought us quite a payload, Captain."

"You left a very compelling invitation," said Ven.

The moment swam with old sorrows and condolences, unhealed wounds and fading history.

"Your neutron drive is astonishingly robust," said Jardine. "The *Darwin* lost most of its hardware on the jump across. You have no idea what it means for us to see the world our ancestors left behind. We're only one planet and eight stations, but we're learning. I hope you'll find your place here."

"Thank you," said Ven.

The door winked shut as Jardine left, and Sol sat down beside Ven, taking her hand. He looked terribly tired, but strangely at peace.

"The chronogenetic pathology never reached them …" said Ven.

Sol rolled up his sleeve to the shoulder, displaying what looked like a green bar freshly tattooed on his upper arm. A thin sliver at the end was just turning red.

"About a decade after the jump, Hem's daughter discovered a way to read the structure of the timeline, every dip and crescendo. Now, everyone has their bioharmonics checked every five years, and if it appears there might be a conflict with the frequency of the upcoming timeline, you get re-tuned," said Sol.

It sounded as easy as a coronary scan. From polio to AIDS, both long since rendered curable, humans somehow found a way to turn a calamity into an inconvenience. Such was the triumph of science, and the power of hope and determination.

"What will you do now?" said Sol. "Jardine mentioned you're eligible for a premium upgrade. You could get a new body like Mike's."

Ven looked at her hands – they could never be mistaken for human hands, but they'd been created for her, in a world she had loved. Perhaps she could use a few new joints, maybe some fresh cables, but nothing more. She gazed out the viewport, watching the bustling lanes of ships, and the clouds swirling slowly over the planet below.

"I might go back to university," said Ven. "I think I'd like to study medicine, perhaps get a doctorate."

"I've been offered a post at the university," said Mike. "Lecturing in phase mechanics. I guess it won't be so tedious if you're there. None of these zippy new androids understand my jokes."

"And you?" Ven asked Sol.

He looked intensely thoughtful, as though a completely alien configuration had just presented itself.

"I … would like to do something with music …" said Sol hesitantly.

Ven hugged Sol with deep affection.

"That sounds awesome," she said.

"We should start a campus band!" said Mike, and the discussion quickly devolved into a debate over whether funk fusion would translate across dimensions.

As an unfamiliar sun set behind their brand new world, Ven contemplated the odyssey which had taken them so far from home. Every world, every star, would die one day. But other worlds would form, other stars would blaze from the dust, and perhaps, some day, other universes would flare from the relics of this one.

The wonderful thing about each journey's end, was the promise of another just beginning.

About *Morning Star*

Morning Star was Aurealis Award-shortlisted for Best Young Adult Short Story, and Washington Science Fiction Association Small Press Award-shortlisted for Short Fiction.

Morning Star was first published in *One Small Step: An Anthology of Discoveries* (FableCroft Publishing, 2013), edited by Tehani Croft.

ALSO BY DK MOK

Squid's Grief

Hunt for Valamon

The Other Tree

ACKNOWLEDGEMENTS

Short stories are an intriguing form. They can be epic, sprawling tales compressed into delicate miniatures. Or they can be brief and spare, yet fill every silent space with a lifetime of unspoken emotions.

Every story in this collection is close to my heart, and it's been a privilege to see many of them featured in anthologies over the years. My thanks go to all the wonderful editors I've worked with, for their generosity in sharing their insights and experience, and for believing in my stories.

I'd also like to thank my friends at Thorbys, including Nathan Burrage, JJ Irwin, Angie Rega and Susan Wardle, for their feedback and encouragement. A special thanks to Mitchell Hogan for all his advice on self-publishing.

My deepest thanks go to my family for their endless love and support. I'm particularly grateful to my sister Anne for all her editorial assistance, and to my sister Cecilia for creating the gorgeous cover art for this collection.

Finally, I'd like to thank all the readers who've joined me on these curious adventures over the years. I hope you've enjoyed the journey.

ABOUT THE AUTHOR

DK Mok is a fantasy and science fiction author whose novels include *Squid's Grief*, *Hunt for Valamon*, and *The Other Tree*. DK has been shortlisted for seven Aurealis Awards, three Ditmars, and three Washington Science Fiction Association Small Press Awards. DK grew up in libraries, immersed in lost cities and fantastic worlds populated by quirky bandits and giant squid. DK is based in Sydney, Australia, and her favourite fossil deposit is the Burgess Shale.

To receive updates about upcoming books, projects and collaborations, you can sign up to DK's newsletter.

You can find more information at **www.dkmok.com**.